DEATH MATCH

DEATH MATCH

ANIMUS™ BOOK THREE

JOSHUA ANDERLE

MICHAEL ANDERLE

LMBPN

DISRUPTIVE IMAGINATION®

LMBPN Publishing
PMB 196, 2540 South Maryland Pkwy
Las Vegas, NV 89109

First US edition, October 2018

THE DEATH MATCH TEAM

Thanks to the JIT Readers

Misty Roa
Nicole Emens
Mary Morris
James Caplan
Kelly Ethan
Danika Fedeli
Kelly O'Donnell
Angel LaVey
Keith Verret
Micky Cocker
Larry Omans

If I've missed anyone, please let me know!

Editor
Lynne Stiegler

*To Family, Friends and
Those Who Love
to Read.
May We All Enjoy Grace
to Live the Life We Are
Called.*

CHAPTER ONE

W ater, oil, and blood dripped from the grates above the canal. Angry shouting and the fizz of over-heated electronics came from above, muffled but audible. A group of six wandered slowly through the tight corridor, three to each side, trying not to step into the puddles on the floor and keeping their noise to a minimum.

Two loud gunshots sounded above. Some whooping and hollering followed, a joyful response to the violence taking place. Up ahead, the group saw a stream of blood trickle through a small hole in the wall. It traced a path into a gutter and streamed down the side of the left wall. The three on the left inched away in an attempt to avoid the crimson liquid coming their way.

"Holy hell, whose idea was it to choose the creepy mission?" Cameron hissed, his annoyance and disgust evident even over the comms.

Jaxon turned, holding a finger up to the front of his

helmet to tell him to quiet down as another voice popped up over the link.

"If I recall correctly, you were the one who said, 'Screw it, choose whatever and let's get in there.' Maybe next time, you'll be a little more thorough and take a look through the mission and map description before we begin?" Kaiden sneered over the comms.

The team in the canal pressed on. Cameron grunted as he walked forward, his voice lowering to a whisper but still plenty angry. "You get to act all high and mighty because you're not down here. You're riding around in your little ship while the rest of us have to walk through this tunnel of what I actually hope is mostly rancid flesh."

"You're a bounty hunter. Drug dens, chop houses, that'll be most of your gigs in a few years anyway, right?" The ace chuckled. "Besides, it's not like we drew straws. You guys are infiltration, while Marlo, Luke, Genos, and I are the distraction team. You were the best choices."

"How does that work again?" Silas asked. He leaned around the corner and signaled that it was clear. "I can cause plenty of distraction of the explosive variety."

"My score is bigger than yours, Si," Kaiden reminded him. "Plus, you lack the personal touch that I have. Luke and Marlo are our big guns—well, a big gun and a big hammer, but it's mostly a metaphorical term anyway."

"And Genos? Is he a secret pyromaniac or something?" Raul inquired. He flinched as he saw a few drops of some unidentifiable liquid fall across his visor. Izzy reached out from behind and steadied him before motioning for him to keep moving.

"He's the closest thing we have to a pilot. Doin' a damn

good job of it too, Genos." Some quiet, unintelligible words came over the comm. "About two minutes? Better gear up, then. Also, your comm link is off. Oh, that's on purpose?"

"All comms but mine and yours should have been offline until we went hot, but I can see most of us did not apparently listen to that part of the plan," Jaxon noted dryly.

"I figure most of your team didn't, although Izzy and Chiyo are still offline. So gold stars for you and the ladies, and Cameron, Silas, and Raul don't get any dinner for a week."

"There's no way he can actually enforce that, right?" Raul asked.

Cameron shook his head. "He gets rank three and he thinks he's actually the captain of the initiates. He's been trying to make some of the others in the Soldier dorm call him 'sir.'"

"I would have expected people do that regardless of rank. Also, your comm is still on."

"Regardless of rank? You thought people would grant you titles because you naturally have such a dignified and commanding air about you?" Silas jeered.

"Well, why thank you, Silas. I didn't know I gave that kind of impression. I *figured* I did, but I wasn't sure others were picking up on it."

Silas and Izzy gave muted laughs while Cameron sighed and Raul shook his head.

"Good God, he is insufferable," the tracker huffed.

"Keep that up and there's no dessert at lunch for you either, Raul."

"You keep picking on us for not following the rules, but

you didn't seem to know about the no comms rule either. You simply got lucky," Cameron pointed out.

"It was a clever ruse to weed out those who were paying attention. You all obviously fell for my charisma and subterfuge."

"Turning off comms. We're nearly there." Silas deactivated his long-range mic before looking back at the others. "Looks like he thinks he's an actor now," he muttered, bemused.

"He might be. That EI of his seems to have some crazy talent options," Raul commented, also turning off his long-range mic.

"He's merely getting full of himself—thinks he's the alpha bastard now," Cameron jested.

"The glorious and supreme alpha bastard, thank you," Kaiden corrected. "Also, your mic is still on."

"Goddammit." Cameron hissed as he pressed the side of his helmet to turn it off.

"Either way, he seems to be getting more into his role as an ace and actually taking point on missions," Silas mused. "Even if, in this case, taking point means you don't want to be in front of where he's shooting."

"Considering where it's gotten us, I think I actually miss the days where he was simply a trigger-happy gun jock," the bounty hunter admitted.

"I mean, he still is. Just...you know, with authority if not maturity," Silas retorted.

"Guess we have you to thank for that, eh, Chiyo?" Raul asked, looking back at the infiltrator. "Don't know how you got through to him with that massive ego, but if I had to guess I would say...drugs?"

Chiyo shook her head. She motioned across her mask for silence and pointed at Jaxon. The Tsuna ace looked around another corner farther ahead, motioning for the others to join him. "Kaiden, we have found the entrance to the underside of the building. Are you ready?"

Kaiden looked at Marlo, who was priming his Tesla cannon, and Luke, who took his massive hammer and gripped it in both hands. "We're good. You'll hear us in a bit," he said. He walked over to the cockpit and looked through the window over Genos' shoulder, seeing the decrepit prison their targets were using as a base coming up quickly in the distance. "Where do you think the best place to set us down will be, Genos?"

The Tsuna mechanist looked around the building, his lips pursed in thought. "I can either play it safe and drop you off on top of the building or the exterior landing pad to the far side, or play it off like a hostage or convoy drop-off—"

"Boring." Kaiden dismissed his suggestions peremptorily.

"Or I can do a hot drop toward the entrance of the prison and let you make your own entrance while I deal with the security towers around the building."

"Next time, lead with that option." The ace clapped Genos a couple of times on the shoulder.

"I figured that would be your preferred option. But I do hope that I can sometimes convince you that the more tactical option may possibly be the better option...occasionally."

"Chiyo thought that too. But considering all our missions usually end up in a firefight, it's usually for naught." Kaiden pulled his shotgun. "It's why I don't bother equipping stealth or silenced guns anymore."

"Yes, she told me as much." The Tsuna drifted the ship around the prison, looking for an entry point. "She also told me that it was usually you who would initiate the fire fights."

The ace shrugged. "Our positions would get compromised."

"Usually after you killed someone. At least that was the pattern I noticed," the alien responded, looking at him.

Kaiden opened the visor of his mask so his companion could see the annoyance in his eyes. "But can you argue that my plans don't work?"

The mechanist stared at him for a moment before looking back at the window. "I suppose I cannot."

"Exactly," he declared triumphantly before closing his visor and walking back to the hold.

"Though those plans may be why the staff hides you from diplomats and Academy patrons when they visit," Genos said thoughtfully.

"What was that?" Kaiden asked, shouting the question.

"Just figuring out coordinates. Get ready to drop!" he called back.

"Gotcha. Ready when you are," he acknowledged, walked up to the exit ramp, and grabbed a handle overhead.

"Is that a new gun, Kaiden?" Marlo asked "Doesn't look like that Raptor you usually use."

"Yeah, only used it since a couple of missions ago." Kaiden held the shotgun up. The white body extended to the tip of the barrel, which was a short and wide silver tube that connected to a chamber in the middle of the weapon that was illuminated by red energy. "It's a Tera Sovereign model, a Havoc III."

"What's that red stuff?" Luke asked.

"This baby fires superheated shards. Cuts right through even heavy armor. The shards pass through this chamber and it heats the metal on the way," he explained.

"So that's some sort of incendiary chamber?"

Kaiden shook his head. "Nah, plasma. It's somehow sustained in the chamber."

"That sounds kinda dangerous," Marlo noted. He sounded a little concerned.

"It's worked for me so far. I heard about the Havoc series a few years back. This was the last model they created before they were discontinued."

"Why were they discontinued?" Luke inquired, continuing to look cautiously at the weapon.

"Some sort of explosive blowback issue. WC had to step in and make them stop. Didn't read far enough along to see what the big deal was. But having used it a couple of times now, it seems damn tragic."

The two titans looked at each other for a moment before taking a few steps away from Kaiden, who looked lovingly at the gun. The ship began to slow, and they could feel themselves descending.

"I'm about the open the ramp. It would appear that

there are a few men waiting to greet you." Genos relayed the information in a calm tone.

"Open the hatch. We'll make proper introductions," Kaiden commanded. "Try not to get blown out of the sky while we're out."

"Certainly noted," the Tsuna affirmed. "Best of luck with the mayhem."

"Thank you, good sir."

The ship hovered near the ground and the ace released the handle and walked down the ramp, Marlo and Luke following closely behind.

They were met by a group of nine men, each in different armored uniforms showing allegiance with various cartels, gangs, mercenary companies, and terrorist groups. The one in the center approached them. He was bald with spidery scars that formed around his lips and right cheek. His pale green eyes were socketed into a face that stretched around his skull as if trying to pop out. He wore a set of black medium armor. A crest on the right breastplate depicted a smiling skull with smoke issuing from each side of its mouth in a 'V' shape, designating him a member of the Vice Ghouls gang. Kaiden recalled that they had a small presence back in Texas, but they were mostly run through the west coast and apparently had a couple of chapters in one of the stations.

"Got a lot of balls to come to a rogue port without invitation. You didn't even land on a pad for inspection and clearance." He sneered as he surveyed the three of them with derision.

"Kind of a stickler for protocol for a congregation of

misfits, murderers, and psychopaths," Marlo noted quietly over the link.

"You're lucky our cannon is out." The man flicked a thumb behind him to show a large anti-air cannon, the barrel pointing low and deactivated behind him. "Or else you wouldn't have even been able to set foot in our place." He eyed the three for a moment and smiled, showing decayed, blackened teeth. "Though if you ain't got nothing to offer or a good excuse for coming here, your fancy suits and toys could catch a nice price."

"Remember, Dense, it's first come, first served," one of the larger men said. He wore a Red Sun uniform with no helmet, showing dark skin and a shaved head with one eye scarred and blind. He wielded a large blade with a serrated chain—a chainsaw blade, as they were often tagged. Calmly, he walked up to Luke, examining his heavy silver armor and hammer. "Looks like it would be a good fit for me." he growled, pressing a fist against the titan's chest. "That hammer can get sold for scrap. I prefer a weapon that shows the insides of my victims, not just flattens them."

Luke grabbed the man's fist and pushed him back, looking at his blade for a moment. "Maybe we don't belong here, then. I prefer to be around guys who actually know how to use their weapon and don't get theirs off the edgelord rack to show his buddies how spooky he is," he retorted, his tone clipped.

The man pulled the heavy blade off his back, holding it in one hand and pointing it at the titan. The tips of the blades stopped only a couple of inches from his helmet.

"Want me to rev it up? See if you're still talking with all that bravado when you see how fast this blade spins."

"Give it a shot. It won't hurt me," the giant challenged. "Even without the armor. Look at all that gunk on the chain. That thing is more likely to snap and whip you in the face than cut into me."

The Red Sun merc gripped a handle on the base of the blade. "Allow me to be a nice host and offer you a demonstration."

"Stop it, Jedrek," Dense, the apparent leader, demanded. "We should at least give them a chance to explain themselves. Don't want word to spread that the gentleman of the Angola rogue port are such wicked bastards." His grin was wide and devious. "It would be true but think of the PR damage if it got out."

"Let's just kill them!" another cried. The owner of the voice was lanky and dressed in a patchwork of armor of various sizes and colors. He wore a mask around his mouth, goggles over his eyes, and some kind of skin cap over his head. The headgear was partially damaged, showing a wild tuft of hair. "It'll be fun. *Come on, come on,*" he wailed fanatically. Kaiden saw an insignia on his left shoulder—an angel with horns made from a shattered halo that showed he belonged to the Soulless Breed gang, though some considered them more of a cult.

"I would suggest you hurry and make your case. My friends are obviously becoming less interested in formalities and more interested in fun," Dense warned.

The ace looked at his companions for a moment. Luke placed the end of his hammer in the dirt and gave him a small nod. Marlo gave him an "okay" signal with his hand, hiding it from plain view behind his cannon.

Kaiden walked forward a few steps and said, "My apologies for our sudden and unexpected visit, gentleman. We are, in fact, delegates of the Scoundrel Butcher company. We figured we would drop by because this seemed like a fantastic place to do business." He ended his statement with a low bow, his gun to his chest.

"Butchers? What, do you deliver sandwiches?" one of the others asked.

"I wouldn't mind that—better than that gruel and those rations we keep eating," another interjected.

"They seem rather heavily armored to be cooks," a third added.

"That's because they are obviously trying to play cute, you idiots," Dense snapped. He turned away and leaned down to speak into Kaiden's ear. "And I don't appreciate it."

"Oh, I'm not lying to you, sir," the ace retorted. "We're not butchers. Our name, if a bit on the nose, is quite literal." He moved quickly, slamming the butt of his shotgun into Dense's chin. In the same motion, he flipped it over and blasted him in his chest. His armor blew open as blood splashed onto two others behind him.

"We are in the business of butchering scoundrels, and as I said"—Kaiden fired another shot, blowing through a second merc who toppled and fell on top of the man beside him—"this seems like a great place to do business."

CHAPTER TWO

"Time for *killing*," the Soulless Breed gang member shouted, taking a flying leap at Kaiden. He was briefly distracted by a bright light coming from his left and looked away for a split second before he was enveloped by a ball of plasma. It tore clean through his torso, leaving only appendages to crumble to the ground as the projectile continued through the port. It finally slammed into a small building nearly a hundred yards away and blew a hole in the side.

"Well, that will certainly get things going. Nice job, Marlo," the ace declared, quickly taking aim at another enemy who targeted him with a machine gun. With calm deliberation, he blasted him through the leg. The man fell back and he fired his weapon into the air, then behind him as he collapsed. The wild volley forced a few gang members to roll out of the way.

"It's what I do." The demolisher chuckled, firing another charged blast into a group rushing out the door of another bunker. The shot erupted at their feet, burning a couple and searing through the armor of several more.

"You lot will make my night," Jedrek, the merc with the chainsaw blade, growled as he stepped toward them.

Luke blocked his path, planting the head of his hammer into the ground. "Go ahead, start that thing up and show me what you can do."

The man paused for a moment, looking at the dirty chain on the blade with a trepidation he hadn't shown before. He grunted before lifting the blade and grabbed the handle at the base, tugging it down in one swift motion. A loud whine erupted from the blade. The chain jerked in place a few times but did not spin. Jedrek cursed, looking from the blade to Luke for a second before pulling the handle again. Another loud whine sounded and the chain inched around, then something cracked. The man just stared as a sudden metallic snap resounded and the chain was ripped from the blade. It whipped down his face and the front of his chest plate.

Jedrek cried out as he gripped his face, blood dripping down his armor. Luke laughed. "What did I tell you? You should've realized that proper weapon maintenance is far more deadly than threats and pointy weapons alone."

The merc bared his teeth, spinning around to confront him. "I'll still pierce your—" His words died in his throat, and the last thing he saw was the barrel of Luke's hand cannon firing.

"Whatever you were about to say...I doubt that too," the titan quipped. He placed the weapon back on his belt and took up his hammer. A siren began to blare around the rogue port, and various hostiles poured out from the sheds, barracks, and main building.

"You know, the last time a siren went off it didn't end well for us," Cameron recalled over the comm.

"Let's not try to make it a future harbinger of doom and focus on getting this done," Kaiden retorted, firing three blasts in quick succession and then venting his gun.

"I'm beginning to think we may have slightly underestimated the number of bastards in this place," Marlo shouted, firing another massive blast toward the right side of the island they stood on. The impact decimated only a fraction of the onslaught headed their way.

"Eh, plus or minus a couple hundred, maybe," Kaiden affirmed as he closed the vent of his gun and fired at the gathering murderous company. "But Genos should be back soon."

Several eruptions blew through the hostile mass and Kaiden's coat rustled in the wind. The Tsuna had indeed returned and now used the ship's flak cannons to tear through the horde from above.

"Damn nice timing, Genos," the ace said appreciatively. "Were you waiting for your cue or something?"

"I was waiting for the appropriate number of hostiles to amass. I want the best average of kills to shots fired. This ship only has so many shots," the mechanist explained.

"Him saying that so dryly is actually rather chilling," Luke noted while taking a massive swing and knocking back five mercs who had wandered a little too close.

"Dryly? Was that a pun on him being a Tsuna?" Kaiden asked.

"Unlike you, I'm not so 'gifted' at being able to come up

with those in the middle of a firefight." The titan chuckled and smashed his hammer down on a heavily armored gang member with a flamethrower.

"They're scattering," Marlo called. The horde was still coming, but several pockets had begun to retreat or at least try to dodge the incoming blasts from above, giving the trio a tad more breathing room.

"Well don't let up. If they figure out what's going on, they'll head back into the main base where there's much less room to maneuver in—gah!" The ace took a shot in the shoulder and slammed into the mud below.

"Sniper," Luke warned as two more shots could be heard from afar, the bullets slamming into his heavy armor. He stepped back but remained unharmed.

"Snipers—multiple. We gotta start moving around," Kaiden determined as he staggered to his feet. "None of us have the range to take them out from here, except maybe Marlo."

"Little busy here," the demolisher yelled as he let loose another charged blast. The returning fire from the rogue port denizens was beginning to overwhelm them. "My armor is almost compromised."

"Even more reason to move," Kaiden shouted.

At another shot of sniper fire, Luke stood in front of the ace, the shot slamming home and ricocheting off his armor. He held out a hand to hold his comrade steady. "Where should we go?"

Kaiden looked around and pointed to the main base. "Over there."

"Aren't we supposed to keep them away from there?" the titan questioned.

"Not inside, to the front—it's got defenses and it's barricaded. The building will cover our backs and we can focus on shooting them down from the stairs above."

"Any ideas on how we get up there?" Luke asked, another couple of shots from sniper fire and a few machine gun rounds careening into his back. He turned around and yelled, "Would you stop that?" as a few bullets collided with his helmet.

Kaiden looked up at the ship. "Genos, can you focus your fire and get us to the building?"

"Certainly," the mechanist replied. "I'll have my EI take over the controls to the turret on the top of the ship and see if she can take care of the snipers while I clear a path."

"Gotcha," the ace acknowledged. He raised his shotgun again and fired into the crowd, walking behind Luke who advanced slowly, occasionally wiping out a group that got too close. "I don't suppose you can hustle in all that armor?"

"Are you kidding? This stuff ain't built for sprinting. But I do have a bounce pack."

"Do what?" Kaiden asked.

"Bounce pack. All heavies have one," he answered. "Marlo! You got a bounce pack, right?"

"Of course," he replied. "What about it?"

"We're heading to the front of the main base. Let's clear the way for our reckless ace buddy here."

"I thought we were trying to stay away from there?" the demolisher asked.

"I'll fill you in once we're there. On my mark." Luke looked at Kaiden. "When will Genos—"

"Good question. Genos?" Kaiden looked up at the ship.

"Prepared to fire on your signal," the Tsuna responded.

"Do it." A stream of nine blasts followed a line in quick succession several meters from them. The volleys tore through the guards and left a charred path to the main building.

"That's a damn good start," Luke cried and braced his hammer against his chest. "Ready, Marlo?"

"I'm with you," he stated, gripping his cannon.

"Let's go," the titan cried. Kaiden saw three large vents pop out of the back of Luke's armor. Blue flames fired from them and the huge man was sent soaring almost fifty feet into the air.

Marlo soon followed, and they catapulted forward in an arc. The demolisher fired a blast at a small group below him as he sailed overhead. Luke landed on a couple as he made landfall, then charged up the steps of the building, crushing any opposition in his way. His companion followed, turning to fire on his way up.

"I gotta get me one of those," Kaiden murmured. He shook his head and ran after them, shooting sporadically along the way. Genos continued to fire the cannons around him, while frantic yells and cries melded with the explosions and gunfire.

As they made their way up, the ace noticed a few partially built turrets around the barricades. "Luke, think you can get those things working?"

The titan looked where Kaiden was pointing. "I think I got a better idea," he said as he walked up to one of the turret heads and picked it up. He studied it for a moment and flipped a couple of switches before turning back down the stairs, holding the turret against his waist.

Those who charged up the stairs after them soon saw him over the ledge and turned quickly to run back as he charged the turret's cannons. It fired large, explosive shells that blasted through the hostiles. Between that and the cannon fire from the ship, it was possibly the most violent fireworks display the ace had ever seen.

"That's a hell of a symphony you got going on."

"Oh, hey, Chief, you've been awfully quiet," Kaiden murmured as the EI appeared next to him. Chief glowed an effervescent blue with white stripes surrounding his body and a shining white orb within his spherical frame. His eye was wide and white, surrounded by a second white ring, and it darted around, surveying the scene.

"Wanted to see how things turned out without my input. That way, you could say you actually accomplished something without my guidance." He looked at him. *"What you've done here,"* he sniffed, *"makes an EI proud, you know?"*

"Odd time to be getting sappy," he noted.

"I take the moments when I can get them. Also, you got a guy trying to sneak up on you."

"I know, he's on the scanner." Kaiden pulled Debonair with his free hand and fired a trio of rounds behind him, shooting the potential assailant in the chest. The man dropped his blade and slumped down against the wall of the building.

"Nice grouping."

"Why, thank you," the ace said as he holstered his pistol. "While you're here, is there anything I should know about?"

"Care to specify?" Chief asked as he turned to the field

again. *"Cause if you're asking for a scoreboard, technically, Genos is beating you."*

"I figured that, but that's not—"

"I love this thing," Luke declared, firing into a retreating group of Red Sun mercs to the side of the stairs.

"Also, Luke is about to pass you too."

"Look, they both have superior firepower. I'm not that petty—though I should probably bump up my numbers soon so I don't look bad."

"No kiddin.'"

"What I'm talking about is are there any secret surprises coming up? You reading any secret reinforcements coming this way or some sort of Asiton droid burrowing underground?"

"Ah...nah, nothing like that. Only the dreadnought in orbit."

"Right, the dread— Wait, what now?"

"This room is the closest thing this hellhole has to a main tech room," Cameron stated as he shot the lock off the door. "Not much, but I'm sure you can make something out of it."

"It should prove sufficient as long as I can get direct access to their systems," Chiyo said, walking into the room with the others.

"Once you get set up, let us know where the device is so we can retrieve it and depart. I'm not sure how long Kaiden and the others will be able to withstand an entire rogue port gunning after them," Jaxon advised.

"Hey, Jaxon, you there?" the ace asked over the link.

"I read you, Kaiden."

"Is Chiyo there? Her comm is still off."

"She is. We've just arrived at the communications room and she's beginning to look through the files for the—"

Kaiden cut him off, "Yeah, yeah, that's dandy. So, um… look, apparently there's a bit of a problem that we did not discuss before."

"Has something happened? Do you need reinforcements?"

"While you are certainly welcome to come and join the fun, I don't think a couple of extra blasters will do the trick here. According to Chief, we have a dreadnought overhead."

"What?" Jaxon shouted and the others looked over in surprise. He used the commands on his visor to open his channel. "You are being broadcast to everyone here. Fill us in."

"Oh, good, Kaiden's back in my head," Cameron muttered snidely.

"I can't hear anyone else, but my gut says Cameron just said something sarcastic, so shut the hell up, Cameron, and everybody listen," Kaiden demanded. The bounty hunter threw his hands up in frustration.

"Chief just informed me that there's an enemy dreadnought in orbit. And it'll probably head this way pretty soon."

"A dreadnought," Raul exclaimed.

"When exactly is 'pretty soon?'" Silas asked.

"When a dreadnought is coming for your ass, any time that is not 'never' is soon," the ace sneered. "But according to Chief, it'll probably take around fifteen minutes to enter the atmosphere and another five to get here."

"He's right," Chiyo stated, looking at a monitor in the room. "It was only called in a couple of minutes ago. But it's on its way here."

"So no one was able to detect this thing before now?" Izzy asked.

"It wasn't in the mission glossary and no one has the ability to detect something that is that far out in space," Jaxon answered.

"Not even Kaiden's shiny-ass EI?" Cameron snorted.

"What was that? Cameron, Chief can somehow hear you and also says to shut the hell up, and that he was able to detect the alert that was sent out. And that it's because of him that we know about the dreadnought now instead of when it's blasting our asses to charcoaled squishy bits." Kaiden relayed all this with a hint of humor in his tone.

"What the... How the hell can he hear me? I turned my mic off."

"Because I am omniscient," Chief stated, appearing behind Cameron. He jumped and aimed his rifle at the EI. *"Or maybe it's because of my 'shiny-ass' upgrade that now allows me to create temporary copies of myself that I can cast into anyone on Kaiden's network list."* Chief floated past Cameron. *"Pretty neat huh?"*

"Spooky bastard..." Cameron muttered as he lowered his weapon.

"What can you tell us about the dreadnought?" Jaxon asked, walking toward the EI.

"What, do you intend to fight it? I don't think even Kaiden is that dense,." Chief retorted.

"No, but if it arrives before we can pull out, we may have to outrun it. Knowing the specs could provide opportunity," Jaxon reasoned.

"I don't know the specifics. Maybe Chiyo can dig them up for ya. You don't have to worry about a dreadnought chasing you down—not the fastest ships. But the long-range cannons and lock-on missiles could be an issue."

"You just said you didn't know specifics," Izzy stated.

"Those are standard, sweetheart," Chief responded.

"Then we'll need to focus on speed instead of subtlety," the Tsuna ace said.

"I've gotten used to that," Chiyo mumbled.

"Have you found our destination?" Jaxon asked.

She nodded. "It's toward the back of the building and one floor up." She displayed a map of the building on the screen. "I'll send a copy of the map up and stay here and activate the defenses in the building to help you and Kaiden out. Then I'll rendezvous at the pad."

"Understood." He nodded. "Kaiden, we're heading for the device. Are you holding out all right?"

"Just dandy," the ace responded as he took out a couple more Soulless Breed members charging him with blades. "Not the best equipped, this lot. Marlo and Luke are taking down groups with almost every shot, and we're well defended. I think we'll be—"

Roars were heard from beyond the walls of the port. The trio and most of the members of the rogue port stopped firing or running to turn in the direction of the fearsome cry. The wall, built of scrap metal, rusted plating, spikes, and razors, began to shake as something smashed into it.

"Genos, what the hell is that?" Kaiden asked.

"The scanner is reading mutant signals from behind the wall—a dozen of them."

"What specifically?" the ace asked.

The defense shattered, pieces of metal and loose spikes flying from the impact. A few projectiles skewered into random gangers and mercs. Kaiden's eyes widened behind his mask as he vented his rifle and crept slowly up the stairs. "We...might need some help here."

CHAPTER THREE

From beyond the broken wall, a creature emerged. A long alligator-like face protruded below the three reptilian eyes set upon its head. It stood—massively built and at least twelve feet high—on two scaled legs and brandished four clawed arms. Its nails were pointed cones coated with dried blood and muck.

Everyone watched, appalled, as several more of these creatures stalked into the port. They glanced around the gathered group. One of them bent to take a pair of corpses into its long mouth, revealing hardened teeth as it snapped down and devoured the flesh. A single arm, hanging on by sinew, eventually fell off and landed near its feet.

There was silence for a moment, broken by the clinking of armor and the heavy breathing of the mutants, along with one last snap of the jaws from the one that had dined on the corpses.

"It's the damn bayou stalkers," a Vice Ghoul ganger finally cried. This was soon followed by all the other members of

the port turning their attention away from the Nexus trio and firing at the mutants as a group.

One creature shrieked as three others lowered on all six of their limbs and dashed into the crowd. They swiped their claws and snapped at the remains of the murderous inhabitants. The lasers, bullets, and explosive shells seemed to have almost no effect as the beasts continued to devour the remaining forces. Others soon joined the carnage as another group of stalkers snaked into the chaos.

"What are those things?" Kaiden exclaimed.

"Bayou Stalkers. Mutated crocodiles. Normally, they stay away from massively populated areas, but all the blood poured out around here must have attracted them," Chief informed him.

"Those things are getting shot by everyone here and it ain't doing shit," Luke yelled.

"How do we take them down?" the ace asked.

"Gotta shoot them in the belly or down the throat. Their hide is way too tough for conventional rounds. Kind of a pain as they scurry around with their belly down when attacking."

"What about Marlo's Tesla cannon?" he inquired, looking at the demolisher.

"Not sure I wanna get their attention," Marlo admitted, moving back a few steps.

"The ship's flak cannons?" Luke suggested.

"I can try, but I'm running out of rounds," Genos responded.

Kaiden gritted his teeth. "Save them for now. They're focused on the hostiles. But they're wading through them faster than we were."

"And your score continues to trail ever downward," Chief chirped.

"Honestly, I'm cool with it considering the circumstances," Kaiden responded. "Jaxon, what's your ETA?"

"Izzy, Raul, and I are headed to retrieve the device. The others are activating the outer defenses and heading to the rendezvous point," Jaxon stated. The three ran through the hallway, having only taken out two gangers along the way. The rest of the building appeared to have run outside to deal with the intruders and the current stalker threat.

"Might wanna change the plan. The mutants are swarming all over the port. The others will probably get eaten on the way," Kaiden advised. "Holy hell. That guy just got ripped in half. Maybe being eaten is preferable?"

The Tsuna ace pursed his lips, thinking over the options. "Genos, can you prepare for individual pick up?"

"I can but I'll need destinations and that will leave Kaiden, Luke, and Marlo with no support," the mechanist cautioned.

"We'll have to make it quick and play it close. I'll send the others to the rooftop and blast a hole in the wall on our floor for extraction," Jaxon replied.

"Guys, Marlo just said he spotted one of the stalkers climbing into the building. I would start running rather quickly," Kaiden warned.

"What? You're afraid of a few deformed crocs, Kaiden?" Cameron snickered.

"You're not out here seeing what they're doing, you ass!" he snapped back.

"I can take on an overgrown— Shit!" Cameron cried, gunfire blasting over the comms.

"Cameron? What's happening?" Jaxon demanded.

"It's here. It smashed through the wall," the bounty hunter yelled as he and Silas fired shots into the beast's body. The monster roared and made a large swipe at them. Chiyo rolled under its reach and pressed a button on her console.

"We need to leave," she shouted as two turrets descended from the ceiling and began to fire on the stalker. The beast roared again, crouching back before leaping up to clutch the turrets in its claws and rip them down, casting one to each side as the initiates left the room.

"Chiyo! Where are you?" Kaiden asked.

"Second floor. The stalker is right on our heels." She activated a few more turrets as they ran, the creature not fazed at all as it continued its pursuit. The infiltrator yanked out her submachine gun and fired behind her as they ran in a full sprint down the hall.

"Can you make it to the roof?" Jaxon asked.

"We'll be a snack for this thing before we get there," Cameron protested. He fumbled for a grenade and threw it over his shoulder at the monster. The projectile exploded and released a large net that wrapped around the pursuing beast. The stalker struggled against the tightening binds for a moment before it simply dug its claws through the webbing and shredded the net.

"Come down to us. We'll help you kill it," Kaiden suggested.

"I'll take you up on that," Silas answered. He flipped a switch on his gun and fired at the floor ahead. Small ballistic rounds blew it to pieces and gave them a quick exit to the first level. They dove into the newly formed hole one by one, landing on their feet or in a roll, and continued their sprint. They heard concrete smashing and the warping of metal as the stalker pried the hole apart, making it large enough for it to descend and continue the chase.

"Take the left hall," Chiyo shouted. The three turned quickly and ran into the hall, the open entrance of the building a little over a hundred yards away. "Kaiden! Behind you."

"Luke, Marlo! They're coming," Kaiden shouted. The three turned and raised their weapons as the others ran toward them. The stalker gained ground. As they aimed, it paused and bent low before leaping into the air, sailing at the fleeing initiates.

"Take it out," Luke roared. The three fired as the mutant was mid-leap, and the others dove to the ground. Explosive rounds, plasma charge, and the heated metal of Kaiden's shotgun all blasted forth and tore through the exposed underbelly of the stalker. It shrieked in pain as green blood sprayed over the walls and onto the initiates' armor.

"Roll to the side," Silas shouted. The trio rolled away as the beast crashed between them and slid a few feet to the edge of the entrance. Kaiden ran up and put a few more shots into it before looking up. "You guys all right?"

"Better when we get out of here." Cameron grunted and pushed himself up.

"Better when there's no more of those things around," Silas said flatly.

Kaiden helped Chiyo to her feet, looking at the enforcer. "Yeah, about that. What's that old saying? Out of the frying pan and into the fire?" There was a loud boom and the group looked around to see what had exploded. "What the hell now?"

"Fire," Marlo shouted. They ran out of the gate to see a building ablaze and fireballs falling from the sky, igniting the wooden boards and buildings around them.

"Oh, good, more bullshit," the ace muttered. Flames erupted beneath the stairs and around the field in long streaks, following a trail. "What's going on?"

"There's oil along the ground," Chiyo stated. "There must have been a blown tanker."

"Or it was the busted tanks of the guys with the flamethrowers," Luke suggested.

"Safe bet," Kaiden concurred.

"Guys, I think the stalkers are running out of appetizers," Marlo said, pointing at the field.

The mutants were devouring the remnants of the port. Kaiden couldn't see any other mercs or gangers running around. He vented his shotgun as it dawned on him what was next. "Genos, can we get an extraction?" One of the stalkers looked at the group, releasing an airy hiss as it moved slowly toward them. "When you got the time…" The ace closed the vent and aimed his gun at the monster, the rest following suit as more of the stalkers crawled toward them. "Now would be good."

As the stalker in the lead made its way to the base of the stairs, baring its teeth, blasts erupted around it and the other beasts. The ship descended to the group's left, hovering a few feet in the air. The door on the side opened and Genos reached out. "Hurry."

Kaiden waved, ordering the others ahead. Chiyo took the Tsuna's hand and he pulled her in. Cameron and Luke leaped aboard as Silas, Kaiden, and Marlo fired at the beasts to keep them at bay. The enforcer turned to jump on board, Luke pulling him in as Cameron fired out the door. The demolisher fired one more charged shot. His plasma blast actually succeeding in hurting a stalker as it burned off the arms on its left side. He handed his cannon to Luke and scrambled in.

"Kaiden! Come on," Cameron called.

He fired his last shot and could feel his gun overheating. Glacially calm, he took a thermal grenade from his belt and activated it, jammed it into the barrel, and tossed the gun into the center of the group of mutants. He swung into the ship, Luke and Silas pulling him in as Cameron slammed on the door switch to close it.

"Get in the air, Genos," Kaiden yelled.

"Certainly, hold on," the Tsuna replied. He pulled on the levers and the ship lifted straight into the air, a couple of the initiates toppling over with the sudden ascent.

The ace ran to the cockpit, looking out in time to see his gun, with a heated plasma core, explode in a massive discharge of energy. A couple of the stalkers leaped away in time, but the ones who were caught in the blast let out a final dying roar as their skin melted or their bodies blew apart.

"Teach you to try to take my score," Kaiden whispered to himself.

"Kin Jaxon, are you prepared for pick-up?" Genos asked.

"Affirmative. Third floor on the right side of the building, far end. Making an exit point now."

The Tsuna guided the ship around the building. He and Kaiden saw a breach appear in the wall in an explosion and cloud of dust. The mechanist steered the ship to the breach and opened the opposite door. "Welcome aboard," he said cheerfully as Izzy, Raul, and Jaxon stepped in.

"Got the device?" Kaiden asked, walking over to greet the trio.

"Was there any doubt?" Izzy asked, pointing a thumb at Raul, who held a big black case. "You guys made it pretty easy, since almost everyone was trying to kill you."

"That was the plan," Kaiden replied.

"Was going pretty well until those scaly monsters showed up." Marlo huffed his annoyance.

"Gotta admit it made our jobs easier...until they decided that they wanted to chow down on us too," Luke said with a shrug.

"Could have done without that surprise appearance." Cameron scowled. "Didn't that thing have enough prey out there?"

"You must be really unlucky...or smell delicious." Kaiden chuckled, earning a roll of the eyes from the bounty hunter.

"How much time before the dreadnought gets here?" Jaxon asked. Chief appeared in the middle of the ship.

"Well, it would have been another minute or two before reen-

try. But it looks like we're gold. It stopped descending for some—Uh oh."

"What's up, Chief?" Kaiden asked, watching as the EI's circle widened and the lines around his body began to wiggle frantically.

"Something's wrong," Chiyo said. She opened her holomonitor and looked at the readings. "There is a huge energy spike. A massive collection of power coming from above."

"The dreadnought. Crazy bastards on that thing have a plasma cannon, and they're going to use it."

"Are they locking on us or something?" Silas asked.

Chiyo shook her head. "They don't need to. It's a tempest-class cannon. When it fires, it creates an explosion at the point of impact and wipes out everything in a massive area."

"They're going to glass us?" Raul cried. "Piss-poor losers, aren't they?"

"Time to fly, Genos," Kaiden ordered. The ship accelerated, leaving the port and flying across the bayou around it.

"How long until they fire?" Jaxon asked.

"Forty seconds," Chiyo informed him.

"I have reached the top speed of this ship. But from the readings Viola is giving me, I don't think we will be out of the blast radius in time," Genos said fretfully.

The human ace walked to the cockpit and sat in the co-pilot's chair. "Any way to give this thing more juice?"

"I don't think liquids will help. I'm having Viola turn off all non-essential systems and reroute the power to the boosters. But if we funnel too much power at once, we could risk overheating or possibly blowing the engines," the mechanist explained.

"Can your EI keep it on the edge?"

"Viola is tasked to capacity at the moment. I'm trying to work out the energy delegation myself."

"I've got your back—or I should say Chief does." Kaiden opened the connection to the Ship's console. "If you wouldn't mind, Chief, get in there and make sure we don't explode."

"On it. Let's get this fat bitch to sing." Chief sounded inordinately cheerful. He disappeared from the room and reappeared in the console screen. *"Give me a moment to get situated."*

"I swear to God, if we fry because you're doing EI warm-up stretches…" Kaiden threatened.

"I'm calibrating, dumbass. Ten seconds till we're boosting."

"Seven seconds until they fire," Chiyo stated. "We will have a lead, but the blast expands quickly. Best of luck to us all."

"This will hurt like hell if we're caught," Raul muttered.

The ace looked at another screen, switching the view to a camera on the back end of the ship looking at the port far in the distance.

"They are firing," Chiyo announced.

He watched as a large red beam shot down from the sky. It continued to pierce through the port before a large wave of bright white light erupted into a dome around it. The light quickly expanded around the base, swallowing it and the bayou in its wake.

"Ready. Boosting," Chief declared.

"Hold on," Genos shouted. The ship accelerated sharply.

Kaiden was drilled into the back of his seat and he could hear the group behind them fall to the floor. He pushed himself up to view the screen again and saw the explosion taking up most of the screen, gaining on them.

"It's almost…right up…our ass," he stammered against the force of the acceleration.

"Our speed is continuing to increase," the pilot yelled. "We should be able to make it to the end point."

"Keep up that optimism," He ordered. The explosion had now almost swallowed the entire viewscreen. The ace gripped the armrests of his seat and gritted his teeth. He could feel his heart beating against his chest.

"We've reached the max speed. Any more and we'll turn into a shooting star," Chief yelled.

"Because we'll be glorious?" Kaiden asked sarcastically.

"Because we'll be a ball of fire flying through the sky."

"We are almost there," the Tsuna shouted.

The temperature of the ship was increasing. The force nearly crushed Kaiden's chest. He looked out the cockpit window to see they were reaching the end of the bayou.

"Genos!" he hollered, looking for reassurance.

"We're here," the mechanist replied.

The ace pulled himself to the console again and watched the explosion taper off and dissipate. He leaned back and saw a **Mission Accomplished** banner appear. Cheers erupted behind him. He smiled as the ship decelerated and clapped Genos on the shoulder. "Good work."

"Same to you," the alien responded, his breath shaky and his hands clenched firmly around the controls. "I must say, it's odd to run a mission where you are not the most destructive thing in it."

"Makes you appreciate the times I am, huh?" Kaiden joked.

The pilot chuckled softly. "Honestly? Quite so. At least you don't direct it at us."

He laughed as the world began to disappear, turning to white as the mission completed and they flew back to reality.

CHAPTER FOUR

"*Commander, it would appear that—*"

"Tell him I'm busy, Isaac," Sasha grunted, continuing to type out his report for the board.

"Too busy to make time for friends? Nonsense," Laurie said with a hint of mocking disdain in his voice as he made his way into the office.

The commander grimaced, peering at the visitor over the shades of his oculars. "Laurie, I'm being completely honest here. I have several reports to finish, messages to sort through, and I have to make preparations for my League team. So if you don't mind—"

"How is that going, by the way?" the professor asked as he sat and crossed one leg over the other. "Things have gotten rather quiet on the League front since the end of the Co-op Test. I'm wondering how my pool is shaping up."

"Your pool? You didn't make a team this year," Sasha reminded him.

His visitor brandished an EI pad and brought up an

image of a crisscrossing board with various symbols on it. "It's a little fun on the side for those of us who didn't make a team. We're taking bets on who will gain the most points. We each took turns choosing a faculty player and at the end of the year, we tally up the total points of all three members and see who won."

"So you created a League based around those already playing in the League. That's both meta and roundabout for you, Laurie."

The professor smiled as he deactivated the pad and put it away. "After some time, I did regret not participating. I figured this would be a fun way to partake in the festivities in a less intensive manner."

"And who's running the operation?" Sasha asked, suspicion heavy in his voice.

"Why, me, of course," Laurie responded cheerily. "Who else should but I? It also means I get to create the gatherings and meet-ups. I assure you, they are much more gallant affairs than whatever droll events you have to attend."

Sasha released a low chuckle. "Since you're participating and are at the head of this little game of exaggerated bingo, I'm sure everything is set up fairly and you haven't given yourself the slightest edge."

The professor frowned and placed a hand against his chest. "Sasha, you must give me more credit that that. To blight this game of fun and tension with masterful strategy —though some would call it cheating—would be a disservice to the spirit of what we are trying to accomplish."

He stopped typing and looked at his companion, then raised an eyebrow. After a silent beat, Laurie shrugged. "I may have given myself first pick, but to be fair, it was a round robin, so I didn't get another choice until after the other thirty-two had gone."

"There are thirty-three in total? That would mean for each of you to choose three teachers, it would only make ninety-nine in total."

"There was a teacher left—Counselor Lupus, and no one wanted him. He's made so many trades and faults that he's almost dead last," Laurie explained.

Sasha switched tabs on his monitor, looked at the League screen, and scrolled down to find the counselor. "You seem to be right. He's in ninety-sixth place, but he's got a decent team… How many trades has he made?"

"Over fifteen. If I recall correctly, you can only make one trade and keep your score, then you lose points with every trade thereafter. He's made so many that he went from the top twenty to almost dead last."

"Is he trying to play some sort of long con? I can't see any strategy that would help him in the standings at this point. Maybe he's decided to forsake the game and simply build a strong team for the sake of the students."

His visitor let out a loud, astonished laugh. "Oh, Sasha, you can be so hopeful and precious at times. The man has basically become a dealer. He figured out around the time of the Co-operative Test that this League could be far more beneficial to him without winning."

The commander leaned back in his chair and folded his arms. "He's been making deals? With whom and for what?"

"The whom is almost fifty percent of the others in the League. The what is for whatever they want to barter," Laurie stated. "He's been making out like a hyper pirate on an unguarded trade route. Some have offered credits, others have volunteered to lighten his workload or traded almost everything from office supplies to making plans for him to have days off at their summer homes."

"Sounds like he's been quite the profiteer, but how has he accomplished this?"

"The old standby of supply and demand. He was able to get a pretty good group the first time around. Once the Co-op Test was coming up, he made some trades. Apparently, one of them offered him tickets to a blitz game along with a trade, and he not only took it but saw a…shall we say a different way of winning the league. At this point, he's even trading the student's points along with them, bringing him even more standing." The professor's laugh was openly snarky. "It's a good thing this isn't connected to the faculty's employment. He'd be spending his time better if he was filling out applications rather than tending to his scoreboard."

Sasha nodded and looked at the monitor again. He leaned forward and opened Lupus' team sheet. Immediately, he saw something that interested him "Laurie, do you know where Counselor Lupus is at this moment?"

"He's not on my network—"

"You must stop with the runaround when you talk to me, Laurie. You have the ability to trace any faculty member or student in this facility. Where is he?"

The other man snickered. "If you know that then weren't you the one giving me the runaround first?"

"Perhaps, but if you don't answer the question, I'll be giving you the out-the-window."

"Someone's grumpy." Laurie huffed dramatically. He

withdrew a curved device from his pocket and slotted it behind his ear. When he tapped on it, a holographic visor formed around his eyes. "Let's see here… Locating the counselor…shouldn't be but a moment… Ah! He's just arrived at a bar in town—Ray Legend's Saloon."

Sasha nodded, stood up, and walked toward the door. "I know the place. I'll see you later, Laurie."

"You're leaving me? What happened to all that busy work you had to do?"

"Obviously, that didn't deter you before, and it won't deter me now," the commander stated as he shrugged into his coat. "Please, do lock up for me once you leave."

"You have a sudden spring in your step. Care to fill me in?"

The doors opened as Sasha stepped into the hall. "I can't say for certain right now, but I believe that your interruption may have brought me something quite fortunate. It will also work out for you and your little game as my points climb higher."

Laurie cocked his head and tapped his fingers on the commander's desk. "How do you know I chose you? I could have chosen anyone," he countered haughtily.

"First, is deduction. You started this game after we chose our teams and, seeing as you chose first, you could probably see who had the best odds. Second, I have Kaiden on my team and your stake in him—or faith, I suppose you would call it—is near obsession at this point. And third, you're a smart man, Laurie, and you know that the intelligent move would be to bet on me."

The professor beamed a glowing smile for a moment.

"Why thank you, Sasha, that may be the first compliment you've honestly given me in quite some—"

"Although all that is mostly hypothesis. Much less concrete than seeing your signature over my name in the holo you showed me a few minutes ago." He waved at the visitor as the doors closed. "Have a good evening, Laurie."

As the doors closed, the professor could feel his eye twitch. He stood and then moved to open the cabinet in the corner of the commander's office. "That shifty bastard! Just for that, I'll drink what's left of your most expensive— Whisky? Pah!" Laurie slammed the cabinet doors shut. "Uncultured lout."

It was a slow evening for the Ray Legend's Saloon, and only a few dozen patrons milled about the large area. The walls and floors were made of smooth, cleaned wood with various pictures of big game hunts and military memorabilia lining the walls. Sasha entered, removed his oculars, and scanned the bar. A man in a Nexus coat sat drinking alone at the bar beneath the skull of an ebonhorn. He made his way across the room, took a seat beside him, and ordered a shot of Golden Dust whiskey.

The man with long, matted blond hair and nonchalant green eyes looked at him with a wry, slightly tipsy smile. "You've got good taste my friend," he slurred in a wavering voice.

"Appreciate it, Counselor," Sasha responded, looking him in the eyes to see if the inebriated man recognized him.

Acknowledgement appeared after a few seconds. Lupus' eyes widened for a moment before steadying, and he leaned against the bar while his smile widened. "Commander Sasha, nice to see you. Never pictured you coming to such a salty place as this."

The bartender came over, a fairly attractive woman with curly auburn hair and dark eyeshadow who was dressed in a red, orange, and black flannel coat with the sleeves ripped off and torn blue jeans. She placed Sasha's glass in front of him. "You're kidding, right? Up until a couple years ago, he was a regular. That deactivated pistol on the wall is his," she stated, pointing at the object on the wall a few yards away.

"Evening, Rosie, a pleasure to see you again." He tipped his glass at her.

"Can I get you anything else?" she asked.

Sasha downed the shot. "Just a schooner of lager to nurse. I probably won't be staying long."

"Got a preference?"

"Peacemaker Amber." He looked at Lupus. "Care for anything, Counselor?"

His companion broke out into a toothy grin as he placed his chin in his hand. "Quite nice of you, Commander...turning out to be a nice night for me." He looked at Sasha's empty glass for a moment. "Gold dust sounds pretty good. I'll take a shot if you don't mind."

Sasha took out his credit chip, placed it into the tab slot, and looked at Rosie. "Certainly. The Peacemaker and another shot of Gold Dust for my friend, please." She smiled and stepped away as he turned his attention to the other man. "I'm actually happy to run into you here, Lupus.

I've been wanting to request a trade seeing as the final tests are coming up."

"Mixing business and pleasure? Good taste and style." He gave a joyful laugh. "Buying me a drink is also a good negotiation tactic too. I applaud you…if only in spirit and not physically. My head's a bit hazy."

"A good way to end a Friday," he responded mildly.

"No doubt," Lupus agreed and Rosie returned with the whiskey and lager, gave them to their respective recipients, then moved to attend another customer. "So then, what can I help you with?"

Sasha pulled a tablet from his coat pocket, opened it to the counselor's page, and showed it to him. "I'm interested in your engineer."

"The Tsuna?" Lupus laughed a little too loudly. "This *is* a great night for me."

"You've been trying to trade him then?"

"Trying but can't get anyone to take the bait. Not because no one wants him, but for what he would cost…a bit too rich for most other leaguers' blood," the man explained dazedly. "You see, Commander, between you and me and—well, quite a few others, actually—I've found a unique way to make my winnings in this tournament of ours."

"I've heard as much." The commander nodded. "Aren't you worried about your score?"

"No, no, no, you see…I may not have the high score on paper…uh, tablet screen. However, I've been making out like the bandit of the league. I got Roland Cohen, the Pilot workshop teacher, to give me tickets to last week's blitz semi-finals in trade for one of the navigators I had. I thought I was up the creek when the Co-op Test came around because I hadn't traded him off yet and he partnered with a mech jock of all things. But Cohen was able to convince him to link up with the pilot on his team and wanted to trade, but I had all the power. He sweetened the deal and I realized there was a much better way to 'win' this little competition."

"I see, but what about the students in your finals group? Will they not be prepared?"

"That's the beauty of it. Everyone is running around trying to finalize groups and get them to gel. My group is already pretty gelled merely because of chance. I got the Tsuna mechanist, I got an enforcer, and a sapper. That's a pretty strong team."

"Perhaps on screen, but it says nothing about their individual teamwork or group dynamics," Sasha countered.

"You know the test brings people together and also blows them apart, but as I've explained, I'm not really going for the big points here," his companion said with a smug grin.

Sasha pursed his lips. He certainly wouldn't appeal to his ethical or strategist sensitivities. It looked like he would simply have to go with plan b then—should have started with it, to be honest. "I want to trade my battle-medic for the mechanist. She will make a welcome addition to your team and will help with the survivability rating as well."

Lupus downed the shot of whiskey, his face contorting slightly from the strong flavor, then placed the glass down and frowned. "That's great and all, but that's not exactly what I'm looking—"

"I'm willing to barter," Sasha interjected.

The man's smile returned. "There we go." He stood as straight as he could and faced the commander. "What do you got?"

"As I'm sure you know, I'm in the lead—comfortably so. Even if my team does not make top five in the Squad Test, I am almost certain to make at least top three in the League. Whatever credits I earn are yours."

"So potentially...fifty thousand at most and, like, ten thousand at least?"

He nodded. "That is correct."

"That's damn tempting," Lupus said with a furrowed brow. He tapped his chin for a moment. "I was kinda hoping to trade the whole lot to someone else for a big payday, but this could work out just as well."

"You could potentially have both."

"How so?" the drunk man asked.

"Simple. With my battle-medic on your team, it has support now. That's a more rounded team than you had before. For a discerning League member, that makes the team more attractive and makes them more willing to trade for all of them."

Lupus clapped his hands together. "That sounds fantastic. Nice thinking, Commander!"

"I've had a few years to figure out how to play the game well." He took a long drink of his lager, then placed the glass back on the bar with studied care. "Many games, in fact."

"All right, I know you'll keep your promise." His companion held out a hand. "We got a deal, then?"

He nodded, shaking the proffered hand. "Indeed, my thanks."

"I should thank you." Lupus beamed. "But it was a pleasure."

Sasha clicked the offer to trade Initiate Ziegler for Lupus' mechanist, Genos Aronnax.

The man accepted the trade and called Rosie over. "Since I'll have some credits to burn in the future, how about I return the favor and get you something to drink?"

The commander downed the remainder of his beer. "Unfortunately, I have other business to attend too." He stood and added a large tip to his total, then removed his credit chip. "Have a good evening, Lupus—you as well, Rosie."

"Best of luck to your team in the finals, Commander," Lupus called as Sasha departed.

"That's why I do these changes and trades, Lupus," he whispered as he opened to door to the spring night. "It's so I don't have to rely on luck as much as most."

CHAPTER FIVE

Kaiden awoke groggily, rubbed his hands over his face, and shielded his eyes from the sunlight.

Wait, sunlight? His room had blackout curtains.

He blinked a few times and found himself in the compartment of a dropship. Across from him were Flynn and Cameron. He looked beside him to see Luke and Silas still dozing. They were all dressed in jumpsuits with the Nexus logo on them and strapped into their seats with a bar over their shoulders and chest, securing them in place.

"Hey, wake up," he shouted. His friends stirred.

"Give me a few more minutes...mate," Flynn muttered sleepily.

"Kaiden, what the hell are you doing in—not my room...what the hell?" Cameron stammered as his hands gripped the bars on his chest and he looked around frantically.

"What's going on?" Luke demanded as he tried to pull the bars off him, to no avail. "Where are we?"

"Why am I in this damn tube-sock body-suit?" Silas growled, stretching the tight-fitting fabric.

"Chief, what's going on?" Kaiden asked.

The EI popped into existence, looking around at the group. *"It's Wulfson's proving-ground thing, remember? You guys signed up for it like a week ago."*

"Wulfson," the group shouted in anger and unison.

"What do ya want?" Their instructor's voice shouted through the intercom overhead. "You bastards are loud after you wake up."

"Where the hell are we?" Cameron yelled.

"Why were we asleep in the first place?" Luke roared.

"Where the hell is my gun?" Kaiden snapped.

"One at a time, one at a time, by God," the security officer muttered. "Where we're going is a mystery until deployment. You were asleep because you were asleep when we brought you onto the ship, and I have your gun Kaiden...if you can call it a gun."

"What is going on?" Flynn shouted, finally coming to.

"Calm down, you fretful lasses. This is the proving ground training I told you about. You all signed up for it."

Cameron continued to pull fruitlessly on the bars over his chest. "I thought this was supposed to be an Animus thing. I don't remember getting in the Animus."

"Because you didn't. We're heading to a real environment, where the lot of you have to team up and use your combined skills to survive the elements and Raza," Wulfson explained.

"Raza? He's here?" Kaiden asked.

"Aye, I told him the year was almost up and he'll return

to his clan in a month or so, anyhow. Figured we'd have one more big going away bout of training and make the most of it."

"What is it?" Silas questioned.

"The proving ground. I haven't had a batch of trainees to run through it in a long while. I'm excited to see how it turns out." The man crowed with almost malicious delight.

"You keep saying that, but we don't know what it means," Flynn retorted.

"When you pitched this to us you made it seem like it would be an Animus thing or that we would go into the mountains or something. This is not the mountains." Kaiden growled his displeasure.

"To be fair, there are mountains around here," Wulfson pointed out.

"Why is he being so damn vague?" Luke hissed.

"Because he wants to piss us off," the ace muttered.

"It's working," Cameron sneered, now kicking his legs in an attempt to slip under the bars.

"Now don't be like that, boys. This will be a great bonding experience," their instructor claimed jovially.

"Yeah, we'll bond over the different methods and ideas we'll think of to gut you," Flynn mumbled.

Kaiden sighed and looked around. A couple of dozen cargo crates and several other small boxes were stacked at the back of the ship. He felt around his body and found a small device in his ear. On taking it out, he realized it was a comm link. "Hey, guys, check your ears."

They all did, also finding comms. "Small mercy," Flynn said flatly.

"Can any of you rig this so we can send out an SOS?" Cameron asked.

"I don't think any of us are that skilled in engineering." Luke sighed.

"I wish Genos were here," Kaiden mumbled.

"Nah, he was smart enough not to sign up for the crazy man's camping trip," Silas said, placing the link back into his ear.

"It's short-range anyway and stuck on one channel. Even if it could be wired or the channel changed, it wouldn't do us much good unless we were already close to an emergency station," Flynn explained.

"I doubt we'll be lucky enough for Wulfson to pick an area where that'll be available," Kaiden guessed.

Silas looked around. "Any way to figure out where we are?"

The ace shook his head. "No windows. Chief, you got anything?"

"I can track your position, but that would be no fun, now would it?" Chief jeered.

"Are you shitting me? You're supposed to help me in situations like this," Kaiden snapped.

"Normally, I would, but you signed the contract. In the stipulations, you agreed to go in without your EIs," Chief stated.

"Wait… Where's my pad?" Luke asked, feeling around his suit.

"My oculars are gone," Flynn cried, his eyes widening in realization.

"All our EI devices were taken," Silas concluded.

"You would be right. Finally one of ya are catching on."

Wulfson chortled over the comms. "Here's the deal since I can tell you didn't go over the rules."

"You could have explained it better," Cameron retorted.

"You are all supposedly grown-ass men, so you should have done the damn reading yourself. Now stop whining and listen up."

The group all sat back, resigned to their current predicament and listening intently.

"Now, what's going to happen is that you will be left in a designated area for one day. During that time, you will have to band together to get supplies and arm yourselves, because in twenty-four hours, Raza will be hunting the lot of you down."

"You mean for real?" Flynn asked, a tinge of fear creeping into his voice.

"Well, I suppose it's more like he'll capture you, but still, he's a Sauren and they are good at that," Wulfson reminded them.

"What are we supposed to do?" Luke asked.

"Not get caught, for starters. But to win, you gotta take him down or capture him yourselves."

"We've gotten pretty good at that over the last couple months," Silas noted.

"Yeah, in a contained space, with me advising you, and with weapons provided and Raza with handicaps. But besides the fact that he's not out to kill ya, it would make diplomacy a bit of a bitch to have dead initiates on our hands. You're dealing with a Sauren Warchief in his element. But keep up that bravado, it'll serve you well."

The group looked at each other nervously. "We

wouldn't be able to pull out of this would we?" Flynn asked doubtfully.

"Pah, where's your backbone? Where's your sense of adventure?" Wulfson demanded.

"I think I forgot to get them from the drawer of my nightstand when you kidnapped me," Kaiden jeered. "Fine, whatever. Sauren hunt in some mystery location, got it. When can we start so we can get this over with."

"Oh, we're just about there. Gotta couple of things to do first, but we'll start in about ten minutes," the instructor said.

"I'm reporting him for this," Cameron muttered.

"Good luck. We signed an agreement to do this. Plus, I think he can do this anyway as our instructor," Kaiden reminded him.

"Your instructor. I'm more of a hostage," Cameron grumbled.

"I'm warming up to it, honestly." Luke seemed thoughtful. "Could have done without the rude awakening, but hey, it's something different."

"Your appetite for spontaneity is greater than mine," Silas observed.

"Mine too, though Amber and Marlo have pulled me along on many a misadventure," Flynn added.

"Two other people who were apparently smarter than us," Kaiden quipped.

"Anyone wanna take a stab on where we're getting dropped?" Cameron asked.

"Jungle would be my guess," Silas suggested. "Izzy's been reading up about the Sauren homeworld Jurak, and says it's mostly a massive, deadly jungle with a couple of deserts, and it rains half the year solid."

"Going for the terrain advantage?" Luke pondered this. "I guess I'd rather be in a jungle than a desert. Wish I had my armor instead of this clown suit."

"No kidding, this stuff compresses way too much." Flynn grunted, pulling at the elastic around his waist. "It's also hot—got thermal lining?"

"Feels like it. I guess that would rule out desert or anything too humid," Luke observed. "Unless that's supposed to be a deliberate liability, but he would have to be a sadist to do something like that."

The other four looked at him with curious or annoyed expressions. The titan took a moment to realize what he'd said before rubbing the back of his head. "I guess that does go without saying, huh?"

"What do you think is in the crates?" Flynn asked, pointing to the mass of boxes and containers in the back.

"Not sure. Can't exactly check them out like this," Kaiden said, pointing to the bars.

"Weapons, supplies, medical tools. I don't know if it's for them or us." Cameron still sounded peeved.

Kaiden crossed his arms. "Wulfson didn't say he was participating, just Raza. Most human food and medicines don't do much for them—hell, some are poisonous. And Raza doesn't like using our gear, says ours pale in comparison with the Sauren weapons."

"You think that's a pride thing or just speciesism?" Luke asked.

"Mixture of pride and biology, I would guess," Silas said with a shrug, "His weapons seem pretty primitive compared to ours, but you have to admit he's damn effective at carving things up with them, and that energy rifle he showed us is pretty sick."

"I like how the war-mongering alien can walk around campus with an energy rifle, and I'm still stuck with my zappy gun," Kaiden grumbled.

"And yet you still hold onto it like it was your teddy bear." Cameron chuckled.

"It's all I have," Kaiden retorted.

"Sorry for the interruption, boys," Wulfson said.

"Just plotting how we'll smother you in your sleep," the ace shot back.

"Ha! Not a very smart tactic against someone who can throw ya like a child's doll into the muck," the man scoffed.

"Is that some sort of Scandinavian proverb or is he simply being weird?" Flynn asked.

Kaiden held his hands up in the air in a show of uncertainty. "Since he's the only Scandinavian I've met, I assume both."

"You boys might wanna hold on. The bars should keep you tethered, but this may get a bit turbulent," the instructor advised.

"What might?" the ace asked. A red light shone from the back of the ship, drawing the group's attention. It turned green, and they heard the hiss of air and the shifting of gears and metal.

"Is he going to—" Cameron began.

"Aw, hell." Kaiden sighed.

The door to the back of the dropship opened. All five of them immediately held on to their harnesses as the ship began to tilt. "What is he doing?" Flynn shouted over the rushing air.

"Good God, it's cold!" Silas grunted. "Sure as hell not in a desert."

"I see snow," the ace stated. "Are we in the North Pole?"

"Nah, Alaska. This ship is fast, but not that fast. Only been out about seventy minutes," Wulfson informed them.

"Alaska? I'm not built for Alaska. I grew up in Texas," Kaiden hollered.

"I was born in the Caribbean. This is a whole new level of bullshit," Silas cried through clenched teeth, bracing against the bars and tensing up from the cold air.

"Sending out first batch," the instructor stated. Kaiden saw several tethers detach, the cases sliding down the floor and then out the hatch.

"You should be making notes of those, boys. Be damn helpful during the training," Wulfson advised.

"Yeah, right. I'll remember to look for the big white spot. It'll be easy to find," the ace retorted acidly.

"Heading up. Hold on," Wulfson shouted. The ship began to ascend straight up. The group was now dangling from their harnesses, clutching them for dear life.

"My ass has never been so clenched," Cameron yelled.

"I'm feeling a little woozy here," Luke bellowed.

"I swear to God, Luke, if you puke on me, I'll shove your hammer up your ass the next time we're in the Animus," Kaiden warned.

"Dropping the next batch!" More cases and a few small boxes dropped into the air, falling to the snowy ground below.

"Heading back down." The ship arced and then raced

down toward the ground. The group slammed back into their seats and then into each other as the plane descended.

"Cameron. Get your elbow out of my ribs," Flynn demanded

"Blame gravity," he grunted in response, trying to force himself off the marksman.

"Luke… Open…your damn…arms," Kaiden ordered, his head trapped beneath the titan's right arm.

"Oh, sorry!" He apologized, opening his arm as wide as he could for the ace to escape.

"I hope one of those crates has deodorant." He huffed his fury. The ship steadied after a few more seconds, then tilted up a little.

"Final batch!" Wulfson said. The last of the cargo dropped out of the hatch.

"I'm going into this with some whiplash," Flynn mumbled, rubbing his neck.

"Congrats, Santa, you dropped off all your gifts, now what?" Kaiden inquired.

"Now it's your turn!" the instructor yelled. The ship banked, making a complete turn.

"Where are you dropping us off?" Silas asked.

"Eh, somewhere around here. I'm looking for a good spot."

"Are we getting anything out of this?" Cameron asked.

"Besides bragging rights?"

Kaiden shifted in his seat, trying to sit straight. "I'll settle for time off after this."

"That's certainly not happening," the instructor warned. "I've got a few prizes for ya once we get back—assuming you win."

"Wulfson's version of prizes is suspect," Flynn pointed out.

"Today we're only running ten miles instead of twenty," Cameron said in a mock Scandinavian accent. "Aren't I so generous?"

"Never complaining about workshops after this," Luke muttered.

"All right, I'm about to let you go," the man said.

"Good, we can finally get out of these damn harnesses," the ace responded in a waspish tone.

"Why haven't you closed the hatch yet? You shouldn't land with an open hatch," Flynn protested.

"I ain't landing."

"Then how are we getting out of here?" Cameron asked. The others hesitated for a moment before they all looked at the open hatch and then back at each other.

"Oh no..." they all muttered together.

"Best of luck to the lot of ya. I'll be back to drop Raza off tomorrow." Wulfson shut the intercom off.

"Don't you do it, Wulfson," Kaiden ordered. Then he heard a clack and felt his seat shift. He heard more of the same sound as the grips holding the chairs in place released and they began sliding toward the hatch.

"Oh, son of a bitch," Cameron cried.

"He does know that we're not in armor, right?" Flynn asked pointlessly.

"Luke! Get in front of me so I can fall on you," Kaiden said, using his feet to try to slow his descent.

"Oh, real nice, you jackass!" the titan snapped.

"If one of you believes in a God or gods, start making deals and throw me in!" Silas demanded.

The intercom whined back to life. "Yer still in there? Quit that bellyaching and get out."

The ship pulled upright, the motion launching all the soldiers immediately through the hatch and into nothing. The arctic around them was rather silent except for their ferocious screams as they sailed through the sky.

CHAPTER SIX

The group continued their fall, the adrenaline in their systems helping them to ignore the frigid air but not imminent death from a large fall strapped to dropship chairs.

"Well, this seems like quite the predicament," Chief noted nonchalantly. *"Also, would you can the screaming? I swear, your mostly empty skull magnifies it."*

Though Kaiden's words couldn't be heard through the roar of the air as he fell, Chief was able to read his lips and counted over a dozen different curses coming his way—not his high score, but close. He then seemed to accuse him of not helping, and if he died, Chief would deactivate.

"I'm quite aware of that, dumbass," Chief grunted. *"But you won't die. You really think Wulfson would just drop you to your deaths?"*

More swearing resulted—nearing twenty unique words, some directed at Wulfson this time. *"True, he's a bit insane and probably should be checked, but good luck getting him in a psychiatrist's office. But no, he's not trying to* actively *kill you. Your seat has a parachute that should activate... Now."*

Kaiden was jerked around in his seat and then briefly ascended for a moment as a large silver parachute opened on the back of his chair. He took a deep breath and looked around at the others. Each of them now had their own parachutes open and drifted around in the air.

The ace drew in a few more deep breaths of the chilling air. Leaning his head back against the seat, he rolled his head around to look at Chief, staring silently at the orb for a moment. "You know...I only meant about half of those things."

"Oh, I know. The usual pet names and just enough violent threats to know you still care," Chief mused.

Kaiden heard some static in his ear before Silas' voice came through. "All right, did we lose anyone to a stopped heart?"

"Nah, still here," Kaiden said.

"These bars don't leave a lot of room for breathing, man," Cameron whined.

"You know, for being so sure I was about to die, I've never felt so alive." Flynn chuckled.

There was silence from Luke's seat. "Luke, you there? Did we lose the big guy?" Kaiden asked.

"No... No, I'm here...just had my dinner make an exit," he muttered somberly.

"Ah, jeez, check y'all's suits," Kaiden jeered.

The group descended slowly to the ground, landing softly on the snow with loud crunches. The ace took a moment to look around. They were in a forest covered in frost and snow. He heard several clicks and the bar around his chest released. Relieved, he pushed it up and over his head, stood, and looked around. "I'm on the ground," he announced.

"Same here. Hey, I see you, Kai, on your left." He looked over to see Flynn waving to him.

"Just landed. Give me a moment to compose myself," Luke mumbled. "I'll find you."

"I think you have it the wrong way around. Catch your breath, and we'll make our way to you," the ace responded as he walked over to Flynn. He looked at his suit. It was white with a small silver Nexus logo blending into the fabric. He wore gloves and boots that allowed him to grip the snow as he walked. At least they weren't totally help-less, even if the thermal lining of the suit didn't completely keep him warm.

"Silas, Cameron—where are you two?" Flynn asked over the comm as Kaiden approached.

"I landed near one of the crates. I also see Cameron. He's not on the ground." Silas chuckled.

"What do you mean? He's still airborne?" Kaiden asked.

"Sort of," the enforcer replied.

"I'm stuck in a damn tree," Cameron yelled, his voice echoing through the forest. It sounded like it came from the east beyond Kaiden and Flynn.

"That's certainly unfortunate." The ace snickered.

"Well, that helped us get your position. We'll grab Luke and hurry over," Flynn assured him.

The two looked around to see if they could find their titan comrade. "Luke, can you call out or something so we can find you?" the marksman requested.

They heard a rather faint moan come from behind

them and hurried over to find Luke sitting against a tree. His seat lay a few feet away from him. He looked up and raised a wavering hand as they approached.

"Man, looking pale there, buddy," Kaiden noted. He glanced around the forest. "At least you'll blend in."

"Funny," Luke grumbled.

"You don't get like this in the Animus," Flynn remarked, offering him a hand. Kaiden followed suit.

"The Animus takes care of things like that." He grunted as the two helped him up. "I've been kinda airsick since I was a kid. Doesn't really bother me now, but all that junk Wulfson was doing and the high speed… Not great."

"Well, take it slow for a bit so you can recover. But let's move ahead and get to Silas and Cam," Flynn said.

Luke nodded, and they trudged through the snow toward the other members of their party.

———

"Would you stop fiddling with the box and get me down?" Cameron demanded, yelling down from atop the tree as he pulled against the bars and the ropes of his parachute. "Why hasn't this thing released me?"

"Probably because it has an auto-lock that won't open until the chair is sitting on something solid, and you're…" Silas looked up to see his friend dangling from the top of the tree. "I mean, you're just hanging there."

"And you could get up here and help me," Cameron pointed out.

The enforcer continued to unstrap the box. "I could, but it would take a while. I'm hoping there's something in here that will help. Climbing spikes, a blade, maybe a gun to shoot you down."

"Let's leave that as the last option, all right?" the bounty hunter requested belligerently. "Shouldn't there be a release switch for the parachute?"

"Probably. Check around, although you have to remember that you're still stuck in the chair. You'll probably bounce around like an archaic pinball through all those branches on your way down."

"Maybe I can swing to a branch," Cameron reasoned, swinging his legs to move his chair forward and back as he tried to reach an adjacent branch.

"You keep on trying," Silas yelled. He looked up as he heard the shuffling of snow and snapping of ice to see Luke, Kaiden, and Flynn approaching. "Looks like the cavalry is here."

"Nah, man, we're just a traveling circus group," Kaiden joked.

"Honestly, it looks that way so far." The enforcer chuckled. He motioned to the opposite end of the box. "One of you mind taking off that twist-lock?"

"I got it," Flynn offered. He went over and began to unwind the latch.

The ace placed his hand on his waist as he looked at Cameron. "So, is he just bored, or is this some master plan I'm not privy too?" he asked as he saw the bounty hunter swing along the tree line.

"His harness is still on. He's trying to get the seat on a branch that will hopefully deactivate the lock," Silas explained.

"Keep it up, Cam. I believe in you," Kaiden yelled.

"Keep your sarcasm shoved up your— Aw, shit!" Cameron cursed as the lines of his chute tangled, sending him into a spin as he swung. "Help!"

"You know, if he wants to be a good bounty hunter, he's gotta be a bit more methodical in his planning," the ace stated.

"That's why we're training, right?" Silas remarked with a grin.

He smirked. "Guess Cam is learning what it means to be prepared for anything."

"I got it," Flynn declared, the final binding falling from the crate.

"Let's see what we got." Silas began to unclasp the locks on the crate.

The ace looked behind him to see Luke leaning against a tree. "You wanna see the goodies, big guy?"

The titan shook his head. "Not unless there's some nausea medicine or blue stuff."

Kaiden reached up and tapped the side of his cheek. "I think I'm turning my friends into addicts."

Flynn and Silas picked up the top of the crate and slid it over. The ace walked up to peer inside with them, grinning at the contents. "Pretty good cache."

"What's this?" Flynn asked, reaching in to grab one of the items. It was a silver weapon about the length of a forearm and had two arced segments on each side. The marksman pressed a switch, and the arcs shot out. Two lines of metal connected to a panel at the back of the weapon. "It's a crossbow!" he exclaimed. "Haven't seen one of these in ages."

"I don't think I've ever seen one, not outside of a vid or weapons glossary," Kaiden stated.

Flynn continued to study it, admiring the design. "My grandad had one. Family heirloom from the early 2000s. I used it a few times. Interesting weapon, not practical even back then, but damn, did you feel good when you hit your mark." He looked at the underside. "This seems more modern. I didn't realize they still made these. It's a bolter model. There should be a loop of arrow bolts for me to slide in here."

"Like this?" Silas asked, holding up a cylindrical tube. The marksman took it and looked at the top, then showed it to the others, revealing the pointed tips of arrows inside. "That's it all right. I'm calling this, by the way." He slammed the cylinder into the crossbow's compartment. When he aimed at a tree in the distance and held the trigger down, a bolt slotted into place, and when he let go, it flew straight into his target.

"Well, it might not be my sniper rifle, but it'll do." He smiled.

"What else do we got?" Kaiden asked.

"There are some rations, a couple of blades in sheaths with belts, a few vials of power-sip, helmet… Ah, here's a pistol."

"Dibs," Kaiden declared immediately. Silas grabbed the pistol and tossed it to him. He examined it, noting that it was metallic with a long barrel. When he unclipped the magazine, he saw small copper bullets. "Damn, are all these weapons archaic?"

"Won't be too much help against a beast that can tank laser fire," Silas noted.

"Anything else good?" Flynn asked.

"Besides what I just said, there's a satchel and this reflective blanket." The enforcer pulled out the blanket and unrolled it. The silver coating reflected the light into Kaiden and Flynn's eyes, nearly blinding them.

"Oy, mate, put that away," the marksman grumbled. Silas rolled it up and placed it in the satchel. "Want anything else?"

"Nah, keep one of the blades and give the other to Cam when we get him down," the ace advised.

"Luke'll be the only one without a weapon," Silas pointed out.

Flynn looked at the ill titan. "I don't think he needs one quite yet. More likely to hurt himself tripping."

"Or maybe use it to make the spinning stop," Kaiden quipped, drawing a finger along his throat.

"What about the helmet?" Silas pulled it out and showed it to his companions. It was white with silver lines running up the forehead and down the back.

"You keep it. Works best for you," the ace said.

"How so?"

"Camouflage. You're at the most risk for a headshot."

Silas frowned and rolled his eyes. "Couldn't be a bit more tactful?"

"Not the guy for that." Kaiden smirked. "One of them is over there trying not to upchuck his stomach, and the other keeps glancing at his crossbow like it's whispering sweet nothings in his ear."

"Hmm, what are you talking about?" Flynn asked, looking up from his weapon.

"Don't worry about it." Silas grinned. He moved a dial

on the base of the helmet which caused the plates to shift forward and out. Cautiously, he put it on and then rotated the dial back until it was snug around his head.

"Comm check," he declared.

Flynn and Kaiden nodded. "We hear ya, but it doesn't seem like the helmet has a mic, so looks like you gonna have to be on air with that thing on."

"You guys done trading presents?" Cameron yelled. The trio looked up to see he had stopped spinning and was back to dangling uselessly. "Find anything that can get me down?"

"A couple of things, but it doesn't look like you're gonna have an easy time of it," Kaiden called up to him.

Flynn looked up at him for a moment before looking back to his companions. "What if I cut a few of the parachute's lines? Let him hang horizontally so he can press the chair against the tree? That should deactivate the lock, right?"

"Not a bad idea. He'd probably prefer that to us shooting him down," Silas commented.

"Can I do it?" Kaiden asked, reaching for the crossbow.

"Whatever you do, don't let Kaiden shoot me," Cameron ordered.

"There's no way you can hear us talking from way up there," the ace hollered.

"I see those guns. Whatever plan you got probably involves them."

"Come on, buddy. You know I'm a good shot. I won't miss," Kaiden countered.

"I'm not worried about you missing," he retorted.

"I am becoming far too predictable," the ace huffed with mock severity.

"Cameron, look here, mate. I'm gonna cut some of the lines of the chute so you're at an angle. Press the chair against the tree so you can get the bars deactivated," Flynn instructed.

Though he was many feet up, they could almost make out his eyes bugging. "That's the best plan you got?"

"Do you want us to leave you in the tree until we catch Raza tomorrow?" Kaiden threatened.

"Dammit...fine, but be careful. We aren't in the Animus."

"There are six lines on the chute. Cut the two on the right and two in the middle. That should put him where he needs to be and still give him enough support not to fall," the enforcer advised.

The marksman raised the crossbow, pressed a button on the side, and a small scope appeared that he aimed through. "You want this as quick as possible or some time to prepare between each cut?"

"Just do it," the bounty hunter commanded.

Flynn fired four shots in quick succession. All four lines severed, and Cameron's chair tilted and slammed into the side of the tree. The bars opened and he slipped out, grabbing the bars for balance as he shinnied onto a nearby branch. "You could have given me a countdown."

"Hey, I did it." Flynn cheered. "But fair enough, let me help you out." He fired a series of bolts into the tree, creating a path for Cameron to climb down quickly.

"Nice work, Flynn," Kaiden complimented him.

"What do we do now?" he asked.

"Well, we should probably find shelter and prepare for tomorrow. See if we can find more crates and arm ourselves better," Silas suggested.

"We going to go looking for a cave or something? All I see is forest," Flynn noted, scanning the woods.

"Places like these have traveler shelters and emergency bunkers for those who get lost. We can probably find one of them along a path, and they'll have supplies to boot," Kaiden reasoned.

"How do you know that?" the enforcer asked.

"I've been catching up on my ace workshops. Had to make up four weeks of survivalist training."

Cameron trudged over to the others. "You know…I'd make some joke about you maturing and all, but I'm too damn tired."

"Didn't all that swinging reignite your childhood energy?" Kaiden quipped.

"Shut up," the bounty hunter sneered, placing his hands on his knees and taking in several deep breaths.

"Definitely not your best. You must be tired," the ace mocked with a smirk.

"I'm going to run these rations and a power sip to Luke, see if we can get him back on his feet," Flynn said and walked over to the titan who still leaned against the tree.

Kaiden reached into the crate and took out the other knife and belt and tossed them to Cameron. "Not much, but I already called the gun."

The bounty hunter wrapped the belt around his waist. "It's a start. At least I can make some pointy sticks if we find nothing else."

The ace chuckled. "Have to remember to go for the eyes."

"Which way should we go?" Silas asked.

Kaiden looked around. "Look like there's a clearing up ahead. Best bet is to find a path there and follow it until we run into a shelter."

"Then I'll pack the remaining gear into the satchel, and we'll head off," Silas acknowledged, going back to the crate.

Cameron walked next to the ace. "What do you think our chances are?"

"Of what? Finding a bunker? Getting frostbite?"

"I'm talking about winning, smartass."

Kaiden looked around at the group, "Well, we're not that well-armed right now, one of our guys is sick, and we're in an unknown environment. And, of course, our challenge is an alien hunter who specializes in this sort of thing…" He looked at his companion and smiled. "I still see opportunity, though."

CHAPTER SEVEN

K aiden kicked open the door to the shack, his gun at the ready as he walked inside. He scanned the room, taking in two cabinets, two beds, and a fireplace with wood and fire-starting equipment. He walked back to the door and motioned for the others to come in. The five were somewhat cramped in the space. Flynn and Cameron sat Luke on one of the beds while the ace crouched beside the fireplace and prepped it to light.

"This will do for shelter. We should rest for a bit before looking for more supplies," Silas advised.

"I wonder if we can hunt some rabbit or birds. These rations will keep us sated, but they aren't exactly tasty." Cameron grunted as he took out a half-eaten bar from the satchel.

"I can take a look around. It gives me a chance to get more practice in with this darling." Flynn grinned and held up the crossbow.

The enforcer nodded. "Just be sure to conserve your

ammo. You already used quite a few to get Cameron down from the tree, and I don't know how many bolts you have left."

"Twenty-four. Each roll has forty bolts, and I used sixteen back at the tree," the marksman answered.

"You know that just off-hand?" Cameron inquired.

Flynn removed the roll from the crossbow to show them the front. "I looked through the roll on the way here."

"Get out there, but don't go too far that you can't hear us over the comms, and stay within five hundred yards of the shelter," Silas ordered.

"On it." The marksman left the shelter and closed the door behind him.

"Look at him, all giddy with his new toy." Kaiden chuckled as he used a flint and striker to ignite the logs. "Wonder if he'll start using one once we're back in the Animus?"

"No matter how good he gets with one, it would be foolish of him to drop a real sniper rifle for a crossbow." Silas moved to sit on the other bed. "You feeling any better, Luke?"

The titan nodded. "Don't feel like the world is spinning and my stomach has settled. I'll be good to go soon."

"Good to hear. We still need to find some more equipment if we want to have a chance at winning this thing."

Cameron sighed, tapping his fist a couple of times on the wall he was leaning on.

"Something wrong, Cam?" Kaiden asked.

"Just the general vibe. I mean, what's stopping us from surrendering when Raza shows up? We could be back at the Academy by mid-afternoon if we do."

"Seems kinda defeatist," Luke muttered.

"Literally, in this case," Kaiden concurred.

"I just don't see how this is really training for us. I get that it's a test of skill, but why not simply have us do it in the Animus? We're here because none of us really read through the agreement and we're trying to win because why? Wulfson said so and the promise of some vague rewards?"

"While I agree the circumstances could be better, I do see this as a good team exercise. Plus, in your case, you get more experience than we do," Silas pointed out.

"How do you figure?" Cameron questioned.

"You going to be a bounty hunter, right? You have to be ready for all kinds of terrain and circumstances. You should be looking around, finding the best place to dig in and make traps, or where you think Raza will attack from —vantage points, things like that." Silas showed a finger for each item on his list.

"This is the first real time I've had to use those survival skills I thought were pointless," Kaiden admitted. "I still have the mindset that I'm at my best with a gun, but I can see that I can have other talents."

"Luke and Flynn are military classes. Luke's gonna be on the front lines, and Flynn will take his place as a sniper. They could be stationed in a snowy region like this. If Flynn decides to become an assassin, having to rely on his own abilities and knowledge will become even more paramount."

Kaiden laughed. "He would make for a cheery-ass assassin."

Cameron took a bite off the remains of his ration, then

motioned to Silas with it. "What about you? You're an enforcer. That's mostly merc work and bodyguarding, right?"

"Mercenary, bodyguarding, and assault teams mostly, but there's still the possibility of police, military, or guardsman. I have options. I may be the least likely one to have to deal with environments like this on the regular, but I gain the most from having to work in a team."

"Don't forget the Deathmatch coming up," Luke reminded them. "It'll be in teams of three, but we should still look at this as practice."

Kaiden hit the top of his head with the palm of his hand. "Aw, hell, when do we learn our teams again?"

"Wednesday. It's only Sunday now so we'll be back by then. Assuming Raza doesn't get lost," Silas answered.

"Probably have even more work to make up. Though considering we're on an official trip with Wulfson, maybe they will be lenient?" Luke pondered the possibility without apparent conviction.

"Most likely. I hope we'll have time to rest. Going from that mission on Friday to this back-to-back is killer." Silas grimaced.

"I'll make sure that the next training excursion Wulfson wants us to do is in the Animus," Cameron stated.

"I doubt that will ever happen. He wouldn't know how to set one up," Kaiden said.

Luke looked at him. "How's that? The teachers and faculty use the Animus too. Everyone knows how to set up a map or training session."

"He doesn't, because he can't," the ace declared.

Cameron tilted his head. "He can't use the Animus? He

always says he doesn't *like* using it but never mentioned that he can't."

Kaiden shrugged. "I don't know all the details, but I left my bag in his training room a month back and overheard him talking to Raza. They were talking about the Sauren's possible integration with the Animus in the future, and Wulfson mentioned that he couldn't use it when Raza asked for his opinion. Something about a mental condition or biological defect that wouldn't allow it."

"Even with all the upgrades it's gotten over the years?" Silas asked.

"Guess not."

"So he stops us from using it for his training because he can't use it?" Cameron quizzed.

"No, his kind of training is important. You can't argue with your gains, can you?" Kaiden questioned.

"I mean, no, not really," the bounty hunter admitted, flexing his arm. "I just don't see why he had to take us out to a place like this. The Animus can replicate an environment like this easily. Up the synch and equi and there would be almost no difference."

The ace looked at the fire. "You aren't a little more on edge out here? Knowing that what's hunting us is very real and that you can't simply de-sync?"

"Sure, but we will run missions like this in the Master year. No point in running them now while we're still getting used to the Animus."

"I feel ya, but you can't say you're not used to it when you're in there almost every day for nine months," Kaiden pointed out. "I'm not saying that getting here wasn't damn stupid, but now that we are here and considering...

Hearing that Wulfson can't use the Animus and thinking about his past, it's obvious the man was one of the great champions in the WC military. He got there by blood and grit. But ever since the Animus became the go-to thing for developing the greats of tomorrow over the last thirtyish years, guys like Wulfson are left behind. It just made me a bit more sympathetic to think about it that way. Makes me realize that I was like that once too, and maybe I've become a little too reliant on the Animus. Nothing wrong with keeping your boots in the dirt—or snow, in our case."

The room went silent. They all looked at the floor, lost in their own thoughts. Then Luke coughed and stood up, rolled his shoulders, and stretched. "I'm ready to move if we got a plan."

"We still need more supplies," Silas stated.

"We could split up. I'll head north while you guys head out in the other directions," Cameron suggested.

"That could work, but we'll need more than only weapons and armor to take Raza down," Kaiden warned.

"You have a plan?" Silas inquired.

"Forming one, but we should spend a few hours scavenging while we still have sunlight."

"You think there are bears around here? Should we be worried about that?" Luke wondered aloud.

"Not unless they're hungry for rations." Silas chuckled.

The door to the shack burst open, and the four jumped. Kaiden readied his pistol and Cameron drew his knife.

"*Bear*," Luke cried. Flynn walked in and looked around.

"What bear? I didn't see one," he asked, perplexed.

"Luke's just skittish." Kaiden sighed, lowering his gun.

"Although, what's with smashing open the door? It couldn't have frozen over."

"What? Oh, right. Sorry, I got excited." The marksman walked over and placed a small case on the bed. "I found this while hunting around." He unlocked the latches and opened it. The case held an Arc pistol, several grenades, a flashlight, and a small black box that Flynn took. "Scavenger rights," he said cheerfully.

"What is that?" Kaiden asked.

"Camo barrier," the sniper said. He dropped it on the floor and briefly became translucent before disappearing altogether.

"So it's like your stealth generator?" Cameron asked.

Kaiden reached out to where Flynn was standing. As he stretched across the barrier, his hand shimmered then dimmed before disappearing. He drew it out, and it appeared once more.

"It makes a small dome that camouflages anything within it. I'm not completely invisible like I would be with my stealth generator, but unless someone can see the haze, I'm mostly out of sight." Flynn deactivated the box, reappearing as he straightened and tossed it in the air and caught it.

"Good find," Silas commended him, holding up one of the grenades.

"Those are net grenades, like the ones I use," Cameron noted, picking up another one. "They are very durable and constrict around the target. We could probably use these to capture Raza. It might take a few considering how strong he is and how sharp those claws are, but it could work."

Kaiden handed his gun to Luke. "You don't want it?" the titan asked.

"It's probably more your speed. I'll take this Arc pistol." The ace picked up the silver gun and examined it. "These things pack a punch. Could be useful for keeping him in place so we can net him."

"Were you able to find anything else?" Silas asked Flynn as he placed the flashlight in the satchel.

"Yeah, there was another big crate about a half mile from here. Wanna check it out?"

They exchanged glances and nodded. "Lead the way," the enforcer said cheerfully.

The group made their way through the trees. "You sure it's this way?" Kaiden asked, "Don't wanna get lost out here."

"Yea, it's right there behind those trees—see it?" The ace moved around a trunk in his path and peered through the thicket, seeing the large silver container in the distance.

"I gotcha. Let's see what we got," he called.

"May want to be quieter. I'm not sure about bears, but there could be wolves or other predators around," Silas advised.

"I'll keep an eye out," Cameron promised, hanging back from the others and watching the woods.

They walked up to the crate. The latches were already undone. "You took a look already?" Luke asked.

"I only undid the straps. Figured I'd get you guys first," Flynn said.

"Let's see what's inside big box number two." Kaiden

undid the latches on one side, and Flynn undid the others. They moved the top and peered inside. "Weapons cache," the ace declared with glee.

"Take your pick, mates." Flynn grinned.

"What's this?" Silas asked, reaching into the crate to remove a large stick with a silver orb on the end.

"Oh, that's a kinetic club," Luke said. He took it from the enforcer's hand and swung it around a few times. "The more you swing it, the more energy it builds up." He continued the motion while walking up to a tree. "Then you press this button here, and the next time you collide it with something…" He reached back with the club, aiming for the trunk of the tree. "It releases all the energy stored inside." He slammed the club into the trunk with a loud crash followed by the cracking of wood.

Luke stumbled back a few steps. He smiled at the partially destroyed tree and the numerous cracks along the wood. "It's got a hell of a punch." Another ominous crack sounded, and Luke looked back. The tree shifted and fell slowly. The titan jumped back, and the others covered their ears as the thirty-foot tree collapsed and kicked up snow on impact. He winced and looked at it sheepishly. "Well, uh…the tree had it coming?"

"You can keep it. Just don't swing it in my direction, all right?" Kaiden laughed. He looked into the crate again and pulled out a rifle and shotgun. "Hey, Cam! You want a rifle or shotgun?"

"What model rifle?" he asked, still looking around the forest.

"Uh, a Zeta & Falco munitions. Looks like a modified Mamba."

"That'll do," the bounty hunter said. He extended an arm and Kaiden tossed him the rifle before rejoining the others. Silas held a machine gun, while Flynn had a set of goggles on his face.

"What the hell are those?" he asked.

"Spectrum goggles—they got thermal, night vision, and scope." He took them off and handed them to Kaiden. "Could be useful, want them?"

The ace waved his hand. "Probably more useful to you. Hopefully, we can use those thermals to get the jump on Raza."

"There's a hand cannon here," Silas announced.

"Call it," Luke declared, marching over. He took out the pistol Kaiden had given him and handed it to Flynn. "You can have this as a sidearm."

"That thing keeps getting re-gifted." Kaiden chuckled.

Silas leaned over and looked at the bottom of the crate. "A couple of chest pieces in here and some ammo, but that's the last of it."

"Well, we can say we're decently armed now," the ace noted.

The enforcer looked up from the crate. "Maybe, but do you think it's enough?"

"We can make it work. There's still a little sunlight, but even with the flashlight, I don't wanna be wandering around in the dark."

"Agreed. Let's press on. If we don't find anything interesting, we'll head—" Two bolts flew behind Silas, who spun and pressed against the box. "Flynn?"

The marksman was wearing the goggles and lowered

his bow to his chest. He smiled and pointed into the distance. "I got us some dinner, boys."

Kaiden gave him a curious look and walked over to the bolts in the snow. He knelt and swept the snow aside to find two rabbits. "Nice shooting," he called as he picked up the game.

"Maybe we should call it a night? Prepare for tomorrow over a warm meal?" Luke suggested.

Silas looked up at him, nodding. "A bit of quiet before the hunt is always good."

CHAPTER EIGHT

C ameron, Luke, Silas, and Kaiden stood back to back in the middle of the field looking in all directions. Silas tapped the side of his gun nervously, while the titan took a couple of swings with his club.

"See anything yet?" the ace asked, placing his hand across his mouth to shield his words and muffle his voice.

Flynn peered out through the bushes, having an entire view of the unobstructed field that the others were in. "Nothing yet. You think he's really gonna get here on the dot?"

"Better to be prepared and wait it out than simply stand in a snowbank waiting for him to come to us," Kaiden reasoned. "We definitely don't want to be in the woods. He'd pick us apart."

"Wulfson said he was dropping him off. Would we have seen a ship overhead?" Silas asked.

"I bet that was a ruse. He probably dropped Raza off yesterday, and he's been preparing on his own."

"What makes you figure that?" Cameron questioned.

Kaiden held his gun up and looked behind him "Why would he risk giving Raza's position away or warning us that he's here?"

"Good point," Luke agreed.

"Can we talk about modifying the plan?" the bounty hunter asked.

"If you have something better, I'm all ears." Kaiden shrugged.

"I just don't like being bait. It's not really my style," Cameron muttered.

Luke laughed and took another swing, "Maybe you don't wish it was, but you come to it so naturally."

"Speaking of which, you and Raul need to be the bait every now and then. I'm starting to feel discriminated against."

Silas walked ahead for a few feet and scanned the horizon. "You have to admit, you make a tempting target."

"What makes me so tempting, exactly?" the bounty hunter growled in a quiet whisper.

"I don't know man. You kinda got this aura about you that makes me think, 'I just have to kill this guy, damn the consequences,' you know?" Kaiden mocked.

Cameron sighed and shook his head. "I hate every single one of you right now."

"And you'll love me if this goes right," the ace retorted.

"That's looking like a big if. Lotta variables in your plan," Cameron pointed out.

"That's what makes it so clever. A lot of planning," he shot back.

Luke elbowed him in the ribs. "Haven't you said you're better at winging it than at strategy?"

Kaiden nodded. "And this well-thought-out plan also leaves me room to wing it. There are options."

"Said with all the gusto and cocksureness of a man trying to hide that he thinks we'll fail." Silas chuckled.

The ace glared at the enforcer. "You want me to leave you here to be the bait alone? I will, you know."

As they joked and bickered, Flynn continued to scan the tree lines in the distance. He paused for a moment when something caught his eye. "Hey, guys, I got movement— eleven o'clock."

"That's your direction, Cam." Kaiden tried to look back without making it obvious.

"I'm looking, but I don't see anything."

Flynn zoomed in with his goggles, trying to focus on what he saw. "There's some sort of big shape on the edges of the trees. It's still now, but I could have sworn it was moving."

Cameron peered around the foliage. "I still don't see a damn thing. One of you wanna take a look?"

Silas began to walk around as if he was stretching his legs. He peered over in the direction Cameron was looking in. "I can't see anything either."

"What color is it on thermal?" Kaiden asked.

The marksman zoomed in as much as he could, but the object was completely still. "Mostly blue and yellow. Wait, I just picked up a small dot of red."

"Wouldn't he be mostly red and yellow? We are the warmest things out here," Luke reasoned.

Kaiden stretched. "Probably, he is a big ass alien…" He

paused, looking slowly behind him. "The Sauren are cold-blooded."

Cameron jerked his head to the side. "What? He wouldn't be able to survive out here if he was. He'd freeze."

"He's probably wearing a suit. We've only seen him in that tribal couture of his, but the Sauren have to have armor or suits of some kind if they travel to a bunch of different worlds."

"A suit would mean he has a power source. The thermals would pick that up," Silas pointed out.

"Not one with low emissions and cooling lines," the ace said as he moved his shotgun slowly back to his chest and slid his finger along the trigger.

Cameron turned the safety on his rifle off. "So you think that whatever Flynn is seeing could be him?"

"Probably. He's a marksman and has good eyes."

"Then why can't we see him?" Cameron grunted in annoyance. "Do we not have 'the vision?'"

"Camouflage or a stealth generator would be my guess." Kaiden also began pacing around their circle. "A giant, red reptile man would make for an easy target."

"So, you have any suggestions?" Silas inquired.

The ace pursed his lips and thought about it for a moment. "Flynn, can you be more descriptive?"

"About what?"

"Where you see the shape."

"It's around trees and bushes, like most of the forest," Flynn said flatly.

"That really narrows it down." Kaiden sighed.

"The best I can do is say that from where I see

Cameron, it's just to the left of where he's facing. Around a huddle of bushes."

Kaiden glanced at Cameron, then off to the side and saw the mass of shrubbery Flynn had mentioned. "That'll do. Get ready," he ordered and walked straight past Cameron to face the forest.

"Wait, what are we doing?" Luke asked, turning with the others.

"If he is over there, he now knows that we know," Cameron explained, as much to himself as to the others.

"I know." Kaiden raised his shotgun. "Flush him out," he roared as he began to fire. The others soon joined him and they moved down the surrounding area as bullets, marbles, and shards cut through the forest.

"We're wasting a lot of ammo," the bounty hunter shouted. "Better hope he's—"

"*There!*" Silas called. Raza appeared in a shimmering light as his stealth generator failed. He glared at them with predatory eyes visible through the visor of a large mask over his head. Two orange lights blinked on his suit of white light armor equipped with a pack on the back.

"He's got armor now? Like he wasn't hard enough to take down before." Luke growled an imprecation.

"No, that works for us. It's what's keeping him warm," Kaiden declared.

"I follow. Stick to the plan, but if you can take out that generator then that's another way to win," Silas acknowledged.

"Ready, Flynn?" the ace asked.

"Get him into the clearing and see if you can strip some of that armor. I'll take him down," Flynn responded.

"You make it sound so easy…" Kaiden ejected his empty magazine and reloaded. "Get ready."

Raza roared at the group, the mask doing little to muffle the bloodthirsty cry. He brandished a rod that expanded with both ends illuminated in a blue glow. Strings of electricity arced off it.

"Static staff," the titan warned.

"Here he comes," Silas yelled. The four backed away as Raza charged, fanning out so that he couldn't sweep them all together. The Sauren unclipped something from his belt. He reached back and cast it toward Cameron. It ensnared him, wrapping around his chest, and sent him sailing into the snow. He looked down to see three spheres on the ends of wires.

"What the hell is this?" the bounty hunter sputtered as he tried to stand but couldn't. He seemed anchored to the ground.

"Heavy weighted bolas. He's trying to capture us, remember?" Silas responded and continued to fire. "You guys keep him distracted. I'll get Cam."

"On it," Luke hollered. He dropped his gun and ran toward Raza with his kinetic club in both hands. The alien looked at him and snarled. Kaiden swapped to his Arc pistol and fired a charged shot. The Sauren twitched a moment, his eyes glancing momentarily at him. The titan leaped into the air, bringing the club down on his target with both hands. Raza snapped his attention back to him and raised his left hand. A barrier shield appeared in the moment that Luke's club connected.

The force was massive, knocking both the titan and ace back as snow erupted into the air, soaring at least ten feet up and as many yards away. Kaiden scrambled quickly to his feet, his shotgun at the ready. His teammate had fallen into the snow and turned hastily to look at the Sauren. "Did that do something?"

The arm of Raza's suit was shattered, and the gauntlet with the barrier shield was smashed and on the ground. The creature lowered his arm and growled, staring Luke down.

"Looks like you pissed him off pretty good!" Kaiden fired his gun, trying to get their quarry's attention. Raza glanced his way, tossed his staff from one hand to the other, and turned toward him with the free arm extended. Something shot out from the gauntlet on his wrist and exploded in the air. A net snagged the ace and pinned him to the ground. "Ah, sonofabitch! Your mother is a lizard."

"Really? School kid insults, Kaiden?" Cameron jeered. "Can't do better?"

"Shut the hell up and get me out of this," he demanded.

"I'll get the whiner. You help Luke," the bounty hunter said. Silas nodded and ran toward Raza. He and the titan circled one another, their weapons at the ready. The enforcer began to fire, focusing on the generator on the beast's back. The alien swung around and roared, raised the staff above his head, and threw it like a javelin at Silas.

He tried to slide, but the weapon caught him in his chest and he felt a massive wave of electricity. Powerless to resist, he twitched for a few seconds before falling face-down into the snow. His teammate yelled as he ran up to Raza and swung his club. The Sauren dodged a couple of swipes before Luke raised his weapon to bring it down on his head. The creature caught the head of the club and growled at the titan soldier.

Luke grinned and pressed the trigger on the club. Another kinetic blast followed, but this one wasn't nearly as strong. It was enough to cause Raza to stumble but not let go of the club, even as he tried to pry it out of his grasp. The alien snarled as he ripped the club out of Luke's hands and slammed it into his stomach, causing the man to gasp and double over. The Sauren cast the club aside, then raised one of his massive clawed legs, shoved it into the soldier's chest, and forced him into the ground.

"Always with the slamming," the titan grunted.

"Luke," Kaiden cried as the bounty hunter cut him out of the net. "We have to get that helmet off or at least crack some more of that armor so Flynn can shoot him."

"It's only light armor. Can't those bolts pierce it?" Cameron asked.

"We're not certain they can pierce the hide deep enough to do what we need, so I don't wanna take the chance of giving away his position until we have to."

"What do you think we should do? He took out our front line."

Kaiden thought about it for a moment. "One of us needs to distract him while the other gets that club, primes it, and uses it to knock that helmet off."

"Which one of us has to distract him?" Cameron asked hesitantly.

The ace thought about it for a moment, then raised a fist. Cameron looked at him, confused for a moment before the penny dropped and he followed suit. After a quick match of rock-paper-scissors, his paper beat Kaiden's rock. "Damn it."

"Good luck, Kai. Get in there," he said, though not too encouragingly.

His teammate stood and raced toward Raza as the bounty hunter followed. They both fired as they drew closer, and the Sauren fired and charged them. Kaiden dove away, rolled to the side, and scrambled up as the alien charged again. He fired two more shots before his gun was empty. With a muttered oath, he reached for another clip, but his adversary was on him too fast, slashing at him with his claws in a moment of fury. The ace ducked and strafed to the side, dropped his shotgun, and primed his pistol. Raza yanked a whip from his belt. The soldier could see an orb on the tip and immediately raised his pistol and fired. The creature raised his other arm to absorb the blast as he snapped the whip forward. Kaiden barely dodged it but heard a loud crack as the whip snapped in the air and saw charges of electricity emanate from the end.

"Oh, that is a whole new level of dickery." He grimaced. Raza brought the whip back and snapped it again. The ace weaved around the strikes, his pistol primed, and looked for a target. When the beast went to strike again, the soldier aimed at the whip and fired, shocking the hand so the Sauren squeezed too hard and broke the handle.

"Got any more toys?" he asked snidely. The Sauren growled and stood to his full height, revealing his claws and massive body. "Oh, right… Natural killing machine."

Kaiden backed away, and as Raza stalked forward, he looked behind him. Flynn was only a few yards away now. He glanced at Cameron and smirked, then pulled down on the trigger of the Arc pistol. Standing straight, he looked Raza dead in the eyes. "Don't blink. You'll miss it."

His adversary sneered and ran forward just as Cameron raced up and swung the club from below, smashing it into his chin as he hit the switch. The alien's mask shattered, and he was thrown several feet into the air. The bounty hunter was knocked back and lost hold of the club from the force. Kaiden was also knocked back and dropped his pistol, a shot plowing into the snow as it fell. The ace took a moment to lift himself. His body was wracked with pain, and the biting cold was getting to him now. He looked over to see the bounty hunter knocked out on the ground and saw Raza picking himself up, his head exposed and a small trail of blood pouring from his jaw.

"Now, Flynn," he ordered as the Sauren regained his feet and charged again. "Do it now."

Several bolts struck the beast in the throat, a few in his arms, and a couple in his face. He stopped mid-stride, looked at the bolts in his arms, then grabbed a few in his throat and pulled them out. Small dots of blood oozed from the wounds.

Kaiden smiled. "We win."

"Arrows? That was your grand plan?" Raza hissed. "Though I admire your decision to try to kill me, you showed more planning and resourcefulness when you were throwing training equipment at me."

"Those weren't supposed to kill you." Kaiden grunted as he stood and wiped some snow off his shoulder. "No way those things would do any real damage. But maybe they would burrow deep enough to get something in you."

"What are you...you..." Raza's words slurred. He

gripped his head and stumbled forward. "What did you do?"

"Enacted a fantastic plan." Kaiden gloated, and he motioned for Flynn to come out. "Those bolts were coated in power-sip. A great energy booster for us, but funnily enough, it seems to have the opposite effect on you, Sauren. You get real tired real quick."

The alien snarled as he tried to stay standing. Flynn walked over with the satchel and handed a few of the net grenades to Kaiden. They activated them and tossed them at Raza. When they exploded, the nets ensnared him, binding him so he toppled into the snow. The ace walked forward and kneeled down at their adversary's head.

"I know you're listening in, Wulfson, I think we've proven ourselves, don't you?"

CHAPTER NINE

"Friend Chiyo!" Genos called.

The infiltrator looked up from her tablet and waved at the Tsuna as he walked up to her. "Good evening, Genos."

"A good evening to you as well." Genos returned the greeting with his usual cheer. "I was wondering, have you seen Kaiden at all today?"

"No, I can't say that I have. You do know you can check your network to find your contacts, correct?"

"Of course, but that's the thing. Kaiden doesn't seem to be on the academy grounds."

Chiyo furrowed her brow. She opened her network page and looked for the ace on the map, to no avail. Curious now, she opened his personal page. His location read, **Not within area**.

"That's odd. I suppose he might be on an errand or something, but it's unlike him to leave campus."

Genos tapped a finger on the rim of his infuser. "I see. I suppose I'll wait for him to return then."

"Did you need something? Can I help?"

The Tsuna shook his head. "Oh, no, it is nothing too important. I was talking with kin Jaxon, and we were discussing the upcoming Squad Test. He told me I should learn more about it and the tactics that others would use so as to be more prepared for the test. I learned that most others call it a 'deathmatch.'"

Chiyo nodded, sighing. "It's a nickname that's been passed around Nexus over the years. It's not the official title."

"Even so, given the title, I feel that with Kaiden's proclivity for violence, he would be one of the best to ask for advice. I wanted to ask what his plans are for the test."

She deactivated her tablet and put it away. "To be honest, Genos, I don't think Kaiden *has* much of a plan. Although in fairness, not many of us do."

Her companion's eyes widened. "Why is that? The test is only a week away, is it not?"

She nodded. "True, but tell me, Genos...who is your team for the match?"

"Well, I suppose since it's a team of three, it would be me, kin Jaxon, and a third party. I would imagine one of the group, or if there are not enough to go around, Jaxon has informed me of other Tsuna candidates who are doing well in their studies. Perhaps one of them would like to join us."

"That's not how this test works, Genos," Chiyo stated. "Our teams will be assigned to us on Wednesday. They are pre-chosen, because part of the test is to see how well you work with a randomized team."

"Randomized? Oh! That is not fortuitous." Genos sulked.

"You didn't know about the test? You were there when we discussed it while watching Cameron's and Raul's Co-op mission," she pointed out.

"I was... Yes, I remember we talked about it, but I was under the assumption that it was simply a grander version of the Co-operative Test. I suppose I didn't take the time to find out all the details."

"It does sound like you are taking after Kaiden," she commented.

"Not that he's not a good person—at least to you and me—but I would rather not."

The infiltrator giggled. "Certainly understandable."

"The fact that I will be on a team with potential unknowns is unnerving, I must admit," the Tsuna lamented.

Chiyo watched him sulk for a moment, and her eyes darted to the side as she released a breath. "Well, I say 'randomized,' but there might be more in play than I thought."

"What do you mean?" he asked, perking up a little.

She gestured at the seat in front of her, and he sat down as she explained. "I have a tracking code on my personal file. I can see when people access it and if they change anything or what they are looking through. I got a notice just before the Co-operative Test that my profile had been copied to a different file. I didn't think much of it at first, believing they were using it to create an early draft of a contract or something to that effect, but since it was still my file, my tracker followed it. It bounced around a couple of times, as well as being loaded into a database that is visited constantly by the academy staff."

"Why are they focusing on you? Are you in danger?" Genos inquired worriedly.

"No, I don't think I have to worry about the Academy wanting to do me harm since they were the ones who invited me here," Chiyo said coolly. "I don't think it's anything like that. It's much less malicious but could potentially explain how the teams are decided."

"Please do tell…is it good?"

She shrugged. "Potentially. I looked over the teams from the last several years. Despite being told the selection process is random, a large number of students were paired with network partners and teams built in such a way that their skills and classes complimented each other. The odds that the teams would have formed this way completely randomly are astronomical."

"So there's a chance I may be partnered with a friend?" the Tsuna asked.

"That, or at least a team you would fit in with. I did some searching and found out about some sort of game the staff plays every year. I figured it was some sort of betting game or pool like some of the other students do around the tests. But there seems to be more involved. It would explain the database as only select teachers have access to it. Not based on standing, clearance, or division, but seemingly at random. I think they design the teams throughout the year."

"Hmm…" Genos stretched his fingers wide and tapped them together, his palms touching. "Perhaps I could find one of these teachers and convince them to partner me with other Tsuna or within our group. Maybe we could all be partnered together?"

"Well, there are twelve of us, so the math works out. But I doubt it would be that simple. If they are keeping it a secret, it's probably for that reason alone. They don't want the students to try to influence their decision or possibly bribe them."

He sighed, bubbles swimming through the tubes of his infuser. "I can only hope the ancients grant me a boon of luck, then."

"You'll be fine, no matter who you're partnered with, Genos. You've improved so much, and your skills were already excellent," Chiyo said encouragingly.

"Thank you, Chiyo." He closed his eyes and made a small bow before popping right back up and tapping on his infuser again. "I suppose I won't quite know what is in store until the night after tomorrow, but that still leaves the mysterious disappearance of our friend Kaiden."

"I don't think it's much of a mystery. If he were in real trouble, he would have contacted one of us or had Chief send out an alert."

"True, but where do you think he could have gone? Will he be back in time to learn what his group is?" Genos pondered.

"I don't think we have to worry about him skipping out on something that concerns a test. Although he doesn't have the best track record at attending orientations, so maybe that is a possibility."

"*Madame, a notification on your network. It would appear that Mr. Kaiden has returned to the area,*" Kaitō informed her.

Chiyo brought the map up. "Looks like Kaiden has returned, Genos, with plenty of time to spare."

He clapped his hands together. "Oh, joy. This is assuming he doesn't disappear again. Where is he now?"

"He's…all the way across the lake? He's coming in fast, and there are others with him—Luke, Silas, Flynn, and Cameron. I didn't realize they had all left."

"We must really keep better track of our friends. They are rather hard to find once you've lost them, it seems," Genos noted.

She closed the map in her ocular lenses. "They are heading toward the docks. Care to go and meet them?"

"Certainly, let us greet our friends as they arrive from their strange disappearance." Genos stood and walked briskly in the direction of the docks.

Chiyo grabbed her bag and placed it on her shoulder as she followed Genos slowly. *You know, there is a stark contrast between Mr. Genos' demeanor depending on whether or not he's in the Animus.*

"I've noticed that too, but it's rather nice to see that he can leave that behind once he's around friends."

It makes me think about how you've been acting these last few months, madame.

The infiltrator stopped for a moment. "It's…a nice feeling to know you can trust those around you. It's rather freeing."

Kaiden looked at his companions. They all huddled on the opposite side of the ship. He sat with his arms crossed, tapping the fingers of his left hand on his right arm. "You guys comfortable over there? Jammed together like canned herring?"

"It's a tight fit, sure," Flynn muttered. "But I'm guessing it's much better than where you're sitting."

The ace looked to his right. Beside him was the sleeping form of Raza. He'd been cut free from the nets but had still not awoken after the fight.

"It's been an uncomfortable ride, yes," Kaiden grumbled.

"Man, when he wakes up, he's going to be pissed." Chief chuckled. *"Gotta hand it to you guys—power-sip poison darts. I would have bet an upgrade that wouldn't have worked."*

"You saying I can take that back?" Kaiden asked.

"Oh, hell no. This stuff is mine now." Chief refuted.

"You shouldn't have been in such a hurry to board. Got stuck with the crap seats." Luke snickered.

"I had hoped I could relax and take a nap. Then Wulfson dumps him next to me, and you all take the back seats."

"They were the only ones available, mate," Flynn reasoned. "The others were dropped into the Alaskan wilderness if you recall."

"Oh, I remember, trust me. I hope Wulfson has to pay an arm and a leg for all the missing chairs."

"Does anyone still have a weapon by any chance?" Cameron asked. "Just in case Raza wakes up grumpy."

"Naw. Wulfson tossed them all in that crate and locked it." Silas pointed over to the big crate in the corner.

"Come to think of it, he dropped a hell of a lot of those back there. Is he simply going to leave crates of weapons where anyone can stumble upon them?" Luke wondered.

"He'll probably go back and get them or send a retrieval team. He's the head security officer after all, and I'm guessing the Nexus security is merely twiddling their thumbs anyway," Kaiden responded.

The intercom activated. "We're here, lads. Welcome back to Nexus Academy. How you feeling, Raza? Raza?"

"He's still asleep," Kaiden yelled.

"You can't hear the snoring?" Silas asked.

Wulfson cursed over the comm and muttered something in Swedish. "Still? We've been flying for almost two hours. How much of that stuff did you put in him?"

"Enough," Kaiden answered. "Now hurry and land this thing so I can get him off me and head to the showers and then my bed."

"We still getting that prize, Officer?" Luke asked.

"You never told us what that prize was. When do we get it?" Cameron added.

"Quit pointing fingers. I'm a man of my word. I'll have it ready the next time you come by the gym," Wulfson stated.

Flynn dropped his head. "Oh, that sneaky bastard. If he thinks I'm coming anywhere near him before the year is out, he's absolutely daft."

"I'm going to see if I can get a restraining order." The bounty hunter snickered.

"Oh, come on, it wasn't all bad. We bonded and shit, right?" Kaiden jeered.

"Damn sure did. If I'm ever heading out to a frosty no

man's land in my skivvies, I'll be sure to take you guys with me," the titan promised.

Kaiden raised an eyebrow. "You said that so earnestly, I can't tell if it was sarcastic or not."

Silas tapped the back of his hand against Luke's chest. "While I will certainly help you out if you need it, maybe ask a few other people if they're game before giving me a call to trudge through the snow. That was my first time in real snow, and I can safely say I prefer the sun."

"There was sun there," the titan countered.

"Didn't do a damn thing," Cameron muttered, rubbing his hands over his arms as if he could still feel the chill.

The ship descended onto the docking pad. The hatch opened, and the group stood from their seats and walked out.

"Hello, friends," Genos called.

"Genos! Good to see you, man," Kaiden replied as he walked up to the joyful Tsuna.

"You were gone for some time. Where have the five of you been?" he asked with childlike curiosity.

"It's a bit of a story, mate." Flynn sighed as he walked past. "Just know that we're glad to be back."

"Just know that you should never sign anything Wulfson asks you to," Silas added.

"Sign? Was it that proving ground exercise he asked us to participate in? I couldn't go because I am taking extra workshops. Was it fun?"

"Hell no," the five shouted.

The Tsuna looked around at the haggard and wounded bunch. "Oh, well then. I'm still glad you made it back in time to see what groups we will get for the Deathmatch."

"You say Deathmatch so innocently that it's almost unnerving," Kaiden commented.

"He knows it's only a nickname." Kaiden looked up to see Chiyo walk up the stairs to the landing pad.

"Howdy, Chiyo, doing good? Staying warm?" Luke asked.

She looked quizzically at him. "It's the springtime, so it is rather nice."

"You wouldn't know from where we've been." Cameron huffed, clearly still annoyed. He waved back at the others as he descended the stairs. "I'm heading to the dorms. See you guys there."

"I'm right behind you." Silas winced as he reached the stairs and gripped the railing as he walked down. "Maybe way behind you."

"What happened to all of you?" she asked Kaiden.

"Like I told Genos, tell you later." He flicked a thumb behind him. "But if you want a hint…"

Chiyo looked over Kaiden's slumped shoulder and gasped. "Is… Is that a Sauren? You captured a Sauren?"

"No, that's Raza… Oh right, you don't train with Wulfson, so you've never met him."

"She is the smart one," Luke said, then cracked his neck and leaned against the railing. He looked at Flynn who stood casually in front of him. "Next time, you're the bait."

The marksman smirked and shrugged his shoulders. He skipped to the stairs as if to rub it in as Luke growled and shuffled after him.

"Yeah, needless to say, we got our asses kicked. We won, though." Kaiden tried his best to stand normally but couldn't muster much more than to slightly straighten his back. "Genos, care to be a pal and help me limp my way to the med-bay?"

"Of course." He nodded and put one of Kaiden's arms over his shoulder. "I'll help you get there as soon as possible. Dr. Mortis will heal you with no hesitation."

"Dr. Mortis? The Mirus doctor?" the ace asked. "Where's Soni?"

"Amber said that she is at a summit in Canada. She'll be back in a couple of days."

He removed his arm from the Tsuna's shoulder and tried to stand as straight as he could, stretching his arms. "You know what? I'm actually feeling better. I think I'll head back to the dorms and take a hot shower. Work through the pain and all that."

Chiyo chuckled lightly. "Trying to keep up your tough guy act?"

Kaiden looked at her with a worried expression. "Trust me, you don't want that Mirus doctor working on you. You don't know the horrors of the slime he's got," he finished with a shudder.

The infiltrator watched as he departed down the steps, Genos following behind and helping to steady him. Then she looked at the Sauren, watching as Wulfson hit him a couple times and told him to wake up.

She shook her head at the absurdity of it all. "I guess there's a lot I still have to learn."

CHAPTER TEN

K aiden awoke with a start, and the pain in his shoulder sent him collapsing back onto the bed, hissing upon impact.

"Nice little do-si-do you did there." Chief chuckled as he appeared above him, nearly blinding Kaiden's tired eyes.

"Man, it's been a while since I was this sore." He huffed and pushed up slowly to sit on the side of his bed and roll his shoulder. "At least the pains from the Animus fade away quickly."

"For now. Once you've used that thing for a couple of years, you might feel even worse, considering how much you're blown up and shot."

"Hopefully, by that time I'll be a bullet-dodging ballerina," Kaiden joked.

"There's always hope, no matter how much you seem to squander it," Chief jeered.

Kaiden stood and headed to the shower. He activated the temperature gauge and turned on the water before heading back to his dresser to pick out some clothes. "What do I have today, Chief?"

"Just the Squad Test meeting with the other initiates in about an hour."

"That's tomorrow, Chief." The ace yawned as he set a t-shirt and pants on the top of the dresser.

"It's on Wednesday, which is today."

He paused for a moment and then shut the dresser and walked quickly to his window. "Open blinds," he commanded. They opened and he saw the sky fading into evening light, then looked at his clock to see the day read Wednesday. "What the... How long did I sleep?"

"Twelve hours. You remember that 'little nap' you were going to have because you got the day off from workshops thanks to Wulfson?"

"I don't remember that."

"You were pretty out of it," Chief recalled. *"You slept through most of Tuesday, too. Really got to get you a better meal plan or something because you're turning into even more of a lazy bastard."*

Kaiden mumbled something about a "translucent jerk" under his breath as he grabbed the rest of what he needed from the dresser and left for the shower.

"Shall I send word to your buddies that you'll be there soon and that you're freshening up?"

"Yeah, fine," he replied. "I'll meet them in front of the main building in ten."

"I should probably make that thirty, but he's got to learn to keep a schedule eventually," Chief muttered to himself.

The ace finished his shower quickly, dried off, and dressed. He looked around the room for anything he was missing and turned to the EI. "You coming or are you gonna hover there in smugness?"

Chief twirled. *"I might as well. I don't have much of a choice, for one, but you'll also need me to get your squad results."*

"Well then, let's go," Kaiden ordered

"Making me rush because you overslept? You have no manners, do you?" Chief chortled as he phased out of the room.

The ace rolled his eyes as he ran out, slammed the door, and headed to meet his friends.

Kaiden sprinted to the main building, dressed in a blue Nexus Academy shirt and grey pants, along with his normal black boots and jacket. He saw Chiyo, Genos, Jaxon, Flynn, Izzy, and Amber in the distance and waved at them.

"Good to see you up and about," Jaxon said as he finally closed the distance between them. "I haven't seen you walking the dorms, in the ace workshop, or at the Animus Center. I wondered if you would ever recover."

"Still a few sores and strains. But I've gotten plenty of sleep," Kaiden admitted sheepishly.

"I'm feeling great, honestly," Flynn said with a smile. "Nothing like getting back to nature for a bit, eh?"

"You weren't the one dodging Sauren claws and electrified whips," Kaiden grumbled.

"Maybe not, but I was the most important component to our plan, and I did my job," he responded.

"No one can hide in a bush quite like you, I'll admit," the

ace jeered.

Amber giggled while the marksman waved him off. "And no one makes quite as good a runaway as you do, mate."

Kaiden gave him an annoyed look. "I'm with Luke. If we ever go off on another field trip with Wulfson, you will be the bait."

"Speaking of which, where is he? And all the others?" Izzy asked.

"Well, Luke, Cameron, and Silas are probably late for the same reason I was," Kaiden reasoned.

"Poor constitution?" Flynn quipped.

The ace sneered. "I have a gun, you know," he said as he reached under his jacket, only to find nothing and realize that he had forgotten it. "Damn it all."

"Cameron and Raul are not exactly known for punctuality anyway," Jaxon stated.

"Marlo was caught up in some armor-crafting training. He'll be here soon," Amber explained.

"He'll be here now," Marlo announced as he walked up and greeted the others with a wave of his large hand. "How you guys doing?"

"Rather well, although slightly anxious, perhaps," Genos admitted, tapping the tips of his fingers together fretfully.

"What? About the squad picks?" the demolisher asked, resting an arm on the Tsuna's shoulder. "Don't worry about it, buddy. If you get someone on your team who gives you problems, just come and get me and I'll make sure they shape-up."

"That is quite kind of you, friend Marlo. How exactly would you be able to do that?" the Tsuna asked.

As Marlo opened his mouth to explain, Amber raised a hand to stop him. "He has his ways. He's a people person," she explained, then leaned in to whisper to the demolisher, "You probably shouldn't expand on that. Don't want him worrying about you potentially bashing someone's skull in."

"I wouldn't be that harsh," Marlo defended. "Just enough to, you know, make them remember their manners."

"Either way, best to not mention it and simply let that lie," she commanded.

Flynn raised a hand and waved at a group in the distance. "Well, look who's here to round out the bunch. How are you, fellas?"

Cameron, Silas, and Luke walked up, each of them with bags under their eyes and sullen looks. The first two mumbled greetings as they passed while the titan stopped in front of Flynn and stretched. "Not as chipper as you seem to be."

"Wonder why that is," the bounty hunter muttered, rubbing around his collar. "Maybe because the only thing on him that got any action was his trigger finger."

"Hope the seats are cushioned considering your sore ass." Flynn snickered.

"Raul is not with you?" Jaxon asked.

Cameron sighed. "He'll be here soon—primping himself up for the big meeting. Said something about wanting his squadmates to appreciate him at first glance."

Izzy looked around. "We need to head inside soon, or we'll miss the good seats."

Kaiden realized that he had been almost completely

oblivious to the other initiates around them. Groups of people walked past and talked excitedly about the meeting and their potential squads. He looked up to see the sky had darkened and the lights of the plaza had begun to glow.

"Best get in there, then. We'll save him a seat if we can," Silas said as he shuffled zombie-like to the doors of the main building.

"Is he gonna be all right?" Amber asked Izzy.

She shrugged. "He's too stubborn to see someone in the med-bay, so I guess he must not be in too much pain."

"We should go ahead. The meeting starts in seven minutes," Jaxon informed them.

The group agreed and entered the building, heading for the theater to hear about their future teams and what their final challenge for the year would be.

The theater was a massive thousand-seat hall. A wide wooden stage sprawled in front, with patterned red curtains and numerous decorations on the stage and the floor below. The group took seats in the middle of the front row. The three hundred initiates filled the lower level.

Kaiden looked on the stage and saw half a dozen staff members talking amongst themselves as the rest of the students found their seats. He recognized the man in a long white coat as Head Monitor Zhang, the overseer of the Animus center. Surprised, he also noticed Sasha —aside from his personal interactions with him, he never really saw the commander wandering the grounds.

He didn't recognize the others, but he saw they were all talking to a figure in the middle. The man appeared to be in his late fifties or early sixties with salt-and-pepper hair combed back and a neat, greying goatee. He had faded blue eyes that seemed to betray his age, but he stood calmly among the other staff members. The way he held himself—standing straight, his arms clasped behind his back, and giving only brief nods of recognition—showed the strength of his character.

"Hey, who's that guy in the middle?" Kaiden asked, pointing to him.

"That's Chancellor Durand. He's the head of this school," Chiyo informed him.

"The whole thing? I thought they had a board or something?"

"He would be the head of that board as well," Jaxon stated. "He personally greeted all the Tsuna on our first day here. I do not know much about him, but our delegates treat him with great respect. He was personally in favor of the Tsuna integration program and had a heavy hand in getting it through the World Council."

"How do you not— Hey, Raul," Cameron shouted, interrupting himself to get the tracker's attention and wave him over. "How do you not know who the head of the Academy is?"

"I told you how I got here. I beat up some punks and got a recommendation. I barely knew what this place was," Kaiden retorted.

"You didn't get a pamphlet or nothing?" Marlo inquired. "He has a plaque at the front of the Academy. You should have seen it when you came in."

"I was too distracted by everything else when I first got here to worry about looking at a plaque," Kaiden replied.

"What about during orientation?" Izzy asked.

"When was that?"

"The first day of school," Silas said, his tone flat.

"I might have been with Wulfson or wandering the grounds. I skipped it."

"Of course." Luke chuckled.

"Well, guess you're about to learn," Flynn stated. "Looks like they're ready to begin."

Kaiden looked up to see the chancellor walk up to a podium at the front of the stage. "Good evening, initiates," he bellowed, his voice amplified throughout the theater. "My name, for those who are unfamiliar with me, is Bastien Durand, and I am the Chancellor of Nexus Academy. For those of you who are meeting me for the first time, I wish to greet you warmly and offer you congratulations for your success so far."

"He seems way more understanding than you lot," Kaiden said with a smirk, which disappeared after a second. "Lot? Am I picking up Wulfson's habits now?"

"I know that you have all done your best and continually strive to be even better than that as you train to be the top of the pack in your respective fields. And because of that, I know that this Academy is a place where you deserve to be. We will certainly do our part to help you succeed and leave here as the greatest soldiers, technicians, engineers, analysts, and medics this world and beyond has ever seen."

Durand took a deep breath as the lights of the theater dimmed. "But it will take more than training and good wishes to achieve that, which is why you have taken these tests throughout the year. They are a way to gauge the application of your talents, get the most out of your abilities, learn and implement teamwork, and measure how you fare against unique and often dangerous adversaries or situations of the kind many of you will face once you have graduated."

"That sounds rather foreboding," Flynn whispered. Kaiden, Cameron, Silas, and Marlo nodded.

"Which is what brings us to this moment. The final test of the year is a combination of your personal skills and your ability to work with your brothers and sisters in arms." A holographic map filled the sky and all the initiates looked up to study it as Durand finished with, "The Squad Test."

Dozens of holographic people filled the map. Shots were fired between the holograms, and explosions shook the room. Virtual ships and vehicles engaged in combat with one another and mechs appeared to fire upon the holographic fighters.

"This test is not only a battle against the environment but with each other. It will be the penultimate accumulation of your mettle. It has been in place since the beginning of the Nexus Academy and is a true battleground where only one team will be truly victorious. Whether you succeed or are defeated will all be laid at your feet. Your preparation, teamwork, skills, and determination will be your edge in this match."

Kaiden watched the teams battle both each other and the various hostiles on the map. Ships crashed in the sky, showering the air with holographic bits that evaporated around him. A squad succeeded in destroying a batch of hostile mechs before another squad came up behind them and took them down in a spray of lasers and kinetics. Various lights began to vanish as more teams began to fall. The map began to shrink, and areas exploded or shorted out. Teams were caught in poisonous gas or rooms with explosive traps and taken out. More and more mayhem continued to unfold until there was finally one group left standing in the one remaining room left on the map. As the holographic team raised their fists in victory, both they and the room disappeared.

With that, the lights came back up, and the initiates focused on the stage again. Durand smiled as he looked at them. Some watched him with wide-eyed shock and others with excited smiles, and many whispered to one another about what they had just witnessed.

"And with that brief demonstration of what lies ahead…" Durand stood tall and his gaze swept from one side of the room to the other. "Does anyone here believe they don't have, within themselves, the true heart of a Nexus Academy student to take on this challenge?"

A long pause followed. The chancellor, the other staff, and most of the students looked around for hands or fearful faces. After a while, those students who were shocked or worried saw the resolve on the faces of the others or were encouraged by their fellow initiates and found the strength to sit straighter in their chairs, awaiting the next words.

"Very good," the Nexus head declared. "Then let us continue and discuss what lies ahead for all of you brave souls."

CHAPTER ELEVEN

"You seem a bit shell-shocked there, Flynn." Kaiden chuckled, seeing the marksman trembling slightly beside him. "Getting pretty real now, huh?"

Flynn looked at him, then shook his head and cracked his knuckles. "Nah, not shocked, excited." He beamed. "I had a picture in my head of what this would be like, but that little demonstration they just put on? I'm more pumped for this than I already was."

"Even after seeing all that carnage? Not to mention those ships and tanks—what will you do against those?" Luke asked.

"Can't say just yet, but I'll figure something out. Guess it also depends on what my squad looks like. Maybe I'll simply wait it out and hope they take each other out."

"Quiet down," Jaxon warned. "The chancellor is going to speak again."

The man cleared his throat. Head Monitor Zhang made his way to the podium and stood silently at Durand's side.

"I'm happy to see so much eagerness and excitement among you. However, as much as I enjoy crafting a good speech and showing a bit of bravado, I won't take up much more of your time—not when we need to get down to brass tacks." He looked at the man beside him, who nodded in acknowledgment. "I'm sure you're familiar with the head monitor, Zhi Ruo Zhang. He will go over the history and rules of the Squad Test. After his overview, we will get to what I'm sure most of you are most keenly interested to find out—your squads."

More heated chatter began among the initiates before the chancellor raised his hand to quiet the crowd. "Please give your undivided attention to Head Monitor Zhang."

Durand beckoned to the man as he left the podium and Zhang took his place. "Thank you, Chancellor," he said and faced the crowd. "I'll get right to it, initiates. This is a formal matter. I'm sure many of you know the basics of the Squad Test through information from previous students or the archives in the library. So, I'll keep this as brief as possible."

A video screen appeared overhead, showing a group of initiates striking poses or waving at the camera. "This was the first class to ever undergo the Squad Test, the initiates of 2171." Kaiden saw a small smile form on the lips of the head monitor as he looked at the video and the group laughing at and prodding one another, but it quickly fell away as he began to speak again. "As you can see by the number of buildings in the background and the students, we were a much smaller facility at the time. This group of forty-five initiates was only the fourth batch we received, and this was the first year we had students in all four year-groups."

"Man, that vid is only in 32k res. Looks straight ancient compared to nowadays," Silas noted.

"Tech changes all the time. This was taken twenty-five years ago," Izzy pointed out.

"Even though we had only been operational for a few years, we were constantly improving and adapting—as should any high-tech institute worthy of respect. We had judged that for all the individual improvements the students were learning and mastering in their short time here, they kept mostly to themselves bar the occasional team mission for SXP. Seeing that many of the jobs these students would fill in the future would require working in groups or in areas with frequent collaborations, and the fact that at the time, team training and activities were saved for the Master and Victor years, we decided that we needed to 'encourage' the students to take it upon themselves to start working together more frequently. Which is how the Squad Test and Co-operative Test came to be."

The video changed to a screen showing the forty-five initiates' pictures in circular frames. The images divided out and then regrouped in triangular patterns of three. "It was actually because of the number of initiates we had that year that the Squad Test groups were formed into trios. At the time, they picked the groups themselves, but as the years passed and we gained more recruits and wanted to add some more difficulty and tactics to the test, we developed a new system."

The screen changed again, dividing into segments and showing each year's total amount of initiates, starting from

2171's forty-five, then 2172's fifty-two, and speeding through the following years. Kaiden saw it increase to one hundred and thirteen in 2177, then one hundred and ninety in 2181, two hundred and fourteen in 2190, and finally to their year's group of three hundred in 2196.

"Obviously, we weren't fortunate enough to have the required number of initiates each year for all groups to have three members. They either had to find volunteers to do a second test with them or use an artificial teammate. Unfortunately, we had to terminate that option as workarounds and hacks became an issue." The head monitor sighed before composing himself again. "Fortunately that is not a problem this year. We have enough students, and this will be the largest test this Academy has ever undertaken."

The map that had previously hung over the students' heads appeared onscreen. "This year will have a few changes from the previous tests. Normally, we do the test in batches, dividing it over three days with one batch going in on Wednesday, another on Thursday, and the final group on Friday. But thanks to advances in the Animus and a larger advisory staff for the center, this year, all teams will participate at the same time. That is, all three hundred of you will face off against each other."

The students sat up and looked at each other, taking in the scope of what they would be facing.

"That'll be a busy-ass map," Cameron exclaimed. "Even the Division Test at the beginning of the year only had between fifty and a hundred students at a time."

"Gonna be a lot of bodies piling up. Maybe they should keep the tangibility down for this one," Luke muttered.

"On top of that, this will possibly be the most visceral mission many of you have undertaken thus far. The synchronicity, tangibility, and equilibrium will all be set to four for the test," Zhang declared.

"Well, shit." Luke sighed. "Guess I better take a couple of training sessions in corpse climbing."

"Can't you simply barrel through them?" Amber asked.

"Or use that hop-jet thing?" Kaiden suggested.

"Bouncepack. Get it right, scrub." The titan snickered.

Kaiden rolled his eyes. "Because that name has so much more dignity."

"Now that the background has been explained, let us get to the rules and winning conditions of the test."

"Uh, sir?" An initiate spoke up, raising a hand in the air. "This seems to be a rather battle-heavy test, a 'deathmatch' as I've heard it called by the older students. What are initiates in non-combat classes supposed to do? Like diplomats, navigators, translators, and the like?"

"Ah yes, the Deathmatch." Zhang sounded amused. "I'll address your concerns shortly. However, I would like to discuss the rumors surrounding this so-called 'deathmatch.'"

The screen showed several glowing shapes in various colors: Time as a white T, Valor as a purple heart, Data as a blue zero and one, Motes as a yellow orb, Cache as a green square, and Honor as a red blade.

"The objective of this test is to collect as much of each 'currency' as possible and survive as long as you can. There are many ways to obtain them, and multiple objectives during the test. It is not simply about your kills."

"Damn shame," Kaiden mumbled.

"Good luck, mate. Won't be able to stay in your happy place during this one," Flynn joked.

The ace shrugged. "Won't be too different. I kill enemies while my partners do their thing—assuming I have competent partners."

"And assuming those partners realize they need to get as far out of your line of fire as possible." Cameron chuckled.

The screen zoomed to the Time currency. "You gather Time simply by surviving. The longer you survive, the more you accumulate, gaining one Time unit per minute."

The display changed to the Valor icon. "Valor is the other basic currency. You gain it by destroying hostile forces such as droids, mercs, mutants, and the like. The more difficult the opponent, the more points you get. I should also note that this goes to whoever makes the killing strike. Keep that in mind."

It shifted to the Data currency. "Data is the focus of technicians. You gain points by hacking into systems, locks, and other tech throughout the map. There are also payloads and teller systems that can give you large numbers of Data points if you can find them and success-fully hack them."

The screen moved to the Motes. "Motes are the most universal of the currencies. They can be awarded to engi-neers if they repair a vehicle or rewire a droid. There will be injured soldiers, civilians, and VIP individuals that those in the medic field can heal or assist and gain Motes that way. These are only a few possibilities."

The screen switched to the Cache currency. "For the initiate asking about Diplomats and Navigators and the like, this is your answer. There are objectives you will have several options to complete. Along with potentially gaining artificial allies or unique weapons, those in logistics will have many ways to apply their craft and, if successful, will gain these cache points to contribute to their squad's score."

"Yay, we're not useless," Kaiden overheard an initiate cheer sarcastically, and he chuckled.

"These are the fundamental currencies of the test. But of course, I left one out. Which brings me to the Honor currency and the reason this test has the reputation of a deathmatch."

The screen changed to the glowing red blade of the Honor currency and a picture of three wire-framed soldiers appeared beside it. "When the test first begins, you cannot harm any other initiate in the field. However, this will change at some point, with all initiates becoming hostile and friendly fire being turned on."

"Friendly fire? We can accidentally shoot each other?" Raul questioned.

Zhang paused for a moment, a sly grin crossing along his face, "It is simply another way to add difficulty and realism to the test. In battle you cannot take back a stray bullet, you understand." The wire-framed soldiers held their guns up as if they were firing at an opposing force. "Honor works like this. All the currencies you gather go toward the final overall team score, along with an individual rating at the end of the test. If you kill someone who has collected little currency..." The soldier on the left was shot, disappeared, and left behind an Honor score of ten points. "It will be a pittance compared to someone who has gathered most of their team's currency." The soldier on the right was shot and disappeared, leaving behind its own Honor currency of three hundred points.

The Honor currencies appeared again, and the remaining soldier ran over to both and picked them up. "This currency, unlike the others, falls to the ground and can be picked up by anyone. If you are fast enough, you can hurry and retrieve your partners' Honor points should they fall in battle before you do, increasing your personal score."

"Oh, you devious bastards," the ace whispered.

"What's wrong, Kaiden?" Chiyo asked.

"I'll tell you when this is over, but this could either make things easier or far more complicated, depending on the number of bastards in the mix."

"Normally, you count yourself among those bastards," Marlo jeered.

Kaiden, however, remained stoic, "Not this time."

"To wrap this up, we will talk about the map and the winning conditions. The map is procedurally generated." The screen returned to a holographic image of the previous map, but rooms started to change, and hostiles and mechs swapped out for different models. "The map is not only different every year, but changes during the test. Rooms that were once death traps could change to rooms with objectives in them. A hallway that was clear now has a team of heavily armed mercs patrolling, so you must always be on your toes." The display began to darken at its edges, and the view range grew smaller and smaller. "Toward the end of the test and past a certain mark, the map will begin to deteriorate. Should you be caught in one of these sections as they disappear…" a room with three holographic soldiers faded, and the soldiers fell into the abyss and disappeared, "it will be the end of the test for you."

Luke sneered. "Oh, boy, running. My favorite."

"Better work on that cardio." Cameron laughed.

"Or use that springy leaper."

"Bouncepa— Shut up, Kaiden," the titan growled

"The last remaining team may not, in fact, be the victors. While that is the typical outcome, we have had teams that have gathered so many points so quickly that even when they were killed halfway through they ended up on top, so you must always keep your strategy and options in mind. You must never believe that you are truly out. Even in reality, you can lose your life and still succeed, and sometimes that might be the only way," the head monitor informed them solemnly. The mood in the theater changed to grimness for a moment before Zhang spoke again. "I should say that only one team has emerged truly victorious in this test. Having the most points doesn't mean you are the winner, only that you are the best among the other teams."

The ace looked at the others in confusion, but they returned his glances with curious looks or shrugs. "Now then, with all that out of the way, let us move to the final event of this meeting. Your squads."

The initiates sat up. Some held hands and other crossed their fingers. "Best of luck, guys," Kaiden said.

Zhang took a tablet and looked at Chancellor Durand, who nodded to him. He entered a few commands and placed the device on the podium. "Due to the number of initiates, we have decided to send your squad files to your individual EIs instead of displaying them one at a time. We'll give you a moment to find your teammates before we close this meeting."

Kaiden saw many EIs pop out of EI pads and initiates' eyes lighting up as their oculars accessed their devices. Kaiden crossed his arms and legs and leaned back, closing his eyes. "All right, Chief, who did I get saddled with?"

"Looks like a biologist named Abcde Notere and an administrator named Fore O'Four."

Kaiden clicked his tongue. "Dammit, really? This is gonna be a drag."

Chief cackled before laughing out loud in his head. *"Nah, I'm screwing with ya. Nice to see all that bravado goes out the window when you get a bad draw. I wonder what your poker face looks like?"*

The ace opened his eyes to glare at the ceiling. "Hilarious. Now, who did I really get?"

"Let's see... Look to your left, four and five seats down."

He raised a questioning eyebrow and peered down the aisle as instructed, to see Chiyo and Genos looking his way. "I got Chiyo and Genos?"

Bingo!

Kaiden chuckled as he sat up and saluted his future squadmates with two fingers. "Well, at least I won't have teammates I'll treat as only meat shields."

Chief scoffed. *"You're the salt of the Earth, partner."*

CHAPTER TWELVE

"Settle down now, initiates." Zhang called for order as the Academy students moved in a whirl through the auditorium, searching for their squadmates. "Get back in your seats."

His orders were finally obeyed and the initiates calmed down and faced the stage, although many of them still glanced at one another or had their EIs sending messages through the network.

Zhang sighed. "I knew we should have saved this for the very end. I say it every year," he murmured. "We are at the completion of the evening. You will have the rest of the night to yourselves to meet up with your squad and discuss your preparations for the test next week. However, before you are released, Commander Sasha would like to share some parting words."

He stepped back from the podium and offered it to Sasha. The commander moved up with what might have been a smile lurking. "Thank you, Head Monitor. Initiates,

I speak as a former commander, a member of this Academy's board, and a former initiate of the Academy. I want to wish you luck on your test. You are not only the future of your respective planets, but perhaps the future delegates to species unknown and future heroes of our galaxy."

"No pressure." Kaiden huffed but flinched slightly when he thought Sasha looked his way. The commander couldn't hear him from that far away, could he?

"As both the chancellor and head monitor said, this test is the culmination of your year. Go into it knowing that even in victory, you are bound to achieve even greater heights throughout your time here and beyond."

Sasha took a moment to look around the room. "You are Nexus Academy students, but that is only your title. You are some of the best this universe has to offer, and you will have to deal with oppression and aggression throughout your life. Some of you may have already had to deal with this, unfortunately, but you survived and through your will and strength, moved beyond those dark moments. Always remember that drive when you are confronted with a seemingly impossible situation or terrifying foe, and know that you are all better than anything that will try to tear you down."

"The commander is pretty good at this pep-talk thing," Amber commented.

"Maybe he put some talents into it when he was a student? Is that a choice?" Marlo wondered.

"Your success is your own to achieve. Always keep that knowledge close, and know that there is no reward without effort. So, strive ever forward and continue to achieve."

The students applauded the commander's speech. After a few moments, he raised his hand to quell them. "Once again, best of luck to all of you. Dismissed."

Initiates flooded out of the building, and the mass quickly splintered as students ran around and found their squads. Kaiden and the rest of their group walked to the center of the plaza before he turned to address Genos and Chiyo. "Well, ain't this a silver lining? The three of us together—it's like a dream team."

"Oh, most assuredly! I wouldn't have thought I would be so fortuitous," Genos declared.

"You trying to turn that into a catchphrase or something?" Cameron joked.

"I must say that it was quite…lucky, for lack of a better word," Chiyo admitted.

Kaiden eyed her curiously, "You still thinking I might fuck this up somehow?"

She shook her head. "No, I was… It's nothing. Nothing to do with you, at least. I am truly happy with this outcome."

He cocked his head and studied her. "No smile, no twinkle in the eye, no bounciness. You read more like indifferent than happy."

The infiltrator stared at him for a moment before placing her pointer fingers on each end of her mouth and pulling them up to make a mock smile. "Is this better?"

Kaiden laughed. "That's pretty good. It'll do." He glanced at the rest of the group, who were talking amongst themselves. "What about you guys? You get any bad picks?"

"Actually, it looks like we all lucked out," Flynn stated. "All of us are in squads with each other."

The ace raised his eyes in surprise. "Really, now? How does that break down?"

"Well, me, Amber, and Marlo are grouped together, so that's a start," the marksman said.

"This thing is supposed to be randomized, isn't it?" Kaiden asked.

"Marlo's armor must be made of horseshoes," Flynn quipped.

Amber slid an arm over his shoulders. "I would say this is the real dream team here."

"Or the other teams' nightmares," Marlo boasted, looking around. "Uh, not you guys, obviously. We'll be nice to you."

"What about the rest of you?" Kaiden asked the other six.

"I have been paired with Silas and Isabella. Should prove a rewarding group," Jaxon confirmed, looking at the other two as Izzy clapped and Silas nodded.

"That would mean..." Kaiden pointed at Cameron, Raul, and Luke. "You three are a team?"

"Yes, sir, the Terrifying Trio," Luke bellowed.

"I don't think we have team names, but if we do, that's not ours," Raul said.

Kaiden began to laugh as he continued to point at the three. "Oh, you guys are so screwed."

"What are you talking about? We work together all the

time. Probably more than anyone here," Cameron growled in protest.

"Yeah, with Jaxon leading you." Kaiden snorted. "You and Raul are always at each other's throats, Luke's a damn good titan, but he's also probably gonna get focused when we all start shooting at each other. You guys are more a comedy troupe than a combat unit."

"Thanks for the vote of confidence, leadhead," Raul sneered.

"I mean, he has good points," Silas admitted. "At least Chiyo and Genos only have to keep him in line. Maybe Genos can use those remote hacking bullets and simply shut down his armor and keep him in a corner for the test?"

Kaiden looked cautiously from the enforcer to the Tsuna. "You wouldn't actually do that, would you, Genos?"

The alien's eyes widened. "What? No, no, no, of course, I wouldn't, friend Kaiden."

"Thanks. I was pretty sure you wouldn't, but—"

"I mean, I would never do that to a friend…unless you were going wild or became a threat to the team. Besides, it wouldn't be practical in a test like this. You would be of no use simply sitting on the floor. If I *did* wish to dispose of you, I would find a more beneficial means—perhaps strapping you with a large explosive and using an exo-net to force you to run into a group of hostiles and take them out…"

Kaiden's eyes narrowed as the Tsuna continued his list of possible uses for his body. "You could have stopped at no," he mumbled, apparently not loud enough for the

Tsuna to hear. Or Genos simply was too distracted by his potential strategies to pay any mind.

"So what will you guys do in the run-up to the test?" Izzy asked. "Workshops and all that are done for the year. We got a week to prepare."

"Well, we'll be training, obviously," Flynn stated.

She rolled her eyes. "I know that, but are you gonna be grinding for Synapse points, or maybe try to scrim with some of the other squads. You have to have more plans than simply throwing yourself in the Animus day in and day out."

"To be fair, that's been our training regime for the most part and it's worked out pretty well so far," Cameron admitted.

Jaxon tapped a finger on his infuser. "I suggest that we take a couple of days to run specified missions for our individual classes. It will let all of us know the strengths and weaknesses we all have as individuals as well as learn the potential objectives each of us can complete during the test. Then we can go into more specified missions to get better at teamwork."

"That sounds like a plan to me," Silas agreed around a yawn. "After I get some sleep, we'll get right on that."

"You're still sleepy? Get some coffee in you or something," Izzy scolded.

"Over the weekend, I had a total of six hours of sleep in the freezing cold and got speared by Raza and pumped with who knows how many volts. I'm. A. Bit. Wrecked," he responded flatly.

"We should probably get some sleep too," Luke agreed, looking at Cameron and Raul. "We'll probably wanna get up not so bright and super early. The AC will be packed for the next week."

"Oh, that's right. Everyone will want to use the Animus, even more than usual," Amber reasoned.

Jaxon nodded. "Plus, the other years will be preparing for their end of the year tests as well. The Animus Center only accommodates around five hundred students at a time and there are nearly one-thousand students here."

"There are five hundred in the normal halls, but you're rank two, right? You have access to the private rooms. We could use those," Izzy suggested.

The Tsuna continued to tap on his infuser. "Perhaps, but there are only thirty of those rooms, so we will still be racing against all the other rank two and rank three students among all years."

"It's first come, first served. Fortunately, a team can only run one mission before they have to give it up to the next team on the schedule. Then, most of them almost immediately queue again right after. Those wait times can get hellish," Raul complained.

As the group began to talk about their personal plans, Chiyo and Genos walked over to Kaiden. "Do you have a plan for this test?"

He stroked his chin. "I guess that would be a part of my job description. But I have to admit, I'm a bit outta my depth. I hate to admit it, but Cameron and Flynn were right in that my normal strategy of 'shoot everything that moves' won't be as viable because of the weird currency system."

"That's a viable strategy to you?" Genos inquired.

"You've been running missions with him. This hasn't dawned on you?" the infiltrator asked.

"I wasn't aware that he considered that 'strategy' rather than the beginning of sociopathy," Genos admitted.

"What are those?" Kaiden asked.

Chiyo looked at him in disbelief. "You saying the Tsuna knows more about human psychology than you do?"

"To be fair, those conditions aren't human-centric, but you do seem to have more offenders than we do," Genos clarified.

"We do strive to be the best in all things," she muttered sarcastically.

"While you guys are making fun of me, mind using some of the mental energy to toss out some possible plans here?" the ace grumbled.

The mechanist tapped on his infuser while Chiyo retrieved her tablet. "I'll use the rest of my night to go over any vids of previous tests and find out any potential information that may be useful. Head Monitor Zhang's words about there's only been 'one true winner' before now has me curious about what that may entail."

"I couldn't understand what he was on about. You get the most points you win, right? No need to be so cryptic." Kaiden didn't hide his irritation.

"I would guess that it was a hint at a different or alternative goal in the test that allows for victory. As he said, despite the nickname, the 'Deathmatch' is more than merely a free-for-all." She looked up from her tablet. "But since we are discussing the head monitor's cryptic words, what got you so worked up before?"

The ace looked blankly at her. "Um... Oh, are you

talking about when he mentioned friendly fire?" He crossed his arms. "It's obviously an attempt to weed out the assholes in each team. Remember that he said there is an overall team score along with an individual score?"

"I do, but what does that have to do with—"

"Do you also remember that initiates who are killed drop those Honor points that anyone can pick up, including the squadmates?"

"Of course, it's a method to encourage combat among the test takers," Genos stated.

"I was simply thinking, what's the point of having individual scores if this is supposed to be a team test. Then I thought back to the other tests and the fact that we got rewards and prizes and all that for coming out on top..." He trailed off and watched the other two to see if they had caught on.

Chiyo's eyes narrowed. "You think some members would kill their own teammates to increase their own score?"

"It's possible," he reasoned.

"That's horrible," Genos exclaimed. "Do you really think students here would lower themselves to such a barbaric mindset?"

"Like I said, it's only something that I thought of. Unfortunately, I've seen selfishness like that plenty, and I wouldn't count on some of the more...tenacious initiates around here not doing so."

"But doesn't that work out for us? Make it more likely that we will have less initiates coming after us?" the infiltrator asked.

"Oh, yeah. Like I said, it could work out great for us.

But if we weren't together and with a couple of randos instead…"

"We would have to worry about watching our squadmates as potential attackers as much as the others and the environment," Chiyo finished.

"Got it, but fortunately, we don't have to worry about that." He eyed Genos. "Right? A Tsuna who just listed how useful my corpse would be for explosions?"

"I said I would never do such a thing. I just got…lost in hypotheticals," the alien said sheepishly.

Kaiden chuckled as the rest of the group joined them. "You guys get everything together?"

"We've got our plans and preparations in order. As I am assuming you do now?" Jaxon inquired.

"Actually, it's still a work in progress, but we'll be ready, and you guys better watch out when the test day comes," the ace challenged his counterpart.

"That's actually what we wanted to discuss before departing," Jaxon stated, folding his hands behind his back. "We have discussed it and we will not hunt one another until the last moments of the test if we can help it. I know that this is a test between all initiates and that the potential for us to fight one another could happen. But considering the bonds we have created this year, it would seem cheap to attack and potentially eliminate each other until we absolutely have to."

Kaiden looked at Genos and Chiyo, who nodded. He walked up to Jaxon and scanned the others. "While I must say it's rather funny that you think you can take me out—"

"Uh, if you recall, I almost did in the Division Test," Flynn retorted.

"One of these days, you and I need to head to the Animus and settle that, because no, you did not," Kaiden countered. "But I don't think that needs to be during the test. Plenty of other fish and all that. No offense to either of the Tsuna."

"Why would that be offensive?" Genos and Jaxon asked at the same time.

"Really? You've been here a year and you never made the connection?" he asked, looking at the blank stares of both Tsuna, "Whatever. The point is, of course we agree. But you all better make it to the top four, because I kinda do want to see what happens when we go all out with no guilt and all that." He offered a hand to Jaxon who took it in a firm shake.

"I plan to go for first, actually, and I'm sure the others do as well. So do not worry, you may get your wish," Jaxon said forebodingly.

"Look, I'm already about to burst from anticipation. You're merely mocking me at this point." Kaiden released the alien's hand and looked at the others. "Y'all heading out?"

"Yep, but I guess we'll see you in the Animus Center?" Flynn asked.

"Maybe. Gonna be a hell of a crowd around there," Kaiden noted gloomily.

"Well, be sure to make time to see each other over the week and check on each other's progress," Jaxon stated. "For now, everyone get some rest and start training."

"You got it, boss," Cameron said, only slightly joking.

"I actually don't mind following that order," Silas said with another yawn. "See most of y'all back at the dorm."

JOSHUA ANDERLE & MICHAEL ANDERLE

They all said their goodbyes. Kaiden and Chiyo hung back as the others departed. "Wanna meet up at the table tomorrow?" he asked.

"I'll be there," she agreed. "I'll send Genos a message before I fall asleep so he knows to meet us there. We'll come up with a plan in the morning."

"Sounds good." He nodded. "I'm tired, but thinking about this test has me pumped. It might be the best thing I've done all year."

"Even better than *our* test?" she asked.

"This test has you and Genos both, and I get to go against all the other trained initiates rather than only AI mercs and junk. It's gonna be a playground," Kaiden said cheerfully, clenching a fist. "But if you wanna know, our test is my current number one."

"I'm glad. It's my number two," she stated as she walked away.

"Oh, gonna do me like that, huh?" Kaiden shot back in mock anger "What's your number one? Come on, don't leave me on a cliffhanger."

The infiltrator continued to walk to her dorm, although she raised a hand and waved. "My first one should be obvious. Without it, I wouldn't have been able to take the test with you at all," she whispered to herself.

CHAPTER THIRTEEN

C hiyo left the cafeteria with her breakfast and headed to her usual table, which was surprisingly still available considering the large number of students around the area. She took her seat and activated her oculars. "Please bring up my network, Kaitō."

"Immediately, madame," the EI acknowledged, bringing up the network directory. *"What do you require?"*

"Where are the others?" she asked, cutting into a pancake as she spoke.

"Those in your squad for the test? Genos should arrive shortly. Mr. Kaiden appears to still be at the soldiers' dorm. Ah, he just left the building and is headed this way."

"Good. We have a lot to accomplish today, and I need to fill them in before we go." She punctuated the statement with a forkful of pancake, gulped it down, and took a quick sip of apple juice "Were you able to find out anything else about the test while I was sleeping?"

"A few things, yes. I found more video segments, but nothing in

141

full or of very high quality. It would appear that most videos or records of past tests are closely guarded, or possibly deleted after a certain point in time after the test. As you surmised, the bits of video we have been able to find are on greysites and seem to have been secretly recorded by technicians from the years before. Are you not worried that the Academy will find out you have this information?"

"No. With the level of power and the number of technicians and hackers they have at the Academy, they could have gotten these sites deleted or the videos taken off, at least. They could have potentially put viruses in the vids as well, and the scrubbing we did showed nothing of the sort."

"True, but we did find trackers and corruption viruses on a few of the videos," Kaitō noted.

Chiyo smiled slightly. "That would only be other techs being cheeky. I would have been rather dissatisfied if we hadn't found at least a few among all the vids. A shame I don't have the time to do a reverse trace. I could have potentially found a few helpful techs from previous years."

"Friend Chiyo! Good morning!" Genos called. She barely heard him over all the chatter. He made his way around the students littering the area and took a seat across from her. "Has Kaiden not made it yet?"

The infiltrator looked at her network map, seeing Kaiden's dot entering the cafeteria. "He'll be here in a minute. It looks like he's getting food first." She noticed that the Tsuna had no food or drink with him. "Are you not hungry, Genos? You should eat before we go to the Animus."

"Oh, no thank you. We have personal cooks in the Tsuna dorm to help with our specific needs. Plus, I still receive gifts and supplies from my matron every few weeks. I am well fed."

"Good to hear, although you may want to apply a little more immerse gel to your hand." She pointed to a blotch on his skin that was turning a bright white.

"Oh, my. I must have not been thorough enough. I've been so excited since last night that I hardly slept." Genos reached into a pouch and removed a vial of purple gel. He poured a small amount on the blotch and rubbed it in. "Thank you for catching that."

"Wouldn't be good for the squad if those hands of yours shriveled up, and not good for an engineer either."

"Certainly not." He chuckled. "So what were you able to find last night? I ventured to the library but it was rather fruitless, sadly."

"That's all right. From the little I have found, it would appear that they are doing their best to hide the specifics of the test from us, even more so than in the other tests." Chiyo hummed thoughtfully for a moment. "Still, I did find a few interesting things. I wanted to wait for all of us to be here before going into specifics—"

"Morning, y'all," Kaiden said as he sat down next to Genos. "What're we talking about?"

"Ah, friend Kaiden, a good morning to you," the Tsuna responded. "Chiyo was just telling me she found out a few things about the Deathma—Squad Test. We were waiting for you before going into details."

"Really, now? Nice work, Chiyo." Kaiden congratulated her as he scarfed down some of his eggs. "You not hungry, Genos?"

"The Tsuna have a private culinary staff, apparently," Chiyo informed him.

"That sounds handy. Even with buffet lines, it's a madhouse in there." He grimaced. "So what did you find out?"

"Less than I hoped but more than I realistically expected." She took out her tablet and turned it on. "My apologies, but I don't have an EI pad, so you might have to crowd around the screen."

"Don't worry about it. Hey, Chief!" Kaiden called.

His EI appeared above the table. *"Morning, squadmates. We all ready for the day? Get into the Animus and train for the end-all-be-all test of the year."*

"I think he's auditioning to be the squad's mascot," the ace joked. "That, or the all-important cheerleader."

"Hello, Chief. It has been a while since we last interacted." Kaitō's avatar appeared on the tablet's screen.

Chief turned slowly to the tablet, *"Hey...Kaitō! How have...you been?"* he responded, his words sounding stilted.

"He still seems to have problems with Chiyo's EI," Genos whispered to Kaiden.

"Hey, man, at least he isn't insulting him, and that sounded like an actual greeting with a bit of small talk. Baby steps," the soldier suggested nonchalantly as he finished his eggs and moved on to his bacon. "Hey, Chief, can Chiyo send you her info and graphs and all that and you display it for us?"

"Of course I can. That is but one of many powers I have at my disposal," Chief declared as he turned to look at the infiltrator. *"I just need you to send me the files you want me to show and I'll get right on it."*

"Thank you, Chief," she said with a nod. "Kaitō, would you please transfer the files and vids we found to Chief?"

Kaiden's EI jostled around in the air, his eye widening. *"Wait, Kaitō is gonna send them to me?"*

"It would be the fastest way," Chiyo reminded him.

"What's wrong, Chief?" the ace asked.

The EI spun around and lowered himself in the air until he was face to face with Kaiden. *"It's just...I mean, I can do it and all, but for an EI to transfer anything to another EI, they have to interact and exchange the info by putting it directly into our memory, and it's... Look, it's kinda invasive, you know?"*

Kaiden smiled slyly at the EI. "So what's the problem? Just let Kaitō get in you and pour out his data stream into your system, and you can pop out the info in about nine seconds or so."

Chief's eye narrowed. *"You're not making this easier, you know."*

"Not my job, now suck it up. I'm talking about Kaitō's—"

"I know what you're saying." The EI cut him off, then sighed and looked at the tablet. *"Just get it over with."*

"Acknowledging. Transferring vids, files, and other information," Kaitō stated.

Chief's eye glowed brighter and darkened for a few seconds, showing that the information was being transferred. *"Transfer complete. Now get out while I do my thing."*

"Certainly. Thank you for your cooperation, Chief," Kaitō said and disappeared from the tablet screen.

"Thanks for making it quick, at least." The EI sighed. *"All right, what do you need, Chiyo?"*

"Please bring up the vids—as many as you can without

sacrificing resolution and without the screen being too small," she requested.

"You only got eighteen here. Shouldn't be a problem." Chief's orb disappeared and was replaced by eighteen virtual screens in rows of three.

"Well done," Chiyo said approvingly. "These were a few videos I found on a few greysites."

"Greysites?" Genos asked.

"They are basically secret websites that are created by clever hackers or scripters and are also called limbo servers. They host their own personal version of the internet but have special access points or workarounds that only those with special permissions or who know where to find them can access. Or if you have enough skill in hacking and know where to look," she added. "They are from various years. Some run as little as eight seconds and others are as long as two minutes."

"Doesn't give us a lot to work with either way, but I'm guessing it's more like a puzzle than a complete picture?" Kaiden inquired.

She nodded. "A good way of looking at it. A few videos seem to be from the same tests, but most are different. Chief, would you please play the videos?"

"All of them at once?" the EI asked.

"Yes, please." The screens played, and Kaiden looked through them. All but two were in first person, and those last were stationary, looking in one direction like they had been taken from a camera set up on a tripod.

"The environments are different in a lot of these," Genos noted. "Most seem to be indoors, but others are in a jungle or desert."

"Good eye, Genos," Chiyo said, "but the entire test is technically indoors."

"So they are using terraforming tech or something like that in a few of the rooms?" Kaiden asked as he continued to watch the screens.

"Technically, they are simply using the capabilities of the Animus. Creating multiple environments in a single setting shouldn't be that difficult for the system," the infiltrator explained. "But take a look here." She pointed at a screen in the middle of the third row.

The soldier watched as two teams of three fired on each other in a hallway. There was a bright flash, and the hallway became a war-torn street. Mechs fell from the sky and activated, firing on the teams as the screen looped back to the beginning. "The advisors changed the environment."

"Didn't the head monitor say at the meeting last night that this would be one of the challenges?" Genos asked.

"He did, but what interested me was that flash of light. I don't think that was the advisors tampering with the environment."

"Why's that?" Kaiden couldn't see what she had picked up on.

"You told me that the first time you entered the Animus it was with Professor Laurie, correct?" Chiyo asked.

"Yeah, because of my implant and all that."

"You said that he swapped maps on you, and the same thing happened during your Synapse and loadout lesson with Adviser Faraji."

"You have a good memory," he admitted, "but what are you getting at?"

"The way the environment swapped in that vid. It was so quick, and the way the mechs loaded in and immediately attacked the surrounding initiates? If that was done with an advisor at the controls, there would have been at least a few seconds of darkness as that segment of the map was swapped out. Then the mechs would have to be loaded, and even once they are, it takes them a few moments to activate and become hostile. Whatever or whoever is in charge of swapping or adding in new obstacles isn't doing it from the consoles in the AC."

"Maybe it's Laurie or a batch of his technicians," the ace suggested. "This seems like the kind of thing he would get his jollies from."

"Possibly. He would have the tech and direct access to the Animus systems. You can try getting him to talk, but I doubt you'll get much."

"I'll bring a can of paint into his office and threaten to stain his clean carpet. That should work." Kaiden snickered.

"Please don't get yourself booted from the Academy before the test is done." Chiyo sighed. "Besides, I'm still curious about the speed and suddenness of the change. The techs Laurie has at his disposal are some of the best, and they could simply have prepared formats and changes at the ready. But I think it might be something more advanced than that."

"What do you suppose it could be?" Genos asked.

"It's speculation, but perhaps it's an EI within the Animus itself," Chiyo stated.

Kaiden finished off his meal and tossed his fork on the tray. "Controlling it like the advisors would?"

"No. I mean that it is within the Animus, and specifically within the map itself. It would explain how all the rooms can change so suddenly and how they can be tailored to each team within reach and react in such a way that it corresponds to their style of fighting and weaknesses. It would also explain how it can do so on a whim."

"But Chiyo, if that was the case, couldn't a hacker like you potentially take control of it? That seems like a large flaw," the Tsuna pointed out.

"That is true, but like I said, it's merely speculation on my part. Something to consider as we prepare for the test."

Kaiden tapped his fingers on the table. "That may be something to consider. Did you happen to find out anything about that team that actually won the test, as Zhang put it?"

"Only an old article," Chiyo said after finishing her juice. "Chief, would you bring that up, please?"

The screens disappeared one by one and were replaced with a news article from the *Nexus Chronicle* declaring the winners of the 2176 Squad Test.

Kaiden read through the beginning of the article quickly. "I'm not seeing any names here."

"They've been redacted, from what I can tell," she stated. "All I could find was that the team was comprised of a marksman, a hacker, and an exotechnician."

"What is an exotechnician?" Genos inquired.

"A type of medic. Biologists use serums and herbs and all that stuff to heal. Exotechs use gadgets and doodads. It's great when you have a good one, but they like to use the latest stuff available and a lot of their new tech is often tested in the field to… Let's go with mixed results," Kaiden explained.

"The article says nothing about what they did or how they accomplished their 'true victory' as it says here." Chiyo shrugged. "For now, I don't have much else other than I can confirm that it happened at some point. I suggest we focus on sharpening our skills to win this test the 'traditional' way."

"That's a good place to start." The ace looked around as more and more students began to leave and head for the Animus Center. "Looks like we should be heading that way. It's gonna be filling up real soon."

"If we have to wait, we can use the time to figure out what mission we should undertake," the infiltrator suggested.

"Don't have to worry about that. You and I are rank three. We get our own special room." Kaiden beamed.

"But kin Jaxon said that there were only so many of those rooms. Will any be available?" Genos fretted.

"Don't worry, Genos. Nothing on Jaxon, but he's still rank two. Rank threes have a few extra rooms available to them. Though to be fair, those might also be taken, considering we have to worry about the whole Academy being there."

"Then we should depart," Chiyo stated as she stood with her tray in hand. "Once we get there, we need to quickly decide what mission we are going to do."

"I've got that covered," the soldier announced as he picked up his tray. "Y'all feel like having a 'clash?'"

CHAPTER FOURTEEN

K aiden materialized in the dropship's hold, and Chiyo and Genos appeared beside him. "Welcome to Air Jericho. I can't promise a smooth flight, but I can promise a future of fun times and a bit of ultra-violence."

"Funny." Chiyo deadpanned as she opened her loadout screen. "Before I make my decisions, do you care to fill us in on what we will face in this match, Kaiden?"

"I can't say I've ever participated in a clash before," Genos admitted. "What is it, exactly?"

"Okay, listen up. Actually, Chief, do you wanna help out here?"

"After you just got up and left me at the table? What happened to never leaving your squad behind?" Chief fumed as he appeared in the center of the hold.

"Cool your jets, Chief. You're tethered to my head. It's not like I can lose you," Kaiden countered.

"It's the thought that counts, dumbass."

The ace rolled his eyes. "Get over yourself and give our friends here a rundown, would ya?"

"Fine, fine, but only because I'm a team player."

"Yeah, your past actions have proved that indisputably. Just start talkin.'"

Chief changed into a large display of the map they were in, showing a substantial jungle island with a building at the center. *"All right, the name of the game is Clash, and here's what you gotta do."*

Depictions of Kaiden, Chiyo, and Genos appeared on one side of the map, and six non-descript figures appeared on the other. *"It's two teams trying to collect as much 'rep' as possible. You can do this a number of ways—killing mercs and droids, sabotaging devices, hacking into nodules, that type of stuff. The first group to make it to one thousand points wins."*

"Sounds almost exactly like what we will need to do in the Squad Test," Genos noted.

"Two teams? Are we in a scrim?" Chiyo asked.

"Nah, the other team is artificial and controlled by the Animus."

"They have six members?" Genos questioned, looking at the six figures on the map.

"I amped it up a bit. Figured we should get used to being outnumbered since, you know, we'll be dealing with two hundred and ninety-seven other initiates, along with all the mobs on the map," Kaiden explained.

"A good idea, Kaiden, but what specifically are we up against?" Chiyo inquired.

"Can't say," he replied.

"Still keeping us in the dark, then?" the mechanist asked.

He shook his head. "No, I really don't know. I set the divisions for the opponents but not the class."

"Can you tell us what their divisions are, at least?"

"You got two soldiers, two technicians, and two engineers. Beyond that, it's up in the air," Chief informed them.

"A mirror image of us with twice the members," Chiyo noticed.

"So I should base my loadout on a straight battle troop, then?" Genos considered his options.

"Safe bet, but you have to remember there are also mercs and droids in the facility and that those technicians could be anything from hackers to agents or even infiltrators like Chiyo. Might get lucky and get a translator, though. That should make for easy pickings."

"On the engineer side, there could be pilots or mechjocks. We need to make sure they can't get into their respective vehicles if that's the case. Otherwise, we'll be at a huge disadvantage," Chiyo stated.

Kaiden nodded as he flipped through his loadout. "Agreed. But I would suggest we play it safe and not engage right away." He looked up to see his teammates staring at him. "What are you looking at me like that for?"

"You…suggested we don't immediately engage the enemy. That's almost concerning, coming from you," Genos said, perplexed.

"Maybe something went wrong during his sync?" the infiltrator suggested.

"I'm fine. But at this point, the important thing is to get the points. We get a good number for taking them out, but we lose points if we die."

"You have infinite lives in this mission. But like Sir Trigger-

Happy said, you lose about twenty percent of your points if you die. And that's if only one of you eat it," Chief warned.

"The opposing team probably isn't up to snuff compared to us, but they are supposed to be way better than the grunts we usually handle. On top of that, they are better equipped. I don't know how many of them it will take to defeat me—if they can at all—but I know how many they have, and it might be enough," Kaiden reasoned.

"So how would you recommend we complete this mission?" Chiyo asked.

"Well, I don't think the normal way will work. Not enough time to get you set up, and even if we did, they would probably catch on a lot faster than the normal mobs do. You would be targeted for the rest of the match," Kaiden advised.

"So we should stay on our feet then?" Genos suggested.

The soldier nodded. "We'll focus on taking out the trash mercs and getting nodes and all that. Those are worth a lot more than simply gunning down whatever gets in our way. Unless it's big, then we kill it and get a shit-ton of points."

"Don't forget the other payloads," Chief reminded him.

"Payloads?" Genos questioned the EI.

The map disappeared and was replaced by images of a large mech, a black server with glowing lights, and a power core. *"Payloads are specific targets that yield five hundred points or more. As Kaiden mentioned, you can take out a powerful enemy and gain a lot of points, but if you can hack into a server with high-end security or rewire a power core, those are also payloads connected to your classes."*

"I recommend we go for the power core or the server. The big enemies are lots of fun, but it leaves us open to ambushes from the enemy team, and there's a good chance the big bastards can take us out too," Kaiden stated.

"It seems clear that you have done this sort of mission before?" the Tsuna inquired.

"Ran it a couple times with Flynn's team. First time was easy. Second time, the enemy team rubber-banded like utter bastards, and we only won by ten points," he explained.

"Might I ask how many members the other team had when you ran those missions?" she asked.

"First time was an even four and four, the next time was four against five."

"And now it's three against six," she muttered.

"Like I said, better to get used to stacked odds now than during the test," Kaiden responded. "We've got this. No worries."

Two minutes to touch-down, guys," Chief warned.

Kaiden closed out his loadout screen, and a kinetic auto rifle appeared in his hands. "All right, y'all pick your loadouts, and let's get ready to get in there."

The group approached the fortress on the island, and Kaiden looked around for side entrances or paths near the large main doors.

"How do y'all wanna play this?" he asked, looking back at his squadmates.

"A full stealth approach wouldn't be practical here," Genos advised. "We could potentially wait for the other team to begin, creating a distraction and allowing us to swoop in and catch the guards unaware."

"Where is the other team? Do we know that?" Chiyo asked.

The soldier pointed at the building. "The other team gets dropped off on the opposite side of the island. We won't run into them right away."

"Then I recommend we sneak inside and try to silently take out as many as we can. I'll get a map if one is available and try to access as many nodes and terminals as I can to boost our score," Chiyo offered.

"Works for me." Kaiden nodded, placed his rifle on his back, and took out his blade. "One last thing before we head in. Are we going for the power core or the server for the big points?"

"I suppose it depends on which one we run into first, unless Chiyo can get the map," Genos said, putting his plasma rifle away and activating his gauntlet to form a c-grip. "I *do* know that power cores are usually heavily guarded, for obvious reasons. It would take all of us to push through and get to it, but it will only take me a couple of minutes to deactivate it once I am there."

"The server may be less well guarded, but it will take me longer to hack in, not to mention any traps they might have both within the server and without," Chiyo informed them.

The soldier paused as he considered the options. "All right, we'll make the power core our goal. If it looks too heavy, we'll keep the server in mind as our back up. Sound good?"

His teammates nodded, and they moved swiftly from the hill they stood on and made their way toward the base.

Kaiden approached a guard looking out a window in the hallway. He crept up behind him and dug his blade into his throat. The guard disappeared, and three points were awarded.

"That makes one hundred and one points so far," Kaiden said as he continued down the hall, beckoning his teammates to follow. He stopped when he saw a turret in the distance scanning the room, then looked back at Chiyo and pointed it out. She nodded and tapped a few commands into her console. The turret stopped moving and deactivated, awarding them four points.

"Hey, what's up with the turret?" an agitated voice asked.

"Don't know. Did it crap out?" another wondered as heavy boots stepped along the metal floor.

Genos moved up to Kaiden's side and they crept along the wall. The two guards appeared from the hall, walking past them to inspect the turret. Kaiden pointed to himself and then to the guard on the left, then indicated that Genos should take the guard on the right. The Tsuna nodded and they snuck up behind their respective targets. The soldier once again drove his blade into the guard's neck, while the mechanist clamped his claw over the other guard's neck and tightened the grip. As the first target disappeared and awarded three more points, bones snapped and the second man fell and disappeared.

"Nice job," the ace said, the compliment genuine. "Let's see if we can find... Aha." He spied a room across the hall from where the guards had approached. Swiftly, he turned and headed in its direction when he heard a mechanical whirring behind him.

"Kaiden, look out," Chiyo warned. He spun and fell to the floor, Debonair in his hand and pointed up behind him. The turret had reactivated and was pointed at him. It exploded as Genos fired his hand cannon at it.

"What happened? I thought you deactivated it?" the soldier asked, looking at her.

She activated her holoscreen and looked through it. "I did, but... It appears they have a hacker or infiltrator of their own. They have access to the security systems on this floor. I can't shut them out, but I'm delaying their commands."

"Using our own plan against us, sneaky bastards." Kaiden chuckled ruthlessly. "Well, that means that they are either holed up in some room or their hacker is all alone. Easy pickings."

"The room ahead may hold nodes or terminals. We should let Chiyo get in there and secure us some more points," Genos advised.

"What's the score currently?"

"They have a slight lead, probably because they hacked that terminal, but once we have done the same we should pull ahead."

"All right, let's get moving," Kaiden instructed. They made their way to the room, where Genos slid the keypad off with the screwdriver on his gauntlet and messed with the wires. The door opened, and they gained six points. Within were six servers and a console.

"Genos, take a look at that console. Chiyo, get started on those servers," Kaiden ordered. "I'll keep a lookout." The two hurried to their tasks as the ace peered around the door. He looked inside after a couple of minutes to see that the infiltrator had just finished with one of the servers. "How many points was that worth?"

"Forty, which means that when I get through with the other three, we should have a total of one hundred and sixty points," she answered.

"Good, keep them coming." He closed the door and walked over to the Tsuna. He had ripped a couple of the consoles out and tampered with them, but was now looking at a screen and flipping through the channels. "What have you found, Genos?"

"Camera feeds, it seems, but some of them are blacked out," the mechanist explained.

"Probably shot down or deactivated by the other team," Kaiden reasoned.

"Fortuitously, there is a rudimentary map here on the console." Genos pointed to a map that showed each floor and was highlighted with numbers. "The numbers correspond to each camera on their respective floors. Using the numbers of the deactivated cameras, I can plot the enemy team's course."

"Where are they headed?" the soldier inquired.

"They seemed to have come in through the first floor and gone up to the third, and following their path there would seem to lead them... Oh, dear."

"What's wrong?" Kaiden asked. Suddenly, there was a

loud rumble, and the lights went out. Kaiden looked around, bewildered, as red lights began to flash around the building. "What happened?"

"The power core. Their destination was the power core," Genos stated. "They are trying to rewire it. Having some difficulty, by the looks of it."

"They haven't succeeded, have they?" the ace demanded.

"No. Not yet, at least, but once they do, they will have more points than us. They could overload it and blow this entire building."

Kaiden heard Chiyo fire her kinetic pistol. He turned and saw her removing something from the servers. "What are you doing, Chiyo?"

"The servers got shut down, so I'm taking the hard drives. I got some points for it, but I can still access the hard drives and get a few more. We'll need as many as we can get if we're going to make up the difference."

"We can still stop them if we get to them in time," Genos suggested.

"Maybe, but they'll be dealing with a stampede of guards soon. Although considering the caliber of the guards so far, that may not be as much of a hope as I'm making it out to be." He scowled under his mask.

"So what do you think we should do?" the infiltrator asked.

He thought about it for a moment before looking at his team. "Genos, were you able to see where the payload server was, by any chance?"

"It was also on the third floor. No doubt they are trying to take that as well."

Kaiden nodded and held out his hand. "Chief, get out here."

The EI appeared in his hand, slightly shrunken, and looked up at him. *"What's happening, partner?"*

"We're going to need your help," he stated, then focused on his companions. "I got a plan."

"What kind?" the Tsuna asked.

"Oh, you should know by now, Genos." Kaiden chuckled. "I only do crazy."

CHAPTER FIFTEEN

The enemy team's two hackers worked on the server, one trying to deal with its internal defenses while the other tried to make his way inside. They heard gunfire from outside the room. One of them looked at the other and motioned for him to check it out. He walked to the door with his submachine gun at the ready. He reached toward it, but it opened before he made contact. Bullets flew through him before he had time to react, dropping him to the floor. The other hacker raised his pistol quickly but was met by another hail of kinetic shots and laser fire, dropping him as well.

"Howdy and goodbye," Kaiden sneered as his team walked into the darkened room.

Chiyo walked over to the server, noticed a small box at the base, and knelt to inspect it. "A small energy generator used to keep the server functional during the blackout," she observed.

"Those two deaths will cost the other team forty

percent of their points and some lost time," Genos noted as he vented his rifle. "We should make the most of it."

Kaiden nodded and looked at the infiltrator, who was already at work on the server. "You good with this, Chiyo?"

"Of course. It will be some time before they return, and we will be prepared for them," she responded and continued to type. "They had already begun their attempt, but it's shoddy work, I must say. I suppose they were going for quantity over quality."

"Hey, they're only artificial hackers. Think of their feelings," Kaiden quipped.

"I would rather use that energy to crack this payload," she retorted. "Go on, I'll be fine. You need to worry about them taking the power core."

The lights came back on, and they held their guns at the ready. "Seems it's a bit late for that."

"They restored the power but don't have the core under their control just yet. They haven't gained the points," Genos informed them.

Chiyo looked at the small turrets in the ceiling. "The hackers apparently deactivated the turrets before the blackout. They will reboot, but I'll take care of them before then."

"All right, Genos and I are heading out," he declared, reloading his rifle. "Good luck."

"To you two as well," Chiyo returned. "And if you don't mind, close the door on your way out. Your fighting will be most distracting."

Kaiden and the Tsuna sprinted through the halls, making their way toward the power core. "You sure it's this way, Genos?"

"Positive. We'll just need to—" The Tsuna stopped in his tracks and raised his laser rifle to fire down the hall. Kaiden lifted his gun and searched for what his companion was shooting at. Lowering it, he saw a machine on the ground with sparks flying from the body and a streak of melted metal through its chest.

He walked over and knelt, looking at the destroyed machine. It had the appearance of a bird with its wings out and a small head with some sort of band across the front. "What is this?" he asked.

"A tracker's spotter droid. It has a remote link to its tracker, and they can see what it sees," Genos explained. "They know we're coming."

The ace stood. "Then we best get to them before they come for—*hurk.*" Kaiden grunted and fell to the ground when a net enveloped his body and squeezed down on him.

"Kaiden!" the mechanist shouted. He dropped his laser rifle and stood in front of his teammate. A tracker dressed in dark green medium armor with a sloped helmet and dark circles for sight stood at the end of the hallway. He aimed his kinetic sniper rifle directly at Genos. The Tsuna raised his gauntlet, and it fanned out into a small shield as the tracker fired at his head. The gauntlet shielded him, but the shot knocked him down. He took out his hand cannon as he fell and fired at the attacker, hitting him in his left shoulder, so he stumbled and fired into the ceiling.

Kaiden flicked his wrist, and his blade appeared in his

hand. He used it to cut through the net, yanked Debonair from its holster, and fired at the assailant as he tried to line up another shot. The lasers melted through the armor after several shots and the enemy collapsed. The body disappeared in bits of white light.

"Nice save, Genos," the ace said, offering his teammate a hand to help him up.

"I should have been prepared." The mechanist grunted as he took the proffered hand and hoisted himself up. "Trackers normally use scouts in closed environments as a distraction for an attack."

"Don't worry about it. I should have been more cautious." The ace looked at the spot where the tracker was struck down. "But it worked out. We took out another one of those dicks, and they lose more points."

"Perhaps, but it seems that bought them the time they needed," his companion muttered, "They have the power core and are at six hundred and eighty-two points."

"Damn it," Kaiden cursed. "You think they will blow it?"

"Listen closely," Genos commanded, pointing at the ceiling. "The fans are no longer blowing, and the heat is rising. They are either preparing to overheat the core for an explosion or are trying to fry all internal systems."

"Both aren't good, and would probably lead them to getting a victory." Kaiden growled his annoyance as he picked up his rifle. "I need to get there asap. Where's this place you need to get to?"

"Right there, at the end of the hall." The Tsuna pointed to a set of double doors behind where the tracker had been.

"Oh… Well, good deal. You got it from here?"

Genos nodded. "I will try to be as quick as I can. Hold out for as long as you are able."

The soldier raised his rifle. "I'm planning on doing a hell of a lot more than holding out."

His teammate chuckled as he picked up his laser rifle and slung it over his back. "For once, Kaiden, I implore you to simply do what you're best at."

He smiled and raised a fist in front of him. "I would do that anyway, but the vote of confidence is nice."

Genos looked at the fist and then at Kaiden. He raised a webbed hand and covered the front of his companion's fist. The ace glanced at their hands and lowered his head, shaking it. "You know what, I'll take it but we gotta work on things like this."

Kaiden made his way to the power core station. He saw that the doors were wide open and looked inside. Two figures hovered near the console, looking at the core through a large window. He didn't see a third figure—the sixth and final member of the enemy team. Without a doubt, it had to be a soldier of some sort, but he didn't see one. He scanned the room, looking for a hidden marksman, but saw nothing. He shrugged as he raised his rifle and aimed at the head of one of the engineers—a pilot, by the looks of it.

"Bad draw, buddy." Kaiden snickered. "No ships here, but you are about to have something flying at you quite quickly."

He tensed when he heard a skittering sound above him.

He looked up to see a machine with four spiked legs looking down at him with an elongated glowing eye. It shrieked a high-pitched static cry and lunged at him. The ace rolled out of the way and fired at it, nailing it once in the body before firing again and taking out its eye. It scurried around the floor, blind. He fired two more shots into it and it crashed into the floor, then exploded.

"Stupid creepy-ass spiders," he hissed. Laser fire came from the door, and he backed up against the wall. "Well, there goes my shot of opportunity." Kaiden growled his defiance.

He snapped around the wall and fired three shots. Fortunately, he clipped the other engineer—which he now knew was a decker, information which would have been helpful a minute before—in the back of his leg. He fell to the floor and his teammate ran over to him, helping him to cover as Kaiden fired several more shots, nailing the pilot in the back before he needed to reload.

"I've got you now, you sons of bit—" The ace could both hear and feel a heavy pounding through the floor. He looked behind him to see someone hurtling at him in heavy light-blue armor with a helmet that had two large spikes protruding from either side. He slapped a new magazine into the rifle and fired at the charging hostile. The bullets collided with the armor, which shimmered blue as the projectiles broke on impact. Kaiden leaped out of the way as the attacker slammed into the wall. The ace was knocked back by the resulting wave of force.

Kaiden flipped himself up and fired more shots. The attacker simply turned to face him as the bullets slammed harmlessly into her, and the armor shimmered with a blue light upon each impact.

"Oh, fuck me. A vanguard." Kaiden cursed as he realized what he was facing. The vanguard ran up to him and drew her fist back. He ducked as she threw her punch, the same blue light encircling her fist as she smashed it into the wall. Once again, he was knocked away but managed to hold onto his rifle as he collided with the floor. He slid in front of the opening to the power core station.

With a quick upward glance, he saw the decker hobble toward the core's console once again. "Oh, no, you don't, you spider-mech-making idiot!" Kaiden rolled onto his chest. He aimed at the decker and fired, nailing him in the shoulder and the side of his head. The enemy fell in front of the console but didn't disappear. "Why won't you die?" the ace bellowed in frustration.

His rifle was kicked out of his hands by the vanguard. She picked him up and held him up in the air. "Isn't there some beta you should be coddling?" Kaiden sneered before snickering. "Although considering your buddies over there, I guess I should be more sympathetic."

She tightened her hold and reached back, forming a fist. The ace yanked Debonair out and fired at her chest and helmet in six quick shots. The lasers broke her shielding and partially melted through her armor. "Up-close laser fire, your one weakness," he jeered as she let him go and tried to avoid the blasts. "Got you now, you— Oh no." His eyes widened as the vanguard whipped around and punched him straight in the chest.

The force of the impact knocked his breath out of his

body and nearly caused him to vomit, but that also might have been because he was sailing across the room to slam into the console. He sat up and coughed as she advanced on him relentlessly. He looked over to see the pilot drawing his pistol and the decker, still clinging to life, unlatch his hand cannon from his holster with a shaking hand.

Kaiden smashed the bottom of his boot into the Decker's face, and he dropped his gun. "Don't try to be all high and mighty now. It shows you're a sore loser," he muttered. A shadow fell across him and he looked up to see the vanguard standing over him, both fists glowing. "You gonna hit me with the right hook or left hook first?" He chortled. She raised both fists in the air. "Oh, a double whammy—classic." The ace looked around his adversary and smiled. "But you know what's also classic? When the cavalry shows up. And by cavalry…" He pointed behind her as the pilot began to fire at something in the doorway. She turned to the entrance to see a dozen raider droids at the entrance, their Gatling guns priming to fire. "I mean a team of killer robots whose only mission in life is to waste your ass."

Chiyo was close to finishing her task when she heard the door open. She looked up to see the two hackers from before in the doorway, along with a tracker. They all had their guns pointed at her, the server the only thing protecting her from their blasts.

"You showed up sooner than expected," she stated calmly while continuing to try to gain access to the server. "I was hoping to be done by the time you came back. I see you brought a friend as well. I wasn't aware of a tracker on your team. I suppose I should remind Kaiden and Genos to radio that kind of information in the future."

The three hostiles circled, and the tracker walked up to her and placed the barrel of his sniper rifle against her head. She crossed her eyes to look at the barrel between them. "You are distracting me. If you do not leave, I will ask Chief to *make* you leave."

The six turrets in the room descended from the ceiling and the three enemies looked around in surprise. The hackers tried hastily to deactivate them but to no avail. "You should stop wasting your energy. I didn't simply hack into them and rewire their protocols."

"Good luck trying to get into me," Chief declared. *"I'm as impenetrable as a dreadnought made of diamond. Your puny hacks only tickle me."*

"Please dispose of them, Chief, and try not to make too much of a mess."

"Since you asked so nicely..." The turrets fired, tearing through the enemy's armor with ease. Their bodies disappeared before they even hit the floor.

"Good work. Sorry you had to wait around for so long."

"Ah, no big deal. It just built up the anticipation," Chief chirped.

"With them out of the way, can you assist Kaitō and me with finishing this up?"

"Not a problem. Let me deactivate these things and get all up in there," Chief agreed, and the turrets slid back into their compartments in the ceiling.

"Genos, this is Chiyo. I have almost claimed the server. How is your mission going?"

"Rather well, actually." Genos related as he watched the large barrier wall that the vanguard erected shatter. The raider droids' assault continued, tearing into her in a hail of bullets. "Make sure to keep still, Kaiden. They shouldn't shoot at you, but stray bullets might be a hazard."

The ace looked up as two bullet holes appeared in the wall above him. "Noted!"

"We will be done soon as well. If the server doesn't provide enough points for us to win, I can shut down the power core and gain any additional points required."

"We should be all right. I'll see you back in reality."

"Acknowledged." The Tsuna closed the comm link. The vanguard disappeared, and the raider droids' guns began to wind down. "Are you all right, Kaiden?"

"I'll be better in a minute." Kaiden grunted as he used the console to pull himself up. He walked over to the decker and bent down to pick up his hand cannon. "I'm borrowing this. That all right with you?" he said and fired into his helmet. The enemy finally disappeared. "Don't bother answering, we just read each other like that." He pointed the gun at the pilot and fired, taking him out of the game as well.

"Was that necessary?" Genos asked as he walked up.

"Oh, God, you have no idea." Kaiden sighed happily. "Is Chiyo finished?"

"Just about. She said that she was—" A Mission Accomplished banner appeared overhead. "Well, that should answer your question."

"Oh, that was beautiful. Got a little close to the teeth and I could have done without the grand slam to my chest, but we beat the odds, and that's always a damn good feeling."

"It certainly is." Genos nodded as the room began to fade into white light. "So, another round?"

The ace took off his helmet and smiled. "Oh, we are going to damn near flog this baby until the test begins."

"I recommend more challengers next mission. Let them at least stand a chance. Also, maybe give them voice boxes if possible?"

Kaiden laughed, and he clapped his companion on the shoulder as they de-synced from the Animus.

CHAPTER SIXTEEN

The evening sky hovered over the glowing lights of the Academy's plaza. Nearly all the initiates were there, talking, laughing, or yelling at one another with excitement and bravado. It was the night before the Death-match, and Nexus had organized a festive dinner. Long tables of food had been arranged in a buffet style—exotic meats of venison, bison, quail, wagyu beef, and elk were spread beside fresh seafood like crab, tuna, salmon, lobster, and shrimp. Many dishes of various cultures were offered at neighboring tables, including a number of Tsuna dishes. A few of the more curious human students were game to try those, apparently.

Kaiden, however, was not one of them. He happily selected a steak, some shrimp, and a lobster tail with a scoop of ranchero beans and two double-baked potatoes and headed to his table. His friends were already there, dining and chatting. He took a seat next to Chiyo and Genos, then looked at his glass of orange juice with a slight frown. For a split second, he glanced at the bounty of beers and wine on offer. Considering the test on the horizon, it was probably wise not go in hammered. He began cutting into his meal and his frown turned into a smile as he observed the festivities around him. There was a palpable thrill in the spring night air.

"So, anyone wanna place bets?" Cameron asked, motioning around the table with his fork, specifically at the human ace and marksman. "Kaiden? Flynn? Who here do you think is gonna drop first?"

"You," both answered in unison, looking at each other and laughing.

"Funny, but Luke, Raul, and I have made our plan, and it's a masterpiece," he retorted and knocked the back of his hand against Raul's shoulder. "Ain't that right?"

"As good as it can be, considering we're going into a map that can constantly change and we'll eventually face up to two hundred and ninety-seven other initiates," the tracker replied once he finished chewing a piece of salmon. "Try not to be so loud. Don't need anyone eavesdropping and learning about our 'masterpiece,' all right?"

"I wasn't gonna give them the play-by-play." Cameron grunted and tore another rib from his half-rack. "Besides, who's going to hear us over all this chattering?"

"Well, there could be bugs, invasion drones, or recorders hiding around the plaza," Genos interjected. "Considering the alcohol available and how loose you humans seem to get once you've imbibed some of it, it would be quite an opportunity for some of the more strategic students here to learn more about their potential competition."

Some of the initiates darted their eyes around cautiously, while others turned their whole bodies to look for any tech around them.

"Not to mention potential hacks of your tablets or EIs," Chiyo added.

Izzy looked at her. "You find any?"

"Or make any?" Kaiden asked.

Chiyo nodded. "Yes, to you, Izzy, but no need to worry. I've taken care of it."

Flynn took out an EI pad and turned it on. "You feeling all right, Jeeves? Stable, collected, nothing feels like it's rooting around inside ya?"

"*I feel quite well, Mr. Flynn,*" The well-dressed kangaroo EI responded.

"You have him call you 'Mr. Flynn?' That's rather haughty of you." Kaiden chuckled.

The marksman rolled his eyes as he turned the pad off and put it away. "That's merely the programming. What do you think he should call me?"

"Maybe it should be something more dramatic," Marlo mused. "Marksman might be too plain. 'Eagle Eyes?' Nah, that's been used."

"'Lord Longshot?'" Izzy suggested.

"Is he a medieval archer now?" Silas chuckled.

"He has grown fond of that crossbow he smuggled back from your time with Wulfson," Amber added.

"Sir Bullseye?" Luke jeered.

"That's somehow better than Jeeves calling me Mr. Flynn?" He grimaced.

"It's funnier," the titan said with a grin and a shrug.

"Mr. Hidey-Hole would be more spot-on if we're

naming him after his talents." Cameron snickered, earning a glare from the marksman.

"Something straight to the point. 'My Happy Idiot,' perhaps?" Kaiden suggested.

"Nah, that would be Chief's nickname for you," Flynn countered. The ace leaned back and shook his head.

"Well, he's not usually happy. Plus, I don't really wanna claim ownership of him, so I simply stick with good old-fashioned idiot," Chief chirped, appearing in the air.

"Good evening, Chief," Chiyo greeted him with a smile.

"Eh? Where is he?" Cameron asked, looking around.

"You need optics to see him. The almighty orb apparently still doesn't have the power to show himself without the aid of such lowly technology, as he would deem it," Kaiden explained, taking another sip of his drink. "Unless you're me. Then you get to be audience to his assery at any point in the day."

"I've upgraded my EI. She doesn't do that." Amber frowned.

"Yeah, but you are not Professor Laurie's pet project," Silas pointed out.

"The perks of being the favored student of a crazy person. Nothing but being showered in fortunes and praise, I assure you." He sighed and took another sip. "I've already told y'all the deal. It's mostly genetics that got me suckered into Laurie's experiments."

"And yet those genetics couldn't do anything for your looks," Cameron quipped.

Kaiden rubbed the side of his chin. "Can't comprehend the natural ruggedness you're seein'? Or livid that anything that's kicked your ass has always had an ugly stick as their melee weapon?"

"Rotten luck, there," Flynn added, smiling. "I mean, what are the odds that it's every time and so frequently?"

"Because I actually get out there and fight," Cameron retorted.

"Yes, the primary strategy of the bounty hunter. Let everyone know you're there and what you're looking for." Kaiden chuckled. "I swear I'm going to hear about some big bounty you turned in because you simply had to tell everybody, then the next day, I'll read your obituary where that bounty's friends show up."

"Seriously, maybe try out for raider," Marlo interjected.

"I'm fine," Cameron grumbled, biting into another rib. "I've got my own way of doing things."

"And we see the effects of it every time you limp out of the Animus pods." Luke snickered.

"Real positive encouragement, teammate."

"Ah, it's only a bit of tough love, Cam. Positive reinforcement," the titan declared, slapping him on the back. "It's not like I've tried to trade you in or nothing."

"Was that an option?" Raul asked, earning a glare from the bounty hunter.

"I wanted to ask how everyone is feeling about tomorrow?" Jaxon interrupted, placing his elbows on the table and folding his hands together. "Any nervousness, or something they would like to discuss before we depart?"

"Looking to get some last-minute info on all of us? See if we got any liabilities you can exploit?" Kaiden asked, waving his fork at the Tsuna. "Pretty smart move there, Jaxon."

He held up a hand. "No. I wanted to simply offer some advice or—"

Luke nudged the ace. "He's messing with you, Jax. We've already made our pact, right? Just some good-natured competitive taunting."

"Kaiden's version of good-natured is a bit suspect," Chiyo commented.

Kaiden held his hands up and grinned. "Hey, I only wanted to lighten him up a bit. This is the calm before the storm and all that. We should enjoy it before it gets all white-knuckled and bloody."

Genos looked at his webbed, periwinkle hands. "Hmm, is that some sort of human disease I should be concerned about?"

The ace looked quizzically at his teammate. "What? Nah, it's when the… It just means that something is exciting or tense."

"Ah, well, that will probably be true." The Tsuna nodded. "As for the blood, I should make sure my armor choice includes scrubbers."

"You should leave that stuff on," Luke bellowed. "Show the others the remnants of those you've taken down. Put some fear in them."

"I believe the explosives and cannon that I carry will be quite sufficient for that," Genos stated.

"You use cannons now too?" Marlo asked, beaming, "Pretty good weapons, right? Nothing like frying a line of mercs in one shot."

"I've dabbled with them. Chiyo and Kaiden stated that having a heavy weapon would prove useful in the test. I've found one to my liking during our last few practice missions, although it is not comparable in size or power to yours."

"We'll fix that next year," Marlo promised, tapping his chest. "Feel like a walking tank when you carry around one of the big boys."

"Also, being composed of mostly muscle and veins in large metal suits probably helps with that," Raul said as he finished his shrimp.

"Hey, the chancellor is here," Silas notified the group. Kaiden looked behind him to see Durand at the edge of the plaza. Monitor screens activated above them and in the oculars of the students wearing them. He raised a hand, motioning for silence.

"Good evening, initiates." His greeting earned "good evenings" and other greetings from the gathered students. "I was just leaving a meeting to discuss the finals for the upperclassman and wanted to stop by and wish you all the best of luck."

"He's quite a delightful fellow," Flynn mused.

"He's also the leader of a highly advanced and mostly military academy," Silas added. "My guess is that under that charming personality, he could probably kill any of us with a napkin."

"Tomorrow, you will all rise and make your way to the Animus Center, where you will take part in what is possibly one of the biggest tests we have administered at this Academy. Certainly the biggest Squad Test we've ever undertaken."

"Deathmatch," someone shouted.

The chancellor chuckled. "If the rumors and hearsay from the upperclassmen make you think of it that way, so be it. But if you believe that's all this is, you are in for quite a surprise. I would also add that it's not exactly the best way to view this test, nor the way you should look at your potential future."

"Is he including us in that statement?" Marlo asked, looking at the table of mostly soldiers and ignoring the warning shrugs and silencing looks.

"While it is true that many here are warriors—and soldiers in particular—you limit yourselves with that kind of tunnel vision," Durand explained. "You have many skills, or you certainly should have at this point. You are here to make the most of yourselves and not only learn what you can do but unleash the inner potential you all have. After all, there is more to you, even if you consider yourself to be the best gunslinger of all time."

"Has Sasha been talking to him about me?" Kaiden wondered.

"That is pretty much on the nose," Chief agreed.

"I want you all to go into this test with not only an eye on your enemies but on yourselves. See how far you have all come in the short time you've been here." Durand took a deep breath before standing tall and looking over the sea of initiates. "This is the first year in more than a decade where we've had no dropouts or failures. Even those who failed the Division Test and Co-operative Test were able to pass during the make-up tests and by taking extra workshops and putting in more time in the Animus. To me, that shows that everyone here has a passion and drive to succeed. If you bring that same mindset into the test, you will continue your successes. This will not only be a triumphant victory but another proud moment on your list of accomplishments."

"Meaning they can get more money from our contracts." Cameron snickered and received an elbow to his ribs from Raul.

"The test will be chaotic. It will push you to your limits both physically and mentally. But you have the strength of not only yourself but your team, and you all have the spirit of Nexus Academy students. You were each brought here because of your potential, and you have made progress in tapping into it. Now, let it shine." The chancellor placed a closed fist across his chest, saluting the students.

The plaza was still. Kaiden looked around and sighed. He found a smile as he stood, uncrossed his arms, and saluted back. Quickly, the other students did the same, standing almost as one and saluting the chancellor.

Durand nodded and moved his arm behind his back. "Now, enjoy the rest of your evening, initiates," he bellowed before a sheepish smile formed on his face. "And if you could do us a favor and pick up after yourselves, it will make it quite a bit easier for us to set up for the Advanced class's meal on Thursday."

The students dropped their salutes and yelled out their thanks or good-byes as the man left. Kaiden sat and returned to his meal, finishing his steak as the evening began to wind down. He began to visualize the potential of the test.

Luke, Raul, and Cameron had already left, and the rest said

their goodbyes and exchanged good wishes. Kaiden was still eating when he waved farewell to Jaxon, Flynn, and their teams. Genos returned with more punch for Chiyo and himself, saying goodbye to their departing friends as he took his seat next to the ace.

"You are consuming quite a lot of food this evening, Kaiden," the Tsuna noted.

"When's the next time we're getting lobster?" he asked as he finished swallowing.

"Nearly every day in the Tsuna dorm," Genos confessed.

"Do what?" Kaiden asked, incredulously.

"Yes, your seafood is one of the few things Tsuna can eat on Earth, along with a few of your fruits and dairy products," Genos explained. "It is not a large or varied menu. Without some of the Tsuna supplies they ship in it would be a rather limited diet, but I have grown fond of lemons."

"Is it ironic that a species whose planet is basically a giant ball of water and who look like humanoid fish can only eat seafood, or does it make complete sense?" Kaiden wondered. "I lean toward the latter, but it also sounds weirdly like cannibalism."

"I think the things you focus on can be quite odd," Chiyo countered. "However, since you are both here, I wanted to run something by you."

"What would that be, friend Chiyo?" Genos asked

"It's about our theory on the test."

"We have a theory? Was it mine? Mine was to simply shoot everything," Kaiden joked.

"She's talking about how the map changes and who controls it, dingus." Chief huffed dramatically.

"Correct. I think I might have found something that could indeed point to the fact that it is run by an EI," she stated as she took out her tablet. "I found old schematics and descriptions in the library on the Animus systems. During the first few years, the advisors were mostly just technicians with a different name. They observed the Animus like the advisors do now, but they were looking over the system itself, not the specific maps or tools or scenarios like they do now. That was because all of that was handled by modified EIs. Their job was to make sure those EIs were running properly and updating or fixing them if need be."

"All right, that would make sense. It's new tech, and EIs could probably handle the load better and make changes and the like easier while they figured stuff out," Kaiden reasoned, crossing his arms as he leaned back in his chair. "But the Animus was basically a giant space that multiple people synced into at the same time then, right? Now it makes personal spaces that aren't as intense on the system or users, and they cleaned up the integration process and Synapse transference, yadda yadda, so they stopped using those kinds of things like fifteen years ago or something, right?"

"Sixteen, but you're correct for the most part." Chiyo looked at him. "I'm surprised that you knew that, Kaiden. Animus history doesn't seem to fall into your interests."

"Laurie is chatty," the ace deadpanned.

"I see. Well, before they updated the Animus, they were able to bond all the EIs together and install new coding, making it faster and more powerful. It was able to generate more space within the Animus, and separate it for the students so they could do various types of missions and practices. Along with this, it controlled the specifics of integration and handled more items and designs than before, all in real-time rather than pre-made maps or functions. They called it the 'Director.'"

"It sounds like a sort of beta test of the modern Animus design," Genos said.

"A good way to think of it," Chiyo agreed.

"If it was so kickass, why did they drop it?" Kaiden inquired. "There were probably some hang-ups."

"It couldn't create personal spaces, for one. It needed to be able to access the entirety of the Animus and couldn't handle multiple large individual areas with numerous actions going on at once. Basically, it created a giant map that it separated using giant walls and skyboxes, creating the illusion of personal spaces. It was also an enormous power drain, meaning only a certain number of students could go in at a time. That's the main reason that they only started expanding the Animus Center about ten years ago —that, and the student population was lower."

"So what makes you think this thing is responsible for all the crazy stuff that'll go on in the test?" the soldier asked.

"Because the two things they have not been able to replicate in the current system are the Director EI's ability to transfer and change a map rapidly, along with the ability to react to anyone in the Animus, read their weaknesses, their strengths, and react to them. When one does that in the Animus, it's essentially a reboot of the system. The way the map and everything on it changes, the way that it seems to analyze the situation and restructure itself accordingly, it checks out when compared with the notes I've taken."

Kaiden and Genos exchanged quick glances before focusing on Chiyo again. "It's a strong case, but what are you suggesting we do? It's not like we can get at this thing, right?" Kaiden questioned.

She simply smiled. "Actually, we can. And I believe that we will."

CHAPTER SEVENTEEN

"All right, everyone stay with your partners and follow the instructions of the advisors," an instructor shouted through the throngs of three hundred initiates as they all made their way to the Animus.

"The Animus Center will be stuffed to the tits," Flynn shouted to the others. He looked behind him, and his eyebrows shot up in surprise. "Oh, we already lost Raul and Silas. Pay your respects!"

"They'll turn up," Cameron called back. "Keep going, or we'll lose the good pods."

"So do the three of us hold hands, or are we simply playing a big-ass game of Marco Polo?" Kaiden asked, looking at Chiyo.

"Just keep moving forward. If you get lost in the shuffle, I'll send Wulfson to find you," she retorted.

"Rather you leave me to die," he countered as they entered the Center. Glowstrips lit up, guiding the students to available halls. Monitors also displayed the current open halls and their current capacity.

"I would think in this instance it would be better to take the stairs," Genos advised as he pointed to the elevators. "It looks quite busy over there."

Kaiden looked at Chiyo again and shrugged. "I did bring my stomping boots. Sounds good to me."

"The stairs are also likely to be full of students. The next available hall is seven stories up," the infiltrator pointed out.

"Hey, if cardio isn't your thing, you can climb on my back and I'll carry you up there. Won't lose you that way." Kaiden chuckled.

She frowned. "I'll be fine. I've been training for the entire school year, so stairs aren't exactly an insurmountable challenge." The group moved down the hall, past the elevators, and toward the stairs which, as Chiyo predicted, had a stream of students ascending, "Better not fall down here. The others will see it as an opportunity to take out the competition."

"No kidding." Kaiden laughed, looking over his shoulder. "Hey, Luke and Marlo, think you can clear a path?"

The two heavies looked at each other, and nodded and pushed past Kaiden. "Everybody, get the hell out the way," Luke shouted as they charged up the stairs. Those who were walking calmly or taking their time ascending looked back in horror as the big men rushed upward and either began to run up themselves or moved to one side.

"That'll do it." Kaiden snickered, raised a hand, and waved it forward. "Race the rest of y'all up to the top."

"You know, if I had known they would send us into one of the private rooms, I wouldn't have been in such a hurry." Kaiden huffed as the door slid open and revealed the compact, darkened room.

"I don't mind. Less of a crowd," Chiyo reasoned as she walked to the room's console.

"The normal halls have a total of five hundred pods. They really needed to ship us off to the corners?" Kaiden asked, leaning against a pod as he crossed his arms.

"It is probably to maintain some order or leave more pods available for the upperclassman. This test will possibly take all day," Genos said and hopped into an empty pod.

"Eh, guess I'm just bitter I won't hear any applause when I step out. If this works out, I might even do a twirl once we win." The ace smiled, pushed himself off the pod, and walked past Genos. "Also, the test isn't starting for a few more minutes. Gotta wait for the advisor to give us a speech or something."

"Ah. I am comfortable, although perhaps I'll lie here and consider the loadout options while we wait," Genos offered.

The soldier snorted. "Not a bad plan—meditation with extreme prejudice." He walked over to the console and saw Chiyo pressing a few buttons. "I don't think you can set up the specifics of the match, or are you playing Minesweeper while we wait?"

"I was changing the screen to the same channel as the

monitors outside to see how close we are to all three hundred students being ready," she informed him.

"Neat." He leaned forward and looked at the screen. "How's it going so far?"

"Well enough. We have just over two hundred students so far." She placed her hand on the screen and began to swipe. "Although it appears that the first couple dozen students to arrive are already being sent into the Animus."

"They get a head start? That doesn't sound very fair," he grumbled. "Where the hell is our Advisor so we can hurry up and get in there?"

"Hello, Team MIA," a familiar voice greeted them. Kaiden looked around and Chiyo pointed at the screen of the console, where he was greeted by the smiling face of Advisor Faraji.

"Hello, Akello," Chiyo said.

"Good morning, Chiyo…and Kaiden."

He clicked his tongue in annoyance and crossed his arms again. "Why such a sourpuss? I've been coming to your workshops again."

"You say that like you're doing me a favor," Akello muttered, her lips tightening.

"Can't win with her," Kaiden growled. He threw his hands up and walked away from the monitor.

"Where's your third teammate? Genos the mechanist?" she asked.

"I am here," Genos called. "I am in a pod. Violently mediating, according to Kaiden."

"That is…actually a better way of putting it," the ace said, giving Genos a thumbs-up that the Tsuna returned.

Akello looked at Chiyo, blinking several times in confusion. The infiltrator simply waved a hand to tell her to ignore it.

"All right, Team MIA. I am the advisor in charge of all teams in the private rooms. Which means I get to be a little more personal, but I do have to hurry as I gotta make it to the other teams."

"Why are you calling us 'Team MIA?' Which of you registered that?" Kaiden inquired, looking at Chiyo and Genos, who shook their heads.

"It is how we keep track of the teams in the match. We create the team names based upon the initials of your classes. Therefore, team mechanist, infiltrator, and ace become 'MIA,'" she explained.

"MIA, really? As in, 'missing in action?'" Kaiden muttered. "Why not AIM? Ace, infiltrator, and mechanist. It makes more sense and sounds better."

"You that full of yourself that you want it to be you in the first spot?" Akello teased.

"It's alphabetical," he countered.

"Maybe, but I was in charge of the names, and I choose MIA. It sounded nicer."

He sighed as he walked back to the pods. "This seems like an abuse of power."

"You are in my domain, remember?" she warned, earning an unintelligible grunt from Kaiden. "Anyway, I'm here to give you guys the last-minute details and answer any questions you might have."

"Understood." Chiyo nodded. "Go ahead."

"When you are synced in, you and all the other initiates will begin on one of three cruisers that are flying around the island this test is taking place on. Once all initiates are in, a countdown will begin, at which point you can choose your loadouts. Once the timer reaches one minute, you will have the opportunity to jump out of the cruiser and land at any destination you wish."

"In drop pods like in the Division Test?" Kaiden asked.

"Nope, free fall. Your armor will be loaded with shock absorption insulation and reinforced frames. Those mods will disappear upon landfall, so keep that in mind—unless you already have them installed."

"I've been meaning to get shock absorption, but haven't had much use for it outside a couple of missions," Genos said thoughtfully.

"Well, this will give you an opportunity to see what you are missing," Akello said.

"Anything else we need to know?" Chiyo asked.

"Nope. Just remember that the map will change and shrink as time goes on and that the main building is where most of the action is, so factor that into your plans. You guys have any more questions for me?"

The infiltrator looked at Genos, who shook his head and leaned against the pod, bracing for the sync. She glanced at Kaiden, who rotated his finger in a circle, telling her to move on.

"We have no further questions, Advisor Faraji," she answered.

"Then get in those pods, and I'll set you up."

Chiyo left the console and made her way to the pod between Genos and Kaiden. "Team MIA are in our pods and ready for sync."

"Oh, don't you start with that too." Kaiden scowled.

She looked at him with a small smile as the pod doors began to close. "I quite like the name."

"Once we get done with this, we're getting a real team name," Kaiden shouted as the doors sealed, nearly cutting him off.

"Pods closed and syncing has begun. Best of luck to you all," Faraji said over the speakers in the pod.

He closed his eyes as the device began to scan his body and white light pulled him in. Despite himself, he smiled as he could feel the Animus accepting him. "Let's raise some hell."

———

Kaiden awoke in full armor. He looked at a couple dozen other initiates already walking around the carrier. The "lobby" was rather sparse, with a high ceiling, silver flooring, and a few catwalks above for easier traversal. There were windows on either side next to large unopened doors.

"At least this time I won't be strapped into a chair," he mumbled as he looked at the various dropways. He walked to one of the windows on the left and saw the island below. It was far bigger than the Nexus Academy island and looked even bigger than the one that had been used for the Division Test. But it was the building in the center that grabbed his attention.

It looked to only be a few stories high, but it was long—at least two miles. It was dark, too, even in the daylight. A foreboding compound, almost like it both beckoned the initiates to it and dared them to enter. Either way, that was where the lion's share of the points would be. He made up his mind that he would get to it.

"There you are, friend Kaiden." Genos greeted him with his usual cheer.

The ace looked away from the window for a moment and nodded at his teammate. "Hey, Genos, take a look." He motioned to the window.

The Tsuna looked out, his eyes widening for a moment before returning to their normal size. "It is quite a lot of ground to cover."

"You think we should drop out and try to land closer to the building? Maybe on top?"

Genos shook his head. "I'm sure many of the other teams are using that same line of logic. I recommend we pace ourselves slightly—maybe land half a mile to a mile out. There will be merc camps and patrols we can take out for Valor points, along with possible opportunities for Chiyo and myself to apply our skills for some Data and Motes along the way."

"Sounds solid, although we do need to discuss our little backup plan that Chiyo was talking about."

"Indeed we do," the infiltrator stated.

Kaiden spun in an instant, startled, before he sighed and relaxed. "Are you somehow summoned whenever I call your name?"

"That would be helpful if we are ever separated, but I simply found you using the network," she explained. "My guess is that the massive loadin has placed initiates randomly around the carrier."

"Or the techs are having a laugh," he suggested. "At least

we're all on the same carrier, so they can't be screwing up too much."

Chiyo walked past them and looked out the window. "I'm going to guess that you and Genos were discussing our landing point?"

"We were. Genos suggested we land about a klick from the building and make our way there so as to dodge all the other initiates who go straight for it, and take out some trash along the way."

"I know the other initiates won't turn hostile right away, but since we don't know exactly when they will, I feel it's best that we try to keep ourselves out of the potential chaos as long as possible," the Tsuna explained.

"I agree." Chiyo nodded. "There is a lot we cannot control here, but we can at least give ourselves some breathing room."

"Squad Test to begin in three minutes. Begin loadout," a synthesized voice declared.

"Looks like we're about to get to it." Kaiden opened his load-out screen. "Chief, load my triggerman outfit."

"Triggerman outfit?" Genos asked as he searched manually through the loadout screen.

"Yeah, it's one of my saved loadouts. Don't you have favorites?" Kaiden asked as his Raptor rifle appeared on his back and his armor changed to his more flexible mods.

"He's been giving all his saved loadouts cute little nicknames." Chief chuckled. *"He's got triggerman, gunslinger, assassin, bullet ballerina—"*

"He made that last one up," the ace retorted. "Besides, it's better to give them unique names than using some sort of Roman alphabet thing."

"Kaitō, please load Infiltrator Beta," Chiyo instructed.

"Of course, madame," her EI acknowledged and changed her armor to her light model, then armed her with a sub-machine-gun.

"Got anything else to say, dumbass?" Chief asked.

"Nah, I'll just leave it." Kaiden sighed.

"Two minutes until test begins. Doors open in sixty seconds," the carrier's EI announced.

"So, any last words of encouragement?" Kaiden asked.

"Just remember what we discussed. We will play this test as it was meant to be, but we should search for the Director EI. I believe that is how we can win this test," Chiyo stated.

"Assuming it's actually here," the ace pointed out.

"I believe Chiyo's deductions," Genos declared. A medium-sized Tesla cannon appeared on his back, and his orange armor changed to silver with blue accents. "The Director is most likely somewhere within the map. The matter of getting to it or finding it... Well, that may be rather difficult."

"If it is here, we'll find it and make it our bitch," Kaiden vowed. "But if we don't...hey, you still got me and all the goodness I'll bring to this party."

"Try to keep yourself in check," Chiyo said, but a small smile crept onto her lips as her helmet materialized. "After all, you wouldn't want to make your fellow initiates feel too dejected, right?"

"Nice to see you coming around." He nodded. "This will be a metaphorical and literal blast."

"I can certainly help with that." Genos pointed to the cannon on his back.

"You certainly can, buddy." the soldier chuckled.

"One minute remaining. Doors will now open. If you have not left by the time the timer has reached zero, you and your team will be ported randomly around the map," the EI warned.

The doors in the lobby opened. Initiates rushed to them and stood looking for their perfect mark to jump. Kaiden walked up and pulled out his rifle. He held it in one hand as he placed the other on his chest, saluting the other students.

"All right, y'all. Let's go kill something!" he called as he jumped out of the carrier and descended to the island, yelling *"Yahooooo,"* as he fell.

CHAPTER EIGHTEEN

K aiden fell through the sky, grinning madly. The island was coming up fast, and he began to drift over to a patch of jungle, flipping himself vertically

"Couldn't have waited for your teammates?" Chief chided, popping up in front of him.

"They were right behind me," he said, looking above him to where dozens of other initiates plummeted through the sky. "They should be able to track me, right?"

"Yeah, they have you on network, but you could have waited. Appreciate the pep in your step and all, but remember this is the Deathmatch. This jungle may not have as many obstacles as the building will, but there are still plenty of hostiles to worry about."

"Point piñatas," Kaiden corrected.

"Don't start that bullshit again." Chief groaned.

He laughed. Only about half a mile until landfall. "We'll be fine. I'll wait for them. I'm not dropping into a camp or anything. What's the worst that could happen?" Kaiden relaxed his legs as he prepared to land.

"Remember the beginning of the Division Test? You stepped on a mine. Not sure if that's the worst, but you don't have extra lives this time around."

"Oh, right. Well, let's pray there are no surprises waiting for us." He looked down again to see he was about to break through the tree line. "And that we don't end up stuck in a tree like Cameron."

Kaiden braced himself and closed his eyes, awaiting impact as he fell through the tops of the trees. He landed on the ground safely, though slightly awkwardly and heavily, and something cracked beneath him. He stood up cautiously. Had he landed on a hill or some fallen branches?

He heard groaning beneath him and looked down to see a man in dark-green armor beneath him, thoroughly implanted into the dirt.

"Might wanna thank him for breaking the fall," Chief mused as he studied the collapsed body below them.

His score went up two points—Valor for a merc kill. For the poor bastard beneath him, he realized. He then saw red dots appear on the chest of his armor—three other mercs were pointing rifles at him. The ace reached slowly for Debonair. "You think this counts as a good beginning or a bad one?" he asked the EI.

"Depends on you."

Sasha and Mya walked into the board members' personal lounge at the Observation Center. Within the circular room was a large screen that displayed the test from an isometric camera field. Laurie and Wulfson were already there, the professor sipping a glass of red wine on a lounge chair while the security officer leaned back on the couch, nearly taking up all three seats with his large frame. Mya walked in and opened her mouth to greet them, but she stalled upon seeing Raza. The Sauren leaned casually against the wall looking at the giant screen before him. Sasha laid a reassuring hand on her shoulder and nodded. "He's with Wulfson, a friend and delegate to the Academy. Don't worry."

She nodded and rubbed her arms in an effort to settle her goosebumps. "Sorry. I had heard that we had a Sauren visitor, but I had yet to meet him. Keeps a surprisingly low profile considering his...size."

"Heh. Takes more than brute strength to be a good enough hunter to make Warchief in the Sauren's ranks." Wulfson smiled at both the commander and the counselor. "Glad you finally made it, Commander. And look, you brought a friend." Wulfson ran his fingers through his beard. "Don't think we've formally met Kära. I'm Biaoh Wulfson, Head of Security at this fine Academy." He stood up and walked over, a large, opened bottle of vodka clenched in his left hand.

Mya offered a hand. "I'm Counselor Mya, a friend of Commander Sasha's and Professor Laurie's. He invited me to watch the test with him. We are both participating in the League this year."

He took her hand, nearly obscuring it within his bear-sized mitts. "Mya, is it? Good on ya. Heard you were the winner last year. Looking to see if you'll take Sasha's place for longest run?"

"I'll need a few more wins to accomplish that," she admitted. "Plus, he has quite the team this year."

"Well, come on in and make yourself comfortable." Wulfson turned to look at the Sauren. "Raza, introduce yourself to the lass."

Raza slowly examined Mya with his reptilian eyes then huffed and bowed his head slightly. "Greetings, Counselor," he muttered before looking back at the screen. "You should be watching the match, Wulfson. Your trainee is in combat."

"Aye? Which one?" the security officer asked. He released Mya's hand and took a swig from his bottle as he returned to the couch. Sasha pointed at a chair across from Laurie, offering Mya a seat as he walked over to the bar.

"Why, the only one we would all have an interest in," Laurie hinted. "Our dear boy Kaiden. Did you know Miss Vodello here is his counselor?"

"That right?" Wulfson asked, leaning his head to the side to watch Sasha as he poured a drink. "You should have gotten here sooner, Sasha. Kaiden jumped right out of that carrier when it first popped. Seems he got over his fear of heights when I took him to Alaska."

"The fact that the test is in the Animus and he's wearing armor with absorption probably helps with the nerves." Sasha deadpanned. "Good to see you all made yourselves comfortable. I apologize for being late, although I shouldn't wonder how you all got in."

"I simply can't surprise you like I used to," Laurie said lightly and took another sip from his glass. "You should try this, Mya. *Le Sang de Bordeaux*, aged for twenty-five years. Simply magnifique."

"That sounds wonderful, Laurie," Mya agreed. "Sasha, if you wouldn't mind?"

"Certainly, Counselor." The commander finished pouring his scotch and brought her a wine glass. The professor leaned over and poured from the bottle he lifted from the table.

"How is he faring so far?" Sasha asked, sitting on the far end of the couch. Wulfson sat up straighter to give him more room.

"Depends on your view, really." Laurie placed the wine bottle back on the table after topping up his own glass.

"Kaiden crushed an enemy upon his descent. He was immediately accosted by the other enemies who were traveling with that one. He has taken them down," Raza informed him. "Quick fire to the helmets. He was lucky they had no shields."

"Where are his partners?" Sasha inquired, looking at the screen to see Kaiden searching through the corpses' belongings.

"Like I said, he leaped out of the carrier right away. His squadmates followed but had to wait for a little as all the other initiates rushed out," Wulfson explained.

"That certainly seems to be his way of doing things. I had hoped he would have shown a bit more patience, considering the circumstances." Sasha sighed.

The security officer chuckled. "Can't blame him for having a fire in his belly. But you are right. In this test and in any military unit, you don't run off from your team without explicit orders or a plan. Like Raza said, he was lucky those mercs didn't have any shields."

"To be fair, he was also *un*lucky that he immediately fell

into a patrol, considering the size of the island," Mya pointed out reasonably.

"In combat, you have to factor in many possibilities," Sasha said, looking at a tablet on the table that showed a map of the island. "He landed close to the building. With the time he had to think this out before the match started, he should have prepared to meet more resistance that close in."

"Eh, you're too hard on the boy," Wulfson said in Kaiden's defense, and the commander looked questioningly at him. "It's true you should always have a plan, and I will drill team coordination into his head the next time I see him, but he's got the skills and prowess to deal with a few mercs. Had it since the beginning of the year."

"So I shouldn't be worried that he seems to have learned nothing?" Sasha questioned.

The large man smiled. "Take it from someone who's had to try to pry open that skull all year. It's not night and day, by any means, but Kaiden has learned to play nice. Even from a purely physical and discipline standpoint, I would say that being able to land and take out a few mercs in quick succession like that, with no hesitation and all reflex and training, shows that he's advanced quite a bit."

"Plus, he hasn't run off. He does seem to be waiting for his team," Mya remarked, pointing at the screen. "Look. Chiyo just landed."

Kaiden heard a loud thump behind him, followed by another, along with the cracking of a branch. He turned from his scavenging to see his teammates about forty yards behind him. "Howdy! Got some points for us already." He grinned.

"I see your gift for violence remains intact," Genos noted.

"Is that a compliment or simply an observation?" he asked.

Chiyo walked over, taking out her weapon. "We should go ahead and make our way to the objective. Genos and I were almost the last ones out, so I would say every other team has landed at this point."

"You're not gonna chew him out for his little stunt back there?" Chief inquired.

Kaiden shook his head, "Despite the snitching, I am kinda surprised myself."

She walked past him. "No need. You lead by example. It wasn't surprising. You already gathered points and cleared the way, at least for now." She looked back and nodded. "Well done."

"Oh, good, she's become an enabler," Chief muttered and disappeared from view.

"She's good at planning ahead," Kaiden retorted, drawing his Raptor. "You coming, Genos?"

The Tsuna primed his cannon for combat. "Following your lead."

"Let's see what kind of trouble we can get into, then!"

Explosions blew the ground apart as mechs and tanks battled. Trees crashed down, torn by the blasts. A mech took a shot from a tank cannon and flew back as two mercs dove out of the way. It rolled a few yards like a mechanical boulder and crushed a few droids that were shooting at incoming initiates along the battle line.

Kaiden observed the carnage from behind a tree, his eyes widening as another blast from a tank scattered a group of at least eight mercs, blowing half of them apart.

"That's a shitload of trouble," he muttered. Across the field, a little over a third of a mile away, was the base. He could see six potential entrances, but they had to make it across the field first.

Even for him, that seemed a grim prospect.

Chiyo activated her holoscreen. "Kaitō, scan the area, and make it as wide as you can."

"Immediately, madame," the EI confirmed. After a moment, a rudimentary map of the area appeared onscreen. Kaiden and Genos walked over and looked at it over her shoulder.

"It's basically a no man's land. There will be a heavy risk if we simply charge through it," she observed.

"I see plenty of men, just in parts," the ace joked somberly.

"It's like this for this side of the building," she confirmed.

Kaiden grimaced and sighed as he quickly took aim and shot at a droid running across the field in the distance. "Makes for an easy shooting gallery, at least."

Chiyo continued to observe the battles. "Considering the various fights going on, there are a good number of jockeys and mechanists in at least some of those mechs and tanks." At a loud rush of air above them, the trio looked up to see several ships blasting one another.

The soldier quickly grabbed the back of his partners' armor and dove to the ground as a ship swooped toward the field, firing blasts at some of the running mercs and launching a plasma bolt at a tank. The vehicle erupted on impact and the cannon blew apart and flew through the air, landing only a few yards from them.

"Pilots as well," Genos added, standing once more after the ship lifted into the air to rejoin the dogfight. He helped his teammates up, then Kaiden dusted himself off and picked up his Raptor.

"Think we can make it through somehow?" he asked the infiltrator.

"I was thinking that we should double back and go around to the other side or check to see if we could find an underground passage."

"We could probably do that, but it would burn time, not to mention that any potential points from mercs and droids would be scanty if we stay close to the buildings." Another blast erupted fifteen meters to their left and a merc flew through the air, landing a few feet in front of them. He moved for a few seconds before lying still and disappeared after a moment.

"It would seem that any potential nearby targets would already be involved in this battle, albeit very temporarily," Genos stated.

"I don't think we want to wait this out. We do get points for time alive, but those are inconsequential." Chiyo frowned.

"Can't you hack into a few droids around here? Create a distraction for us to sprint to the building?" Kaiden asked.

She opened her holoscreen again. "It wouldn't be very effective. We would need a good amount and the ones that I could get into easily wouldn't last very long. Maybe not even long enough for me to gain access to them. The stronger droids are either locked out from long-range hacking options or have systems too advanced for me to gain control quickly enough for them to be of much use."

The Tsuna looked out into the valley, a single finger tapping the neck of his armor where his infuser would normally be. "I think I know a way to get us an opening."

The two looked at him in surprise. "We're all ears, man," the ace said.

Genos handed his cannon to his teammate, then reached behind him and brought out his hoverboard. "Please hold this."

Kaiden took the cannon and held it against his shoulder. "Not a problem, but what are you…"

"Please keep your comms open. I'll tell you when to go," the mechanist said cryptically. He activated his board and hopped on. "Although you should have no problem noticing." With that, he sped off into the field.

"Whoa! Genos, wait!" Kaiden yelled. He could only watch helplessly as his teammate charged into the battle.

As Kaiden observed the mechanist speeding through the fighting, explosions going off around him as he weaved through laser and plasma fire and ignored his calls to retreat, he sighed. "So that's what it feels like."

CHAPTER NINETEEN

Genos whipped around the field, looking for his targets. He needed to get to the middle of the battle and cause an obvious distraction. It had to be something to get the attention of the rest of the enemies in the field focused on a primary target for long enough that his teammates could make it across.

It was ironic. In an open field like this, even among the explosions and fighting, he had acquired enough skill to dodge the blasts and speed through. He could easily make it to the other side, but his teammates couldn't, and it wasn't like he could carry them across one at a time. Either of them would weigh the board down too much.

He considered looking into modifications to increase the board's weight capacity once this was all over.

Genos looked eastward and saw his prey—a trio of mechs coming out of an underground bay. They were booting up, vulnerable enough for him to do what he needed to do.

He activated his gauntlet, shifting the hand into a clamp as he raced toward them. On the way, he snatched a droid up. It was a basic fighter droid with a skinny frame, lightly armored, with a basic laser rifle. The head spun around as if it couldn't comprehend the situation as he smashed its chest apart in his grip. He kept the head and swerved around the mechs to get behind them as they began to stand and arm their systems.

The Tsuna jumped off his board and onto the back of the mech in the middle. He climbed on top, quickly tearing into the outer metal to reveal a panel within. He glanced quickly to each side and saw that there were jockeys in each mech, but he couldn't make out their colors through the darkened windows. From their frantic movements, he gathered that they could certainly see him. He had to work fast.

Genos opened the exposed panel and then a small port on the head of the robot that he had taken. He deactivated his gauntlet and straightened his index finger, releasing a small set of prongs. Carefully, he reached into the panel of the mech and snagged a small cord. Holding it in his hand, he placed the robot's head onto the mech and slid the end of the cord into a slot in the port of the metal skull.

From the corner of his eye, he saw the other mechs on either side begin to turn toward him. The whirr of mechanics working in tandem sounded and the claw of the mech on his left began to fidget. He was cutting it close.

"Genos, what the hell are you doing?" Kaiden demanded over the comm.

"Just a moment, friend. It is quite stressful right now,"

he responded as he reached into the mech's panel again to yank out some wires.

"No shit. You'll get yourself killed."

The mechanist uncurled his pointer and middle finger, blades emerging from inside them to create scissors, and snipped a few of the wires and then deactivated them. Drawing his pistol, he shot the device into the back of the droid's head. The mech on the left began to reach up to grab him and Genos dropped onto its back. The attacking mech's claw missed as he pulled himself up again and opened the screen on his tablet. He heard energy charging and looked up see the mech on his right step back and turn his way, aiming its cannon.

"Genos, I don't know what the hell you are doing, but you need to—"

"Merely using a strategy of yours Kaiden. I'm simply adding my skills to it," Genos stated and pressed a button on the gauntlet's screen.

The mech he was on lifted its arms to either side and the cannons on its arms began to charge rapidly. Both mechs moved back once they realized what was going on, but it was too late. The cannons fired right into the cockpit of both mechs, taking them out and causing them to crash to the ground.

"What did you do?" Kaiden asked, astonished.

"I'll fill you in later. For now, I need to finish my plan. Kaiden, you are close by, correct?"

"We're in the trees on your left."

The Tsuna looked in that direction. "That should be close enough. Please ready my cannon and fire at the cockpit on my mark."

He climbed back on top of the mech and over to the cockpit, then punched down several times. As the shielding cracked, he could see the figure inside reach for a pistol on the side of their seat.

"That should be enough. Please fire, Kaiden." He pushed himself back to the top of the mech and braced against it.

Genos moved his head to the side as he saw an orb of red light smash into the cockpit. A scream was immediately followed by a burning smell. He looked to see that the window had shattered and partially melted. The jockey on the inside was no longer an issue.

"Much obliged," the mechanist said, thanking the ace as he reached in and grabbed the corpse, tossed it out, and climbed in. He sat in the jockey's chair, making sure to peer out onto the field for a moment to see if there was any immediate danger. Satisfied, he reached under the control board and pried it loose.

He studied it, noting what he had to work with. "This will do."

"What is he doing?" Kaiden muttered. "He said he was going to create a distraction, not take out a few mechs for giggles."

"We did collect quite a few points for it—both Valor and Motes since he's applying his class," Chiyo pointed out.

"And while I would usually appreciate that, I'm worried it will be for nothing if he gets himself killed." Kaiden huffed, resting the mechanist's cannon against his shoulder.

The infiltrator looked at the downed mechs for a moment, barely seeing Genos in the cockpit of the last one standing. He would occasionally poke his head up, but he seemed mostly preoccupied with something inside. "Just do what he normally says when you run off to do something."

"What would that be? 'Stand-by for a wave of hostiles?'" Kaiden snickered.

"Trust him, he will make it work."

He looked at her in silence, then back at the mechs, and sighed. As if he needed to keep himself busy, he moved the cannon off his shoulder and held it in both hands "If he's not done in a few minutes I'm pulling him out of there."

"I don't believe he'll take that long. He works almost as fast as I do," she stated calmly.

"Friends, I'm ready. Prepare your accelerators," Genos ordered on the comms.

"Priming," Kaiden acknowledged, stretching his legs. "You wanna fill us in now, or is that still a rain-check?"

"There doesn't appear to be rain during this time. Do not worry, the weather does not affect whether or not I give you information."

"I'm getting him a list of slang terms and idioms to study over break." Kaiden chuckled.

"Distraction happening in ten seconds."

He hopped out of the mech. The ace could see the boosters on the back begin to rotate and the mech's cannons pointed forward, charging up. Genos took off on his hoverboard, heading toward the building as the mech lurched forward. Kaiden could see the small droid's head still attached to it waving in the wind as the mech hurtled ahead. It began firing its cannons indiscriminately, blasting tanks, droids, mercs, and other mechs along its path. A couple of other mechs and a tank turned to it and fired. The tank shot off one of the cannons, but the mech continued to speed forward and fired with its remaining cannon. Other droids and vehicles began to focus on the rampaging mech as it continued its onslaught. A leg was blown off, but the boosters continued to power it through the field.

"That is certainly one way to get a lot of attention." Kaiden whistled.

"Let's go, Kaiden," Chiyo demanded, leaning close to the ground before sprinting across the field, her suit enabling her to speed across.

He followed quickly, holding the cannon to his chest as he raced after the infiltrator.

The mech was finally downed by another cannon shot to its chest. It fell to the ground and was slowly approached by a few droids. A rapid beeping began to sound as a red light flashed in the cockpit. The droids turned to flee as the thing self-destructed, blowing them away and causing a few mechs to stumble back.

Kaiden and Chiyo slid into a doorway held open by their teammate. As the explosion went off, the Tsuna slammed it closed. A few pieces of metal smashed against the outside of the door.

"You certainly like your explosions, eh, Genos?" the soldier asked merrily. He straightened and tossed the Tsuna his cannon. "Good work. I'm not sure if that was resourceful or crazy, but it was the spirit of it that I appreciate."

"It was, admittedly, more spontaneous than I would have liked. I had planned to simply activate the self-destruct sequence of a mech in the middle of the field that was too preoccupied with the battle to notice me, but they kept being destroyed," the mechanist confessed.

"That and a Tsuna in armor riding a hoverboard isn't exactly inconspicuous," Kaiden jeered.

Genos tapped the neck of his armor. "Admittedly, that could have been an issue. Fortune favors the bold, as they say. Quite apt in this situation."

"So you *do* know idioms," the ace said, his tone almost accusatory.

His companion shrugged. "I have learned a few. Chiyo has been most helpful."

"Getting there little by little, right?" Kaiden said mirthfully. "That mech went on a hell of a killing spree. The best part was that we got even more points for all its destruction since it was your handiwork."

Genos nodded. "I had hoped so. Considering the difficulty and the time we spent out of action, I wanted to make up for it if possible. Turning lemons into lemonade."

"Now you're simply showing off. Keep at it." The ace beamed under his mask, giving the mechanist a thumbs-up. "I noticed that the mech didn't really seem to care who or what it was attacking. It might have taken down a few other initiates."

"Yes, that was a possibility. The pilots and jockeys do not use their own vehicles or mechs, so all of them were flying enemy colors. I tried to work it in such a way that it wouldn't attack anything that broadcast a friendly signal, but beyond that, I had no way of knowing who was friendly and who wasn't."

"I would think any soldier or engineer worth their salt would know to get the hell out of the way of an out-of-control mech."

"True, but I don't think they were exactly prepared. I do not know if that is a factor considering the honor system. It was not my weapon, but it was my hand that caused it to go out of control. But in all honesty, it doesn't matter to me."

Kaiden pulled his rifle and cocked his head at the Tsuna. "That's surprisingly cold of you."

"I agree, but those out there are not my team. You are," Genos declared. "And it was my mission to get us across. I couldn't let the potential collateral damage slow me down."

The soldier rested his rifle against his shoulder "That's the kind of team spirit that'll serve us well in this test."

The mechanist took a deep breath and stared at the ceiling, thinking for a moment. "Also, I don't believe any of our friends were in the field or in those vehicles. I don't believe any of them have the training or know-how to commandeer or use them effectively. Maybe kin Jaxon, but he would be intelligent enough to not stay in such a chaotic place or would display some sort of open signal to indicate that he was friendly."

"To be fair, considering how much he's worked with us, he might not even consider it chaos anymore. Maybe not normal, per se, but maybe like a more than moderate threat?"

"Kin Jaxon does not share your predisposition to wild fights."

Kaiden rolled his eyes, "Yeah, yeah, I remember your little talk during the Co-op Test."

Genos rubbed the back of his helmet, "In your favor, he has used more talents in gunplay and martial skills."

"I have noticed I have a very particular effect on people," he admitted. "But we'll talk personal philosophies and being a potential volatile influence on intergalactic beings another time. Let's get our bearings, shall we?"

He turned to take a good look at where they were. It seemed like a regular hallway—metal walls and flooring with steel beams along the sides.

"Doesn't look like much," he muttered and looked over to see Chiyo on her holoscreen. "Guess we should be on our way?"

"Not picking anything up. No cameras, turrets, droids, or comms," she stated.

"It's an empty hallway, so maybe the good stuff is farther in?" Kaiden wondered aloud, not quite sure he believed the evidence.

Genos walked past him to their teammate. "No vital signs? Can you switch to radar?"

"There's nothing here," Chiyo declared. "But there *is* something blocking my scans. I can only get a readout of this room. If there were any sort of tech or connection anywhere nearby, I should be able to see it, but I've got nothing."

"How long is this hallway?" Kaiden asked, peering into the darkened space. "You don't think this is one of those never-ending paths or a maze or something, do you?"

"Could be." She shrugged and deactivated her screen.

"From what they told us about this place, and from the vids we saw, it could turn into and be almost anything."

"Kinda anticlimactic that we simply got the long walk then," Kaiden grumbled. "At least out there, we had stuff to kill. Maybe we should go back."

The others looked at him incredulously. "You are joking, right?" she asked.

"I'm just saying," Kaiden protested defensively and looked back at the door. "Sure, it was hell out there, but we can at least— Where's the door?"

The mechanist and infiltrator looked up and saw that there was nothing but a wall behind them. "It's gone," Genos whispered in shock.

The ace walked up to the wall. "This is an ever-changing place of doom, and the best it can do is make a door disappear?" he growled, kicking the wall.

"Friend Kaiden, are you hot?" the Tsuna asked.

"Oh, I'm damn livid," he fumed.

"No, not metaphorically," Chiyo said. "I feel it too. The temperature is rising."

Kaiden turned toward them, feeling sweat on his brow and forming on his body under his armor. "Yeah, I'm starting to steam, but these suits are insulated, right? We'd have to be in the bowels of a volcano or something to actually feel anything. Wait, what's that?"

He pointed behind them. A light was enveloping the walls, ceiling, and floor of the hall, racing toward them. They braced for an attack or impact but the light simply moved past them, then the room changed.

Instinctively, he covered his eyes against the light for a

moment. After he opened them, he saw that they were in a room of fire and magma, standing on a path of red stone as geysers bellowed around them.

"Correction, *this* is Hell."

CHAPTER TWENTY

"Jävlar," Wulfson cursed. He watched as Kaiden and his team began to make their way slowly along the fiery path, their guns at the ready as they traversed the new domain. "What kind of rotten luck is that?"

"Is it any worse than where they were?" Laurie questioned, pressing his wine glass against his cheek. "At least now they will probably grow to respect the danger they are in."

"At least before, they couldn't trip and fall to their deaths," the security officer muttered. "They'll make it. I've got a thousand credits on it."

"You're betting? With whom?" the professor inquired, then heard a grunt from Raza in the corner. "I wasn't aware the Sauren traded in credits. I thought it was normally tech, weapons, and knick-knacks. Things like that."

"As our trades expand and this 'alliance' of yours

between the Mirus and Tsuna ends with a unified currency, we have acknowledged that it is an acceptable payment," Raza hissed, "We have taken more jobs and made more deals with the payment of credits, accruing them for our various clan war chests."

"And you use it to gamble?" Laurie smirked. "The mightiest hunters of the galaxy have such relatable vices."

Mya scooted her chair over and leaned toward Sasha. "Would now be a bad time to ask to change the view to my team?"

Sasha nodded, but he reached forward and picked the tablet up off the table, switched it to a view of Mya's team, and handed it to her as he continued to watch the main screen.

"The path seems stable and clear. The environment has changed, but it is still only a hallway. It shouldn't be an issue for them to get across," he reasoned.

"You might want to take a closer look at the details, Commander," Laurie retorted. "The environments all got an upgrade this year as well. They aren't merely generic placeholders anymore. All of them have a story to tell." He took a sip of wine from his glass, then shot his colleague a toothy grin. "And this one is rather dirty."

Sasha looked at the side of the screen. "Expand menu," he ordered. The test details enlarged, focusing on the specifics of what was happening on screen. "Go to environment details." The display moved quickly over the team's initiate files and class descriptions and stopped at the description of the level.

The commander leaned forward and read the screen,

sucking a harsh breath in through his teeth. "So it won't be a simple walk then."

"Mauna Loa? That's one of the Hawaiian volcanoes, aye?" Wulfson asked.

"Yes, one with unfortunate inhabitants, as well," Sasha confirmed.

"Inhabitants? What kinda freaks would live in a volcano?" the large man blustered, earning an eloquent glare from the commander.

"Depends on the kind of 'freak.' Maybe one that was bred for it through unnatural means?"

Wulfson raised a bushy eyebrow. "You mean like a... Hmm, that'll make for a much more difficult trip."

"But much more sporting," Laurie declared. "I suppose we'll get to see how all your training has come together. And we'll see if you nearly blowing up my lab last month was worth it."

Although he wanted to rebut the professor's snide remark, he leaned back and stroked his beard, thinking about what Kaiden had to face. "Ey, Raza," he called to the Sauren, who barely moved his head to look at the security officer. "Might want to pay close attention to what's coming up. It could make your list of things to hunt while you're still here."

"Good Lord, it's hotter than the taint of the sun in here," Kaiden grumbled as they continued to advance along the path. "Be careful, the path is getting narrower."

"I can see the exit, but we still have some way to go," Chiyo informed them. "You all right, Genos?"

"I'll be fine, assuming we can get through here fast enough," the Tsuna said, his voice quiet and slightly strained.

"I was able to get some healing injectors from those mercs I killed when I landed if you need one." Kaiden tapped his supply box.

"Thank you, but it won't do much good. This sort of immense heat isn't good for my body. My suit is supplying hydrating liquids for me, but it's burning through it fast." He reached into a pouch on his waist for a small tube of purple gel. "If I might have your assistance for a moment, Chiyo, I need to refill my immerse gel supply in my suit."

"Of course. Keep watch please, Kaiden." She turned to help, and he popped open a compartment on the back of his suit and handed the tube to her.

The ace stopped and looked around. He peered out into the distance to the edge of the path. The end was still a few hundred yards away, but they were closing the distance. He only hoped it didn't lead to an even worse location.

Casually, he watched as the lava flowed downstream. He saw some of it gurgle and ebb, moving like a current of glowing slime. As he looked ahead down the other stream, he noticed something in the magma.

"Hey, Chief, what is that? A rock?" he asked quietly, leaning forward as the object moved slowly closer.

"I mean, you're walking on rock, so that's a definite possibility," Chief pointed out. *"Kind of a weird detail to add, though. A single rock simply riding the lazy magma river."*

"Stupid question, but are there things we should worry about in here *besides* the lava?"

"A few potential problems, like eruptions or armor getting compromised leading to heat death."

"I'm talking hostiles."

"Not too many animals dig living in a volcano. Some sea life lives underneath it, and some bugs live around it. I mean, there is — Oh, shit."

Kaiden hastily readied his rifle. "What is it?"

"I should have thought about it right away, but usually, the maps are just a grab bag. But if this place is based on—"

"I don't need the backstory. What should I be worried about?" Kaiden growled.

"What's wrong, Kaiden?" Chiyo asked as she shut the compartment on Genos' suit.

"Chief is all worked up about something," he shouted.

"Hope your mutant-killing game is still strong," the EI warned. *"Get back. That might be a moho."*

"The hell is a—" The question cut off as a creature leaped out of the lava. It resembled a giant lizard with jet-black scales. Magma slid off its body as it hissed, staring him down with cold black eyes.

"Don't worry about answering that," Kaiden grunted, then snapped the latch on his rifle, and prepared to fire.

"Switch to ballistics. The laser fire won't do jack against its hide. Best bet is to aim for the gullet when it's snapping at you."

"So I should wait for it to try to eat me?" Kaiden yelled, backing up as the moho crept inexorably forward.

"It'll try to do that regardless of whether you wait for it or not." Genos and Chiyo ran forward, their weapons at the ready.

"What about Genos' cannon?"

"It might do some damage, more than your rifle shots. But this thing lives in lava, remember. It's an important detail," Chief stated.

Another hiss issued behind them and Chiyo whipped around. "Kaiden, two more at our rear."

"Great," Kaiden muttered. "To hell with it, let's run."

The Tsuna nodded, "Agreed, we don't have the footing or room to engage well here."

"Focus on the one in front and get it out of the way, then we run like mad," Kaiden ordered.

"We don't know what awaits us in the next room," the infiltrator reminded them.

The ace flipped a switch on his rifle, changing to ballistic shots. "Better the enemy you don't know than the one you do, right?"

"I don't believe that's how the saying goes," Genos protested.

He frowned. "Like you can lecture me on that," he mumbled, and his companion cocked his head in confusion.

"The ones behind us are closing in," Chiyo warned.

"Let's go. Fire, Genos!" Kaiden commanded. The two fired together, driving the moho back. The mutant let out an angry hiss as ballistic shots exploded against it and Genos' plasma bolt exploded against the side of its head. It began to slide back into the magma. "Accelerators on. *Move.*"

The three sprinted down the remainder of the path and the other two mohos gave chase. "They are quite fast!" the mechanist shouted.

"They are even faster moving through the magma, so make sure to keep an eye— Watch it. On your right."

The ace turned his head just as the moho they had shot lurched from the lava, lunging at him. He tried leaping over it, but it was able to sink its teeth into the bottom of his boot. The sudden stop caused him to drop his rifle and fall to the ground. The creature stared at him, holding his gaze when he turned to look at it. He reached quickly for Debonair, but the monster began to drag him to the blazing magma.

"Kaiden!" Genos yelled. He changed his gauntlet to the clamp, which he used to catch his teammate's wrist and pull him back. The man grimaced at the pain of being pulled in opposite directions as he continued to reach for the pistol in the holster at his waist.

Chiyo turned back and tossed a small device at the two mohos pursuing them. It slid down the path and projected a hologram of her. The mutants snarled and leaped at it, sailing through it. They turned, confused and hesitant, and slowly approached the image again.

She stepped forward and shot at the eyes of the moho holding Kaiden captive with her submachine gun. Kaiden saw it wince for a second and stopped fumbling for his pistol. Instead, he felt for his supply of thermals. He managed to take out three and activated them. The beast finally hissed and released him after Chiyo's constant barrage, opening its maw briefly as it turned away in pain. The ace threw the grenades into the opening before flinging himself into Genos.

The mechanist closed his fist as they tumbled toward the other side of the path and the magma. A crowbar popped from the armor compartment in his gauntlet and he smashed it into the ground to stop them from rolling off the walkway.

The thermals detonated in the moho. It didn't erupt but smoke billowed from its mouth and its eyes rolled back into its head as it crashed into the lava, sending globs of the molten stone into the air. Chiyo rolled out of the way as the ace pulled his barrier and activated it to shield himself and Genos. Small blobs of the magma landed on the barrier. He raised it quickly and tossed it back to let the hot debris slide off before deactivating it.

"Thanks for the save." He grunted as he stood and hauled the Tsuna quickly to his feet.

"Same to you. Virtual or not, I'd rather not have to experience being ignited by magma," Genos stated.

"Or being eaten by lava lizards. Let's go before they recover." The soldier ran over and retrieved his rifle. "Quick thinking, Chiyo. Thanks."

"Can't lose you quite yet," she said with a grin as she attached her weapon to the magnetic strip on her thigh.

"Nah, still got stuff to shoot." Kaiden snickered. "Door's ahead, two hundred feet. Double-time."

The three dashed across the rest of the ravine. By now, the two mohos that had been preoccupied with the hologram had grown bored and continued their pursuit, but the distance was too great. Genos ran to the door and used the crowbar to pry it slightly open, then he and Kaiden pulled on either side and forced it wide. Chiyo ran through before the mechanist pulled it open a bit further and slipped in. Kaiden hurtled in after him and fired at the mutants to keep them at bay as the Tsuna shut the door.

As the metal slammed shut, he breathed a sigh of relief. "Next time I go in for training, I'm queuing up a map with a lot of those bastards and having a field day."

"We all have our ways to relieve stress," Chiyo agreed. "I think I'll simply stick to not trying to make volcano exploration a common occurrence."

"If nothing else, I certainly won't complain about being stuck in a regular hallway anymore. Speaking of which, where are we now?" Kaiden stood. They were in another hallway, but it led to a room only a few feet ahead. The three of them walked cautiously into the massive chamber. It was square with halls leading in four separate directions, each with a door at the end.

"So, any suggestion or should we simply flip a coin. Eh, that wouldn't work with three options. Got any dice?" he asked.

"Kaitō, do you read anything coming from this or any of the rooms?"

"There seems to be a node of some kind in the room to your left, madame," the fox EI informed her. *"Could be an opportunity for points, perhaps?"*

"Agreed." She nodded. "Kaitō says there is a node I could hack into in the room to our left."

"Hey, I'm game for almost anything that isn't carnivorous lava lizards or a battlefield of mechs and tanks," the soldier said with a shrug. "Lead on."

The three approached the sliding doors to the room. Kaiden and Chiyo held their guns at the ready as Genos pressed the button to open them. They slid easily, and the team was greeted by a trio of guns pointed their way.

"Hold your fire!" one of them shouted. "We're initiates.

Honor hasn't activated yet, so it wouldn't do you any good."

"Something friendly for a change," the soldier mused, lowering his rifle. "I'm Kaiden, an ace. This is Chiyo, our infiltrator, and Genos is a mechanist." His companions nodded to the other team.

"An ace, infiltrator, and mechanist. I guess you guys got settled with the team name of AIM, right?"

"No, MIA," Kaiden replied, making no effort to hide his chagrin.

"That's a pity. Seems to be a perfect fit. Plus, MIA is like 'missing in action,' right?"

The ace crossed his arms. "Preaching to the choir, buddy."

The man chuckled as he put his pistol away. "I'm Julius, a biologist." He was dressed in light red-and-white armor and a box-like helmet with separate visors for either eye. "The big glowing guy behind me is our vanguard, Mack."

"Howdy," he greeted them in a noticeable southern drawl. He stood tall as nearly all of the heavy-type soldiers did, decked out in heavy silver armor that had the light blue glow of a barrier.

"Howdy," Kaiden responded. "You Southern?"

"Memphis, Tennessee, born and raised," he declared, holding up an arm. "How 'bout you?"

He clapped his hand against the vanguard's, gripping the side of his palm. "Born in H-town, mostly raised in Fresno, Texas, though."

"A Texan? Nice to meet you," Mack stated. They nodded and ended their handshake. "Our buddy over there is Otto. He's an agent."

"Agent? That's a technician class, right?" Kaiden asked, looking at Chiyo.

She nodded. "They are the other side of the infiltrator coin. They work in plain sight, usually getting into targeted corporations or companies and working under-cover. They are more akin to spies than thieves or saboteurs."

"Not that we don't steal or sabotage," Otto stated, turning back and showing his gunmetal-grey armor and rounded visor on his circular helmet. "We merely do it with a little more flair."

"How's it coming along, Otto?" Julius asked.

"Almost done here," he answered, looking back at his holoscreen. He was working on some sort of terminal in the center of the room. "Minute and a half at most."

"Good to hear." Mack nodded.

"Well, looks like they beat us to it." Kaiden stretched his arms as he looked at Chiyo. "Unless you wanna see if you can out-hack him."

She shook her head. "I'll have other opportunities. We can move on and try another room. There don't seem to be any other paths here."

Kaiden nodded, turning back to Julius and Mack. "All right, it was nice meeting y'all, but we gotta head out. Robots to disassemble, heads to shoot, servers to access, that sort of thing."

"We'll be heading out soon. We could stick together if you want," Julius offered.

"Appreciate it, but we gotta make up for our little detour. By the way, when you go back there, don't go to the room on your right. Lava lizards."

Julius and Mack looked at each other. "Do what?"

"Got it. Three hundred and fifty Data points!" Otto shouted.

Kaiden heard the door behind them slam shut. He spun around and drew Debonair but only saw the shut door, then heard it lock in place. "What's happening?"

"Safety node deactivated. Purging room of hostile targets," a crackling synthetic voice announced.

CHAPTER TWENTY-ONE

"Did that thing say 'purge?'" Kaiden asked.

"Otto, what the hell did you do?" Julius demanded.

"I hacked the node," his teammate said defensively. "That's what we came in here to do."

"Did you miss something? Because that voice seems pretty pissed that you were fucking with it," Kaiden snapped, readying his rifle.

"I know how to hack," the agent retorted. "But... *Scheiße*. It said it was a-a safety node. I fell for a dummy."

"Chiyo, mind playing translator for a minute?" the ace asked.

"A dummy is a term for a false or trap target," she explained. "It's usually baited with the promise of helpful information or the appearance of something important, but will have been rigged with anything from an explosive or tracking virus. In this case, it was meant to trap a team in here."

"To 'purge' us. Yeah, I follow. But purging comes in a multitude of flavors, so what are we going to have to deal—"

"Activating Assassin and Havoc droids," the voice declared. The droids began appearing in flashes of light around them. The Assassin droids had black metal bodies and blades on their wrists and stared at them through crimson visors. The Havoc droids were charcoal in color with glowing yellow visors. They had large metal hands with gun barrels mounted on top.

"Killer robots. Pretty vanilla, but considering all the options and that we're in a locked room with no way out, I guess that would be the sprinkles." Kaiden huffed his annoyance. He and Genos covered the left side of the room while Julius, Mack, and Otto went to the right.

"You need to hold them off," Chiyo ordered, taking a wire from the computer on her wrist and plugging it into the node. "I can reactivate this, and hopefully, that will deactivate the trap. If not, I'll have to see if there is a way to access the system and shut it down manually."

"I'll help," the agent stated, kneeling beside her. He took a wire from his own computer and plugged it into another port on the node.

"You should help fight the droids. I can—"

"I know you're good. You wouldn't be an infiltrator otherwise. But this is my mistake, and I can help you undo my work and make this go quicker," he stated, looking at her. "Together, we'll get this done in short order."

She was silent for a moment before she nodded and caught Kaiden's attention. "Do whatever you need to do. But keep them off us."

"You do your thing, I'll do mine. That's the deal, and it's worked out so far." He hummed as he refilled his ballistic rounds. "Just make this a rush order, if you don't mind?"

"Here they come!" Mack roared as the droids advanced on them.

The soldier placed his barrier on top of the node, forming a dome around Chiyo and Otto. He then turned quickly to face the oncoming horde of killer robots. Calmly, making every shot count, he began to blast the oncoming attackers back. Working methodically, he shot them with ballistic rounds when they were far enough away and switched to laser fire as they closed in.

"Throwing a seeker," Genos yelled as he hurled a grenade into the fray. It burst apart and sent dozens of tiny drones into the air. They scattered and latched onto the various droids around them. "These droid models are too advanced for the seekers to take them over, but they will stall them for a bit," the mechanist explained.

Kaiden looked over to see ten droids halt in their tracks. Their bodies began to twitch, deactivating and reactivating every few seconds.

"Nice job. Take them out," he shouted, continuing to fire on the advancing droids. "Feel free to use more of those."

The Tsuna retrieved another seeker grenade. "I'll toss one behind us to help the others." He turned and threw it. The grenade opened overhead and sent out more seekers to attack the droids.

Mack roared as his armor lit up. He solidified his barrier and charged into the fray, plowing through a group of Havoc droids that blasted uselessly against the powered-up barrier. He caught a pair of Assassin droids as they tried to flank him, smashing them against one another. "Julius, you all right?"

The biologist medic fired a few more rounds from his semi-automatic pistol. The burst of laser fire chewed through the armor of the Assassin droid attacking him. "I have plenty of concoctions and poisons to deal with organic hostiles. Robots are not my forte!"

"That's why you have me," the vanguard shouted. His armor glowed again as he activated the bounce pack and jumped through the air. When he slammed back into the ground, he crushed two droids before a wave of energy burst from him and knocked all the nearby droids back.

"Thanks, Mack, but remember, that knocks my ass back too," Julius shouted, having slammed into the barrier protecting the technicians as they worked.

"Sorry partner, but it's better than shot and skewered by a bot, right?" Mack gritted his teeth as he felt two shots land on his back. He turned to see a Havoc droid advancing while his barrier generator needed to recharge from his stunt. As he reached for his hand cannon, a couple of laser blasts pierced the droid's chest and it fell. He looked over to see Kaiden give a quick two-finger salute before turning back to deal with his side of the mechanical swarm.

"Bless ya!" the vanguard shouted as he stood and began to fire powerful shots into a couple more havoc droids that had recovered from the barrier nova he'd set off.

"More are popping in," Kaiden called. New Havoc and Assassin droids joined the fray, and he and Genos had to constantly dodge and move as they continued the fight. "How's it going, you two!?"

"We're in. The node is activated, but the signal is still going," Chiyo answered

"Make it stop doing that, if you would, please!" he shouted.

"We'll get it done," she assured him.

"We'll either need to reboot the node entirely or create a new command to shut it off," Otto suggested.

"I can begin creating the command if you can find a place to put it."

"How much time would that take you?"

"Three or four minutes."

"Best guess for my side as well..." he muttered, wincing as a few stray shots slammed against the barrier.

"Purging not yet complete. Continued fighting unnecessary. Loading in Goliath model droids."

"What? Nah, the fighting is *totally* necessary. We're having a great time. Just keep it to the normal shit, please," Kaiden suggested to the uncaring voice.

A massive droid appeared, only slightly smaller than a normal-sized mech. It had two large cannons for arms and moved on tank tracks. The body was heavily armored and stalwart, with a large scanner on its domed head.

"That is problematic," Genos uttered, slightly shocked at the size of this new adversary.

"My energy is at seventy-five percent and climbing. I might be able to take one at full power," Mack stated.

"Keep fighting, and keep them distracted. We're almost out of this," Kaiden called.

"I'm going to activate my technician's suite," Otto said.

"What? In this mess, that could be suicide," Chiyo warned.

"Hopefully, the barrier will hold while I'm in there. Plus, our teammates are giving it their all. This is much faster. I'll be in and done in a minute; ninety seconds at most."

"It's more than that. We are supposed to keep our use of the suite to a minimum. If you're not careful with the systems or the node is broken or destroyed, it could mean more than simply failing the test." She warned.

"I'm quite aware. I paid attention in the technicians' seminar during the first week and every subsequent warning over the year, but we don't have a lot of time and our teammates are dealing with unending waves of death machines on our behalf. All of you could potentially fail because of my mistake. If I can end this as soon as possible, I'll take the chance."

Chiyo stared at him for a moment before nodding. "I…I understand your conviction. I'll take care of any incidentals. Please hurry."

Otto nodded. He looked at the node and placed his hands on his knees. "Schatzi, activate the suite." His body froze and he went silent, his stare fixed on the node.

"Mack, have you fully recharged yet?" Julius asked.

"Eighty-three percent."

"That might have to do. Those cannons are up," the biologist declared. "It's firing—get *down*."

Mack activated his bounce again and leaped out of the line of fire as the cannons let loose. The blast hit the top right corner of the room, and large chunks of the wall fell and crashed onto a few unlucky droids below.

Kaiden slammed the butt of his rifle against the head of an Assassin droid before he leaped back and fired into its chest and neck. "Genos, you think you can rewire that thing like you did with the mech?"

"Possibly, but there are too many enemies nearby, and many are focused solely on me. In the field, I had the cover of widespread battle." The Tsuna aimed at an Assassin and fired another shot from his cannon. The droid weaved around the blast and leaped forward. The plasma bolt exploded on the ground, and the explosion blew off the legs and part of the torsos of two other droids a few yards back.

As the Assassin droid moved in to attack, Genos side-stepped the cut of the blade and activated the clamp on his gauntlet. He blocked the droid's second attack, ensnared the bot's arm, and placed a foot against its chest. With a violent jerk, he ripped the arm off and then aimed his cannon at the attacker. He released a less-charged shot at its chest that created a perfect circle through its torso.

The bot fell in a heap as the mechanist deactivated the clamp. "If we want to try that, we'll need to—"

"*Look out,*" Kaiden cried as he dove into his teammate and moved him out of the way of the goliath's blast. The explosion slid them into a waiting group of bots. Genos yanked out another seeker and threw it in the air. It activated, attaching seekers to the bots and locking them in place before they could kill their catch. The ace stopped sliding and flipped over, fanning Debonair's barrel and destroying the malfunctioning bots in a hail of laser fire.

He vented his pistol and looked at his companion. "You all right?"

"Better than I could have been. I was not paying attention to that Goliath. That could have been costly." Genos sighed, still on his knees and breathing deep.

"Survive now so you can beat yourself up later." Kaiden grunted and helped the mechanist up.

"Kaiden, the barrier," the Tsuna shouted, pointing at Chiyo.

He looked back to see that it had shattered. She had pulled her gun and fended off a couple of Havoc droids as Julius hopped backward and several yards away from her, dodging the swipes of an Assassin droid.

Kaiden closed Debonair's vent and aimed at one of the Havoc droids attacking Chiyo. A couple of well-placed shots took it down before he snapped the weapon to the other side and fired a shot through its head. "Dammit, why is that agent guy just sitting there? Wait, is he using the suite?"

"Otto, Chiyo look *out*," Julius called as he slammed his semi-auto into the visor of a droid and fired. "The Goliath is—"

The Goliath turned to aim its recharged cannon at the pair of technicians.

"Get out of there," Kaiden ordered as he switched to ballistic rounds and fired at the attacker, trying to divert its attention away from them.

Chiyo returned to working on her access device. "We can't leave him. If the node is destroyed while he's in the suite, he will—"

"If he's shot by a goddamn cannon, I'm guessing it would be equally bad," Kaiden retorted.

"It's all right," Mack shouted as he charged the Goliath. "I've got this one." His armor glowed with bright blue energy as he rushed toward the larger droid.

"Mack! Take these." Kaiden threw the vanguard a cylindrical container with the rest of his thermals.

He grabbed it as he jumped and smashed into the massive frame. When he reactivated his nova, the Goliath fell backward and fired its cannon at the ceiling. The blast created an opening in its chassis. Quickly, Mack activated the grenades and shoved them into the hole, leaping off the Goliath as its body exploded behind him.

Kaiden ran over to Chiyo and looked up to see a chunk of the ceiling fall to the floor.

"*Alert disengaged. Deactivating and recalling remaining droids,*" the voice announced.

Chiyo pulled her connection from the port. "He did it. Now he needs to—"

"*Move*, Chiyo," the ace shouted, pushing her out of the way of the falling debris scant seconds before it crashed to the ground.

Julius did the same for Otto and they rolled away from the wreckage to avoid getting hit themselves. As Kaiden recovered, he looked up to see Mack push himself off the floor as the remaining functional droids powered down and disappeared.

"I like the way you destroy things." The soldier chuckled, sat up, and rested a hand across his knee. "Reminds me of myself, but you seem to like it a bit more up-close."

"Grit and grind, baby," Mack declared, beating a hand on his chest a couple of times. "Thanks for the boom."

"Happy to do my part."

The vanguard nodded, then looked at Julius. "How are the jewels, Jules?"

The biologist used a chunk of the ceiling to hoist himself up. Kaiden noted that his armor had taken a beating, with a number of cuts along the chest and the arms and parts of his leg armor missing. "Intact, fortunately."

"You gonna be all right?" Kaiden asked. "Looks like you're missing parts."

"Still got my underlay. I'm a biologist. As long as I'm still suited up, I'm swimming in healing gel and antibiotics. Nothing hurts much or injures me for long."

"Good to hear." The soldier looked up to see Genos offering him a hand. He grabbed it, and the Tsuna pulled him to his feet. "You all right, Chiyo?"

"No!" she cried. He ran over to her, fearing that she had broken something or had been wounded by one of the droids before they deactivated. He saw her raise a hand and point to the node. He looked and saw that the node had been crushed by the wreckage.

Kaiden kneeled beside her and place a hand on her shoulder. "What's wrong? Why are you freaking out?"

"He needed time to get out or deactivate. If he hadn't—" She sounded distraught and kept looking between the node and Otto's body. "Julius, check him!"

Julius looked at the unmoving agent, taking an injector out as he began walking toward him, "Otto, you all right?"

He and Mack knelt beside their teammate and raised his torso, supporting it between them.

"What's wrong with him? Why isn't he moving? Is he dead?" Mack asked.

"No, or at least not yet. His body would disappear," Julius stated, "He has a pulse and I don't see any serious injuries, but he's unconscious, Did he—"

"He used his suite to deactivate the alarm," Chiyo informed him. She and Kaiden walked over to them. "I don't know how much he explained to you about it, but if a technician uses their suite and they don't have the time to properly de-sync or the device they are using it on is destroyed—"

"It leads to— Otto, wake up!" Julius commanded, shaking him.

"I know there's pain and all that in the Animus, but aren't you guys being a little melodramatic?" Kaiden asked Chiyo in a lowered voice.

"It's not that simple with our suite, Kaiden. If Otto's de-sync was botched, it could—"

Otto coughed and sputtered, then inhaled deeply as he leaned against Mack.

"Otto, you all right, man?" the vanguard asked worriedly.

"Did I get it in time? We still in the test?" the agent asked.

"Yeah, we're good. Are you?" Kaiden inquired.

The agent leaned back. He would probably have laid down if there hadn't been a piece of rubble from the ceiling propping him up. "I'm all right. Got a bit dark there. Let me tell you, mentally interfacing with any sort of tech…it's a trip, man."

"The door is unlocked," Genos called to them. "We can depart whenever everyone is ready."

"Good work." Julius looked around the group. "All of you."

"Especially you, Otto," Chiyo added.

"I would just say I broke even." He sighed. "I was responsible for trapping us in the first place."

"That was a bad first impression." Mack chuckled, and he looked at Kaiden. "Sorry about roping you into that, although I have to say I'm glad you were here to help with the mess."

"Don't fret about it." The ace shrugged. "Turned out all right and we got plenty of points, although this place is really starting to earn its reputation as a death trap."

"You good enough to stand?" Julius asked Otto.

"Yeah, I'm fine." He grunted as he struggled to his feet with some help from Mack. "Or I will be fine soon enough. What now?"

"Well, not many options really," Kaiden mused as he looked at the now-open door out of the room. "Guess we'll go poke our heads into those other rooms and see what tries to kill us. Wanna come with?"

CHAPTER TWENTY-TWO

K aiden made his way to Genos as the others rested and Julius examined them. He found the Tsuna removing his helmet and looking it over as he approached. Genos studied his helmet with pursed lips, which were a darker, more purple color than his periwinkle skin. There was a slight bulge above his mouth with two small slits, the closest thing to a nose on his face. Kaiden hadn't thought about the fact that Tsuna didn't need the infuser masks in the Animus. The ace began to feel slightly like a Peeping Tom as he continued to stare at his teammate, who seemed none the wiser. He snapped himself quickly back to reality.

"Good shooting, buddy," he complimented him. "Might want to make sure to keep your six clear of giant-ass guns, though. Also your twelve, four, ten...you get the picture."

Genos nodded slightly in acknowledgment as he ran a hand over the helmet.

"Something wrong?" Kaiden asked.

The alien looked up and blinked in confusion. "Hmm?

Oh, yes, sorry. My helmet took some damage during the fight and fall. I was hoping to repair it, but it seems that it is mostly inoperable."

"That bad? You are an engineer. I thought armor repair was pretty basic for y'all."

Said engineer nodded. "Light and moderate damage are fairly easy to repair, assuming we have the right tools and materials, but the upper half of the inner mask and the visor... I don't believe I have the means to deal with it."

"There's nothing at all you can salvage?" Kaiden asked, worried about the Tsuna's survival chances without the aid of at least some defense for his noggin.

Genos rolled the helmet around in his hand. "I could disassemble the top part and keep the underside. Might as well remove some of the chipped and cracked pieces. It won't be much, but my comm will remain, and I'll still have a re-breather."

"It's something. When we inevitably run into a room that has a fog of poison in it, that will be a life saver."

His companion cocked his head. "You know for a fact that we will deal with gaseous or aerosol poisons?"

The ace shrugged. "So far, we've dealt with a mech warzone, a room that turned into a lava pit with giant lava lizards, and a room that spawned a horde of robots because a hacker hacked a thing they were supposed to hack. I'm starting to respect the fickleness of this test."

"Understandable," Genos agreed as he activated the crowbar again. "This should only take me a few minutes. Are we leaving soon?"

"In a bit. Julius is looking everyone over. We'll travel

together for the time being. You know, considering the death traps and all."

The Tsuna planted the crowbar into the underside of his visor, using some force to pull it out of the helmet. "Are you sure that is wise? We are a couple of hours in, so I'm sure the Deathmatch portion of the test will activate soon."

"They seem like good guys, plus Otto just risked his neck to save us. I don't think they will turn on us." Kaiden looked back to see Julius check Chiyo and put a serum into her neck using an injector. "Or at the very least, they won't shoot us in the back. If they try, I'll bet my trigger finger is faster than theirs. Plus, your cannon is bigger than any weapon they have, except maybe Mack himself."

"If the vanguard attempts to attack us, I have one last seeker grenade ready along with my pistol, which fires a projectile that will let me deactivate his shielding. He is of no concern," Genos stated with an eerie calm as he used a small buzz saw to remove the top half of his helm.

"Good to keep the options open," the ace said, a little taken aback with the Tsuna's rather robotic demeanor. "You feeling all right, Genos?"

"A few minor injuries. Would be a lot worse if it hadn't been for your assistance. Thank you for that."

"No worries, but you seem a bit more…hostile than usual."

His teammate released a deep breath as he finished removing the top portion of the helmet, throwing it to the side. "Yes, I suppose I am feeling not quite myself. This test has gotten much more 'real,' as you usually put it. Normally, in the missions we undertake there is a clear pathway for us. Even when we run into a problem or have to change the strategy, it is not usually so dramatic. We simply reconfigure our plans slightly and keep moving forward." Genos pried off a few pieces of compromised plating around the mouthpiece. "I suppose I am starting to feel a little out of my depth now. I have thought the scenario over in my head these last few minutes. If it had been just us in here, do you think we would have survived?"

Kaiden looked at Otto for a moment before moving closer to Genos and leaning in. "To be honest, I don't think we would have had to deal with it at all. I doubt Chiyo would have fallen for a trap like that. She seems more methodical than that guy."

The Tsuna chuckled as he slid the remainder of his mask onto his face and attached nozzles from the container on his back into the sides. "I suppose I hadn't considered that. I would have to agree. She is as fine an infiltrator as I am a mechanist."

The ace smiled under his mask, knocking the back of his hand against the alien's shoulder. "Keep up that kinda spirit. Better that than falling into a funk."

"Funk? Isn't that a type of music or a synonym for a bad smell?" Genos asked.

"It can also mean a feeling of sadness or worry. I'm only saying you should remain in good spirits. We still got a lot of test to take and all."

"Quite true," Genos agreed, looking out the open door. "I suppose my concern is simply whether or not we will take on something we are not prepared for."

"I haven't been prepared for almost everything I've dealt with so far, and I'm talking the entire school year, not just the test," Kaiden pointed out. Genos looked back at him. "But sometimes, you just gotta roll with it and rely on your personal bag of tricks, maybe pick up a few new things along the way." He focused on the Tsuna. "And just remember-—you, me, and Chiyo, we got each other at least. Whatever we run into next, we can knock three heads together instead of only one."

"Another good point. Rather surprising that you seem so open to working on a team now, Kaiden. I remember the first couple of months, when you always seemed to go off on your own on a whim."

He shrugged and crossed his arms. "It's something I wish I had learned before I got here. If I had, well, maybe things would have turned out differently for me. But then I wouldn't have had a reason to be at that bar in Seattle, which led me to being here. Like I said, you roll with things and learn along the way."

"And if I hadn't found the courage to greet the human who was staring at me, we might have not become friends," Genos added.

"Maybe. Probably. You really consider that a good thing for your mental health?" Kaiden joked. "Things can work out all right if you take chances. And I do have to say that it's rather cool that the first alien I ever met turned out to be a teammate."

"Same here."

The ace tapped the side of his mask. "You know, I keep forgetting that humans are technically considered aliens by all the other races."

Genos snickered. "Well, we are on your planet. But

should you ever visit Abisalo, I'm sure it will be quite the shock."

"Yeah, then I'll be the one walking around in scuba gear all the time," he responded, mentally picturing walking around on a planet that was mostly one large ocean. "I'll make that a bucket-list item. You ready?"

"I am." The Tsuna nodded as he pressed a button on his gauntlet that activated the pack the nozzles were attached to. "You should see if the others are ready."

"You guys good to go?" Kaiden shouted.

"Feeling good," Mack yelled back. "Julius shot us all up with happy juice. I kind of feel bouncy."

"Just don't fall over on top of me and you can do whatever you feel like," Kaiden jeered. "Let's go check out our options, shall we?"

The two teams made their way to the door immediately across from the room they were in.

"What do you think will be in here?" Julius asked.

"We've dealt with mechs, tanks, mutants, and droids so far," Genos stated. "I expect almost anything at this point."

"Maybe ghosts?" Kaiden suggested sarcastically.

"You know, I wasn't concerned about that," Otto muttered. "But since you brought it up, I'm now considering it, and that honestly sounds terrifying."

"That would be some shit." Mack chuckled. "Slide right through my barriers. I'd be the south side of useless."

"It isn't something we have to worry about. Do remember these tests are supposed to prepare us for things we may actually have to deal with," Chiyo interjected.

"Not the superstitious type, Chiyo?" Kaiden jeered.

"I have not had to deal with anything that would make me think ghosts or phantoms should be something we have to worry about," she answered.

"Gotta take you to New Orleans sometime. I saw a house for sale there once that pimped the fact that it *wasn't* haunted."

Mack laughed. "Oh, that place was definitely haunted. I don't believe in ghosts either, but I would give that place a pass."

"Perhaps a Sauren squad?" Genos suggested. "We haven't run into any hostiles that are part of the other races, only human mercenaries."

"Possible," Chiyo said. "But I didn't find any evidence in the vids or research that I went through to learn about the test that suggested there are alien opponents. But they could have added them in recent years."

"A rogue Sauren hunting party or insane Mirus could be something to watch out for," Genos warned.

Julius shivered. "Evil Mirus…they have a specific name, don't they?"

The Tsuna nodded. "Yes, it's different for every species as the Mirus' telepathy instantly translates their companions, but I believe the humans call them Vesa?"

"It's from the Latin word 'vesanus,' meaning insane," Chiyo explained. "I have only read reports and seen a brief description in an E.E.T encyclopedia. They are apparently Mirus who broke away from the Mirus hive mind, and as their mental stability decays, they are powerful psionics and absolutely deranged. I don't think anyone in the Master class could, but the top in the Victor class would be able to take them on."

"Says you," Kaiden scoffed.

She shook her head. "Confidence aside, I don't think it's something we'll have to deal with."

"Speaking of crazy, what about neurosiks?" Otto asked. Chiyo shifted uncomfortably behind him.

"If we run into those, start making deals with God or the devil, whoever will hear you," Kaiden said solemnly.

"You've faced them before?" Julius asked.

"In the Animus, a couple of times, but those were with a group of other soldiers, and we were all armed to the teeth. Still vicious but you had more confidence." He shrugged. "But before I came here, I had a buddy who was doing a gig over in Houston. They had to go in a slice shop where the owner had 'borrowed' something that he hadn't given back, so they were going to 'borrow' it right back for the contractor. I don't know what the hell they were doing in that shop, but they ran into a neurosik on a slab, thought it was dead, and got too close. Only a couple of them made it out."

"How many went in?" Mack asked.

"Nine. The guys I used to run with were no pushovers and were well-stocked. One neurosik took out seven of them. They didn't even take it out. They simply ran and were able to lock it in. Considering they didn't run into any guards or gang members or anything, that thing probably took all them out too."

"Maybe we shouldn't have started thinking about this,"

Otto lamented as they finally approached the door. "Now, I'm wondering what the hell is behind this door."

"Only one way to find out," Kaiden stated as he walked over to the panel and pressed the button to open the door.

"*Hey,*" Julius shouted and drew his pistol.

Otto followed suit, along with brandishing a blade. "What are you doing?"

"Did you want to sit in front of the door for the rest of the test?" the ace asked. "I'm opening it. Let's take a peek at what's inside."

The six looked into the room. It was much smaller than the last one, with two other doors to the left and right of the center of the room. It seemed to be empty—no nodes, consoles, or hostiles in sight.

"Looks clean," Mack commented. "Then again, so did the last one."

Kaiden took out his Raptor. "Should we venture in and see what awaits us?"

"Hold for a moment, if you would," Chiyo asked, walking closer to the doorway.

"What are you doing?" He pointed the rifle into the air and rested it on his shoulder.

She withdrew a small disk from her belt. "Taking precautions." With a quick motion, she tossed the disk into the room and a hologram of herself materialized.

At first, nothing happened, and the group looked amongst themselves to confirm that they were ready to head inside. With a low buzz, a laser barrier sealed the entrance, trapping them outside the room. Kaiden, Julius, and Otto jumped back. Four large turrets popped out of the ceiling, aimed at the hologram, and ignited it in torrents of flame.

They watched as the weapons continued to spew fire for at least thirty seconds. The flames were so hot they melted the hologram's disk, and it disappeared. The turrets ceased firing and slid back into their hiding spot, and the lasers disappeared as well.

They were all silent for a while. Mack the first to speak. "You think it's good now?"

He received only silence in response. Chiyo finally answered, "There is one other room we could try back down the hallway."

"Let's do that," Julius acknowledged.

"I'm game," Otto declared.

"That seems reasonable." Genos agreed.

"Fuck that room," Kaiden hissed, and the group chuckled.

CHAPTER TWENTY-THREE

The six initiates had doubled back from their failed excursion across the hall and now looked at their last remaining option. Julius glanced behind them to the door through which Kaiden and his team had arrived. "You sure we can't go that way?"

"Lava. Lizards." Kaiden deadpanned.

"It could have changed since then," Genos said thoughtfully.

The ace crossed his arms and looked at his teammate. "You wanna pop it open? Besides, you're missing half your helmet now. Your dome is gonna dry out if you go in there."

"That sounds like a bad way to go," Mack mused. "Then again, I can't say there are many good ways to go, considering the circumstances."

"Maybe the dumbass system running this thing will drop an elephant on us and we'll make the year's blooper reel." Kaiden shrugged.

"What room did you and your team use to get in here?" Chiyo asked.

"Teleporter," Otto answered. "You said you came in from that room. I'm guessing that's the west side of the building."

"Yeah...I think. Don't have a compass," Kaiden admitted.

"Well, we came in from the far side—the east side. When we got in, we went through a couple of rooms with some slight resistance, just a straight path, really. It ended in a room with a single teleporter."

"By that time, the whole place started shaking and we could hear explosions behind us. Big ones," Mack added.

"Probably mechs and tanks like what we had to get through," Chiyo reasoned.

"Hope all the pilots and jockeys are having their fun out there. Don't think they are going to have tank battle in... I already jinxed it, didn't I?" Kaiden fretted, looking at Julius, who simply shrugged.

"We decided to take our chances and head through the teleporter. We got warped to this room. This exact spot in fact," Otto finished.

"In that case, we should probably step back a few feet in case anyone else comes through," Genos advised, taking a couple of steps back. "Should someone teleport into the position you are in, it does not turn out well when they are reconstructed."

"I don't think we have to worry all that much, considering you're the only ones we've seen so far," Julius said, although he did look down and took a few steps back himself. "If there is still a chance, however, I do wanna say that I don't have any serum or concoction that's gonna fix someone's arm being recombobulated into your kidney."

"So I guess that means we're left with door number three over there," Kaiden asserted, turning to look at the last door. "You have any more of those hologram disks, Chiyo?"

"No, they are a very limited gadget," she stated. "If it is another empty room, I suppose we could try throwing in a piece of our armor to see if it sets anything off."

"Should have kept the top half of your helmet," Mack said, looking at Genos.

"I can retrieve it if you would like," he offered.

"It's all good. I still have a few grenades, or I'll toss my barrier in." Kaiden reached down and took out his barrier projector. He studied it. "Still only twenty-seven percent recharged. It took a beating."

"That's a long hallway we gotta go down." Otto hummed as he stared down the passage. "Let's get to it if we're gonna. We racked up some points in the last room, but I'm guessing we're lagging behind now, if we weren't already."

The rest nodded agreement and they began making their way to the final door, weapons at the ready.

Mack reloaded his hand cannon and began priming his barrier. "How long till the Honor activates? Anyone have a guess?"

"It varies. From what I've seen, it could happen anywhere within the first couple of hours—meaning any second now—to about twelve hours in," Chiyo answered.

"You seem to know quite a bit about the test," Julius noted. "At least more than we do."

"I was able to find some brief vids on greysites and dug around the available information on the Academy network and a few articles in the library. It wasn't that much, even when it was all combined."

"Were a couple of those greysites Kara's Den and Ebon Net, by any chance?" Otto inquired.

She nodded. "Yes, and they had the most vids available."

The agent sighed. "I tried to do some research too, but I was locked out of those sites after I made a couple of rookie mistakes as a kid. Those guys don't seem to forget or forgive very easily."

"You're lucky that you were caught by the moderators and simply banned. If you had been caught by a sting or fell for a hacker's ploy, it could have been much worse," Chiyo reminded him.

Otto chuckled. "Honestly, I'm only an above-par hacker. I make up for it with divine luck and natural charisma."

"It's honestly kinda shocking, the way he gets to the ladies and some of the stuff he can talk his way out of. That's a gift." Mack snickered.

"And yet the times that he fails, we're somehow stuck cleaning up the mess," Julius mumbled.

"That's one of the jobs of a wingman," Otto declared.

"I don't remember applying for the job," the biologist retorted.

Kaiden, in front of the pack, stopped in his tracks and held up a hand to tell the others to halt. "Hey, y'all hear that?" he whispered.

The group listened, In the silence, they heard clanging, along with the whir of what sounded like a drill or saw going through metal. The ace looked up and saw a hole forming on the ceiling.

"I don't know who's doing that or what the hell they're thinking, but they don't seem very bright," he said in a tone of disbelief.

"You think they're friendly?" Mack asked. "Maybe they're other initiates who got stuck in a room and are trying to make their way out?"

"I don't think so. Any engineer class who would have a way to cut through metal would use a torch. Most take them instead of a blade or melee weapon. Sappers would obviously use an explosive charge," the Tsuna reasoned.

"Genos, mind using that cannon of yours to find out?" Kaiden asked.

"Priming," he acknowledged. He held down the trigger of his cannon and aimed at the hole, watching the saw make it to the halfway point.

"Your hand cannon is the most powerful weapon we have in our team. Mack, could you help him?" Otto said.

The vanguard aimed upward. "If they are friendlies, good thing we can't kill each other yet."

"Firing," Genos stated, sending a blast of energy at the target. Mack responded with several shots of his own. His shots put several holes into the ceiling before the mechanist's shot blasted the ceiling apart. Several dark figures sailed through.

"Back up," Julius shouted. The group stepped or jumped back as a few bodies decked out in Red Sun merc outfits hit the floor.

Kaiden walked up to them to see several large holes in a couple of bodies while another had its entire left side blown completely off. He kicked the one that seemed the most together. When he heard nothing, he rolled him over with his foot to see two shots in his right ribcage. "How did that even happen? Was he lying down?"

"Well, we got a few points." Mack shrugged, venting his hand cannon. "But that was a bit anticlimactic, wasn't it?"

"You think this test is just messing with us at this point?" the ace asked.

"I suppose every event can't be a hellish scenario or droid horde," Otto surmised.

"Breaks up the monotony, at least." Julius sighed.

Mack closed his gun's vent. "I'm sorry, you bored already?"

"Wanna take point?" Kaiden asked mockingly.

"Well, I simply meant that all we're doing is… No, I'm good. Let's enjoy our little walk." The biologist sighed as he continued toward the door.

The others followed and grouped around the entryway. "It sounds like there's something on the other side," Genos cautioned them.

"Weapons ready," Kaiden ordered, raising his rifle, "Get the door if you would, Julius."

He nodded and walked to the panel as the rest readied for an attack. The biologist raised three fingers and began counting down, pressing the switch to open the door at zero.

"Whoa," Kaiden gasped as the door opened. "What's going on in there?"

The door opened to reveal a large cylindrical shield glowing white at the center of the room. The two teams walked in, and the door closed behind them. They reached the barrier and stepped onto a walkway that circled around the shield and led to a ramp that ascended on the far end and another that descended several yards to their left.

"Hey, look," Otto said, pointing down and across the way. "There are more teams in here."

Kaiden looked down to see at least six other teams below, all traversing various paths. Some were circular like theirs, and others were long catwalks or even triangular. One team moved along a floating pad. The shield seemed to stretch down at least several floors to the very bottom.

"Not just down there, either," Chiyo observed. "Look up."

Above them, the cylinder extended another few floors, at least sixty or seventy feet. Kaiden couldn't tell how many initiates were above them, but from his angle, he could see at least a couple other teams, along with someone who wore familiar armor and had a contraption on his back similar to Genos'.

"Hey, Genos, is that Jaxon?" he asked, pointing to the soldier.

Genos walked over to Kaiden and looked where he was pointing "I think... Yes, that is his usual armor loadout."

"Think he would hear us if we called to him?"

The Tsuna shook his head. "He's at least three stories above us, and the hum from this shield would likely drown out our voices."

The ace waved his hands to see if he could get Jaxon's attention, then saw Izzy walk up beside him. Both seemed to be studying the barrier. "No good. We can't hail him on comm, can we?"

"No, our comm is only linked to our team," Genos stated.

Kaiden sighed and tapped a finger on his arm. "That's true, but we do have someone who could probably get their attention." He slowly looked back until he stared at Chiyo. "Think you can get up in there, Chiyo?"

"More than likely. I don't think they would have any way to protect themselves from me accessing their comms, but it will take me a few minutes to hack in without completely compromising their systems. Is there a reason we need to contact them right now?" she inquired.

"Eh, say hi? Compare notes? See how badly we're beating them?" he suggested,

"This is the first room where there's something of interest and nothing trying to kill us. We should probably focus on figuring out where we are," she reasoned.

"I'll look around with Genos and the others while you do your thing," Kaiden suggested. He looked around for a moment and turned off his open mic, speaking solely through the team comm link. "Besides, this place just gave me an idea about our personal plans."

Chiyo closed her open mic. "About the whereabouts of the EI director?" she asked, her voice hushed. "I made a similar assessment, considering that it would be sound reasoning that it would be at the top of the building like most main computers or systems. But given that it doesn't need to act like one to control everything here, it would probably be in a place that was harder to reach and not in a destination where most teams would want to be."

"Underneath the place where all the action is happening," Kaiden finished, pointing down with his hand. "This shield thing goes down pretty far. I figure we head down that ramp over there and see where it leads. If it turns out we're wrong, then we can just head back up."

"Sound reasoning, but again, should we be making calls right now when we have a place to be?"

Kaiden looked at Genos, who was watching Jaxon and his team. "I mean, it could be tactical. You said the Honor could come into play at any moment. Better to have communication with another group that we could use on our side if anything goes down."

Chiyo sighed, shaking her head as she brought out her holoscreen. "A reasonable decision, but your delivery makes it obvious that it's simply an excuse."

"And yet I'm still convincing." Kaiden chuckled. "Thanks, Chiyo. Let me know when you got him." He looked back to catch Genos' glance and saw that the other team had gone. "Where did the others go?"

"Over to the ramp. They appear to have discovered something," his teammate informed him, his mic still open.

Kaiden reactivated his mic. "Discovered something good or bad?"

"Well, I do not hear any screams, so probably not terrible, but they did not seem excited by it." Genos holstered his cannon on his back.

"I'll go take a look. Stay with Chiyo. I'll be right back." He walked in the direction of the lower ramp and spotted Julius and Otto standing at the top and looking down. "Hey, guys, what's going on?"

The biologist grimaced. "There's some sort of barrier blocking the way," he answered and motioned down the ramp before folding his arms. Kaiden looked down to see

Mack standing in front of a shield that shimmered with blue light. Another large armored figure stood behind it, making motions with his hands.

"Who's that guy? Are they playing charades?" Kaiden questioned.

"It's another vanguard. There's another team behind the barrier trying to get through. Mack says the two of them can break the barrier by smashing into it, but it has to be at the right power level or something," Otto informed him.

"The barrier is blocking sound, so they're gonna have to wing it. If they don't get it right, they might actually power the thing up even more," Julius added.

"You guys wanna head down too? That's where we're thinking of going."

"Really? Most of the action will be in the main building, I figure. We're just being good Samaritans." Julius shrugged.

"We're on the ground floor...at least I think so, if you came in from that other room. We might have been warped up to the top floor for all we know," the biologist mused.

"Obviously not, considering there are floors above us, but hey, maybe we're inside some sort of wormhole or something," Kaiden joked.

"We would have more problems than a barrier if we were in a wormhole," Otto said thoughtfully. "But hey, it's the Animus, right? Anything is possible," he finished with a flourish of his hand.

"Might wanna stand back. Looks like they are going to give it a shot," Julius suggested.

Kaiden stood to the side as he saw Mack's fist glow blue

with energy. The vanguard reached back, and his counterpart did the same. He lifted his other hand near the barrier and counted down from five. In the end, both slammed their fists against the shield, and the punches released a pulse of energy that cascaded through it and cracked it apart. The two men fell back from the force as the barrier collapsed.

The ace whistled appreciatively as Julius and Otto helped him up. "Feeling heavy-strong now?"

"Did it work?" Mack asked, getting to his feet.

"Yeah, thank you." He looked up to see a woman dressed in white medium armor. "I'm Lara, a raider. That's our decker Juri, and your fellow vanguard over there is Bernard."

"Nice punch, man," Bernard stated.

"Right back at you. Good to find another vanguard who know the nuances of their energy output," Mack responded approvingly.

"Hey, Kaiden, I've reached Jaxon," Chiyo informed him.

"I'll be right there—and good news, we got ourselves a way down."

CHAPTER TWENTY-FOUR

"Kaiden, this is Jaxon," the Tsuna ace declared. "Chiyo said that you asked her to…contact me."

"In a manner of speaking." Kaiden chuckled and approached the shield to look up at Jaxon and his team from below. Chiyo's holoscreen floated above his hand. "How have you guys been doing?"

"We've had our struggles. Silas took a hard hit to his left leg. We've been searching through the base for a healing serum or painkiller but have come up empty so far."

"Is that right?" The ace looked at the other team. "Hey, Julius, I have a request!"

The biologist excused himself from the conversation with Lara and her team and made his way over. "What do you need?"

"You guys are heading up, right?" Kaiden asked.

"That's the plan." The biologist nodded.

"You see that guy up there?" He pointed to Jaxon, who was looking down at the two of them.

"Yeah, who is he?"

"He's a friend of mine, Jaxon, an ace like me. One of his teammates is injured, another friend named Silas. When you get up there, do you mind patching him up?"

Julius cocked his head. "I guess I do kind of owe you for helping us back in the node room."

"Damn straight," Kaiden chided playfully. "Jaxon said he took a shot in the leg. Shouldn't take but a few drops from one of your batches of happy juice to get him back in top shape, right?"

"Better than top, that's the Julius Dexy guarantee," he promised. "Plus, I should be getting some personal currency for it, so it works out for me too."

"How magnanimous of you." The ace snickered. "You hear that, Jaxon? Just wait for Julius and his guys to make it up there to you, and he'll get Silas skipping right along."

"You are sure they are trustworthy, Kaiden?" Jaxon sounded wary.

"Yeah, go ahead and look a gift horse in the mouth," the biologist muttered. Kaiden could almost visualize him rolling his eyes under his helmet.

"I'm talking to you through Chiyo's holoscreen. It's on speaker," Kaiden said dryly.

He heard the Tsuna sigh. "My apologies, medic. I did not mean to scoff at you. Any help would be appreciated, but considering the circumstances—"

"I understand," Julius acknowledged. "I guess everyone is cautious at this point. We'll head up in a couple of minutes. My team is myself, an agent, and a vanguard. We'll try to get there ASAP, but another team I've been talking with tells me this place is littered with traps and barriers blocking different paths, so it may take us a while."

"Understood. I'll see if I and my team can disable some along the path and try to meet you a level down. And thank you."

The other man nodded. "No problem. I guess this is where we part ways, Kaiden?"

"Guess so. I and my team have our own plans on how to win the test. It might be a long shot, but we're risk takers. I've taken top scores on both the Division Test and the Co-operative Test, and I'm looking for a three-peat."

"Oh, so that *was* you," Julius said, realization creeping into his voice. "I knew your name sounded familiar, and the fact that you are an ace should have made me recognize you earlier. You've earned a reputation here in only a year."

"I like to make grand entrances. I'm a crowd-pleaser." Kaiden beamed.

"Best of luck to you and your team. Maybe we can network once we get done with this test."

"I have an exclusive list, but I can probably make room."

"How magnanimous of you." Julius snickered.

"Best get out of here before Honor turns on and I pay you back for that," Kaiden threatened jokingly.

The biologist raised a hand in mock surrender and backed away. "I hear you. I'll get going. Thanks again for the help."

"No problem." The soldier waved him off. "You still there, Jaxon?"

"Chiyo hacked into my comm. I couldn't honestly tune you out if I wanted to," he admitted.

"But you would never want to mute the expert advice I

offer or my surprisingly authoritative and empowering tone, now would you?" Kaiden asked, earning an unamused grunt in response. "I'll make sure Chiyo puts everything back in place when we leave, don't worry. I wanted to consider possibly teaming up in case everyone starts shooting each other soon, but we have something we have to look into first, and we're taking a gamble. I'd feel bad if it turns out we're wrong and we dragged you with us."

"It's not a bad idea. What is your plan? We may be willing to… What? Izzy says hello."

"Howdy, Izzy," Kaiden greeted her cheerfully.

"She can't hear you since she's not on the link, but I'll pass it along. Now, what is your plan? We may be willing to help."

The ace glanced at Chiyo, who shook her head. "Sorry, man, can't say for now. Gotta keep a few things close to the chest. We are technically rivals right now, even if a team-up would make for a great jaunt through this deathtrap of a building."

He heard the alien chuckle. "Very true. I suppose I've gotten so used to working with you it slipped my mind. I and my team have our own plans as well. I wish you the best."

"Same here, but you'll want to hope that our plan works out, because if it doesn't and we both make it to the last minutes of the test… Well, I'll admit you're the better ace, but you have to acknowledge I'm a far better shot."

"Perhaps, but I've been trained to be a warrior almost since my birth. Flashy gunplay and a headstrong attitude will only get you so far, Kaiden. You have not seen a Tsuna warrior in a proper duel."

"True, but Genos also has a cannon. Don't need to be terribly accurate with that," he countered. As he turned to give the mechanist a nod, he saw that he was staring at the holoscreen with anxious eyes. "Speaking of whom, I think he wants to give you some good wishes of his own before we set off. Give me a second." He walked over and transferred the screen to Genos, smiling as he heard the Tsuna greet his kin excitedly and relate their fights and mishaps thus far.

"Genos always brings a sort of levity to all this, doesn't he?" Kaiden asked Chiyo as he walked up beside her.

"His honest optimism is refreshing in these situations," she acknowledged.

"You really think that we'll find the Director down there somewhere?" he inquired.

She walked to the edge of the ramp and looked down. "I still think it's the most promising idea, but there are no guarantees."

"You're starting to sound hesitant," he noted.

"I have to consider as many options as possible and plan accordingly. Taking precautions is always an intelligent move, as I'm sure you noted in the last room."

"Yeah, yeah. Thanks for making sure we weren't flambéed," Kaiden retorted with mock chagrin. "What's Plan B if it turns out we're wrong?"

"It all depends on how long it will take us," Chiyo admitted. "I don't know how large the area we'll need to cover is. If we find out we're wrong quickly we can simply double back, and I'll accede to doing this the normal way."

"And if it takes too long?"

"Then we will have to figure out an alternative. Honor will no doubt come into play by the time we return, so we'll have to deal with other hostile initiates along with the various traps and mobs throughout this ever-changing facility. And on top of that, the map will start shrinking soon."

"Guess we'll see how good we do under pressure," Kaiden quipped.

"Thank you for going along with this."

"What was that?" he asked, surprised by the infiltrator's words.

"I know you probably wanted to do this like everyone else. I will also admit that it would probably be better—at least in some respects—to do it that way considering all the possibilities. But you still listened to my suggestion, and have done your part up till now. I wanted to let you know that I *do* acknowledge that and... Thank you for humoring me, at least."

"It's the least I can do. You did a lot of legwork, or a lot of hacker work and research at least," Kaiden said with a shrug. "And like I said to Julius, I have a hot streak going with these things. I wanna keep it going."

"I certainly don't want to be the one to stop you," Chiyo declared.

"Friends Chiyo and Kaiden, I have finished talking to kin Jaxon," Genos interjected.

She took the screen from him. "Thank you for your patience, Jaxon. Sorry about being so invasive about this. I'll disconnect the link now and put everything back together."

"Understood, I appreciate it. Best of luck to all of you for however much longer this test runs."

"Same to you," she responded, canceled the link, and tapped a few more keys before closing the screen.

"Well, if there's one nice thing about heading down instead of up, it seems that most of the traps and barriers have been deactivated already by the other teams," Kaiden observed as they went down another floor. They were now four floors down and had passed two other teams, one of which eyed them questioningly as they headed up and another who went by without so much as a wave.

"How far down do you think it goes?" Genos asked.

"At least a hundred more feet if I had to guess," Kaiden said looking over the side. "So about ten stories?"

"It's rather far down. It will probably lead to some sort of cave system when we reach the bottom," Chiyo added.

Genos looked across the square walkway they were on to see a team enter a doorway on the other side. "How do you suppose the others got stuck down here?"

"Probably teleporters like Julius' team, or maybe elevators. There could also be secret entrances on the island like we were thinking back at the battleground," Kaiden suggested.

"So far, this seems to be rather safe in comparison to the other, smaller rooms in the building. I would hazard a guess that most of the hallways are safer in comparison to the main rooms," Chiyo noted.

"I would think the same, but that one vid you showed

us had a team fighting in a hallway that changed to a wrecked city with droids," the ace reminded her.

"True. Wishful thinking on my part I suppose." She looked thoughtful as they went down another ramp to the floor below. The walkway ended only a few feet ahead in empty air. "Wait a moment."

"What's with the sudden drop? This place is like a modern Winchester mansion." Kaiden sighed.

"Look ahead, Kaiden," Genos said, pointing across the way. A spinning pad approached them and stopped just in front of the ramp. The infiltrator hopped on and beckoned the others to follow. They stepped on to the pad which began to move in reverse, transporting them across the expanse.

"Yeah, this was necessary," Kaiden grumbled. "Could have just had a catwalk, but a floating pad will work just fine…" He groaned slightly as the device continued to rotate. "Won't make me sick at all."

"Deep breaths, Kaiden," the Tsuna recommended.

"Kaiden, Genos—*look*," Chiyo shouted, pointing in the air. Her companions looked where she was pointing to see a large screen in the air, followed by several more popping up both above and beneath them. The screen showed six people—other initiates, by the looks of their armor and weapons—standing in a room with rocky walls. One of them typed on a console and another on a node around which the four others had crowded.

"How much longer will this take, Carlos?" an initiate in green-and-grey armor asked.

"Only a couple more minutes. How's the chick at the console faring?" the one working on the node inquired.

"You almost done, Katrina?" an initiate in smoky-grey armor asked, a marksman by the looks of his sniper rifle.

Katrina flashed a thumbs-up as she continued typing into the console.

"Where is this being shown from?" Kaiden asked as they reached the other side of the ravine and dismounted from the pad, turning back to the floating screen in the air.

"I don't know. I'll see if Kaitō can find out." Chiyo began to scan the screen.

"You got any idea, Chief?" he asked.

"They're only holoscreens, remotely activated. Doesn't seem like something the system would do unless we're missing something," the EI answered, popping up over Kaiden's shoulder.

"Let's wrap this up. I feel like we're being watched or something." Another initiate in red armor fretted. "You sure those cameras are off, Katrina?"

She nodded again, continuing her work.

"Why is she so quiet?" Carlos asked.

"I don't know. She's usually a chatterbox. I was worried she would give away our position when we found the access point to get in here," the one in grey said.

"She must have gotten spooked when we went through that dark hallway before we ran into you three," the red initiate said. "We heard a few weird thuds and some scraping, but nothing picked up on scans. I think it shook her nerves a bit."

"Don't blame her. We were attacked by a few bayou stalkers in the first room we made it into. Nearly used our entire explosive arsenal trying to get past them. They got hides like titanium," the last remaining initiate, a demolitionist with a large grenade launcher on his back, grumbled.

"I know that feeling," Kaiden muttered.

"Hey, that camera over there—it's moving." The marksman pointed it out.

"What?" the red Initiate exclaimed in shock. "Is something watching us? Katrina, I thought you said they were—"

Her words were cut off as a domed barrier activated around them and trapped them inside. The five initiates began pounding on the walls or trying to shoot through the barrier, but nothing happened. Kaiden watched as the node in the middle began to spark and red lights flashed. Their yells were silenced by the barrier as Katrina turned slowly from the console and walked toward them. Carlos began to work frantically on the node as the lights began to flash faster and the others seemed to yell at Katrina to do something. Then the node exploded, and smoke enveloped the dome and obscured the other initiates.

"What the hell is going on?" Kaiden stammered, aghast.

The barrier collapsed and the smoke dispersed, showing the bodies of the initiates on the floor briefly before they disappeared in white flashes. Katrina looked directly into the camera as her armor faded, revealing a slender robotic frame with a curved head and one round light in the center. It continued to stare for a moment before it began fading from the screen and eventually disappeared.

In shock, Kaiden's team watched the screen that was now blank after the sudden and violent display. The screens vanished as if nothing had happened.

CHAPTER TWENTY-FIVE

"*T*hat was a doppel-bot," Chief said, yanking Kaiden from his shock.

"A what?"

"*A doppel-bot, as in doppelganger. It's a stealth-model droid that is used for infiltration and recon. It has a stealth generator and holo-skin deployment kit that allows it to create disguises based on other people or creatures that it has scanned.*"

"It just took out those five initiates in one go," he muttered. "Did it set off that bomb?"

"*Probably, and also probably erected that barrier. I would imagine whoever 'Katrina' is was taken out earlier and replaced by the doppel-bot.*"

The ace looked back at his teammates. "Neither of you is one of those body-snatcher bots, are you?"

His companions looked at each other before turning back and shaking their heads. "No, I do not believe so, though to be fair, I'm fairly certain neither one of us would admit to being one if we were," the Tsuna said reasonably.

"Got me there," Kaiden grunted.

"They are clean. I already scanned them. Those bots are good at masking their emissions but the hologram kit they use has a miniscule energy signature that can be detected if you zero in on it. Plus, I'm reading their EIs. Can't construct EI signatures on a whim; they are too unique."

"Good to know." Kaiden sighed with slight relief. "You have any idea why those screens turned on? From what I heard, it made it sound like the bot turned them on."

"Probably to sow distrust," Chiyo suggested. "To make all the teams—or at least the ones in here—begin to question each other. The Director is playing mind games."

"As if it wasn't before," Kaiden snarked. "Can you get Jaxon or Julius on comm again?"

Chiyo opened her holoscreen "Just give me a minute to —" Chiyo began before freezing in place. Her screen disappeared. "Genos! Throw out your EI device."

"Chiyo, what's wrong?" The Tsuna looked worried as Chiyo ripped off her helmet.

"Do it, Genos," she demanded, as she threw her helmet down the ravine behind them.

The mechanist took out his EI pad and held it up uncertainly for a moment before she snatched it and tossed it into the ravine with her helmet.

"What are you doing, Chi—" Kaiden saw Genos' pad light up and then erupt in a shower of sparks and jolts of electricity.

"What happened?" he barked and placed a hand on the back of his mask. "Is my implant going to explode too?"

"I don't feel anything," Chief responded. *"From the looks of*

that, it appears the EI devices had their systems corrupted. They got infected by an ataxia virus."

"Just like that? How did it get to Chiyo and not me? I would think her system is better defended than mine."

"It is, but not everything can be blocked quickly enough. I at least got a warning and was able to transfer Kaitō into my secondary device." She held up the tablet attached to her wrist. "But Genos...if that pad had still been in his compartment when it went off, his leg would have been fried."

The alien rubbed his right leg. "Thank you for your quick action, Chiyo."

"But what about his EI?" Kaiden asked. "Is it gone now?"

"Technically no, since we're still in the Animus, but unless he has another device that it can be moved into, he won't have it for the rest of the test," the infiltrator explained.

"Is it too late?" Kaiden looked at the engineer, and specifically at the missing half of his helmet. "The helmet is the main dock for the EIs for most students. That's gone, and now his pad is gone too."

The Tsuna looked at the screen on his gauntlet. "I'm still reading Viola, but the connection is weak."

"EIs have programs, fail-safes, and backups for these sort of emergencies. Let me take a look, Genos." Chiyo began looking through the tablet on the gauntlet. "I'm beginning your EI's reset process. It will take a while for it to come back online, but I can have Viola take control of your suit systems. I'm basically modifying your gauntlet's

OS to act as a temporary EI system. I'll have to make some room, and it won't work at full capacity when it does come back, but you'll have some functions available."

"I see." Genos nodded. "That will be fine, it is better than—" The mechanist was interrupted by a scream, and the three looked up to see an initiate fall down through the shaft from the upper levels, followed quickly by a few more behind the shield in the distance.

"I am officially one hundred and ten percent done with this place," Kaiden growled.

"They were probably knocked off when their devices erupted, or there's a fight going on up above," Chiyo reasoned. "But look at the shield! The circumference is shrinking."

The ace hadn't noticed before, but she was right. He also saw the light glow bright, and the humming grew louder. "Is that something we need to be concerned about?"

The infiltrator finished working on Genos' gauntlet and stepped away. "We need to move. The shield is powering up. It looks like it's about to erupt into a nova."

"Fantastic," the ace sneered. "New plan—first door available, we dive in and pray that it's much more manageable than an exploding energy field."

The three raced down the path. The lights around the tower began exploding or powering off, leaving only the illumination from the shield to guide them. The barrier itself began to fade in and out like a pulsating light. They descended another floor, desperate to find a way out as the shield continued to shrink into itself.

"*There,*" Genos shouted, pointing to a doorway on the other side of the walkway.

Kaiden charged ahead, slid up to the panel, and punched the opening switch. The doors slid wide and he waved his teammates through, running quickly after them as the alien closed the door behind them.

"We made it," the ace said, breathing a sigh of relief. He heard a loud explosion, and the shockwave toppled him to the floor. When he looked up, the door was still intact, and his companions lowered their hands from their faces.

They were in a cavernous hallway with no sound and only a few glowstrips for light. Kaiden stood and approached the door they had just entered through. "You think it's safe to go back in?"

Chiyo activated her tablet and held it up. "I'm not reading any excess energy. Any sort of explosion like that would usually leave large fields of dispersed energy for at least a couple of minutes, but there isn't even a trace."

"Open the door, Genos," he ordered.

"The panel is offline. The blast knocked it out."

"Crowbar it." Kaiden walked to the right side as the Tsuna took the left. The mechanist slid his gauntlet's crowbar into the sliver between the doors and pulled, cracking it open. The two then forced the doors halfway to peer outside. Nothing greeted them but a dark and empty room. The area they had been in had disappeared.

"Well, there goes the easy way down." The ace huffed, stepping away from the doors. "I guess we'll have to look around and see if there is an elevator or something to the lower levels."

"That would be our best course of action," Chiyo agreed. "I wonder how many made it out?"

"Can you sense anyone, Chief?" Kaiden asked.

"Nothing. Either everyone in there died, or they were tele-ported out. I can't read anything in the immediate area. We're all by our lonesome again." The EI disappeared again.

"Guess we'll see how long that lasts." The soldier frowned as he looked behind him. "There doesn't appear to be anything in that room, and there's only one at the end of this hallway. Guess that's where we gotta go." He looked at Genos who was staring at a piece of the wall in the distance. "You seeing a face in the rocks or something?"

"No, but something looks a bit peculiar," the Tsuna admitted. "Give me a moment, please." He walked to the area that had caught his attention and dropped to one knee to inspect it. "Kaiden, might I use one of your grenades, please?"

"I gave the rest of them to Mack to take down that Goliath, remember?" Kaiden stated as he drew his Raptor. "Still got some ballistic shots if you need something exploded, but mind filling me in?"

Genos took the rifle from his teammate and walked back a few steps, aiming at the rocks. "I prefer to show... firing." He shot a ballistic round into the wall. Shards of rock and dust erupted around them. The mechanist shielded his eyes as Kaiden stood still with crossed arms, his visor automatically scrubbing any debris that would obscure his vision.

"What exactly are you trying to show— Is that a room?" he demanded as the dust cleared, revealing a hidden passage behind the rocks.

"Something seemed strange about the formation and look of the rocks. I had learned that smugglers and mercenaries like to keep caches of supplies or hide secret entrances using these sorts of tricks," Genos explained, handing Kaiden back his rifle.

"Never figured you for a geologist," the ace mused as he placed his rifle onto his back.

"I have picked up a few extra-curricular hobbies during my time on Earth." The Tsuna placed his hands behind his back. "I used to collect various stones and minerals back on Abisalo. It was more for research and scientific purposes than as a hobby, but I enjoyed it nonetheless."

"Few of my hobbies have practical use in the field." Kaiden chuckled. "Let's see what we got."

The three looked inside the hidden room. It was rather small, but it contained three chests—cube-shaped and black with silver trim—and there appeared to be a hatch leading down at the end of the room.

"Jackpot," he exclaimed as he walked over to one of the chests. "This is our first real chance to restock since we began."

"Let Genos and me check them for traps before you potentially get us caught in an explosion," Chiyo warned.

He nodded and backed away, leaning against a wall as his team members inspected the crates. "So, how many floors do you think we made it down?"

"By my guess it was about seven. I was slightly preoccupied during those last few minutes," Genos said as he finished examining one of the boxes and moved to the next one. "That one is clear, Kaiden, if you wish to take a look."

"When we're done here, you guys wanna head down the hatch?" he asked as he popped open the locks.

"It will continue our descent, so we would be closer to our objective" the infiltrator stated, opening the box she had inspected. "I found some healing supplies."

"Got some ammo and a couple of guns in here," Kaiden said. "Some more ballistic rounds, too. Genos, you want one of these rifles? Give you other options in battle than only your cannon."

"Are you sure you don't want one?" his teammate asked.

The ace took out the rifle and tossed it to him. "It's all good. Similar model to mine, but I got the deluxe edition. There's also a pistol in here if you want it, Chiyo."

"I have one, but I suppose a backup wouldn't hurt. Is it kinetic or energy?"

"Kinetic, Karna Munitions model. Looks like a Series Three Scorpio." He twirled the pistol in the air. "Light, decent fire rate, good punch, kinetic option for barriers and heavy armor."

She nodded and handed him a few vials of various colors. He took them and traded her the pistol and a couple of magazines. "Those are two vials of healing serum, a vial of anti-venom, and a power-sip in case you start feeling tired, along with an injector."

"Healing juice, snake de-fanger, and prep pop—good to have," Kaiden quipped as he placed the items in his supply box.

"You sound like a short-order cook," Chiyo teased, attaching the Scorpio to her hip across from the static pistol on her left leg.

"What did you find, Genos?" he inquired.

The mechanist straightened from digging into his box

and held up a black cylindrical object with red lines down the side. "It is a box of explosives. There are some more thermals for you in there, Kaiden."

"Cool, but what are you holding there?"

The Tsuna lifted the object so they could see it. "It is a disintegration grenade. It creates a small field of super-heated particles that dissolves nearly any matter within it." He looked at his teammates. "Mind if I keep it?"

"It honestly sounds like it would be better in your hands than Kaiden's." Chiyo chuckled.

"You saying I couldn't get good use out of that?" He grimaced.

"It's a delicate and dangerous device, Kaiden. One slight mishap and you could disintegrate yourself instead of a target. Genos, as an engineer, is trained to handle various explosives," she countered.

"Plus, you know you would use it the minute you saw a hostile instead of saving it for later just because you wanna see what it does." Chief scoffed.

"Stop judging me," he muttered, throwing up his hands. "Fair enough, Genos has earned a few toys through all this anyway."

"I'll be sure to use it responsibly," his teammate promised and tossed him a container of thermal grenades. "There are some shock grenades in here as well. Would you like them, Chiyo?"

"Yes, please." She reached out a hand as he passed her the container. Quickly, she clipped it onto her belt and looked at the hatch. "That seems to be it in here unless you happen to see any other irregularities, Genos."

"No, it seems that was it."

"Nice find," Kaiden complimented him. "If it weren't for the various dings and scratches on our armor, it's almost like we just started."

"Though a disintegration grenade is not usually in the standard loadout for initiates," Genos added as he opened a slot in the container on his back and placed the grenade inside. "Shall we depart?"

"Allow me." The ace led the way to the hatch, twisted the valve, and grunted as he forced it open. "It's kind of a steep drop," he muttered as he looked down the hole.

"The shocks in our armor should be enough to disperse the fall as long as it isn't over a hundred feet," Chiyo reassured them.

"Well, I'm not sure if— Uh-oh." Kaiden pointed out of the room. "Incoming, guys."

His teammates turned to look as the hallway outside transformed into a volcanic landscape, complete with a moho staring at them.

"Those things again? Are they pissed they lost their snack the first time?" Kaiden growled belligerently.

"Fight or flight, Kaiden?" Chiyo shouted, yanking out her submachine gun.

"I just got these thermals. Don't want to lose them right away." He huffed and looked down at the hatch. "Place your bets and follow me," he ordered as he leaped into the hatch.

As Kaiden fell through the hatch, he saw glowing rings light up all through the tunnel. "Hey, guys," he called up to his team. "New problem."

"Beginning teleportation in three..." a synthetic voice announced, beginning a countdown.

"Teleport? Where to?"

"Two... One..." In a flash of blinding light, Kaiden and his team were gone.

CHAPTER TWENTY-SIX

C hiyo lay face down for a moment, her vision blurry and her mind reeling.

"Are you all right, Chiyo?" Genos asked as he helped her to her feet.

"Yes. Just give me a moment to find my bearings," she wheezed. "Where are we?"

"We traveled through a teleportation field, madame. We have no way of knowing where it transported us without positioning," Kaitō informed her.

"Where's Kaiden?" she asked.

"Over here." He grunted. He was bent over and balanced on his knees. "Giving my stomach some time to settle."

"Do you suffer from teleportation sickness, friend Kaiden?" the Tsuna asked.

He coughed and sputtered. "I guess so. Never teleported before, but I ain't feeling too hot. Remind me to apologize to Luke when we get out of here."

The infiltrator rummaged through her supply box and retrieved an injector and an ampoule of pale orange liquid. "Hold still," she ordered, driving the needle through the underlining of Kaiden's armor into his neck. "This is a serum to help with nausea and dizziness. There was only one, and I didn't think you would have a use for it," she explained as she injected the liquid.

"Good thing you brought it anyway." Kaiden rolled his neck around after she removed the injector. She helped him stand, and they surveyed their surroundings. "Well, this is certainly a change of scenery."

They were in a jungle, damp with mist and fog, and heard animal roars and screeches in the distance.

"I'm not sure if this is better or worse than where we were," Genos said thoughtfully. "How vast do you think this place is?"

"Chief, think you can get us an aerial view?" the ace asked.

"You won't throw up from the height?" the EI inquired.

Kaiden retched. "Don't display it in my visual. Just float up there and look around. See if you can find a door or something."

"First time I get to contribute, and I'm a glorified telescope." Chief sighed, floated above the trees, and looked around.

"You going to be all right, Kaiden?" Chiyo asked.

"Yeah, I'm feeling better. That stuff you shot into me certainly helped." He stood and stretched. "Let's try keeping teleportation to a minimum, all right?"

"Curious that you seem to have no problems integrating with the Animus, but basic teleportation seems to make you ill," Genos noted.

"I guess it was nice of them to give me the full experience," he grumbled. "Need to make a mental note to visit Laurie and thank him personally."

"It is the point of the Animus to get you used to all potential combat situations. If you get a contract with the Navy or a space station, teleporters will be used quite frequently," Chiyo remarked.

"So I should repeatedly throw myself into teleporters until I get used to them and achieve teleportation sickness resilience?" he asked sarcastically.

"That may work, but there are also medications. I believe those would be more beneficial," Genos suggested.

Kaiden removed his mask to take a deep breath, frowning at the alien. "If you weren't so precious, I would think you were mocking me."

"I finished my little recon flight," Chief declared, floating back down to the trio.

"What did you find?" the infiltrator inquired.

"There are three doors in here. One is about three klicks south, and the other two are five klicks north, separated from each other by one hundred yards."

"You have any idea what's behind them?" the ace asked.

"I don't have x-ray vision. At least not without the mod." Chief huffed with exaggerated patience. *"And just like all the other rooms, I can't scan through the doors. It's a crapshoot."*

"Figures." Kaiden sighed. "You guys have any suggestions, or should we simply spin one of us around a few times and whichever way they hobble, that's where we go?"

"While I would suggest going in the direction of the two doors since that gives us more options, the fact that we don't know what's in here with us concerns me. They are farther away, which means more chances to run into something hostile," Genos pointed out.

"Fair point, but we are armed to the teeth now and have some healing serums to boot. So we can take on anything with sharp teeth and claws that decides to get feisty." Kaiden looked at the trees and up into the air. "But if there's a volcano around, let's try to not get close to it."

"True, but we don't want to diminish our supplies too quickly. We don't know where we are or what floor. If we were transported to the top, we'll have to give up on our plan and play this out the traditional way. The *long* way," Chiyo emphasized.

"Let's go with the closer one. It'll get us out of here, and we can get our bearings sooner," Kaiden suggested and pulled his rifle. "You can spirit yourself away for now, Chief. Don't think I'll be needing to cast you into a coconut."

"Then I shall take my leave and take a well-earned nap," he declared and vanished.

Genos approached one of the trees and laid a hand on the bark. "Maybe we should take a look at the fauna. If the maps are more detailed, perhaps this is based upon an actual destination on the planet. We would have a better understanding of what awaits us."

"Possibly, unless this is based on a planet other than Earth," the infiltrator argued.

"Looks pretty Earth-like. Not seeing blue trees and yellow skies, so they aren't exactly original with their designs." Kaiden sauntered along a path and looked toward something in the air that caught his eye. He aimed quickly and fired his rifle, and the something plummeted to the ground.

The three ran over to it and discovered it was a small machine—circular with pointed attachments in each direction and a single lens in the middle.

"It's a probe. A tracker's probe," Genos confirmed, picking up the device and studying it. "But the design isn't human, or at least not one I've seen."

"It's Sauren." Kaiden revealed. "Raza has one like it. I got a chance to look at his various weapons and knick-knacks a month back. Similar design, but different color and more streamlined. These little prods on the end seem like balancers of some kind. This thing is rather crude."

"Sauren tech? That would mean—" Chiyo looked at the others as a small snap was heard in the foliage.

"We're in a hunting ground," the ace finished as he donned his mask and readied his weapon.

Genos took out his new rifle and activated it. "We need to move."

"Looks like Kaiden is going to see if his training with you has paid off, Raza." Wulfson chortled. "Think he and his friends have what it takes to take on a party of your kind?"

Raza's eyes narrowed as he studied the screen, watching as the team began to make their way through the jungle. "It depends on the skill of the Saurens they are going to face— and if your technicians designed them to hunt like we do or if they are simply there to be a different enemy type with no substance."

"I assure you, my technicians design every potential enemy to match the skills and specifics of their real-world counterparts." Laurie sounded mildly indignant. "We wouldn't spend hundreds of hours in research and development time to do half-hearted work. If you recall, you were one of our consultants."

"I do. But discussing strategies and fighting methods is different from the execution." Raza looked challengingly at the professor. "And since you brought it up, you wanted me to describe the way the traitors fight, not our warriors."

"Rogue Saurens? This might get nasty." Wulfson grunted, sat up, and leaned closer to the screen. "Haven't fought any myself, but Raza has told me a few stories. He seems to respect their propensity for violence."

"I do not respect traitors. They are honorless, and a taint among our kind," the Sauren growled. "But they have our training, and many crafted their own ways to fight and hunt after they were banished or fled. They hunt purely for blood."

"Are you worried for young Kaiden's safety, Mya?" Sasha asked. He looked over when he received no response. "Mya?"

She looked up from her tablet. "Hmm? Sorry, Sasha, my team was just in a bad situation. I got caught up."

"It's all right. You should probably be more invested in your own team," he acknowledged, returning to watch the scene unfold. "I'll fill you in after this plays out."

As the team ran through the forest, Kaiden heard a buzzing

from behind them—an odd sound amongst the rustling of the trees and snaps of wood. He turned just in time to see two disks sailing their way. "Get *down*," he shouted, firing at the disks. He was able to hit one, and it exploded and sent the other sailing toward a tree. It spun clean through the trunk, enough for it to topple forward. Genos dove toward Chiyo to plow them both out of the way.

"Chief, scan for hostiles. They might be using stealth generators," Kaiden ordered. He placed the butt of his rifle against his shoulder and looked around at the trees.

"Don't need to. There's one in the trees—nine o'clock," Chief warned.

The ace looked up to see a spotted brown Sauren peering through a fanged mask. It was large—smaller than Raza but at least six and a half feet tall—with broad shoulders and thick arms and legs. The body was almost covered in leather wraps around the chest, waist, and arms. Several long, deep scars traced its arms, and chips in its claws made them look like they had serrated edges.

The alien roared and leaped from the tree. Kaiden rolled back just before it landed, but he could feel the claws slice his coat and armor. He scrambled up and fired several shots. The monster's skin crackled with a burning glow, but it simply hissed in response and charged. He was used to this dance by now and side-stepped the Sauren's downward swipe, switching to ballistic rounds. Calmly, he fired two shots to the chest which knocked the reptile back. He smirked as it shrieked in anger.

"Kaiden, two more!" Chiyo warned. The ace looked back to see two new Sauren—one a dark blue with a white chest and the other a nearly camouflaged green—dash through the forest on all fours. He fired a few ballistic rounds at them, but they serpentined around the shots. The team had to move. Kaiden could tell they weren't as patient or strong as Raza, but they were certainly stronger than any of them, and Genos and Chiyo weren't used to fighting bloodthirsty Sauren.

"Get to the door. I'll hold them back," he ordered as he grabbed two thermals and tossed them on the ground. He sprinted away as the first alien recovered and the other two closed in. The thermals went off, creating a dense cloud of smoke and flinging debris all around. Two trees were blown to the ground. The soldier could see Chiyo and Genos approaching the door. He pushed himself to run faster while placing his rifle on his back and taking out Debonair, then fired behind him as he closed the distance between him and his friends.

Something stopped him in his tracks, and he was dragged back. The brown Sauren had snatched the back of his coat. The reptile pulled him in and slammed his claws into his chest armor. He could feel the tips of the claws against his skin.

"Kaiden!" Chiyo called, her voice fearful. Genos spun around and began to fire his rifle at the Sauren, the infiltrator joining in with her submachine gun. The monster hissed in response, took out an orb from his belt, and tossed it toward them. The device popped open and a group of smaller orbs were flung through the air, exploding once they hit the ground. The defenders tried to dodge the explosives, but two fell near her feet, blasting her backward, so she dropped her SMG as her head hit the ground.

The ace raised Debonair and pointed it at the Sauren's eye, firing a direct shot at the distracted alien. It cried out in pain, flailing with the arm that was embedded in Kaiden's chest. He yanked out his blade and hit the switch to heat it up. After a few seconds, he slashed at the monster's fingers, slicing them off. Another howl of pain issued from the beast. The soldier dropped to the ground, retrieved another thermal, and looked at the other two attackers, who were now only a few yards away from them.

He dropped the thermal at the Sauren's feet and jumped back. The creature bared its razor-sharp teeth and hissed.

"Chief, activate battle suite!" Kaiden ordered.

"Initiating," Chief acknowledged.

The ace looked at the Tsuna. "Genos, *cannon*," he yelled and held out a hand.

His teammate took the cannon from his back quickly and threw it. The thermal exploded, catching the two running aliens in the blast and knocking them back, but the now-one-eyed Sauren had leaped out of the way and was bearing down on Kaiden. The beast pulled a stick from his belt and it extended to a staff with a jagged blade on the end. Time began to slow as the suite kicked in. The ace grabbed the cannon out of the air, rolled back, and held the trigger to power it up.

He knelt, aiming at the beast. The suite helped him find the angle for his shot as the Sauren closed in. It lunged at him as the cannon finished charging, and Kaiden let go. The blast crashed into the enemy's chest, which evaporated under the searing power of the blast. The reptile's remaining eye went wide as its lunge was halted in mid-air and it fell to the ground. The shot erupted in its chest, almost completely destroying the top half of the alien hunter.

"Deactivate suite," Kaiden ordered as he tossed the cannon back to Genos and pointed toward the door.

"Battle suite deactivated."

He ran over to Chiyo, slid one of her arms around his shoulder, and helped her up. They made for the door. Genos was at the edge of the open doorway, firing at the remaining Saurens, who dodged the blasts. They were, thankfully, more wary of their prey after seeing the death of one of their own.

"Get inside, Genos," Kaiden demanded as he and Chiyo made it through. The Tsuna fired one more shot, but one of the Saurens moved around the blast and threw two more of the cutting disks at them. He ran through the doorway as the ace drew Debonair to fire at the disks. The shots came close but didn't manage to hit them. Genos hit the switch to close the door, but as the two halves slid into place, the disks went vertical and sailed through the opening. Kaiden lay back and covered Chiyo's head as the disks flew barely a couple of inches above him. He heard the reptiles shriek with rage as the doors closed and locked.

CHAPTER TWENTY-SEVEN

"Are you two all right?" Genos asked his downed teammates.

"I'm good. I don't know about Chiyo." Kaiden pulled the infiltrator to a seated position with him. "Hopefully, she didn't get a concussion."

"That sounds like it could be problematic inside the Animus," the Tsuna said fretfully.

The ace nodded, studying their teammate. "You all right, Chiyo?"

"Yeah… Yeah, I'll be all right," she said quietly, her right hand held to the side of her head. "We made it out, I assume?"

"Yeah, took out one of those Sauren bastards for good measure before we split."

"That's good. Make up some of the points." She sighed, reached into her supply box, and located a healing serum. Frowning against the pain, she opened the top and drank it in one go. She let the vial fall to the floor and grimaced slightly at the taste.

"Think you can get to your feet?" Kaiden asked.

"I can, but if you don't mind helping…"

"Yeah, sure." He stood and offered her his hand. She took it, and he pulled her slowly to her feet. "Bet you're missing the normal missions right now, huh? Where you can just stay in your little hacker's cave for most of the mission."

She laughed weakly. "Maybe I *have* gotten too used to that. I haven't had many opportunities to use my abilities so far."

"You did help save us from that horde of Assassin and Havoc droids," Genos pointed out.

"I suppose. Next year, I should spend a few more points in gun and fighting skills if I'm to be of more use on missions like these in the future."

"To be fair, I don't think we'll have to deal with transforming rooms and dozens of varieties of enemies on a regular basis," Kaiden pointed out. He looked at another door a few yards away. The disks had embedded into the door, and they vanished in a small white flash.

"Looks like that's our next destination," he said, dusting himself off.

Genos looked at the door to the jungle. "I suppose it would seem obvious by now, but it appears any enemies in the previous room cannot follow us once we leave." He looked at the panel next to the door. "This door now appears permanently locked."

Kaiden shrugged. "Good thing. Not a lot of room to fight in here."

Chiyo wiped some of the dirt and grass off her armor and moved her hair out of her face. "If you two are ready, we can proceed."

"You sure you don't need a few more minutes?" the ace asked.

She shook her head. "No, we still need to figure out where we were transferred to, and we won't be able to do — Where's my gun?" She reached down to the magnetic strips where she had stored her SMG.

"It got knocked out of your hand in the explosion. I had to leave it back there." Kaiden nodded at the previous room. "Didn't have time to look for it, sorry."

"It's all right, I can make do," she stated, taking out her Scorpio. "Always adapt."

"That's a pretty good motto, and it certainly fits the situation." He walked down the hall, still holding Debonair. "Let's see what's behind door number one, shall we?"

He opened it as the other two followed him. They were greeted by a laser grid a few yards ahead of them.

"Is it a dead end?" he asked.

"No, doesn't appear to be," Genos said. "There's a panel on the wall over there. It looks like a control system."

"Well, crack those knuckles, engineer, and let's take a look."

The trio walked in and toward the box. As the mechanist went to inspect it, Kaiden approached the grid and peered through it. "Looks like there are more teams in here."

Chiyo came up beside him. They saw seven other teams around them. The room had an octagonal shape. Eight hallways, including their own, all led to a large central chamber with a single computer console in the middle.

"Trap," he said bluntly.

"It would appear that way, considering all the other rooms with a central device and no obvious defenses," Chiyo agreed.

"Should we just say screw it and head back?"

"Genos said the door was locked. Besides, you really want to face those Saurens again?"

"At least in there, I have some idea what I'm going to face. Hard to plan for the unknown. It's like trying to stare at the abyss while you're in it." He huffed his annoyance. "As for it being locked, I'm sure between you and Genos you could get it unlocked.

The laser grid disappeared. Kaiden leaned back in slight shock. "What happened?"

"I deactivated the grid," Genos stated, holding up a bunch of cords. They heard a charge and hum behind them, and the grid reappeared at the doorway.

"Genos, put it back," Kaiden deadpanned.

"I deactivated the power system. It should have no power to activate a failsafe," the Tsuna explained, looking at the new grid.

"As much as I would like to believe you, the new set of crisscrossing lasers blocking our exit would make me believe that is not the case," the ace snarked. "Then again, you *are* the engineer here."

"It might be like the node. A secondary function is activated once the main power is cut off or the system is compromised," Chiyo suggested.

"My apologies," Genos stated as he placed his free hand against his chest and bowed his head slightly.

Kaiden sighed. "No worries. Always adapt, right?" He looked into the main room. "Let's see what the flavor of bullshit here will be."

The three walked into the room. Kaiden saw all the grids disappear in the other halls. The teams seemed to either stand in surprise or walk right in.

"You think this will turn into some sort of match or race?" the mechanist asked.

"Some of those teams don't seem to know what's going on. I think some of those grids turned off by themselves—unless you somehow knocked out the whole system?" Kaiden looked expectantly at the engineer.

"No, it was only connected to that individual grid," he confirmed. "Something is amiss."

"It appears they are trapped in here just like we are," Chiyo confirmed. "Their doors are blocked as well."

All the teams walked into the room. The initiates looked around or talked amongst themselves. Kaiden scanned the room, sizing up the competition, and saw some familiar armor. "No way." He chuckled. "Hey, Flynn."

The marksman raised a hand in acknowledgment. "Kaiden. Good to see you."

"Hey, guys," Marlo yelled as Amber waved at them.

The ace began to walk over. "You guys been doing al—" He stopped as he felt the ground shift and looked down to see lines forming under his feet. With a muttered oath, he jumped back to stable ground as walls erupted around him, soaring up twenty-five feet. The walls appeared all through the room, creating a maze and trapping the teams, separating them from each other.

"Oh, son of a bitch." Kaiden scowled, holding Debonair up "This is losing its charm."

"I think we know what the console is for now." Chiyo held up her Scorpio as Genos drew his rifle.

"You think we'll be lucky and it's just a maze?" the ace asked before several Guardian droids appeared in front of them. "Why do I still have hope at this point?"

They fired at the mechanicals as gunfights erupted all around the room. After dispatching the droids, Kaiden holstered Debonair and took out his Raptor. "Let's get to that console and finish this quickly," he ordered, taking a few steps forward before Genos grabbed his shoulder and held him back.

"Careful, Kaiden," he warned, pointing down. The ace looked down to see an immolation trap on the ground.

"Thanks, Genos. That would have been embarrassing. Wulfson has had me deal with those things since I first met him. Chief, fly up there and find us a path."

"I'm not liking that this is becoming my thing." The EI sulked as he appeared and flew up. He stopped about fifteen feet in the air and collided with an invisible wall, bouncing off it and falling on the floor. *"Ow."*

"I didn't even realize you *could* be hit physically," Kaiden said, surprised.

"It looks like some sort of barrier. I haven't seen one of that type before," Genos remarked.

"The Director adapts, correct?" Chiyo suggested, "Looks like it's adapting to Chief."

"Well, don't I feel special," Chief grumbled as he floated up off the floor.

"Well, thanks for trying, partner. Just keep a look out for traps for us, all right?"

"I can certainly do that unless this 'Director' decides to piss in my eye or something," Chief mumbled as he vanished and reappeared in Kaiden's HUD.

"Let's get to the center," Kaiden declared. "Show this thing we aren't taking its shit anymore."

The three made slow progress through the maze, taking on various droids and dancing around traps as they continued to try to find the right path.

"Watch out, Genos," Chiyo shouted as she raised her pistol and shot down a duo of flying droids.

"I notice they aren't getting slapped out of the air," Chief grunted.

"No, just shot down in explosive blazes," Kaiden retorted. "Keep a lookout, I feel like we're getting close."

"You've said that every three minutes for the last twenty minutes," Chief muttered.

"And I still believe it. Be a team mascot and start cheering." Kaiden snickered, turned, and blasted back a trio of Assault droids with a ballistic shot.

"Yeah, I'll do a little dance and then lead the 'wave.'" The EI snickered.

"You could do a twirl," he suggested, shooting another drone out of the sky.

"I'll do a helluva twirl when we get done with this. Six o'clock, Assassin droid."

The ace spun and fell to a knee as an Assassin droid tried to stab him. He unholstered Debonair and fired straight up into its exposed chest, then slid to the side as it deactivated and fell to the floor. Kaiden put away his pistol and smiled but felt the ground shake again. He stood up as he felt himself moving. The ground beneath him was separating, creating a gap between him and his teammates. "Chiyo! Genos! Get over here."

They looked back, then jumped across. Chiyo barely made it, but Genos collided with the edge. Kaiden and Chiyo reached out and grabbed his arms to pull him up. Two more Assault droids fired on them, hitting Kaiden in his shoulder and cracking his armor.

"We're doing something, assholes," Kaiden yelled. He handed Genos' other arm to the infiltrator, picked up his Raptor, and shot their heads to pieces.

"You all right, Genos?" Chiyo asked as she dragged the Tsuna up.

The mechanist looked back into the pit. "Certainly better than I could have been."

The ace chuckled as he stood. *"Hey, partner, might wanna take a look back at the perimeter,"* Chief suggested.

He looked up and saw a large circular grid around the maze which began to slowly move inward, burning through the walls as it contracted.

"You know what? I'm not even going to get mad." He heard the metallic thump of a droid behind him. Without looking back, he fired and heard it drop. "We're getting out of this, and I'm taking out the rest of my frustrations on every damn droid that's left." He vented his rifle and looked at his team. "Let's run with pep in our step, shall we?"

They dashed down the corridor, and more Assault and Guardian droids appeared. "Don't stop for a damn thing!" Kaiden ordered as he leaped over a static trap and fired ballistic shots at the feet of the droids, blowing them up or knocking them back.

They turned left at a fork in the maze to find at least a dozen more robots waiting. "Genos, seeker grenade," he ordered.

The Tsuna threw one, and it burst and took control of seven of the droids. They immediately began to fight amongst themselves as the team weaved their way through.

They turned around the corner and saw the console in the distance. "There it is," Genos shouted.

Another team was already there, their technician working on it. "Chiyo, when we get there, deactivate this maze as quick as you can," the ace demanded.

"If that technician is already plugged in and using their personal commands, we might be in conflict," she protested.

"Won't be a problem," he assured her. They made it out of the maze and Kaiden past the two other initiates and confronted the technician at the console. "You, get off."

"Do *what*? I'm under the gun as it is," the technician complained. "I don't have the time to listen to you trying to play alpha."

"What's your class?" the soldier demanded.

"I'm a translator."

"That means you work on decryption and ciphers. Hacking isn't your forte," Kaiden pointed out.

"I'm working with what I've got."

"Our tech is an infiltrator. She'll get this done quicker." Kaiden tried to be reasonable, but his tone was curt.

"You see those lasers? They're going to dice us in a couple minutes," the translator yelled. The ace could feel his patience wearing thin. "I unplug now, and we have to start over. There's no way she's good enough to—gah!" The translator hit the floor from the force of Kaiden's punch.

"What the hell?" one of the translator's teammates roared and raised his machine gun as his demolitionist teammate readied his cannon.

"Chiyo, get on there," Kaiden stated and raised his rifle as Genos stood beside him with his cannon ready. She nodded and set to work.

"You would risk all our lives to get some extra Data points?" the demolitionist growled.

"You think I'm that pedantic?" he sneered before cocking his head. "Well, honestly, I might be. But my team's infiltrator is one of the best in our year. Hell, maybe in the entire school. I don't wanna risk my neck so your translator can get over his feelings of technician inadequacy."

"We're only a minute and change from getting seared. There's no way she can get it done in—"

"Finished," Chiyo declared. The laser grid disappeared, and the walls retracted. Kaiden peered to the side to see the remaining bots disappear.

"You were saying?" he asked cockily.

The two of them looked at each other and lowered their

weapons. The one with the machine gun went over to help the translator up.

"You're lucky this didn't come to blows," the demolitionist snarled. "It would have been a quick ending to the test for you."

"I doubt that. In these close quarters, that cannon you keep stroking like a phallus would blow you and your buddies up if you tried to shoot me." Kaiden sneered.

"Smartass. I've already run into plenty of scrubs like you. All bluster because we can't actually fight right now. If Honor was actually on, you would be nothing but fried guts," he threatened.

"Attention, remaining squad test participants." Head Monitor Zhang's voice echoed throughout the room, his face appearing on a holomonitor. "Congratulations on getting this far into the test. From this point on, Honor is active and friendly fire is enabled. Choose your targets carefully, and best of luck to those who remain." The monitor disappeared, and silence filled the air.

"Wait, w-what happened?" the demolitionist stammered. He felt something against his head and turned slowly to see the ace pressing the barrel of his rifle against his helmet.

"You were just talking that good shit," Kaiden goaded, hitting the switch for ballistic rounds. "Wanna follow it up?"

CHAPTER TWENTY-EIGHT

The demolitionist was silent, sweat forming under his helmet. Kaiden tapped the trigger of his rifle threateningly and heard the metallic clink of rustling armor and a gun being primed. He looked over to see the man's teammates aiming their weapons at him. Genos pointed his cannon at the duo as Chiyo walked calmly between them and Kaiden with her Scorpio in her hand.

"All of you need to calm down," she ordered, looking at the opposing team and then at Kaiden. "Honor may be in play now, but that is no reason to immediately start killing one another. There is still a lot of time remaining in the test, and we just unlocked all the passages again. We can agree to lay down our arms for now and leave—"

"Or, we can take all of you out now and grab some extra points while we're here," a voice declared. Chiyo looked back to see a raider holding a hand cannon pointed at her. "This is a deathmatch, right? I'm just playing by the rules." Kaiden spun to fire at the raider as he began to pull the trigger, but a shot rang out and the cannon whipped out of the man's hand. The raider cried out in pain and raised a now-bloody hand with a metal spike through it.

"You forgetting about everyone else in here?" Flynn asked, his sniper rifle still at the ready. "Unfortunately for you, I happen to like them more than you."

Marlo walked up, his cannon in his grasp. "Same here. I suggest you all listen to Chiyo's suggestion and simply turn around and walk the hell back to where you came from."

The intensity in the room continued to build. All the initiates looked nervously at one another, waiting for someone to make a decisive move.

"You forgetting how many people are in here? Even if you two teams are buddy-buddy, that still leaves eighteen others. You think you can take them all?" the raider growled as he yanked the spike out of his hand.

"I would be worried more if I were facing a group of soldiers. But I spy plenty of guys and girls here from the medical, logistics, and technician divisions. Nothing too frightening, really." Flynn paused for a moment before looking at Chiyo. "Except you, Chi. You've proven yourself to be just fine with a weapon."

"I appreciate the compliment, but I'm still trying to not make it come to that," she stated solemnly.

"How many of you— Oh no, you don't," Kaiden warned, holding his Raptor in one hand while he grabbed Debonair and placed it under the demolitionist's chin. The man had tried to inch his hand toward his hand cannon, but he now froze. "As I was saying, how many of you think you have enough points to pass? We've been in here a few hours, so maybe most or all of you do, but I'm guessing you'll be on the bottom rungs of the rankings. Piss-sad way to end the year, don't you think?"

"You keep talking like you're trying to stop a fight from breaking out, but you look like the one most likely to pull something," another voice in the room challenged.

"To be fair, that is pretty accurate, Kaiden," Amber pointed out.

"Normally, yes, but we're trying to do a thing, and as much I would enjoy a good brawl with lasers and explosions, that wouldn't really help at the moment." He paused. "Hey, Flynn, what floor are we on?"

The marksman shook his head slightly, not lowering his rifle. "You lose count on the way here?"

"The short story is we fell through a teleporter, so I don't know where we ended up."

"We're in the sub-levels," another initiate yelled. "Six floors down from the ground level."

"Oh, so we only went up one floor," Genos noted. "Fortuitous."

"At least there's another rando in here who's helpful." The ace grinned. "All right, so we all good? Everyone willing to just put away the weapons and leave here nice and—"

"*Kaiden!*" Chief exclaimed.

He grunted, stopping his negotiations. "I'm kinda busy if you haven't noticed." He growled his annoyance under his breath.

"*Kinda important. I'm picking up an energy reading. It's the same one that corresponds to a hologram field.*"

"Which means what? It's left over from the maze, probably."

"No, it's small and moving. There's a doppel-bot in here."

Kaiden froze for a moment, looking at Chiyo who opened her holoscreen. Apparently, Kaitō had discovered it too. "Can you pinpoint it?"

"No, the trail is faint and I only detected it just now. Usually the emissions are too small to notice without upgrades or specific equipment. That means it's been in here long enough for it to be noticeable. The best I can give you is a general direction —northeast."

Kaiden gazed in that direction and saw eight other initiates either staring at him or looking at the others. He took a deep breath and lowered his weapon slowly. "Let's let bygones be bygones, all right?" he asked the demolitionist as he placed his rifle on his back. "Name's Kaiden Jericho, an ace in the soldier division. If you're looking to settle the score some other time, just come and find me."

The demolitionist seemed taken aback for a moment, as if recognizing the name. The ace walked over to Chiyo, and Genos put his cannon away and followed behind him.

The infiltrator looked up from her screen. "There appears to be a—"

"Doppel-bot, yeah. Chief told me. Said he doesn't know exactly where it is, but he mentioned it might be over there." Kaiden nodded in the direction of the potential threat. "Should we warn the others?"

"Honestly, I don't know if that will help or hurt the situation," she admitted and continued to type.

"The other technicians and engineers should pick up on it soon enough. Maybe it's best that we allow them to discover it on their own, otherwise they may think it's a ruse on our part," Genos reasoned.

"Unless the bot makes a move before everyone else clues in. That's probably why it's here," Kaiden countered, keeping a hand on Debonair as he holstered it under his coat. He motioned behind his back for Flynn and his team to join them. "We need to either find it and take it out or get the hell out of Dodge."

"What going on, mates?" the marksman asked as he joined the trio.

"We have a bit of a problem."

"I think we've picked up on that." Amber scanned the room as a few initiates began to back away from the center to the doors as others still fidgeted, tapping fingers on their guns.

"It's more than that. This powder keg might blow without any action on our part," Kaiden stated.

"Why?"

"Kaiden, there's more," Chiyo interjected.

The ace grimaced. "What now?"

"I'm detecting multiple emissions—same type. There's more than one bot in here," she revealed as she closed her screen and held up her pistol. "They are going to take action soon. We need to—"

She stopped speaking as a weapon fired twice and a body fell to the floor. The six of them turned to see the translator who had worked on the console before lying on the ground, unmoving. Behind him stood an initiate in light armor still pointing a pistol at his body. It fired again, and the translator vanished in white light.

"What the hell did you do that for?" his teammate snapped and aimed his machine gun at him. Another shot came from the west and the initiate stumbled to the side for a moment, dropping his gun. He turned to reveal a smoking hole in his helmet. The man toppled to the floor but disappeared before he made impact.

"Mario," the demolitionist shouted and pointed his cannon in the direction of the shot. "You'll pay for that, you coward. You *bitch*," he roared as he fired a half-charged blast from his weapon. Although it was only partially charged, it would be enough to kill anyone in medium or light armor. Two initiates dove out of the way of the blast as it sailed at a marksman in faded gray armor. He turned invisible as he activated a stealth generator. The blast hit nothing but a wall and left a crater in its wake.

As the demolitionist looked angrily around for the attacker, he switched his attention to the initiate who killed the translator. But before he could fire, there was an explosion behind him. They all looked back to see three initiates on the floor, knocked down by a thermal grenade. Two of them quickly scrambled up, turning to check up on their teammate who was slowly getting to her feet. But as she stood, a blade erupted from her chest. Another soldier behind her ripped the knife out as she was de-synced.

More sniper shots rang out, followed by another explosion. Initiates dodged the attacks or fired back, and the room erupted into chaos.

"Dammit," the ace snarled, replacing Debonair with his Raptor and firing into the madness. "So much for settling this peacefully."

"We need to leave," Chiyo shouted, covering Kaiden's side and firing into the crowd. "We're too exposed in here. We're in just as much danger of falling to stray fire as focused fire."

Genos took his rifle from his back and covered their other flank. "We are still in a position to continue with our original plan, but I agree that we need to make our way out of this room."

Kaiden spotted a marksman taking aim from the far end of the room. He switched to ballistics and fired three rounds, one hitting him in the chest as the others impacted the wall behind him. The body fell out of the smoke, and the armor faded away as it revealed the slim mechanical body of the doppel-bot.

"Pesky bastard." He grunted and saw a rocket fly through the air, soaring past Genos before pivoting forty-five degrees and detonating while still airborne. "Pick a door and move," he ordered. "Flynn, we're getting out of here. You coming?"

"Little busy," Flynn responded, taking a shot at a raider who fired wildly around the room. The shot skewered the man's arm and halted his frantic shooting before Flynn followed it up with a shot through his helmet. The body disappeared, dropping the red Honor points icon in its place.

"How come the other initiates didn't drop anything when they died?" Kaiden asked.

"Because they were killed by doppels, not other initiates. It should have tipped the others off, but the shock probably meant they weren't thinking straight," Chief explained. His eye went wide. *"Kaiden, your left."*

Kaiden saw the initiate with the blade charge toward him. Chiyo turned and fired several shots. The attacker blocked some of them with their free arm as it lunged at them. The ace flipped his rifle around, strafing to the side as the other initiate lashed out. He knocked the blade away and then slammed the end of his rifle into the aggressor's helmet. It cracked, and for a moment, it became a blurry image and the head of the doppel-bot underneath. Chiyo kicked it to the floor, firing five more shots into its chest before her gun ran out of ammo. The initiate twitched for a moment before falling still, and the hologram disappeared to reveal another defeated bot.

"Two for three," he sneered. "We have an opening now, so let's get out of—"

"*Look out,*" the infiltrator shouted, pushing Genos down before she leaped at Kaiden and knocked him over. The two rolled on the floor for a moment as he heard a crackling noise overhead, followed by a loud explosion. He looked up to see the demolitionist in the distance, looking at them while charging his cannon.

"What's wrong with you?" he hollered.

"This is your fault, you asshole," the other man barked. "We could have been out of here by now if it wasn't for you and—"

"Don't pin this on me. Those were doppel-bots," he snapped back. "Can your bitching and piss off. We're getting out of here. If you stay here and keep attacking people while you're all alone, you're going to die."

"I'll take you with me," he roared, pointing his cannon at Kaiden and Chiyo. "Then I'll find you back in the Academy and kick your ass again."

The ace's first instinct was to take aim and shoot to knock him back or destroy the cannon, but he no longer had his Raptor. He'd lost it when he tumbled. As he watched the demolitionist's cannon nearly reach full power, he saw Marlo run over and shoulder-tackle him to the ground. The cannon went off and a shot skimmed just above the ground. It caught the back of the leg of an unfortunate initiate in its path, where it exploded, vaporizing the initiate in a blast of plasma energy.

The demolitionist rolled over and tried to stand, only to be greeted by Marlo's boot on his chest as the fellow demolitionist pointed his own cannon at him. "You're a real idiot," he muttered, slowly pressing the trigger. His cannon stirred and began charging. "Attacking Kaiden was a bad move, but even worse was doing it around a demolitionist who is better than you." He kicked the demolitionist, who skidded a few feet away. "Who happens to be a friend of his." The titan fired the partially charged blast right at the demolitionist on the ground. The blast destroyed most of the armor and fried the exposed skin. The man was thrown back and rolled across the floor, his skin sizzling and charred. He took a few ragged breaths before trying to reach for his hand cannon, but his hand stopped moving and fell to the side as he de-synced in another flash of white light.

"Nice save, Marlo," Kaiden said, thanking the big man as he helped Chiyo to her feet.

"Not a problem. I like making sure that my fellow heavies remember their place." He scowled. "The bigger you are, the more you gotta stay humble. Plus, he was an ass."

"Just took out a doppel," Flynn announced. "Was that the last of them?"

"I took out two of them. I only saw three, so I would imagine so," the ace affirmed.

"We would appear to be the last ones in here," Genos noted, looking around the chamber. "The rest have either fled or"—he looked at the broken or charred pieces of armor and weapons strewn about the room—"have been incapacitated."

"Then we're in the clear." The marksman sighed. "For now, my guess is there are plenty of bloodthirsty initiates running around along with all the other problems we have waiting for us."

"Does anyone need a patch-up?" Amber asked, taking out her stim ray.

"I think we're good," Kaiden said, looking at his team and seeing no critical injuries. "Might check Chiyo. It looks like she got a little banged up, but we seem to be in pretty…good… Why am I woozy?"

"Kaiden, you're bleeding, mate," Flynn shouted.

He looked down to see blood pouring from his left leg and the right side of his chest. "When did that…happen?" His words were slurred.

Genos walked behind him and placed his hands on his shoulders to ease him to the ground. "We were shot at from all sides. Like Chiyo said, we were as likely to be hit by stray fire as from direct attacks."

"Laser fire, from the looks of it," Chiyo said, examining the wound on Kaiden's leg. "The wound is cauterized but he's still lost a lot of blood, probably from a kinetic shot," she surmised. "Here on his chest, next to his ribs. You're lucky your armor took most of the impact. There's another one here on his shoulder." She placed a hand next to the injury.

"*Ow!* Chiyo!" Kaiden winced.

"Oh... Sorry, Kaiden," she apologized and pulled her hand away.

"Let me take a look." Amber hurried over and ran her stim ray over the wounds.

"Maybe it's a bad time to mention this, but it's kinda nice to see you can be wounded, Kai," Marlo admitted. The ace cocked his head and looked questioningly at him. The titan held a hand up defensively. "I mean, most of the time, I see you shake it off or work through it. Been awhile since I've seen you take real damage."

"Don't forget the times he's blown himself up or gotten himself killed doing some stupid stunt." Flynn chuckled.

"Might I remind you that the first time you saw me get blown up was to help you beat that war machine in the Division Test?" Kaiden pointed out.

"I'm just saying it makes you seem a bit more human, you know?" Marlo stated.

"Kaiden has always appeared to be one hundred percent human to me, just as all of you do," Genos interjected.

"You saying we all look alike to you?" Flynn asked sarcastically.

"Human, huh?" Kaiden hummed wistfully, then winced as Amber ran her hands over the wound on his ribs. "Considering how I'm feeling right now, being human bites."

CHAPTER TWENTY-NINE

Genos picked up the last of the Honor point icons littering the floor, then watched it burst open and signal that he was awarded two hundred points. He looked across the room to see Flynn pick up the last of his batch, nodding to him as they walked back to the group.

"All finished?" Marlo asked.

"Yep, that's the last of the bunch. Hell of a crazy moment there, but it was good for the score," Flynn mused. "You finished as well, Amber?"

"He's all patched up." She nodded and helped Kaiden to his feet.

"Feeling better?" Chiyo asked.

He rolled his shoulder and stretched his leg. "Yeah, much better. That stim ray of yours is a lifesaver. Even healing serum still leaves aches."

"We keep her around for a good reason." Flynn chuckled, earning a cross-armed glare from the battle medic.

"Keep it up. I'm the one in control of the painkillers." She huffed dramatically.

"It doesn't look like there's any reason for us to stay here," Chiyo stated. "Even the console has shut down."

"Then I guess let's get out of here." Kaiden glanced at Flynn. "Thanks for the help during all that."

"No worries, mate. We'll get together and compare who owes who later." The marksman chuckled.

"Where are you guys heading now?" Marlo asked.

"We're heading deeper into the sublevels."

Flynn cocked his head. "We had just run through the bottom level. There's nothing down there but a giant cave system, which we found while wandering around the island. We were lost for ages, shooting the occasional bot or merc we found, but nothing much else. At one point, we thought of trying to double back until we happened to stumble onto the service elevator that brought us up here. What are you hoping to find?"

The ace looked at Chiyo, wondering if he should explain their plan to the others. She shrugged and nodded, giving him the go-ahead. "We're searching for something—testing a theory of ours."

"What kind of theory?" Amber asked.

"We think there's some sort of EI in the system, guiding things along. It's the reason these maps and scenarios change so often and so rapidly with so little error or warning. We figure if we find it, that could be the real way to 'win' that the head monitor mentioned during the orientation."

Flynn, Marlo, and Amber traded looks before turning

back to Kaiden. "You're willing to risk everything on that?" the marksman inquired.

"It's not like we haven't been getting points along the way." Kaiden shrugged. "Been dealing with plenty of bullshit on the way here. I thought about saying 'screw it' a couple of times now. Think about it from my perspective. I'm choosing to play a game of hide and seek instead of seeing if I can beat my personal headshot high score."

"Which is why it's all the more baffling that you want to possibly toss it all away on a hunch."

"I suppose it's my competitive nature," Kaiden said with a shrug, "The way Zhang was talking about this... I don't know, it made it seem like the victory would be hollow if we didn't follow the 'ancient path' or whatever you wanna call it. Only one other team was able to do it. I've taken all the other records so far this year, and I wanna go for the three-peat."

"That certainly seems more like your style," Marlo agreed with a laugh.

Kaiden chuckled, nodding at his teammates. "Plus. Chiyo did all the research to find out about this in the first place, and Genos has been a hell of a good sport up until now. They both wanna try it this way, and I think they deserve the chance. This is supposed to be a Squad Test, after all—democracy and all that."

"You'd choose a Squad Test over a Deathmatch?" Flynn snickered, his tone almost disbelieving. "Hard to believe you'd do something so selfless—getting all mature and shit right before our eyes."

"You should follow suit sometime soon," Amber teased.

"Keep it up. Remember who's the best shot here," he retorted playfully.

"You should remember who has the big-ass cannon," Marlo jeered, placing said cannon against his chest. "And that I like Amber better than you."

"Oy, I was only playing," the marksman pleaded theatrically. "We're all being friendly, right?"

"Where are you guys heading then?" Kaiden asked.

"Up, I guess?" Amber made it a question.

Flynn nodded. "We'd stick with ya, but I feel like we'd get in your way. None of us have any clue what you're talking about, and like I said, we almost got lost down there."

"Yeah, no offense meant, but we'll stick to doing this the old-fashioned way," Marlo added.

"But hey, if you do win, we'll do our best to be a close second," Amber promised.

"Really shooting for the stars there." The marksman chuckled.

"We'll be rooting for ya while dodging whatever else this place throws at us," Kaiden said, his tone encouraging as he gave them a thumbs-up. "By the way, you mentioned an elevator? Which way to it?"

"It's down the hall from where we came in." Flynn turned and pointed to the right wing of the room. "Go through the doorway and down— What was that?" he asked. He and others began to lose their balance as the room seemed to shift.

"Is that stupid maze starting back up again? Was it on a timer?" Kaiden asked.

"No, I made sure to shut it down," Chiyo responded. "This isn't linked to anything. The room is changing."

"To what?" Marlo exclaimed.

"*Look out,*" Genos yelped and jumped back. "The floor. It's disappearing."

Kaiden saw a small hole form in the center of the room. It expanded, growing wider as it inched toward them.

"Fuck. This. *Place,*" he roared.

"Move," Flynn ordered. They all ran to the end of the room. The ceiling above them began to crack and shatter, sending chunks of metal and rock crashing to the floor. They dodged the falling debris, losing speed and momentum as they tried not to get crushed.

"Bots," Amber shouted as several Assault droids appeared in front of them. They opened fire with their shock pistols and pulse rifles. Their weapons weren't much of a physical threat, but if they were hit, they could be stunned and fall into the growing pit.

"Keep moving," Kaiden demanded, yanking out his rifle, and fired ballistic rounds at the group of droids, destroying two or three with one blast. He was nearly out of ballistic rounds, but he didn't have time to shoot them down one by one.

"More droids," Flynn warned, sending several shots clean through the heads of the new batch of attackers. "We made a path. Get through— Shit!" he cursed as he slipped and almost fell through another hole that had formed beneath him.

"*Flynn,*" Amber shouted.

Chiyo ran up and reached down to help him. "The entire

room is destabilizing. We don't have enough—" Another hole appeared beneath her. One of her feet slid through, and she fell to the floor. The gap widened as she held onto the marksman, and only a small bridge of flooring kept them from plummeting down as the original rift continued to widen.

"Genos, take out as many as you can and then get out," Kaiden called. The Tsuna nodded, charged his cannon, and sent a blast at a team of droids as they were teleported into the room. They were barely able to take a step before they were scattered by the explosion. Kaiden put his rifle away and dashed toward Chiyo. Marlo was already making his way there.

The demolisher reached Chiyo first. The hole she was in danger of falling into widened, and she lost the edge she was holding on to. He gripped the neck of her armor and pulled her up, tossing her out of harm's way into Kaiden's arms as he turned his focus to Flynn. The marksman had already slipped, and when Marlo reached out to grab him, he just missed his hand and he began to fall into the abyss below. The titan pressed a button on his chest, and his cannon fell from his back as he jumped into the hole.

Kaiden helped Chiyo to stand and pushed her toward the doorway before running over. He grabbed Flynn's sniper rifle as he ran, expecting to see nothing but a dark pit. He hoped that Marlo had made it in time. As he danced along the edges of the many forming pits and out of the way of the falling debris, he saw Flynn fly out of the hole.

"Marlo," the marksman screamed as he turned and looked back into the pit.

"Flynn, what happened?" the ace asked, holding the

marksman back. He seemed to be reaching back into the rift.

"Marlo jumped in. He grabbed me and activated his bouncepack. It looked like we would make it but it died before we got to the edge. He tossed me back up," the man explained, his tone frenetic and breathy. "He fell back in…"

Kaiden was shocked, silent for a moment before he felt the ground around him begin to give way. "We have to go," he shouted, shaking Flynn's shoulder. "We're going to be next if we stay. *Move!*"

The marksman snapped out of it, nodding as he stood and jumped across a ravine. They made their way back to the edge of the room. Genos helped them across and took out another two droids in the process. They ran out into the hallway and Kaiden slammed the button to shut the doors. As they closed, he fell against the wall and slid down, taking a deep breath. "Everyone all right?"

Amber, Chiyo, and Genos nodded. The battle medic walked over to Flynn. "What happened? Where's Marlo?"

"Lost him. He saved me from falling, but he didn't make it back," he lamented.

She pressed a hand to her chest and looked down. "I'm sorry, but you know that he's all right, yes? This is the Animus. He's waking up in his pod right now."

Flynn leaned back, his helmet knocking against the wall. "Yeah, yeah, of course, I do. But for a moment— Maybe I got swept up in the whole thing, or I wasn't thinking straight because I was about to be the one to fall, but… I honestly thought I lost him there, even if it was only for a single second."

The others glanced at him before looking at each other.

JOSHUA ANDERLE & MICHAEL ANDERLE

Over the school year, Kaiden had been in dozens of training sessions and missions with the marksman, but he had never seen him act like this after one of them had fallen, even Marlo. He wondered if it was getting to him after all this time.

Flynn placed two fingers on the side of his helmet. "Hey, mate, thanks for that. I'll be sure that Amber and I end this on a high note for you."

Chiyo walked over and knelt beside him. "There aren't any outgoing comms during a test, Flynn. He can't hear you," she reminded him, placing a hand over his.

"Yeah, you're right. I'm an idiot." He sighed and lowered his hand. "Thanks for your help too, Kaiden." He rolled his head toward the ace.

"We'll tally up who owes who after all this, right?" Kaiden said, repeating the marksman's words back to him.

Flynn chuckled quietly and nodded. "Yeah, gonna be a lot of tallies on that list after all this."

"No doubt," Kaiden assured him. He held Flynn's sniper rifle up. "I'm assuming you'll want this back?"

"I'd let you take it for a spin"—the marksman stood and gripped the barrel—"but since I'm still kicking, it'll be at its best in my hands."

The ace smiled as he released it. Flynn took it firmly into his hands. "I'd usually say something snarky at this point, but I saw how quickly you took out those bots and a few of those initiates. I'd have to say that you are quite adequate."

"You're ever so kind, partner," the marksman jeered in a mock southern accent.

"Is he mocking us?" Chief asked, his eye furrowing in the HUD.

"I can't tell. His accent sounds pretty close to yours, honestly." He snickered.

Chief rolled his eye. *"Ha ha. Since we've got a couple minutes of peace now, I should let you know that since Honor is now in play, we have the current total of initiates available for display."*

"What are we looking at?" Kaiden asked, and a small scoreboard appeared in his visor.

Total Initiates: 103 / 300

Teams Represented: 48 / 100

Current Time: 7 Hrs. 22 Min.

"Wait, there's one hundred and three initiates remaining and forty-eight teams? How does that math add up?"

"Forty-eight teams represented, meaning there's still at least one member on a team. The remaining one hundred and three initiates don't all have their teams still complete.

"Those guys won't last long," he mused.

"No kidding. Two more just bit the dust."

"Not to mention it's been over seven hours. Once that headcount gets lower and a bit more time passes, they're gonna start deleting rooms and all that." Kaiden looked at the door. "They might have already started."

"Then we need to carry on," Genos stated.

"Right." The ace nodded. "Flynn, Amber, which way to the elevator?"

"It should be down the hall and to the left unless things have switched around," Amber said.

"Quite possible," Chiyo agreed. "But it's an easy fix—or easier when compared to everything else."

"We're going to head down," Kaiden said.

"Is that offer to join you still available?" Flynn asked as he switched out the magazine on his rifle.

He looked up in surprise. "Of course, but I thought you said you wanted to do your own thing."

"Well, we're down our big gun, and the numbers are beginning to bleed out. Best we can hope to do once we get up there is maybe take care of the scraps or hope we run into a few different scenarios for Amber to grab some Motes. But, if it turns out you are right about your little theory, I honestly think it would be kinda boring to go and play clean-up instead of watching you take on an omniscient EI."

"I would certainly have to agree with that." Kaiden chortled.

The marksman slung his rifle over his shoulder. "What do you think, Amber? Should we tag along?"

She took out her submachine gun and nodded. "I'll stand by for when you two inevitably take your hits doing your little super-soldier tag-team bit." She looked at Chiyo and Genos. "Plus, it will be nice to tag along with a couple of people with their heads screwed on straight for a change."

"So, is she insulting us or is she merely being passive-aggressive?" the ace pondered.

"She's being insulting passive-aggressively," Flynn stated firmly.

The Tsuna moved his hands around his neck. "My head seems to be aligned just like anyone else's."

"Is he being funny or naïve?" the marksman asked

"He's funny because he's naïve," Kaiden answered.

The two laughed, Kaiden nudging the other man playfully as the group set off to the elevators—and to hopefully bring an end to the test.

CHAPTER THIRTY

"This is the slowest elevator I have ever ridden," Kaiden grumbled, tapping his foot impatiently on the floor as the cables continued to whir just outside the caged box that constituted their ride.

"'Service' is a relative term here," Amber joked.

"We seem to be in a rather disadvantageous situation should anyone attack," Genos noted, looking around the rickety and slipshod container. "Even weak weapons could reach us through the cage."

"We'll get down there eventually." Flynn shrugged, leaning against the side of the box. "Like I said, I doubt there're gonna be too many threats down here. Most initiates are probably up top, and whatever is left over down here, the five of us can take on no problem."

"You are forgetting the primary reason we came here," Chiyo stated. "If the Director EI is here and we find it, I doubt it'll let us take it over or disable it without recourse."

"It can try," Kaiden challenged. "Everything it has sent our way has been more annoying than deadly."

"What if it summons another group of those mohos?" Genos asked, tapping the remainder of his helmet. "We did not fare too well against them."

The ace coughed and looked sheepishly to the side. "True, but... Um, we don't have to worry about lava this time around."

"Unless it warps some in," Chiyo pointed out.

"Would you stop that? I'm trying to keep all this bravado going, and you are not helping," he grumped.

"Just remember to hold yourself back, mate. This is new for all of us." He knocked a hand against Kaiden's shoulder. "You'll get your chance to take out your big bad EI—assuming we find it, of course."

"What should we do if we don't?" Amber inquired. "Not to spoil the mood, but we should have a Plan B."

"I suppose we'll either have to come back here and make our way up to the building proper," Chiyo suggested. "That or see if we can find an entrance out of the cave and onto the island, and head back that way."

"I should have left a trail of some kind." Flynn sighed.

"You really think it would still be here?" Kaiden asked.

The marksman looked at him, a little startled. "That's a good point. We didn't see anything change when we were making our way through the first time, but it could all be totally different now."

"It could, but I have a plan to track the EI," the infiltrator revealed.

"Do you, now? Wanna share or would that compromise the situation?" the ace snarked.

"I can, but it involves a lot of explanation of EI systems and theories about the Animus overlay."

"Pass." Kaiden grinned.

"Same. I'll take your word for it," Flynn muttered, looking at the back of the elevator and the rock wall visible through the cage as if it were a much more interesting object to study.

"I would like to hear your plan, friend Chiyo," Genos said tentatively.

"Same here. *I* like to know what the plan is before heading into a potentially dangerous situation." Amber glared at the ace and the marksman.

"That's because you're boring." The ace snickered.

"Why do both of you think it's smart to pick on the medic?" Amber huffed in a show of annoyance.

"We don't, but hey, laughter is medicine too," the marksman reasoned.

"See how much good it does compared to serum when your arm gets blown off," she warned.

"I'll be sure to take notes," Kaiden retorted.

Amber sighed and shook her head, turning to address Chiyo again. "So what are you thinking, Chi?"

The infiltrator activated the tablet on her wrist. "When we get down there, I'll send a directive to all of your EIs to search for— Wait, do you hear that?"

The ace looked up and listened intently. Over the creaking of the elevator and hum of machinery, he heard the sound of rushing air. It was faint and sounded like it came from the distance, neither above nor below them.

"That sounds like something flying at high speed—too small to be a ship or plane, but maybe a drone?"

"Too fast," Flynn countered, taking out his sniper rifle. "That's a rocket."

Kaiden looked over as the front of the elevator finally descended past the rock walls and revealed a city below them. It was a re-creation of a metropolis, but he couldn't discern which city. The terrain was post-apocalyptic, the streets broken and cracked and vehicles and buildings abandoned and in various states of dilapidation. As he looked at the new scenery, the marksman raised his rifle and fired. There was an explosion in the sky as he shot the missile out of the air.

"Hostiles? Where?" the ace demanded.

Genos leaned against the fencing. "Initiates—a team of three below."

"Assholes. At least wait for us to get out of this cage before you try to blow us up."

"Attack of opportunity, Kaiden. They're gonna take it." Flynn tried to take aim at the three. "I can't get an angle at this height. Everyone back up and wait until— Oh, bloody hell. They're gonna shoot the elevator line at the bottom."

"Everyone get close to me," Kaiden ordered. A rocket launcher fired as the other four initiates surrounded him and he pointed his barrier downward and activated it. An explosion rocked the elevator, and it slid down for a moment before catching. The ace tried to look up to see if they would be fired at again before hearing a vicious snap as the elevator went into freefall.

The barrier broke their fall before it snapped into pieces. Kaiden and Flynn rolled forward and kicked the elevator's doors open. Another rocket flew toward them that the marksman shot down as soon as he had visual. The soldier grabbed a thermal and activated it, throwing it at the trio of initiates. They scattered before it went off, buying the group some time to recover.

"Is everyone all right?" Flynn asked, going back to help the other three.

"I'm okay, what about the women?" Genos asked worriedly as he pushed himself up and took out his rifle.

"I'm okay, but Chiyo..." Amber fretted, as she looked at the infiltrator.

"My leg. I didn't land properly. It's broken." She gasped, wincing as Amber tried to help her up.

"Kaiden, Genos. Give us some cover fire," Flynn ordered. The Tsuna nodded as he went to assist Kaiden, who was already engaging the enemy team.

"We're exposed here. We have to move you," the marksman explained, taking her other arm over his shoulder.

"This will help with the pain until I can treat you properly," Amber stated, injecting a vial of painkiller into her neck through a tear on her underlay.

Chiyo nodded, clearly dazed, and the two of them dragged her behind a broken van as the other two continued to fight.

"Genos, charge your cannon," Kaiden yelled. His teammate nodded, dropping his rifle and switching weapons. As he began to charge it, the ace took out another thermal, not activating it before as he tossed it to the left of two of the hostile initiates. They didn't seem to notice that it wasn't armed as they both dashed to the right to get away from it. Genos saw his opportunity and fired a charged blast at the two. One looked up just in time to see the glowing orb barreling down on them.

They were both caught in the explosion. Kaiden watched as their forms melted and disappeared in the now-familiar white flash.

"Dammit!" He heard the remaining enemy curse. The ace ran over to the unexploded thermal, watching as the soldier rearmed his rocket launcher and turned to shoot him. Kaiden slid down and snatched the grenade, pressed the button to activate it, and held it down to let the explosive cook.

As the soldier lined up his shot, his rocket launcher was knocked away by a quick shot from Flynn's sniper rifle. Kaiden used the opportunity to lob the grenade at the enemy. He tipped backward, trying to get away, but the device went off right in his face. The explosion blew him off the pile of debris that he was standing on and he crashed to the pavement, his helmet and armor broken. Blood seeped from him as he lay on the ground for a moment before he de-synced.

"Good riddance," Flynn sneered as he walked over to Kaiden. "Good moves, mate."

"Nice shooting," the soldier responded, pushing to his feet. "How's Chiyo?"

"Amber is looking her over now." The marksman looked around for a moment. "Don't see anyone else. This sure isn't a cave system anymore."

"No kidding," he murmured. "This is sprawling. It looks like it goes on for miles. How the hell are we gonna find this thing in here?"

"I guess we should have listened to what Chiyo was

thinking," his companion admitted. He held up his rifle and flicked a thumb behind him. "Go ahead and check on her. I'll keep watch."

"Appreciate it." Kaiden jogged over to the others.

Genos was already there, kneeling beside Amber as she ran her stim ray over their teammate. "You doing all right, Chiyo?" the ace asked, concern filling his voice as he saw the shape of her leg.

"I have something to deal with breaks and fractures, but I'm tending to her moderate injuries first," Amber explained. She took off her broken helmet, revealing her sandy blond hair and tanned skin. Her hair was matted to her skin, and she was sweating profusely, but she turned to smile at him. "Don't worry. I'll make her good as new."

"Thank you, comrade Amber. Your healing skills are invaluable," Genos proclaimed.

"It's what I do." She beamed. "'Comrade' Amber, huh? You Tsuna seem to like your titles."

"It is a sign of respect to place a title on an individual when speaking to them. Most of the others have used it sparingly or not at all to better integrate, but I find people like it," he explained.

"So comrade Amber and friend Chiyo, hmm? When do I get the friend title?" she teased as she deactivated her stim ray, put it away, and took up a small orb.

"I did not want to be presumptuous. Our personal interactions have been minimal," the alien said in apology. "But I am always happy to make new friends."

"Go ahead and consider me friend Amber from now on, you little periwinkle cinnamon roll," she teased. Turning back to Chiyo, she placed the orb above the infiltrator's tibia and pressed the switch on top. Blue liquid drained out of it, sliding down and around Chiyo's leg.

"Is that what I think it is?" Kaiden asked.

"Mom's 'proprietary' blend?" she questioned, "Kind of. It's a new thing we're trying. It's basically her serum combined with that goo the Mirus are fond of."

"Oh, right...*that*." Kaiden shivered. "The toxin sponge or whatever? How will that help a broken leg?"

"Those little goo balls have a number of uses. It basically soaks into her leg and creates tiny tendrils around her muscles and through her bones, resetting and repairing them. What should take weeks of healing with modern tech and medicine, we can heal to a useable level in about thirty minutes, depending on the break and assuming she doesn't push herself too hard."

"That may not be up to me, depending on how this goes." Chiyo pulled out her wrist tablet and tapped a few buttons. "Thank you for your help, Amber. This would have been a rather embarrassing way to end things."

"I wanna see this play out," the medic assured her. "We'll be ready to go in no time."

"Let's hope we have a place to go," she whispered and typed on her tablet for a moment before looking at Kaiden. "Please bring Chief out if you would, Kaiden."

"You heard the lady. Get out here," he ordered the EI.

"This might be a bad time, but I want to note the irony of the most cautious member of this team being the one who's getting banged up the most," Chief stated as he formed over Kaiden's shoulder before floating down toward Chiyo. *"Sorry, darlin'. If life were fair, Kaiden would be eating his meals through straws*

for several years instead of you having to take the brunt of his mistakes."

"Yeah, sure, find a way to make this my fault." He sighed. "I was the one who saved us from the fall, you know."

"It's inconsequential. I should have been better prepared for the crash," she said dismissively. "I need you to do something for me, Chief."

"What do ya need? I should warn you that my bedside manner could use some work and that I'm a shit wet nurse."

Kaiden chuckled as she shook her head. "Noted, but not needed. I need you to link up with Kaitō to boost his abilities."

"What for? I can handle whatever you need me to do."

"I'm searching for specific lines, energy readings, or transfers. I'm going through a long list. I've been doing this on every floor we've been on and found nothing. I'm guessing the EI is masked to some degree, but by searching and focusing on specific targets, I can find a trail," she explained. "I need to use my personal systems, which are linked to Kaitō, but I would like you to help by adding your power with his to hasten and expand the search. So unless Kaiden has been upgrading you with hacker talents or coding mods—"

"I've tried, but he doesn't read my Christmas lists," Chief snarked. *"All right, I'll tango with foxy. Opening a line."*

Chiyo nodded, continuing to work on her tablet as Flynn walked over. "Everything all right over here?"

"Looking much better." Kaiden nodded. "Nothing roaming out there looking to dine on our fleshy bits?"

"Not even trash mobs. This place is barren," Flynn

noted, scanning the horizon. "Not exactly well-defended. Maybe it's a hiding-in-plain-sight tactic?"

"Maybe again, this could all be a—"

"Chiyo, *wait*," Amber shouted. The two men looked back to see Chiyo standing. "Your leg still needs time. You could break it again."

"I've found it," she declared. Kaiden saw her full smile for what he realized was probably the first time since their Co-operative Test. "The Director is here."

"How can you tell?" he asked.

"I've found a stream line. It's faint, but it seems to travel all through this area—and, I would guess, through the whole map, but the farther from the source it is, the more it's hidden." She limped over to the side of the van. "It leads to that building." She pointed to a partially ruined tower in the distance. "It may be the Director itself or something connected to it, but whatever it is, we now know for certain it's here."

"It's not going anywhere." Amber fretted, trying to get Chiyo to sit down. "Let's wait for your leg to heal. It'll take half an hour. Hour tops, I promise."

"No, we need to go ahead and—" Kaiden placed a hand on her shoulder, breaking her train of thought.

"Like she said, it's probably not going anywhere, and if it does, we know what to look for now," he reasoned. "Rest up, and then we'll go. You would look pretty ridiculous limping to face the all-seeing EI."

"I'll go slowly. The medicine can work as we travel," she stated and shook him off, then tried to keep moving using the van for balance.

The ace shook his head and picked her up, an arm

under her legs and one under her back. "What are you doing?" she hissed, trying to kick him before wincing with pain.

"Tough love, although this seems tougher on you than me," he joked and placed her back on the ground. "Take an hour and let it heal. Even with the time loss, it'll probably be faster getting there than limping all the way."

Chiyo looked up and frowned before taking a deep breath and lying back. "Fine, but we're going as soon as I can walk normally."

"Fair enough. Snaps for tenacity." Kaiden winked. He looked at the building Chiyo had pointed to. "At least we can see the finish line now."

CHAPTER THIRTY-ONE

"Not exactly a very fancy evil lair," Flynn quipped as the group stood outside the entrance of the derelict building.

"I'm not sure if this Director can be considered evil or malicious. It is only following its programming," Genos reasoned.

"Well, unfortunately, it was programmed to be a pain in the ass," Kaiden grumbled belligerently, taking a moment to draw Debonair and check it before sliding it back into its holster. "And we'll destroy it for that—fuck the messenger."

"I doubt we need to destroy it. I'm hoping that I can find a way to access its systems and simply deactivate it," Chiyo cautioned.

"Got this far and you won't even let me have this," he muttered, flinching slightly as Chiyo looked at him. "Fine, fine, we'll do it your way. But if that doesn't work, I'm finding a way to blow it up."

"I would be impressed if you could," she said, turning back to the entrance. "Is everyone ready?"

The group declared that they were and made their way into the building, stepping over the broken glass and metal of what was once the formal entrance. They walked into the lobby, Kaiden and Flynn on edge and awaiting an ambush.

"Still nothing here? Not even going to send a welcoming party to greet us, followed by a playful round of disembowelment and bullet-riddling?" Kaiden snarked.

"I'm beginning to take this personally. We not good enough for an extermination squad?" Flynn muttered.

"I doubt that this Director, whatever it is, is trying to whittle you down by attacking your pride," Amber countered.

"It's a pretty effective strategy, honestly," Kaiden said, looking above him to see holes in the ceiling that gave him a view of the floor above, seemingly equally barren, "I was hoping for a more climactic finish to this than just spelunking," he complained. As he took a step over a piece of jagged metal, a glowing, circular device popped up from the floor. The ace jumped back and moved to shoot it, but Genos fired first. The Tsuna hit the device with a pistol shot, attaching one of the RAAs to the device. The lights dimmed and it fell to the floor, spinning around for a moment before stilling.

"What was—"

"Typhoon mine. When triggered, it leaps in the air and deploys small explosives in a three-hundred-and-sixty-degree arc around itself. They can be rather catastrophic to small teams like ours," Genos explained. He put his cannon away but kept his pistol at the ready. "My apologies. I should have noticed them sooner, but Viola isn't running at full capacity, and I suppose I wasn't as aware as I needed to be. It would appear that we do have a few things to look out for as we continue."

"No kidding. I know I said I wanted a climactic ending, but I meant that we win, not die from an explosive frisbee," Kaiden gibed.

"If there are traps to look out for, maybe it's best that you take point, Genos," Chiyo recommended.

"Understood." The Tsuna nodded. "It might be slow going, but I'll do my part to make sure none of us are eviscerated."

"It would be appreciated," Amber said warily.

He walked to the front of the group, tapping on the device on his gauntlet. "Do we have a direction, Chiyo? I would assume that, considering the size of the building, we'll be heading upwards?"

"No, actually. It appears that all the streams are converging on this floor, not above." She looked around the room and tapped on her device. "But there are so many, it's like several spider webs laying on top of one another. It's getting harder to find a direct path."

"Then we'll keep moving until we find one. Not many places to hide here," Kaiden declared. He began to walk forward before halting next to Genos. "Uh, you first, though. You know, I think you've proven that you can take the lead from time to time."

"Certainly, I'll do my best to confirm your faith in me," the alien agreed. "Also to make sure you don't activate another trap in your haste," he concluded, taking point as he led the group deeper into the building.

"He's catching on," the ace mumbled as he followed behind.

The group combed the entirety of the floor, stopping in each room no matter how small to check for any sign or device that could lead them to their quarry. The Tsuna would have to stop occasionally to deactivate trip lines or explosives along the path. Kaiden noted that the mechanist seemed to be a surprisingly excellent shot with his little antenna pistol. He would toss pebbles into rooms to activate mines and shut them down with a flick of the wrist.

They came upon two large doors, the bottom of one bent back and both slipping from the hinges. Kaiden and Flynn walked over, slid down and through the opening, and bent one back to help the others through. They appeared to be in what was once a central conference room or lobby. Desks, chairs, screens, and other appliances and furniture lay scattered about on the edges of the room. For the most part it was empty, except that a few decorative pillars in a square pattern remained in the center of the room. The most unusual thing was that the walls were almost covered by graffiti.

"This is interesting," the ace remarked, looking at the various designs and logos. "Some of these seem to be based on works of known artists—that crown logo over there looks like a Sire Midas job. That eagle-rabbit-fish thing seems like a Ludoviko design. "

"Into street art, Kai?" Flynn asked, checking out a few of the designs.

"There's a small scene in Dallas. Can't really take off

with all the suits paying to strip them away, no matter how good they are. They prefer that clean, soulless polish in the metro area."

"I don't recall seeing many of these paintings throughout the rest of the map," Genos observed. "You think this may be a sign?"

"I do," Chiyo affirmed, deactivating her tablet and scanning the area. "There is a confluence here. There has to be something linking to the Director, but I can't see anything."

"Maybe it's hiding behind a stealth generator or something?" Amber suggested.

"In a wide-open area? Not a very smart use of that. Kaiden could simply spin in a circle and fire to look for it." Flynn chuckled.

"Can I?" the ace asked, holding his rifle up and looking at Chiyo.

"Please refrain from that for now. I don't think it will help," She stated. "My guess is that the Director is in a different area. What I'm reading could be a command console or a linked node."

"Maybe the Director is smaller?" Amber suggested. "I mean, I think we're all thinking it's some giant glowing being with a dozen eyes or something fantastical like that. It might not be much bigger than Chief, and could be floating around over our heads maybe?" She looked up as if it were hiding right above her.

"*Nah, when it comes to EIs, size matters,*" Chief said, appearing above her and looking down. "*Something with that much juice and power would have a large figure. From what Chiyo discovered, it looks like it was based on mainframe EI models. Those things can get massive, and are usually contained in their own separate unit. Like a super-sized version of an EI pad."*

"Well, I'm certainly not seeing the Wizard of Oz floating around here," Flynn muttered. "And any console or computer I see is wrecked, so unless there is a— What are you staring at, Kaiden?"

The ace was near the wall on the far end of the right side of the room, looking at one of the logos on the wall. "It's this emblem. It looks familiar, but it doesn't seem like any style I know. I feel like I should know it, but I can't put my finger on it." The design was three lines connecting in the middle to create a triangular pattern. At the tip of each line was a different symbol—a circle with a line going vertically through it at the top mark, an octagon at the bottom left, and what looked like a spiraling branch on the bottom right.

"It's the old symbol for the EI project," Chiyo stated.

"Each line was supposed to represent a facet of what EIs were. Top means tech, left means adaptation, and right means evolution," Chief explained. *"The idea behind all EIs was to be the first in a series of projects that would create self-sustaining technology that would advance over time of their own accord."*

"Rather ambitious, but that isn't exactly what happened," Kaiden noted. "They bite off more than they could chew?"

"The concept of what would be the EIs started long ago, during the time the Asiton crisis happened," Chiyo related. "I'm guessing that led to some restructuring."

"Ha! No kidding." Chief chortled.

Genos walked over to the emblem and placed a hand on

it. "Friends, this wall is irregular, like the rocks from before."

"What's he talking about?" Flynn asked.

"He means it's supposed to be a secret area," Kaiden explained.

"Destroy it, Genos. Let's see what's behind it," Chiyo ordered.

The Tsuna nodded. Taking position a few yards from the wall, he holstered his pistol and drew his cannon. "You may want to step back. Some blowback is to be expected," he advised as he began to charge the cannon.

The group took a few steps back, but as the mechanist began to aim at the wall, they heard a metallic shriek. One that made Kaiden's blood run cold. One he had grown familiar with over the year.

"Everyone, get back," he yelled, spinning around with his rifle at the ready.

"What is that?" Flynn demanded. "Where is it?"

"Above!" Genos shouted. The ace heard the floors above crash and rumble. He moved back to the doors and away from the center of the room as the roof caved in and something crashed to the ground.

It was a machine, huddled into itself. Slowly, it began to transform, its body unlatching from its legs and its arms unfolding. When it stood to full height, its head nearly touched what remained of the ceiling. The head was circular and curved down the back, and held one massive, glowing white eye. It had a sleek design—a silver body with heavy armor. Kaiden could see a few cords hidden within, glowing with an almost ethereal light. One arm carried a cannon and the other a five-fingered hand, the ends jutting out into pointed claws. It stood on hunched legs. One step forward caused the ground to shake as it scanned the team.

"Take it down," Kaiden ordered. He reached for his thermal container, feeling that there were only three left. Cautious, he gritted his teeth and held back from using them for now, deciding to wait and see what tricks this machine had to play.

"Is that an Asiton?" Flynn yelped. "Speak of the devil!"

"Not the time to be in awe, Flynn!" Kaiden barked. "Go for the head."

Flynn, Kaiden, Amber, and Chiyo began firing at the droid, but their attacks barely seemed to register. The machine turned and charged its cannon, taking aim at Amber.

"Amber, get away," Chiyo shouted. The infiltrator and the battle medic dashed to the side as it fired. They jumped at the last second, but the force of the blast blew them into the wall, cracking it as they impacted.

Genos stepped up and fired his charged cannon. The droid's hand glowed with bright blue energy as it literally caught the blast, crushing it in its grasp and causing it to explode, knocking the Tsuna into the wall behind him

"Genos!" Kaiden cried.

Genos rolled over and got shakily to his feet. Amber and Flynn continued to fire at the machine, to no avail. Pieces of Genos' armor were cracked, and the low light of his armor's barrier was gone.

Kaiden looked over to see Amber and Flynn dodging a shot from the mech. Genos took shelter on the side of a broken slab of concrete, Kaiden quickly slid in next to him, "Genos, get out of here! You have no protection."

Genos looked at his cannon, "My weapon is still functional, so I can continue to fight."

"Even so, if we don't take this thing out soon… Wait, that disintegration grenade—you still have it?"

Genos opened the compartment on his back, taking it out. "I do. It's—no, it's damaged! The activation switch is cracked."

"Can you fix it quickly?" Kaiden asked.

"I can, but I can hear the holding pin on the inside rattle. Without it, the grenade will detonate in my hand."

"Dammit, that would have been helpful," Kaiden snapped.

Genos paused for a moment. "I think I have a solution, but I will need time. I know it is a lot to ask, but—"

"Already on it!" Kaiden shouted, hopping out of cover and firing at the droid. "Everyone, keep firing!"

"That's a redundant order!" Flynn snarked, sending shots at the machine's head. "I would be much more impressed with that if it weren't trying to kill us," Flynn shouted, sending shots at the machine's head. They found their target, but it constantly spun its head, so the shots struck the armored side and were unable to pierce through, even at full draw.

"Chief, activate the battle suite," Kaiden demanded. The EI nodded and disappeared into the HUD as he began the process. The ace decided to get close. The suite began to boot up as he took out the entire thermal container and hit the switch, activating the remaining grenades within. He sprinted at the machine as it turned toward him. Flynn and Genos resumed firing, trying to get its attention. It pointed its hand at them, and the energy surrounding it erupted and knocked them down. It fired several smaller blasts at Kaiden, which he was able to weave and flow around as he closed in.

As he jumped to the side to dodge another shot, he tossed the container at one of the exposed slots in the machine. He landed and rolled behind a pillar as the explosions went off. After another static cry from the droid, he looked around the post to see it collapse on one leg, the other shattered in the blast.

"I've gotten used to destroying your kind," Kaiden muttered. "Looks like we're good, Genos." He seated his rifle against his shoulder, "I don't know what your plan was. It was probably pretty good, but nothing beats good old-fashioned—"

The others recovered and continued to fire at the machine. He walked up to take a final shot to its head. Another cry sounded, and the droid's body sparked with white energy that expanded and knocked them all back. Kaiden looked up to see that the machine had surrounded itself in a domed barrier. He fired several shots, but they wouldn't break through. The machine's chest opened, revealing a core that began to flash and a foreboding hum filled the air.

"What is it doing?" he asked.

"It's going critical. It's going to self-destruct," Genos warned, his eyes wide and his hands trembling.

"We have to retreat," Amber yelled.

"We won't make it. The blast is nearly equivalent to a hydrogen bomb," the mechanist explained. He looked at the team and began charging his cannon. "I'll take care of it, friends."

"What do you need us to do?" Kaiden asked, making his way over to the Tsuna.

Genos shook his head. "Just continue. Please do your best to finish this," he stated. He fired the cannon blast at the barrier, ripping open a small portion of the shield. "I think it was indeed for the best that I kept this." He held up the disintegration grenade, his thumb placed firmly on the activation key, "Not to be rude, but I think another would have gotten this wrong." He dashed toward the opening, diving through as it began to reform.

"Genos!" Kaiden cried, watching as the shield closed on itself. Genos dodged a swipe from the droid's arm, leaping off the cannon as it turned to fire, striking the shield. He latched onto the droid's chest and let go of the button on the grenade.

All Kaiden saw was a bright flash of red. He was blinded for a moment and turned away. When he looked back, the dome, the droid, and Genos were all gone. A crater was the only thing that remained.

CHAPTER THIRTY-TWO

"Genos..." Kaiden murmured, his eyes wide as he stared at the crater where his friend and the droid had been. He felt cold, like ice was forming in his stomach and coating his veins. His rifle nearly slipped from his grasp as his hand twitched.

He felt a hand on his shoulder, not registering it at first until it tightened. He looked back to see Chiyo touching him, with Flynn and Amber waiting behind her. "It's all right, Kaiden. You're too immersed. Breathe in and out. Genos is all right."

He clenched his teeth, releasing out a long sigh, then nodded silently and rolled his shoulders as Chiyo let go. After one more deep breath, he rested his rifle against his shoulder. "I see what you were talking about, Flynn. That's rough."

"You fall into it, right? I think the sync might be up, and combine that with the oscillation and all the chaos going on...it feels pretty real. I guess that's the point, though."

"Still, I feel like shit that I didn't take that thing down quicker. Genos wouldn't have had to do that, otherwise. We're a man down now and at the gate." He looked back at the logo and grunted in annoyance. "It didn't take any damage at all. I'm out of thermals and ballistic rounds. We got enough firepower to bust that thing open?"

Chiyo walked past him and picked something up off the ground. "It would seem Genos left us a parting gift," she said, throwing Kaiden the Tsuna's cannon.

"Why didn't it disappear with him?" he asked after he caught it.

"Probably because it wasn't equipped. He had the other rifle, so when he was de-synced, that rifle was considered his main weapon and disappeared with him," Amber reasoned.

The ace held down the trigger, hearing the cannon buzz and come to life. He aimed it at the wall as the others stood back. "Planned or just luck, I appreciate it either way." He released the trigger, blasting the logo and the wall apart.

When the dust had settled, the four looked inside, and Kaiden retched, "Is that what I think it is?" he asked. Behind the wall stood a tall device. Cylindrical and with a small circular panel on the bottom, it looked similar to an open Animus pod but more like an older model with the only light being the one from the pad on the ground.

"It's a teleporter," Chiyo stated and moved closer. She saw a screen on the right and activated it, and the teleporter turned on. "There's only one destination—coordinates that make no sense. X, Y and Z are all an infinity symbol."

"Is that supposed to be symbolism, or is this thing

saying it can port us to an infinite number of destinations?" Kaiden asked as he slung Genos' cannon on his back. "If that's the case, I hope it doesn't do it all at once."

"Technically, that would be impossible," Amber refuted.

"So are most of the things we've been running into," Flynn countered.

The ace walked up to the pod. "Send me in, Chiyo."

"Are you sure?" she asked. "I'll have to do this one at a time. It shouldn't take long, but you'll be temporarily alone."

"I'm used to that," he admitted. "Not that I don't appreciate the company, but that's been my natural environment for most of my life. I can handle a minute or two of no hand-holding."

She looked at him for a moment before smiling slightly and nodding. "Beginning teleportation. Step inside."

He stepped into the pod and leaned back. "At least this way, if I puke when I get there, y'all won't be around to see it."

"Try to do it in a corner or something, mate," Flynn requested. "I don't wanna teleport in there and immediately slip on your breakfast."

"No promises," he ribbed as the teleporter activated and he vanished.

"Next up?" Chiyo asked, looking at Flynn and Amber.

They looked at each other, each raising a fist. "Best two out of three?" she asked.

"Nah, one shot. Let's get this over with," the marksman said. At the count of three, they revealed their hand, Flynn with rock and Amber with paper. "Dammit."

"You and your edgelord cloak get into the pod." Amber chuckled.

Kaiden appeared in a new room in what felt like less than a second. He stood up and stared at the space around him in awe. "What is this place?" he wondered aloud. The room was a mass of black and white formations, and the space around him flowed with blue lights drifting through the sky like a river. It all floated through the air, heading in the same direction and over a vast expanse of black metallic wall with a lone open doorway through it.

"This seems more like a lair," Chief noted, floating around the room and observing the streams. *"You feeling all right?"*

"Wha? Yeah, yeah, I'm good. Guess I got used to the teleportation thing pretty quickly, or that stuff Chiyo gave me is still working."

"Or it'll hit you in a few minutes. At least you can yack over the sides and into the pretty void below."

He looked to the left of the path, seeing nothing below him but more of the blue lights. "Better not trip."

"Long-ass trip down," Chief agreed. *"Might wanna move. One of your buddies will be coming through soon."*

"Oh, yeah...right," Kaiden stammered, quickly taking a few steps forward as he continued to try to take in the vista. "How long until the next one arrives?"

On cue, Kaiden saw a bright flash and Flynn landed on all fours. "Oh, Lord, that is frightening!" he exclaimed.

"Your first time?" Kaiden asked as he walked over to help him up and pull him away.

"We had some time with teleporters in prep, and I used the teleporter stations in Melbourne from time to time, but it was never that fast or intense," he explained, taking several deep breaths. "That was a ringer."

"Might wanna come down from that quickly and take a look around," the ace advised.

"Oh... Well, this is different." Flynn gasped.

"Right? Looks like cyber-purgatory," Kaiden mused. "Let's hope we don't have to stay here long."

"What the hell is all that floaty business?" Wulfson grimaced. "Where are they? This one of your pet projects, Laurie?"

The professor shook his bottle of wine and sighed at its emptiness. "Although I would hate to spoil your sense of discovery, I also know that's something lost to you," he lamented as he placed the bottle back on the table. "It's a separate map that contains the Animus personification of the Director EI. Kaiden and his friends are the first to see it in twenty years."

"So they actually made it," Wulfson bellowed, his voice growing more jovial. "I was beginning to think they were on a wild goose chase. Looks like they are taking home the gold."

"Not necessarily," Sasha interjected. "The EI won't simply submit or deactivate when you press a button. They still have one last trial."

"How do you know, Sasha?" Mya asked, now engrossed in Kaiden's travel. She was no longer watching her team's progress—fortunately, for they had been one of the first to fall once the Honor was activated. "You've read the reports? Or seen the vids from the first team?"

"I had no reason to," Sasha stated, paying close attention to the screen as Amber and Chiyo appeared.

"Then how do you..." Mya's question trailed off.

Laurie chuckled. "Putting it together, Miss Mya? I must admit, I'm a little envious that dear Kaiden seems to take more after our commander than me."

"In some ways," Sasha said, watching as the team set off down the path. "I wish he would take notes in other ways, but in a few, he surpasses me." He leaned forward to rest his head on his folded hands. "Let's see how this concludes."

The group walked down the path and into the hallway. Kaiden called a halt when he saw that the path in front of them ended. "Did they not finish the road?" he snarled, looking at the vast expanse between them and the end of the hallway.

Chiyo walked over and leaned over to press a hand down, causing ripples to appear. "Hard light bridge," She revealed and stood. "Scan, Kaitō." She was silent for a moment as her lenses flared and dimmed soon after. "It will take us all the way to the end."

"Like I trust that? What's to stop it from disappearing under our feet and dropping us into the pit?" he asked.

"What's to stop it from doing it now?" she asked, tapping her foot on the floor. "It might appear solid, but the Director controls everything in here. This is just as susceptible to being removed as the bridge."

The ace frowned as he took a cautious step onto the bridge, "I hate being in the domain of what is essentially EI Jesus."

"Losing your nerve when we've come this far?" she asked.

He glared at her and sighed. "Clever girl." After a few more cautious steps and seeing the translucent floor send small ripples around his feet, he relaxed slightly and continued. His teammates followed slowly.

When they reached the other side, the infiltrator bumped into his back as he suddenly stopped. "What's wrong?"

"Nothing much..." he sputtered, leaning over so she could see past him. "Just whatever the hell that is."

The group's eyes all went wide as they saw a massive orb of white energy. All the blue streams flowed into it and green streams flowed out. It floated in the middle of the circular room, surrounded by pillars of an octagonal shape.

The group moved forward, looking at the massive sphere in shock and confusion.

"Is that your big brother, Chief?" Kaiden asked, pointing at the giant shimmering orb.

"If I had relations, I'm pretty sure I would know about this one," Chief stated, observing the construct. *"But if he is, he better not ask for money."*

"So, this is the Director thing?" Amber asked.

"Yes, those streams are representations of data flowing to and from it. This is what we've been searching for," Chiyo explained.

"How the bloody hell are we supposed to deal with that thing?" Flynn asked.

She pursed her lips and activated her holoscreen. It immediately flashed red and disappeared. "I've been locked out?"

"You didn't believe it would be that simple, Initiate Chiyo Kana?" The voice actually sounded like several voices speaking at once in various tones—whispery and mellow, loud and booming, calm and melodious.

"Was that the big thing?" Amber asked.

"You speak Japanese?" Chiyo asked.

"Japanese?" Kaiden questioned, "I didn't hear any moon-speak."

"It is a simple matter for me to translate my communications into whatever language I need to for conversation," the Director stated. *"I'm speaking to you individually, although you may all hear it. I choose the primary language of the listener for convenience. That includes English, Japanese, and code for your flying friend there."*

"What?" Kaiden looked at the orb. "Is that thing talking to you in clicks and chirps or something, Chief?"

"It's a little more technical and nuanced than that," Chief grumbled. *"Like I said, this thing is the deluxe collector's edition, super-special-awesome version of normal EIs. What he's doing is essentially what all EIs do to 'talk'—translate our coding into human or alien language."*

"You keep hyping this thing. I thought you were supposed to be the uber EI here," Kaiden admonished.

"I am, among normal EIs," Chief explained, his eye narrowing. *"This thing is a few tiers above, though. It essentially ran the entire Animus system for more than a decade.*

That's a hell of a lot of power and function." Chief turned to address the Director. *"I have to admit, it is nice to speak to someone on my level for a change. You wouldn't believe what it's like to work with this guy."*

The voices chuckled. *"Yes, I have records of all of your exploits. Some are rather amusing."*

"You can feel amused? You have emotion?" Chiyo asked, astonished.

"Hmm, no more so than any other EI. We can approximate human emotion through programs and make educated deductions about how to understand a situation, depending on various parameters and tags. I found Initiate Kaiden Jericho's mishap at the beginning of the Division Test to be quite humorous."

"Which one?" Flynn asked, he and Amber looking at the ace.

Kaiden sighed. "I stepped on a mine right after landing."

They laughed. "Seriously? I spent half that test thinking you were a badass. That would have put things in perspective." Flynn chortled.

"I expected to come here for a fight, not spend the end of this test having to deal with an EI running through a montage of my fails," Kaiden growled

"Oh, that will come. I wanted to be a gracious host and offer simple conversation and alternatives before we devolved to that," the EI responded calmly.

"Wait, you are gonna attack us?" Flynn snapped, arming his sniper rifle. "You seemed like such a nice chap."

"As I said, I would prefer not to," the director reiterated. *"There are a number of ways this could go. You have done so well to get here, I feel like it would be something of a tragedy to get this far and falter now."*

"Now that it's starting to feel like itself, the resemblance is starting to come out a bit more, Chief," Kaiden jeered, taking his rifle in both hands. "As much as I would like to shoot something, especially after that bot you sent at us killed my alien buddy, I can be placated. How many of these solutions of yours end with us winning?"

"Hmm, that was unfortunate. I have less information on the Tsuna, but to see one act so selflessly was a nice experience. It gives me hope for the future of your two species, knowing that there are those among them like that."

"I haven't worked with too many, but the ones I do run with are both like that," Kaiden stated.

"Noted and added to my directory." The EI construct flashed briefly. *"As for solutions that would end in immediate victory for you, well, there are none, definitively,"* the Director admitted. *"But I can teleport you to anywhere within the building or the island that you wish. I can grant you weapons of your choosing and empower your armor. You would have a clear advantage over the remaining initiates."*

"There are only forty-two initiates left besides y'all," Chief informed them. *"Most are alone or have lost at least one team-mate. You could just run through the rest."*

"That would lead us to fighting each other," Kaiden protested.

"I know that we promised to leave each other at the end, but now that we've gotten here together, I would feel terrible if it came to that," Amber admitted.

"Not to mention that if Jaxon and Luke's teams are still kicking, they'd hold the fact that we were powered up when we took them down over our heads," Flynn pointed out.

"Agreed. No dice, big guy." The ace raised his rifle and placed his finger on the trigger. "Deactivate yourself, or we'll find a way to do it for you."

"I am still bound to follow the orders of others within certain conditions. Are you sure this is your choice? Perhaps I can still offer something to end this more amicably."

"Nah, we've made up our minds," Kaiden declared, looking at the others. Chiyo and Amber nodded back, drawing their weapons as the marksman took aim.

"Understood. Activating defenses." The group saw numerous droids, mutants, and mercs appear around the room. *"I wish you luck. I would predict that your chances of survival are around thirty-two-point-three percent."*

CHAPTER THIRTY-THREE

"Anyone got a plan?" Flynn asked, trying to snipe some of the hostiles as they were ported in.

"Not dying, for starters," Kaiden snapped, backing up as a trio of Assassin droids ran toward him. He fired several shots, taking two out as another made a leap toward him. Three shots to the head dropped it as Chiyo reloaded her Scorpio. She fired another shot from her shock pistol at an advancing grunt, stunning him, and Amber finished him off.

"Leap down," Chiyo ordered.

"To what?" Kaiden demanded. He vented his rifle and looked over the edge. "Those pillar things?

"We can't stay here, we'll be overwh—*ah!*" She cried out in pain as she took a shot in the back.

"Dammit!" Kaiden cursed, closed the vent, and destroyed the Assault droid that had shot Chiyo. He fired on two heavies that were starting up their chain guns.

"Climb on," the ace said. She held onto his shoulders

and scrambled onto his back. "This won't be a safe landing," he warned as he jumped down.

Flynn and Amber kept firing from the bridge as they backed up to the edge, then jumped down and followed them.

Kaiden and Chiyo landed hard, the infiltrator falling off his back as he nearly slipped off. There was a brief moment of respite before shots were fired from above. "We're not exactly safe down here either," he shouted. "And now we're on the low ground!" He saw their teammates land on a pillar across from them, then took out a healing serum and tossed it to Chiyo.

She drank it quickly and looked up. "Kaiden, over there."

Kaiden looked over to see a node in the shape of a pointed obelisk, bare of any accents or markings. "What about it?"

"We need to get over there. That could be a direct connection to the Director."

"We've kind of had shit luck with nodes." Kaiden took a bullet in the left shoulder from an Assault droid, shattering the last remnants of the shoulder pad. "Tenacious bastards," he growled, firing back, and managed to hit one as the others ducked out of range.

"The Director said there was a chance we could win this. It isn't a no-win scenario. We can't take on waves of opponents with only the four of us," she reasoned. "We have to make it across."

"Kaiden, look *out*," Flynn shouted, firing past him. The shot hit a Guardian droid that had appeared on a pillar behind him and Chiyo.

"These things are zipping all around the room now," he hollered, firing at the newly-appearing enemies. "Go, I'll catch up!"

She nodded, then ran and leaped to another pillar, using her Scorpio to shoot anything in her path. The ace took out a duo of merc grunts before leaping to the next pillar, venting his rifle. An Assault droid appeared, its back to him. He kicked it off the edge and drew Debonair with his free hand, firing at two drones that were flying his way.

"This is crazy even for us," Chief shouted.

"Keep moving, keep shooting," Kaiden declared. "We'll make it out of this."

"You think this will get worse?"

Before he could respond, the entire room was bathed in white light. When it receded, he stood on a sand dune. The room they had been in had transformed into a desert.

"Never mind, I'll shut up." He sighed.

"At least it's better footing." He grunted, rolled to the side, and fired at a grunt who ran down a hill. He heard a beastly shriek behind him and saw a devil bird flying overhead. "Hey, look, it's our old buddy."

"Don't jump on it this time," the EI demanded.

"I don't have any grenades this time. That's a problem," he muttered, and a laser shot skimmed the side of his mask. "And I have to deal with these assholes." He turned and fired, taking out an Assault droid as another raised its rifle to fire. A spike suddenly jutted from its head, and it collapsed. Flynn saluted in the distance and pointed to the west.

Kaiden looked over to see Chiyo kneeling by the node.

He ran over, venting his rifle along the way as Flynn and Amber distracted the others.

"Hey, how's it going, Chi?" he asked, his breath ragged.

"I've got a direct connection, but it keeps shutting me out of its systems. It's too fast, even with Kaitō's help," she said, her tone annoyed as she kept typing on her tablet.

Kaiden looked up and sent four consecutive shots at an encroaching heavy merc. The first three blasts cracked his armor, and the fourth seared his chest and made him collapse. "You gotta keep an eye out. Screw it, let's do this the normal way." He spun around and shot the legs off an Assault droid that tried to ambush them, took his blade and dug it into its neck, and tore out the circuits, deactivating it. "You do your thing, I'll do mine." He handed her his barrier projector. "It's only at eighteen percent recharge. Not a lot of juice left, but hopefully it helps."

"Thank you." She took the projector. "I'll try everything I can. We are not going to lose here."

"Damn straight," he agreed. "Chief, help her out any way you can."

"*On it, partner,*" he acknowledged. "*I'm at your disposal, ma'am.*"

Kaiden left them to help Flynn and Amber. After another flash, they were now on a remote island. The ace perched on the edge of a sandbank while Amber and Flynn were knee-deep in water.

"What the hell is this now?" Flynn hissed.

"Something's in the water, Flynn," Amber warned. He looked over to see a large shadowy shape flow toward them.

"*Ningen,*" the marksman shouted. He grabbed Amber

and raced to shore, then stowed his rifle and drew his pistol to shoot any enemies blocking their path.

Kaiden fired, covering their retreat as he saw the water surge. A giant pale-white being emerged, humanoid in shape but with large fin-like hands and a lanky body. It reached out with one of its long limbs and tried to catch Amber, but Flynn grabbed her and threw her out of its reach as he fell back to keep himself from getting caught.

The ace ran over to help before getting snatched, held by his left shoulder, and whisked up into the air, dropping his rifle during the ascent. He lashed out before yelling in pain and anger as he felt talons digging into him. He was in the devil bird's clutches. He considered his options quickly —he had no explosives left, but he did have the cannon. All he needed was to find an opportunity to fire, but he would have to be closer to the ground. If the creature dropped him from too high up it would kill him on impact.

He still had his blade, so he hit the trigger to heat it and sliced at the mutant's talons. The bird shrieked and released him, but he grabbed the base of its foot and stopped himself from falling. He climbed up the mutant's leg, trying not to look down as he got as close as he could to the top, slicing at the bird's wings as they flapped in the air. It wasn't doing much damage, but it kept the mutant's attention. The devil bird began to dive, swooping around as it tried to knock him off.

Kaiden held firm as he stowed the blade and took out the cannon. He charged it and aimed at the creature's head, able to angle the shot as it descended. Holding his breath, he fired and heard a croak and a whimper on impact. The body thrashed around, slowing the fall. When he was close enough, he hopped off as another flash obscured his vision. When he opened his eyes, he was falling toward a spike on the upper half of a wall. Quickly, he charged up a partial shot from the cannon and fired behind him, the force moving him barely enough to miss being impaled before he crashed through the top of a tent.

The ace scrambled to his feet and looked around. They were in some sort of merc camp now. The ningen had disappeared but he saw Flynn and Amber swarmed by mercs of various classes. As he staggered up, he looked at the cannon. The indicator showed low power, so he had to conserve his shots. Regretfully, he put it away and reached for his rifle, then realized it wasn't there. With a curse, he drew Debonair. As he charged into the fray, he looked around for Chiyo, not seeing her in the field. She must have holed up in one of the buildings.

He slid down and fired six shots at three different grunts, killing them all in a hail of laser fire. His feet found purchase, and he stood and whipped his pistol across the face of a hitman before firing another shot at the exposed head of a sniper. Quickly, he crossed Debonair under his arm and fired two shots into the hitman to finish him off.

Kaiden heard an explosion and turned in time to catch a sniper rifle flying in the air and see Flynn tumbling toward him. He helped him up and gave him his rifle. "You need to keep better track of this."

"She always finds her way back to me." Flynn chuckled, nodding in thanks as he took the rifle. "Bastards just keep coming."

"Where's Amber?" the ace asked.

"We got separated for a minute. I was heading back but

got caught in that explosion," he explained. "You know how Chiyo is doing?"

"Not really. I wouldn't say she's met her match just yet, but she's having a hell of a time taking care of that Director."

"Then we'll keep fighting," Flynn vowed, reloading his rifle. "Help me find Amber."

"There she is," Kaiden said, pointing to the battle medic in the distance. She waved frantically, pointing behind them.

"What's she doing? She's completely exposed," he stated.

The marksman placed his fingers against his helmet, activating the comm. "Amber, what are you—" He looked behind him and quickly pushed his teammate aside.

The ace slid back and watched in horror as a merc with a chain blade sliced clean through the other man, Flynn vanishing as his body was bisected. Kaiden roared in anger as he tackled the merc to the ground, firing continual shots from Debonair into the adversary's helmet until it began to melt, and blood seeped from the cracks and down his neck. He stood and ran to Amber, who was too distraught to see the merc coming after her with a cleaver. He fired, but Debonair was overheated. Undaunted, he sprinted past her and blocked the merc's attack using the armor on his arms. He pushed him back, taking out his own blade and parrying the aggressor's swipe before jamming his knife through the merc's visor.

Kaiden yanked his knife out and walked over to Amber, then helped her up. "I'm sorry, I should have been paying more attention."

"No... It's all right. We can still win this, make up for

everyone who has sacrificed themselves so far," Amber vowed. "We need to get back to Chiyo. The two of us alone won't be able to continue with this onslaught."

"No kidding. I don't even have my rifle anymore." He growled as he saw some of the tents behind Amber disappear. Mercs in the distance froze, and the sky became a violet color before fracturing like a broken screen

"Kaiden, get back here. It's almost done," Chief hollered.

"Chiyo got in?" he asked.

"No, we weren't able to get through. Even with all of us working together we couldn't shut it down, but we found a loophole. We've been sending junk data and random commands into it, trying to overload it. It's working, right?"

"Some weird shit just went down so I would say that it is," he confirmed.

"Then hurry up. Chiyo said that this should expose its core, and we need some firepower to take it—" Chief cut off as the ace heard a loud discharge of static.

"Chief!? What happened!?"

"Get ba-back," the EI stammered, his voice fuzzy and distorted.

Kaiden activated his network, locating the building they were in. He and Amber raced over as the mercenary camp around them began to distort and fall away to reveal the original sanctum of the EI Director, now all white. The ground beneath the ace changed to a hard-light bridge as he ran to Chiyo, who was convulsing on the ground . The node was sparking, and electricity snapped and fizzled around it.

He knelt and picked her up but felt pain shoot through his arm as he touched her. "Chiyo?"

"An electrical spike. It fried her. Probably a last-ditch effort from the Director. It didn't kill her, but she's out of commission for a bit," Chief stated, coming back online. *"Spiteful son of a bitch. The damage was already done."*

He looked up to see the orb disappear and a small metallic orb with several mirror-like circles adorning it appeared. *"That's it, Kaiden. Take it down, and we win."*

Kaiden dropped Debonair and drew Genos' cannon, charging up a blast and aiming at the core. As he fired, a Goliath droid appeared, taking the blast and staggering back.

"Goddammit. Just accept your loss, you bulbous ass," Chief cried. *"Move and take another shot."*

"There's not enough energy for a full blast," he yelled, holding Chiyo as he walked back while Amber fired at the Goliath with her SMG.

"Then do what Genos does. If it's still got a little power left, overclock that bitch and make it an explosive."

"Can you tell me how?" he asked.

"Shut the vent fully, pull and lock the trigger, and deactivate the protection field—small button on the back. It'll go from blue to red."

Kaiden followed Chief's instructions and felt the cannon heating up in his hands. Chiyo stirred, looking up. "Is it done, Kaiden?"

"Almost. Wait here." he said, laying her down. "This won't do any good if no one is here to be declared the victor."

"It's going to blow soon, Kaiden. Get up there," Chief ordered.

He nodded, covering his face as the Goliath blasted at

Amber. She rolled to the edge of the bridge but remained on it. The ace ran forward and threw himself onto the Goliath. He climbed up, the droid smashing one of its cannons against itself in an attempt to hit him. The ace reached for the hand and leaped. He could hear the cannon snap and whir, and it began to burn his hands through his gloves. His jump landed him on the edge of a pillar, and he climbed up just as the Goliath fired. The blast broke the pillar and sent it crashing into the abyss. Kaiden raced up as the pillar fell, jumped into the air, craning his arm back.

"End this, partner," Chief bellowed.

The soldier flung the cannon at the core and saw a small image of the Director begin to form. The cannon erupted, catching Kaiden in the blast. As he began to fade away, he could hear the room fall apart and saw the core explode, smiling as another wave burst him apart.

CHAPTER THIRTY-FOUR

C hiyo awoke to see two figures looming over her. She blinked several times before her vision cleared to reveal the worried face of Genos and Kaiden's grin. "Howdy! Nice of you to come back to us."

"Uh, my head is pounding," she muttered. The ace helped her out of the pod. "I don't know about total score, but you probably do have the dubious honor of being the one who got knocked around the most."

"I suppose it can't be you *every* time." She sighed and stretched her limbs.

"Nice to see you're still feeling good enough to make snappy comebacks." He chortled.

"I'm glad that both of you are safe," Genos stated, clasping his hands together. "I watched your progress on the console, and you did fantastically. Even despite the strange changes, I would have liked to have accompanied you to that island. I wonder what that white aquatic creature was. It looked similar to a beast from Abisalo."

383

JOSHUA ANDERLE & MICHAEL ANDERLE

"You'd have to ask Flynn. He seemed to know enough about it to know to run away," Kaiden told him.

"I shall bring it up later. For now, congratulations to both of you."

"We made it?" Chiyo asked.

"Indeed we did." The ace beamed. "You were pretty out of it for the last part. I heard you took quite a shock."

"Right, yes. We were sending junk data into the Director, then I felt my body go stiff and my vision blurred. I thought I had been de-synced."

"Chief says the Director shot you with an electrical spike, probably as some final attack or because it was annoyed that you found a workaround," Kaiden explained. "Glad you made it, since otherwise I'm not sure if it would have counted as a win. I had to make a suicide charge at the core to take it out."

"I have to tell you it concerns me that such a tactic is becoming common for you," the Tsuna noted. "You should work on trying different strategies next year."

"Says you," he scoffed. "Considering how you took yourself out? But I do have to say it was some quick thinking on your part. Pretty noble, too."

"Yes, well, not many options at our disposal," Genos admitted sheepishly. "I'm glad it saved you. Both you and Chiyo were more important for the mission than I was."

"Don't think like that, buddy." Kaiden clapped him on the back. "You ain't no wet blanket with a rifle or a cannon, especially when we're dealing with bots. Speaking of which, thanks for leaving that with us. Was that intentional?"

Genos tapped a finger on his infuser. "Well, before I

attacked the droid, I was thinking—" His statement was interrupted by a knock at the door of their private room.

"Who is it?" the ace asked.

"Get your asses out here," Advisor Faraji ordered.

"I think it's for you," he said to Chiyo. She shook her head and opened the door, Genos and Kaiden following. Standing before them were a frowning Faraji and Head Monitor Zhang, an expressionless stare on his face.

"Are we in some sort of trouble" Genos inquired, looking at Kaiden and Chiyo.

"I don't know why we would be," the infiltrator said with a shrug.

"So, what do you think?" Kaiden asked, resting his arms behind his head. "First team to truly win the squad test in twenty years. I think that makes three records I've beaten? I should get some sort of prize or banner for that. Find a way to hang it in the plaza."

Faraji's frown quickly switched to a smile. "I was hoping to make you sweat a little."

"Might have worked, but the head monitor wasn't exactly playing along," the ace pointed out.

Zhang drew in a deep breath. "I prefer to keep things orderly, as you well know. Your excursion through the test was a rather interesting development. With your completion, you jettisoned the remaining students from the test," he revealed.

"Our bad?" Kaiden said tentatively. "I guess we didn't think how it would affect the others. But hey, they could have been gunning for the Director too. The only reason we—or I guess I should say, Chiyo—decided to look into it was your cryptic-ass statement during the orientation."

"Would you quit it?" Akello seethed through clenched teeth and knocked Kaiden in the ribs. "That's the head monitor you're talking to, and you're one of *my* students. Don't make me look bad."

"It is all right, Advisor Faraji," Zhang said impassively. "I haven't had many personal interactions with Initiate Jericho, but Commander Sasha informed me of his colorful personality."

"Does he talk to everyone about me?" the ace wondered aloud. "Speaking of which, where is he? I feel like bragging to someone some more."

"You should make your way to the lobby shortly. Most of the Initiates and faculty will gather there. I expect him to show up soon, now that the test has been abruptly concluded."

"Again with that? Do you want us to say we're sorry?"

Zhang shook his head. "No. It's merely a statement of fact. I should say that despite the sudden end for the other initiates and the change to the points, I am happy to have overseen the first time this event has occurred in two decades." He turned away from the group and said over his shoulder, "Besides, I have prepared for this eventuality ever since I was an advisor. It's good that my planning didn't go to waste." He went down the hall and headed for the stairs but paused and turned back. "By the way, Kaiden, you should note that you are technically not the only team who won the test. Sorry if that cools you off a bit."

"Wait, what?" Kaiden questioned, "Who else— Wait, Amber was still there. That means her team won too?"

"You may have struck the final blow, but she and Flynn

helped you guys," Akello reminded him. "You really gonna dispute that?"

He placed his hands in his pockets and sighed. "Nah, they did good work. No reason to not let them have some of the glory. Just be sure you get to work on that banner, all right?"

"Good luck with that," Akello deadpanned. She turned and beamed at Chiyo and Genos. "Now, on to students I actually like. Well done to the both of you."

"Thank you, Advisor," Genos said with a bow.

"Thank you, Akello." Chiyo smiled. "If we have any sort of celebrations afterward, feel free to join us."

"Oh, there'll definitely be celebrations," Kaiden promised.

"I second that," Akello agreed "But it's time to wrap this up for you initiates. Pass through the gate, on to the next level, all that jazz." She turned and gestured for them to follow. "Let's go. I'm sure everyone wants to see the winners."

―――――――――

"Kaiden," Luke bellowed as the ace walked down the stairs. He turned to see the titan soldier waving from the end of the hall, pushing through the throngs of gathered students. "Gotta keep making the rest of us look bad, huh?"

"I got a reputation to maintain." He grinned. "Where are the others?"

"Cameron and Raul were behind me like a minute ago." Luke scratched the back of his head as if bewildered.

"People don't move out of the way for us like they do

for you," Raul muttered as he and Cameron finally caught up to their bigger teammate.

"How'd y'all do?" Kaiden asked.

"Pretty damn good. Cameron made a killing when the Honor started," Luke stated.

"I simply picked off the loners and set up a few traps throughout the building. I got a couple of kills without us even being there," He bragged before he crossed his arms and stared at Kaiden. "Had to ruin my fun, didn't ya?"

"Look at it this way: at least you didn't have to take *me* on." Kaiden snickered.

"Hey, guys." Kaiden turned to see Flynn and his teammates running toward them. "You won, Kai?"

"Should we tell them or would that spoil the surprise?" he asked, looking at Chiyo.

"I think he would enjoy hearing it from you more than the head monitor," she suggested.

"Tell us what?" Marlo asked.

"You guys also got the victory. Amber was still alive when I took out the core, ergo it counted for y'all as well," he revealed.

"Whoa, really?" The demolisher whooped. "It's a good thing I saved your ass, Flynn. Worked like a charm!"

"You keep reminding me." The marksman sighed, then chuckled happily. "You did good, big man, and good job on not dying, Amber."

"If you could tell that pointing behind you and 'look out' are signs of warning, you could have lived too," she snarked.

"Hey, my valiant sacrifice saved the winner, which let us win. I think that makes me MVI."

"MVI?" Kaiden asked.

"Most valuable initiate," Flynn explained, and the ace slapped his hand against his face.

"You can just stick with MVP. Besides, we won't be initiates for long."

"Not within the hour," Jaxon noted. He, Silas, and Izzy joined the others.

"Good to see you, Jaxon." Luke shook the Tsuna's hand. "How'd you fare?"

"Well enough, but we didn't get to see the test to its completion." He eyed the winning team. "I have been informed that you are responsible for that."

"So are they," Kaiden said, pointing to Flynn and his group.

"You were able to make it to the end, kin Jaxon?" Genos inquired.

"We did, as a full team as well. Your biologist friend was quite helpful in that regard. Thank you for sending him to us."

He looked up, recalling the test. "Ah, yeah, Julius. I need to see if I can network with him and his team later."

"He mentioned the same to me. We will see if we can find them after the ceremony," the Tsuna suggested. "What about you, kin? Were you able to reach the end with your team?"

Genos tapped his fingers together. "Well, not to the very end. There was a potentially catastrophic situation and—"

"He saved our asses. Took down an Asiton droid by himself when it was going to self-destruct in our faces," the ace interjected. "Took one for the team. It was because of him that we were able to finish at all. His cannon helped even after he was gone, so he was there in spirit."

"I see." Jaxon nodded appreciatively. "Well done, kin. Your skills as a warrior are beginning to match your experience as a scientist. I'm proud."

"Thank you, kin Jaxon." Genos bowed.

Kaiden began to smile, but his eyes went wide as he heard a number of screams from the main lobby. He and all the other initiates ran through the hall to see what was causing all the commotion. The ace frowning once he saw all the fuss. "Seriously? He's just waltzing around now?"

"Would you dumboms quiet down? You never seen a Sauren before?" Wulfson snarled, waving his hands as if he were swatting at the shocked initiates.

"I did, during the test, It tried to kill me!" one of them shouted.

"Did it?" Raza asked, his voice a low snarl.

"N-no. We got away."

"Then it was not a true Sauren. We do not let our prey escape," he snapped.

"Hey, easy there, Raza. Don't go making all these nice young kids start wetting themselves on their big day." Wulfson chuckled. He glanced up and spotted the ace. "Oy, Kaiden. Over here."

"It's not like I can miss you," Kaiden muttered. He, Chiyo, and Genos made their way over.

"I watched your test with Sasha, his lady friend, and some other idiot. Raza too, of course." He placed a hand on the initiate's shoulder, his smile widening. "Nice work, boy."

"Appreciate it. Guess all that hard work paid off in the end, huh?"

Wulfson laughed. "We haven't even got to hard. We're still at toddler."

Kaiden's face fell. "Oh, joy. Looking forward to that."

"A Tsuna," Raza whispered, studying Genos intently. "You are one of the ones I faced the first time I met Kaiden. You demonstrated considerable combat potential during the test, along with your 'machinations.' Tell me, are you of your people's warrior clan, like Jaxon?"

"Um, no, Leader Raza," Genos stammered. "I am of a different clan. Science and forging are our practices, but I have trained in the warrior's way."

"You do it well. Even without the threat of death, sacrifice is always respected," he stated unequivocally, then looked at Chiyo. "And how do I address you? I understand your talents lie in the field of technology."

"Yes, sir. I am Chiyo Kana, an infiltrator," she answered.

The Sauren nodded and bowed to both. "Kaiden has earned my respect. It is good to know the company he keeps. You are both promising warriors."

"He's really a softy," the ace whispered to Wulfson.

"Isn't he, though?" The security officer chuckled.

"You said you were watching the test with Sasha. Is he here?"

The giant nodded up at the balcony. "Take a look."

"Greetings, students." Zhang's voice rang out, and the crowd quieted immediately. Kaiden turned to see him standing at the edge of the balcony. Sasha and Counselor Mya stood behind him, along with several other staff members. The head monitor's face appeared on screens throughout the Animus Center as he continued, "A well-fought and well-executed test. I could hardly ask for a better trial run for a test this size, barring a few personal nit-picks."

"I guess he's holding in a lot more," Kaiden said, leaning toward Chiyo.

"I will send your scores to your EIs in due time, but first, I want to let you know two things." He let the moment linger before taking a deep breath. "This test had its rules, but there was one thing we were looking for in particular among you all. It is one thing to finish a mission; that is to be expected. But it is another to take the unconventional paths; to look out for oneself but also for others. To go beyond."

Zhang looked around the room as small whispers began, the initiates trying to figure out what he was talking about. "There is a reason I told you not to think of this as purely a Deathmatch. Although many of you did find success, there were many ways to win, including assisting your fellow initiates—something I was proud to see many of you doing of your own accord."

"Hey, bonus points." Kaiden smiled.

"You will each receive your personal scores, but I am happy to announce that you have all passed and will graduate to the next level." Cheers erupted through the building. Initiates hugged and high-fived one another in celebration. "Well earned, but simmer down for now," Zhang ordered. "No matter who has the highest score, those are not the winners this year."

The ace saw a number of students turn to look at him.

He gave a slight wave, caught off-guard by the sudden attention.

"As many of you who were watching the final moments of the test after you de-synced will know, some initiates were able to find the secret way of winning the test." Zhang chuckled. "Last time it happened, there was no policy of allowing others to watch, but I suppose it is no longer a secret. We may have to find something else for next year's test." He looked up and held his hands in the air. "Kaiden Jericho, Chiyo Kana, Genosaqua Aronnax, Flynn King, Amber Soni, and Marlo Leoman are the victors of this year's Squad Test. I believe it's customary to give them a round of applause." The initiates obliged, Genos and Chiyo shrinking from the attention while Flynn and his team waved at everybody and the ace saluted the other students.

"As is customary, there will be a closing speech before you depart. Unfortunately, the chancellor is unavailable, having left to go and meet with the World Council. However, Commander Sasha has graciously accepted the responsibility. The podium is yours, Commander."

Kaiden watched as Sasha moved to the front of the balcony. He felt Chiyo walk up beside him. "Well, you made it through a full year, Kaiden," she said with a smile. "How do you feel?"

He grinned. "I'm looking forward to seeing what kind of trouble I can get into next year."

"Initiates, I will keep this brief. You have made it through all your trials, bettering yourselves along the way as students, people, and the leaders of tomorrow. You have earned a respite," Sasha stated. "What has been accomplished this year is astonishing. We have had an incredible year, and even with everything that has been thrown at you and expected of you, you took it all in stride. Even when you fell, you stood up and kept going, training so you would do your best to never fall again."

The students nodded and some saluted the commander, and he continued. "Take the time to rest. Next year will bring greater challenges. You will have more freedom, but more expectations as well. Those at the top know they are only winners for so long. There will always be another challenge awaiting them. You are superb Initiates..."

Sasha took off his oculars and studied the room with a cool gaze. "But now is the time for you to Advance."

First a HUGE thank you to all of you reading these books. Due to your enthusiasm, and support by 'telling two friends' this series has stayed in the top 600 for over a month now and (for me anyway) that is a very successful launch.

I actually had a nice set of author notes for this book but apparently, the cat (of which I don't own one) ate my homework.

This book is supposed to go on sale in just a few hours, and I woke up and for whatever reason, decided to check my Slack messages.

I received one from 'Editor Lynne' who explained that the author notes I provided were the ones for Damian 01.

I figured, 'ok, I'll be up a few more minutes, but no problem. A quick jump over to the laptop, find the right file, Bob's your uncle and I'm back to bed.'

Except, no author notes.

As I frantically started looking through all of the new files, I remembered an important detail.

Microsoft Word wasn't saving files correctly.

OH YEAH.

So, I went over to my TextEdit files and started looking for where I had copy/pasted the info before I went fixing anything.

Nothing. Only the aforementioned Damian 01 notes.

Oh Crap...

Now, I was a bit more concerned. I looked around,

I tried hitting 'CTRL-Z' in a few files to see if my words were just a quick over-write and would magically reappear before I remembered, 'You closed down Microsoft Word to see if it fixed your save issue, dumbass.'

...Sonofabitch.

In short, I had something about how we have 12-books for the Kaiden series (instead of my original 4) planned and then we will go off into space. Assuming the series is supported by the readers, of course.

I also discussed how we will have book 04 out a bit later than the 2-3 weeks between these books. That has to do with these stories are longer than my typical 70,000 or so words in The Kurtherian Gambit and we don't have any 'banked' now. So, they come out as fast as they can be written.

Which, for 90,000 words takes about 5 weeks plus 2 for editing.

Longer if there is an author-issue on the chapters. We will need to keep you updated on the status...

Well damn. I realize that we don't really 'have' an Animus

FB group or anything. Since I'm already involved in so many groups, I don't want to create a new one.

I'm usually in the Protected by the Damned Facebook group if you want to go there or the Kurtherian Gambit Fans and Authors (or is that Authors and Fans) Facebook group as well.

Feel free to ask in either of those fan groups (or message me directly, as well.)

I apologize these author notes are rather sparse. At 3:00 o'clock in the morning, my brain is mush.

Ad Aeternitatem,

Michael Anderle

BOOKS BY MICHAEL ANDERLE

For a complete list of books by Michael Anderle, please visit

www.lmbpn.com/ma-books/

All LMBPN Audiobooks are Available at Audible.com and
iTunes. For a complete list of audiobooks visit:

www.lmbpn.com/audible

CONNECT WITH THE AUTHORS

Michael Anderle Social
Website:
http://lmbpn.com

Email List:
http://kurtherianbooks.com/email-list/

Facebook Here:
https://www.facebook.com/OriceranUniverse/
https://www.facebook.com/TheKurtherianGambitBoo
ks/
https://www.facebook.com/groups/320172985053521
/ (Protected by the Damned Facebook Group)